I0676227

Praise for ARCTIC FIRE

"A new twist on a classic battlefield ploy finds an iceberg controlled by a megalomaniac on a collision course with NYC. A provocative blend of fact and fiction that explores issues surrounding a critical natural resource, fresh water, *Arctic Fire* is bound to leave readers thirsty for more."
— **Rick Chesler, author of *kiDNApped* and *WIRED KINGDOM***

"Audacious and ambitious, *Arctic Fire* burns with action, and chills with the possibilities of what the future may hold. A thriller not to be missed!"
— **Sean Ellis, author of *INTO the BLACK***

"A madman's insatiable quest for power could level a major American city and kill thousands, ushering in a New World Order. *Arctic Fire* is a thrill-ride that will leave you breathless."
— **Jeremy Robinson, bestselling author of *ISLAND 731* and *SECONDWORLD***

Fortress Publications

© 2011 Paul Byers. All rights reserved.

This is a work of fiction. Names, characters, places and incidents are products of the author's imagination or are used fictitiously and should not be construed as real. Any resemblance to actual events, locales, organizations or persons, living or dead, is entirely coincidental.

No part of this book may be used or reproduced in any manner whatsoever without written permission, except in the case of brief quotations embodied in critical articles and reviews. For more information email all inquiries to: paulbyersonline@yahoo.com

Visit Paul Byers on the World Wide Web at:
    www.paulbyersonline.com

Cover illustration by Andy Wenner, www.auroraartcompany.com
Cover and interior layout by Stanley J. Tremblay,
www.findtheaxis.com
Editing by Jenn Waterman, Modern Elektra Editing,
modernelektraediting.com
Author picture taken by Star Morris, www.ratstarcreative.com

To my Mom and Dad…
Gertie and George Byers
Thank you.

ACKNOWLEDGMENTS

There are many people I need to thank who helped me bring *Arctic Fire* to life. First, I would like to thank a man who is a dying breed in his skill and knowledge of the written word. He has taught me that words are precious. He is also a private man, who lives a quiet life and wishes no public recognition, so I offer this anonymous thanks to you sir.

To Jenn Waterman, for her editing. Colonel John Frisby and Captain *Carmine R. Bassano,* both retired officers of the United States Air Force, who helped me with the technical jargon for the Red Flag chapter and to Steve Hinton of the Planes of Fame Air Museum (www.planesoffame.org) for his invaluable help with my research for the F-86 Sabre.

Technical thanks to Stan Tremblay for his help in formatting and interior design of the book and in helping me spread the word. It's always good to have an expert in your corner.

I want and need to thank my wife Cheri and my children Alyssa and Adam (you too, Luke) for allowing me the time and space I needed to complete Arctic Fire. Without your love and support, it never would have happened. Also to my brother Mark for his continued belief in me and pushing me to always do better.

A special thanks goes to Andy Wenner for his fantastic design of the book cover. I only hope my story reads as good as his cover looks.

And finally, I would like to thank you, the reader. Thank you for taking your precious time and money and investing it in this book. I hope you enjoy reading it as much as I did writing it.

CHAPTER ONE

April 14th, 1912

"Up scope," the Kapitan called out. As he waited patiently for it to rise, he began humming *Alexander's Rag Time Band* quietly to himself. It was a catchy tune he'd first heard last year when he was in America, assigned as a naval attaché in Washington D.C. Though it was frowned upon in some circles back home in Germany, he was becoming a fan of this new style of American music. When the scope reached chest height, he turned his cap around, flipped down the handles and peered into the eyepiece. Still humming, he slowly turned the periscope, sweeping the ocean, searching for his prey.

It was a moonless night and the sea was a glassy calm, a beautiful, yet somehow disturbing sight. The sea was supposed to be alive, always moving, pulsating, teaming with life, but tonight the waters were flat and stiff, as if she had lain down and died and rigor mortis had set in. In his nearly twenty years before the mast, he could remember only one other time when the sea was this stagnate.

In the old days of tall ships and sailing with the wind at your back, some would have called this a becalmed sea, an omen of bad things to come. But these were modern times; man no longer needed the wind to move across the sea, or in this case, under it. Men of the twentieth century no longer believed in such things as becalmed seas, monsters that rose from the depths to devour whole ships or the likes of the *Flying Dutchman*. But in spite of modern technology and his belief in logic and sound reasoning, he had seen things at sea that would set a prudent man's mind wondering.

Then he saw her, and at that moment, all thoughts of superstitions evaporated in an instant. Even with the moon refusing to show her face, and even peering through the tiny lens of the periscope, it would have been hard for a blind man not to see the magnificence of the ship as she sliced through the plate glass sea.

Festive lights shone through nearly every porthole on the floating city, piercing the darkness and reflecting off the mirror sea, making it look like two ships traveling side by side. He estimated that she was still several kilometers off, giving them plenty of time to maneuver and get into position. These were ideal condition to evaluate the new system.

"Status, Herr Kappel?" the Kapitan said, unable to take his eyes off their prize.

"The boat is handling like a lumbering whale full of blubber, Kapitan. Even with the calm seas, five knots is the best we can manage with all the added weight of the scaffolding and ice, and you can forget about trying to turn. So, if you just want to go straight, and go slower than my dead grandmother, then everything is shipshape... sir."

First Officer Barrett Kappel snapped to attention and mockingly saluted the Kapitan after his report. He then rolled the cigar butt from the left side of his mouth to the right, as if that were the proper military way to do things. Though smoking was never allowed on a submarine, the first officer was never found without a cigar sticking out of his mouth.

Kapitan Claus Haufmann peered around the periscope with amusement in his eyes and a smile on his lips as he looked at his first officer. "Now Barrett, I know you don't much care for this assignment but you know it is necessary. Discontent and unrest are sweeping across Europe like a rising breeze, a breeze that I fear will soon turn into a hurricane, and we must be ready. This observation mission will be critical to tracking the movement of enemy shipping, both military and civilian, and doing it without being seen."

Haufmann paused and stretched as he spoke. He was tall by any standards, but at six-foot-two, he was a giant for a submariner and was constantly bending and stooping as he contorted his lanky frame inside the confining bowels of their steel whale.

"Camouflage," Haufmann continued, as he rubbed the last kink out of his neck, "is the art of seeing without being seen, and what better place to hide than in plain sight? Yes, the scaffolding surrounding the boat and refrigerating unit installed to generate and maintain our facade of being an iceberg certainly weighs us down, but I believe the benefits of blending in with our surroundings outweighs our ability to be able to move faster than your dead grandmother."

"Come, Barrett, see for yourself. Helm, port two degrees, let's get a little closer."

"Port two degrees," echoed the helmsman.

Kappel stepped up to the periscope to look while the Kapitan continued. "Remember, Barrett, this is just a prototype, a training mission to see if it is feasible. But just stop and think about it. How valuable would it be to be able to monitor the enemy's ship movements, to know exactly where their ships are at all times and to be able to strike at will from seemingly nowhere?"

"My God, that thing is big!" Kappel said in awe. He stepped away from the periscope. "I understand, Kapitan, it's just that I'd hate to have our shark turned into a wallowing flounder."

"So do I, my friend, but sometimes sneaking in the back door is better than trying to bash down the front door." Kapitan Haufmann peered once again through the periscope. "She's making good speed. Send up the lookouts. We'll maintain course, get to within two hundred meters, then let her slip past us."

"Aye, sir." Kappel looked toward the back of the boat and barked. "Lookouts one and two, topside now!"

From the stern, two young sailors spilled into the control room like puppies trying to run across a linoleum floor. One was wearing a white, fur-lined parka with white binoculars hanging from his neck; the other was wearing a dark blue parka.

Kappel stared at the two; there was no mistaking that they were brothers. He'd seen it a hundred times before. Country peasant boys tired of the farm, looking for adventure and glory by serving in the *Kaiserliche Marine.* Some of these boys were so wet behind the ears that he feared if he had a crew full of these peasant farmers, they would surly sink to the bottom. Both boys, Thayer and Damien Lehmann, were desperately trying to grow mustaches to make themselves look older, and failing miserably. He couldn't fault them though; he himself had escaped grueling factory work for the freedom of the sea and it had served him well, but these two had a long way to go.

"Where is your white parka, crewman Lehmann? We are supposed to be an iceberg. I have not seen too many dark blue icebergs," Kappel said, shifting his cigar for emphasis. "Have you?"

The young crewman snapped to attention. "No, sir, I tried but I couldn't find my white parka, sir, sorry, sir. I can take it off and go up in my uniform, sir!" Thayer replied.

"What, and have you freeze to death within the hour? I don't think so. This is just a training mission so go on up, but if this had been a combat situation, then I would let you freeze. Do I make myself clear, crewman?"

"Yes, sir!"

"Good. Now go. If they spot you perhaps they will just think you are a giant Dodo bird who has stopped to rest on the ice." Both men scrambled up the ladder and disappeared through the hatch into the conning tower. Everyone felt a wave of cold air invading the control room when the hatched was opened.

Once through the hatch, they closed it and Damien, in the white parka, reached over and slapped his brother on the top of the head. "Nice going, Thayer. You're such a *dummkopf*, but you know what? I do like what First Officer Kappel called you. I think that will be your new nickname: Dodo."

"Shut up, Damien, it's not my fault. I know you hid my jacket somewhere."

Damien had a look of mock hurt on his face. "Now why would I do such a thing as that? Mother said I should take care of you."

"Yeah, she didn't mean it like that." He glared at Damien for a moment then sighed; he could never stay mad at his older brother, no matter what he did. "Let's just take our stations."

Thayer stood on deck for a moment and breathed in deeply, tasting the fresh, crisp salt air. Even though they had only been at sea for a few weeks, the air in the submarine had already turned into a flat, stale taste that lingered in your mouth. Diesel fuel, cooking odors, battery acid and the sweat of thirty-five men crammed together in a tight space made the air so thick at times you could almost take a knife and spread it on your biscuit.

Thayer inhaled another breath then adjusted the hood on his jacket. Even though the air tasted sweet, the wind was still a bitter cold.

"Are we going to take our stations or just stand here and look at the ocean and skip stones... Dodo?" Damien mocked.

Thayer reached over and slugged Damien hard on his shoulder. He looked at him for a moment, then both men burst out laughing. Thayer just shook his head, then grabbed a pair of headphones and climbed into his position on the right side of the mast.

Before him was a strange sight that he still hadn't gotten used to yet: instead of seeing the sleek, dark gray bow knifing through the water, there was a huge, bulky mass of white. A series of scaffoldings and supporting cooling pipes were attached to the hull, making the submarine look like a giant swimming porcupine. White canvas covered the scaffoldings, supporting several inches or more of ice, all kept frozen by the cooling pipes.

When running, the sub would blow its ballast tanks and the whole "iceberg" would raise about two feet out of the water, allowing the submarine to move. With the added topside weight, the sub would sway back and forth in the water, so giant outriggers were attached to the hull and ran to the outer edges of the berg. When they were stationary, the sub would take on water and would "sit" the berg down on the ocean surface.

Damien grabbed the other set of headphones and took up his lookout position on the opposite side of the mast from Thayer. Thayer tapped his brother on the shoulder and pointed behind them to the left. With binoculars raised, both men paid little attention to anything else as they stared in an almost trance-like state, totally mesmerized by the moving city that was quickly overtaking them.

"Damien, I can see people up on the boat deck, see there, just behind the first funnel," Thayer said excitedly. "And listen, I can hear the band playing." For a moment, both men were silent as they just watched the great ship.

"Look, on the main deck, just below the third lifeboat, I see a couple kissing," Damien replied. "Oh isn't that sweet, they look just like you and Gretchen smooching when we left home—kissy, kissy."

"Shut up!" Thayer glared at his brother, then focused back on the ship. "I wonder where they are all going, what their stories are?"

"I know that we'll be going to the brig and that our story will be a court martial if we don't report in." Damien turned on the small switch on his headset. "Lookout to Con, the ship is about three kilometers. Port aft."

"Con to Lookout, aye."

The electric motor whined as the periscope slowly began to descend back into the bowels of the submarine. A moment later they heard the hatch open. The Lehmann brothers looked down to see the Kapitan and the First Officer coming onto the conning tower. Both officers were wearing white parkas. When Damien saw them, he pointed at them, then to Thayer and mouthed the words *Dooo-dooo*. Thayer gritted his teeth and threw daggers out of his eyes, as that was all he could do at the moment with the Kapitan there.

With both officers concentrating on the ship, Damien turned his attention to the surrounding area. After a moment he stopped and stared in front of them.

"Herr Kappel," he said. "Why is there a hole in the sky?"

Kappel looked at the Kapitan and shook his head. "And to think that I was worried about Thayer there. What are you talking about, Damien?"

"Over there, sir." Damien pointed, just off our port bow."

Kappel raised his binoculars; it did indeed look like a hole in the sky. It was as if someone had taken a knife and carved out a section of the night sky at the horizon, removing the stars and leaving a blank, empty hole. Almost immediately, Kappel started screaming.

"You idiot! Were you both staring at the ship this whole time instead of doing your jobs and looking around?"

"What is it?" Damien asked, panic rising in his voice.

"It's an iceberg, you idiot!"

Kapitan Haufmann spun around and raised his binoculars and looked at the iceberg, horror filling his eyes. "Hard right rudder. Now!" he barked, down through the open hatchway to the control room below.

Startled by the intensity of the shouted order, the young helmsmen spun the wheel hard and fast, and despite its bulk, the submarine responded quickly and lurched to one side. So sudden and quick was the maneuver, the outrigger on the left slammed hard into the water. The force of the impact was so abrupt and great, it sent shock waves reverberating throughout the submarine and through the scaffolding, which acted like giant tuning forks. A large block section of ice hanging over the stern broke off and swirled underneath the submarine and hit the rudder, bending it back to port and lodging itself at the hinge point, jamming the rudder.

"The helm is not answering!" came a frantic cry from below deck.

"Full ahead port engine, full reverse on starboard engine!" Haufmann commanded.

The three men were sitting in the engine room playing cards. First Class seaman Elmar Hirsch was sitting near the bulkhead trying not to smile. At last he had a decent hand and hoped to win back some of his money, aces over eights. Chief engineer Dieter Schwab was sitting across from him, also smiling on the inside. He wasn't smiling because he had a winning hand but because he was amused at Hirsch trying to hide his. Mechanics Mate Otto Grün, was sitting with his back toward the forward hatch, ready to fold, it seemed Lady Luck had left him high and dry.

When the chunks of ice fell off the scaffolding, a huge slab tore a long gash in the port ballast tank, then snagged on a cross beam and swung under the hull with such force that it punched a large hole in the engine room. The force of the impact popped several of the rivets, and one shot out like a bullet, hitting Hirsch in the back of the head. He was dead before his crumpled body hit the deck. Schwab sprang to his feet to help his friend but slipped in the onrush of water and went down hard, jamming his knee on the deck and slamming his head again the side of the metal work-table. He cried out in pain and nearly passed out, but managed to struggle to his feet and grabbed Hirsch. He felt a wave of nausea sweep over him as he pulled his hand from the back of the boy's head; it was covered with blood. Grün rushed to help his crew-mates but had taken only two steps before he was slammed against the bulkhead as the rest of the rivets gave way and the hull collapsed. The deluge of water hurled him against the other bulkhead, crushing him in an instant.

"Why are we still moving?" Kapitan Haufmann shouted down the hatch to the control room. At that same instant, the sub lurched back to the left when the ice bent the rudder and jammed it in the opposite direction.

Thayer was still high on his lookout post, paralyzed with fear, staring at the moving city that wasn't wavering from its imminent collision course. Within moments, an immense wall of moving steel was literally within arm's reach and even though he was fifteen feet above the deck of the submarine, he still couldn't see onto the deck of the liner. Thayer looked at Damien for reassurance but instead of finding comfort, he saw the same wild-eyed look of fear that he had in his own eyes. He was even more terrified now because he had never seen fear in his big brother's eyes before.

He vaguely heard the Kapitan shouting something and then the submarine lunged to one side with such force that he heard the scaffolding breaking and saw huge chucks of ice falling off the sub. Suddenly the submarine lurched back the other way and Thayer felt his hands being torn from the railing and then he found himself falling through the air. With a bone-jarring thud, Thayer landed painfully hard, face down, onto a floating slab of ice.

With dizzying, agonizing pain, he lifted his head and watched through blurry eyes as his submarine continued on without him. The last thing Thayer Lehmann remembered was how cold the ice was and wondering why they were leaving him behind.

"KAPITAN!" Kappel shouted.

Haufmann no longer needed his binoculars to see that less than one hundred meters away, 882 feet of steel was bearing down on his tiny submarine at twenty-one knots.

"I need right full rudder NOW!" Haufmann barked out, but he already knew it was too late and that only a miracle could save his submarine now. The words had no sooner left his mouth than the submarine shook violently and the sounds of grinding, scraping, ripping metal vibrated throughout the boat as the two vessels collided.

The scaffolding and piping of the U-boat bent, twisted and snapped away like dry twigs crushed underfoot. The left bow diving plane punctured the hull of the immense ship and suddenly the submarine was being pulled along by the ship, hitching a ride like a flea on the back of a great dane. For a fleeting moment, the Kapitan was beginning to think that they just might have their miracle, that they just might cheat Death and simply bounce off the great ship. But Death would not be cheated; it would not be denied. For tonight, Death was about to go on a gluttonous rampage.

Haufmann felt the submarine jerk as the dive plane began tearing a great gash in the liner's side. In an instant, the wound had grown to several dozen meters, and in that moment, he knew there would be no miracle.

Suddenly the dive plane caught on a main bulkhead of the ship and instead of sheering off, the fine German engineering and crafts-manship proved their undoing as the dive plane held and it twisted the submarine, pulling her onto her side. The remnants of the scaf-folding and ice shattered against the hull of the ship like a snowball thrown against the side of a house.

The submarine continued to roll and the conning tower was dragged under and smashed against the hull of the great passenger liner, like a tin can placed on a railroad track for a passing freight train to crush. The piercing screams of metal scraping metal alerted no one. They were lost, drowned out by the steady, throbbing heartbeat of the giant liner's engines. The cries of help from the men trapped inside the submarine, once their home, now their coffin, would never reach the living. Their muffled screams were softened into melody as they mixed and mingled with the sounds of music and laughter, floating down from those strolling casually on the decks of the ship six stories above them.

Few, if any, of the passengers of the *R.M.S. Titanic* felt the slight vibration as 53,000 tons of swiftly moving ocean liner brushed aside the six hundred ton gnat that was unfortunate enough to get in its way.

CHAPTER TWO

"It's bloody cold out here. I can't wait to get back to the ship; I'm freezing me bum off out here."

"Stow your complaining, Mr. Sanders."

"Beggin' your pardon, sir, but no one could be alive out here now. Everyone knows that a man can only last a few minutes in these waters before he freezes to death, and the ship went down hours ago."

"Thank you for your assessment, Mr. Sanders, but I think we'll keep looking just the same."

"It would be a bloody miracle to find anyone alive out here," Sanders said under his breath.

"It's a bloody miracle they let you in the merchant marine at all." His friend Tully smiled.

"Oh shut up."

Petty Officer Norton turned around from his position in the bow of the longboat and gave both men a less than satisfactory look.

The sun had been up for several hours, finally revealing the true extent of the tragedy that had happened only a short time before. The surface of the sea was scattered and strewn with debris, looking like the room of a spoiled child who had taken everything out of his drawers and thrown them everywhere. Furniture that had once graced the elegant first class lounge now bobbed up and down gently like giant bathtub toys.

Slowly, the longboat made its way along, the only sound coming from the slapping of the oars as they rowed. Earlier that morning, the precious few found in the water still alive had been picked up. Now, to those in the boats scouring the seas, it was not a mission of finding the living, but of gathering the dead.

"Mr. Norton, what's that? Just there, off our port quarter?" Tully said, pointing on the left side of the boat.

"What? That there?" Sanders replied "It looks like a fat seal sunning himself on that slab of ice."

"Hold oars, let's have a look," Norton said as he took out his binoculars.

As they sat there, a woman's hat lazily drifted by. It was adorned with colorful bird feathers, bright reds, yellows and greens, sticking out in all directions, looking as new as the day it had been bought. It was a stark contrast of color to the dull gloom that enshrouded the area.

"Pull lads, pull hard!" Norton shouted. "That's not a fat seal out there, it's a man." A jolt of electricity shot through the boat at the prospect of finding a survivor. The six men rowing responded with a surge of power and enthusiasm as they began churning the water with their oars. Within a few short minutes the rescue boat had sliced through the icy waters and was approaching the ice slab.

"Stow oars," Norton ordered as they drifted the last several feet to the slab. The bow of the boat made a crunching sound as it nudged its way into the ice. The petty officer reached for the leg of the man sprawled on the ice but his fingers fell several inches short of the man's motionless foot. Unable to reach the body, he grabbed the gaff and placed the hook on the man's belt to drag the body toward the boat. Just as the body started to slide, they heard a low moan.

"Sanders, get up here and help me!" the petty officer yelled. "You too, Tully."

"Aye, sir," they replied in unison. Quickly both men stowed their oars and scrambled to the bow of the boat. In their rush they nearly knocked Norton overboard.

"Be careful, you oaf, you nearly sent me into the water, Tully."

"Sorry, sir."

"Grab his leg there, Sanders," he directed. "Tully, pull him back after Sanders relays him to you."

"Aye, sir."

They struggled to haul the waterlogged man off the ice and into the boat.

"Quick, grab some blankets there," Norton ordered. "Let's get this jacket off him. He's soaked to the bone."

"What have we here?" Sanders said as he tugged and pulled the waterlogged jacket off the man. "That's not something you see every day. It looks like a German Navy uniform."

"So, he's a German sailor," Tully answered.

"Just think it's a bit odd, that's all."

"Well, he'll be a bit dead if you don't hurry up and wrap him in those blankets. Tully, grab some of that hot brandy there too," Norton said.

"Aye, sir."

Propped between the two men, Norton gave the German sailor a sip of brandy. He coughed a little and slowly opened his eyes. They were dazed and confused but they were filled with life.

"There's your miracle, Mr. Sanders," Norton said.

With shaking hands the sailor grabbed the brandy flask. *"Danke."* He drank slowly at first, but soon, the few small sips quickly turned into swigs.

"Easy there, lad," Norton said. "We don't want to have a drunkard on our hands." The German sailor smiled weakly. Norton reached into his pocket and took out a piece of hardtack and gave it to the sailor. "You're very lucky, if you hadn't had on that dark colored jacket, we might never have seen you."

CHAPTER THREE

Present day

The hot desert sun beat down mercilessly through the Plexiglas canopy of his F-15 Eagle, turning the cockpit in to an easy-bake oven, a stark contrast to the thirty degrees below zero on the outside. His crew chief had warned him that the A/C unit was not working properly but he wasn't going to stand down because of that. Melting now from the heat, he felt a trickle of sweat roll down the side of his face; now he knew what the ants felt like when he had held a magnifying glass over them when he was a kid.

His breathing was practiced, slow, and steady and the air had a slight rubber taste as he breathed. He could hear each breath as he inhaled and exhaled through his oxygen mask, the sound reminding him of Darth Vader. Today, he wouldn't be using the Force; instead he would be relying on his Raytheon APG-63(V)3 radar and targeting system.

A warning chirp and blip on his radar erased all thoughts of the Force or the heat in his cockpit as he focused on the screen as the one dot turned into two, then three, then four.

"Blackjack Two to Blackjack One. Picking up four bogies, forty miles out."

"Roger Two, I've got 'em. Maintain speed and heading."

"Copy."

Colonel Douglas Madison glanced out of the cockpit of his fighter. The dry desert sands and barren, craggy rocks below painted a very bleak picture of what he would have to parachute into if he were shot down… that is to say, if he survived.

Suddenly, alarms started sounding and his wingman, Lieutenant Pat Packard, burst in over the radio.

"We've been painted, sir, confirmed bandits, they've got a missile lock… they've fired at extreme range. Tracking missiles."

Madison could hear the alarm in Packard's voice, but to his credit, he maintained control. Four missiles from extreme range, yeah, with two-to-one odds, they could afford to spray and pray missiles away, he couldn't.

"Afterburners now," Madison commanded. "When you get a lock, hold fire until you're at fifteen miles then volley one sparrow then toggle to sidewinders. Break hard on my command." Tongues of fire shot out of the Eagle's twin engines and a loud boom rolled over the desert floor as the two planes burst through the sound barrier, rushing headlong into the face of the enemy.

Madison's plan was simple: close the gap between themselves and the bandits, turn hard at the last possible moment to defeat the incoming missiles, split the aggressors up and through superior tactics and airmanship, neutralize the threat and return home safely. Yeah, simple. Maybe he could use the Force about now.

In his mind's eye, Madison could visualize the approaching missiles, probably Russian AA-9 Amos, with their blood-red tips closing on him at nearly Mach 2.5. Two miles a second.

"Fox one, break now!" Madison shouted. Madison broke right and his wingman broke left as they crisscrossed. Madison felt his straps digging into his shoulders as they held him in place as he set the plane on its side in a knife edge turn. He grit his teeth from the strain as he entered the high-G turn and began to feel a little lightheaded. His pressure suit inflated, pushing the blood back to his brain, keeping him from blacking out.

"All missiles defeated... radar shows one bandit splashed," Packard reported.

Madison didn't acknowledge as he concentrated, watching two of the enemy fighters streaking high above his canopy with the third one going low, disappearing under his wing. He was breathing heavier now, drawing in deeper breaths, keeping the oxygen flowing to his tense body, he now sounded like Darth Vader on steroids. He snapped his head around and saw that Packard was swinging in behind him; Madison now switched his mindset from prey to predator.

Madison was below and behind the pair of enemy fighters and watched as they continued to climb, then curiously they began to turn to the right to reengage. Having lost speed in the turn, he could now easily turn on their inside and track for a missile lock. Within moments his computer "sang" to him with a perfect lock-on tone.

"Fox two!" Madison calmly called out. "Missile tracking... tracking... contact hit, splash two." Madison put his head back on a swivel and started searching for the single aircraft. "Where is the low bandit?"

A moment later, Packard called out. "Got him. Four o'clock low, he's trying to get an angle on us, sir."

With one eye on the remaining high fighter and the other on the low bandit, Madison calculated that he would be in firing position on the high bandit about the same time the low bandit would be in position to get a shot off at Packard. He wanted that third plane badly but no kill was worth the life of his wingman.

"I don't like this set up. Break to two-seven-zero degrees and egress west. We'll see if they want to reengage or call it a day."

"Two," Packard replied automatically.

Several minutes went by as they watched the two remaining planes leave their radarscopes. After another five minutes of making sure they didn't double back, Packard let out a huge sigh.

"Man, that was intense. I almost forgot this was an exercise. I was sweating bullets back there when that aggressor was crawling up our six," Packard said.

"This is your first Red Flag, isn't it?" Madison asked.

"Yes, it is sir, I've been looking forward to it for months. They told me in the briefings that it would be realistic but I had no idea."

Madison smiled under his mask. "It doesn't get any more real than this."

During the Vietnam War it was discovered that if a pilot could complete his first ten combat missions, then his chances of surviving and finishing his tour increased dramatically. Red Flag was designed to give pilots that edge by providing realistic training for those first ten missions.

"One hop down, nine more to go," Packard said, a slight cockiness floating in his voice.

"Blackjack Flight, this is tower, we have an unidentified fast mover at your two o'clock, thirty miles out on the edge of restricted airspace. Please put eyes on the target."

"Tower, Blackjack, roger your request," Madison replied, then thought for a moment. "Tower, is this part of the exercise?"

"Negative, Blackjack, bogie is unknown at this time."

"Roger, we're on our way."

"Begging the Colonel's pardon, sir," Packard said, "but it's probably just a corporate jet flying some bigwigs into Vegas for the weekend. Or who knows, it could even be a UFO up from Area 51. Anyway, sir, I've got the weekend off and have plans, if you know what I mean, sir? Besides, my fuel is getting a little low, couldn't we just abort the mission because of fuel status?"

Unlike his wingman, Madison didn't have a hot date waiting for him at the end of the flight. Instead, he had a desk full of paperwork. Even though he knew Packard was probably right about the corporate jet, anything to delay the inevitable was worth it, even if it meant chasing a UFO.

"What's the matter, Lieutenant, don't you want to see a UFO? Turning right to a heading of one-two-zero."

"Roger, sir," Packard replied, trying, but not very hard, to hide his disappointment.

Madison couldn't help the smile that filled his face under his oxygen mask at his wingman's less than enthusiastic reply. Poor kid. But the girls would wait for their flyboy, and he would get at least another ten minutes in the cockpit, which meant ten minutes less time he'd be flying his desk.

Less than five minutes later, the disappointment that had been in Packard's voice was now replaced with astonishment. "I was kidding earlier about the UFO, but is that what I think it is, sir?"

The pair of F-15 Eagles had come up low and slightly under their target, amazement filling both pilots' eyes.

"Are we in the twilight zone, sir?" Packard added.

"No, Lieutenant, that's the real deal there, an F-86 Sabre, the great granddaddy of us all."

The wings and fuselage of the Saber were polished aluminum. Bold, yellow stripes, bordered with black, sat on each wingtip and a matching yellow diagonal band wrapped around the rear fuselage, halfway between the cockpit and the tail. The vertical stabilizer tail section also sported the wide yellow band with a black lightning bolt coursing through it.

"That thing must be, what, sixty years old?" Packard said.

"Haven't you learned yet, Lieutenant, to never guess a lady's age?" an unfamiliar voice said over the radio. "She's fifty-seven, to be exact. Gabriel Pike, gentlemen, a pleasure to meet you."

"Likewise, Mr. Pike. Colonel Douglas Madison. You sure have a beautiful bird there."

"Thank you, sir, she is my pride and joy, the *Yankee Clipper*."

"Mr. Pike, Lieutenant Packard here, I don't recognize your marking there."

Just behind the cockpit was a logo of a top hat, the kind like Uncle Sam would wear, sitting inside a ring.

"That's the 94th Pursuit Squadron, isn't it?" Madison said.

"Yes it is, you know your history, Colonel." Pike answered." It's my small way of paying tribute to our heroes of the past.

"The 94th?" Packard asked.

"Eddie Rickenbacker flew with the 94th in WWI. You do know who Eddie Rickenbacker was, don't you, Lieutenant?" Madison ribbed.

"Yes, sir, Eddie Rickenbacker was the top American ace of the War to end all Wars with twenty-six victories; we were required to read *ancient* history at the academy," Packard jabbed back.

The 94th, also known as the famous "Hat in the Ring" squadron, was the first operational American fighter squadron in WWI, stationed at Gengault Aerodrome near Toul, France in April of 1918, and being the first, they were allowed to come up with their own insignia. Taking the boxing phrase, throwing your hat in the ring, which meant you were willing fight, they choose the symbol of throwing Uncle Sam's hat into a ring, signifying that America was ready and willing to fight.

"Your bird may have been 'hip' in its day, Mr. Pike, but it can't hold a candle to what we fly now," Packard said, ending with a smug tone in his voice.

A smile began to stretch across Pike's face and a twinkle of anticipation flashed in his green eyes: he did love a challenge. "Just because something is old, doesn't make it useless, Lieutenant." Pike snapped on his oxygen mask, took a deep breath then blew it out slowly. He lowered the flaps a notch, yanked the stick to the right and did a barrel roll up and over the pair of F-15s and in less than three seconds had settled in right behind Packard's aircraft in perfect firing position.

"Colonel?" Packard said.

Madison could hear the surprise and irritation in his wing-man's voice. "I thought you said you were getting low on fuel." Madison replied.

"I have enough, sir."

Now he could hear his teeth gnashing, chomping at the bit. "Well I believe the gauntlet has been thrown down, Mr. Pike?"

"Fine by me, Colonel," Pike replied, then thought for a moment and couldn't resist. "If the lieutenant thinks he can handle it."

"Colonel!" Anger now clearly replaced the irritation in the young lieutenant's voice. "Hang on, Lieutenant, let me get out of the way first. Standard rules of engagement apply." Madison pulled back on his stick as his Eagle leapt above the two combatants. He had the best seat in the house and he wasn't about to miss this show.

Pike edged up beside Packard, the two aircraft now flying in formation, looking like a fly-by for a local air show.

"On my mark," Madison called out.

"Roger," both men replied in unison.

"On three... two..." But before Madison had said 'one' Packard broke hard left and fired his afterburners, streaking up and away like a shooting star. Pike turned in toward Packard to follow, although he knew he could never match the speed of his opponent. He knew his only chance was to stay close and use his only real advantage of being able to out turn his bigger and faster foe. He hoped that Packard wouldn't pull straight out a couple of miles and just turn and fire a missile, he had to keep him close.

"Giving up already, Lieutenant?" Pike taunted. "I didn't think you'd turn tail and run quite so quickly. Maybe you're good with missiles, but how long would you last in a knife fight?"

The radio remained silent, but the message had its desired effect as the F-15 pulled straight up and over in a tight loop and came straight back at him. Pike smiled, with that sharp of a yank on the controls, he knew Packard was pushing it for all it was worth, he was mad. Self-confidence, a supreme belief in one's own abilities, and an ego to match were all qualities of a good fighter pilot, but there was one other quality that Packard was missing right now – patience. And Pike was going to exploit it as much as he possibly could.

The two aircraft were two miles apart but closing at a combined speed of over 900 knots. Both pilots had just seconds to react. Pike put his plane in a shallow dive, gaining speed and keeping just enough angle that Packard couldn't get a good firing solution. Pike kept pushing the stick forward, forcing Packard into a steeper angle, putting him into negative G-forces, making it very difficult to maneuver and very, very uncomfortable, even with modern G-suits.

A smart pilot, a *patient* pilot, would continue on in the pass and extend out for another run, Pike was betting everything he had that Packard wouldn't do that, but a little extra insurance never hurt. "Your Eagle can fly fast in a straight line, but can she turn?" Pike said with a measured tone of sarcasm in it. Pike thought he heard the colonel snicker, which meant that Packard could hear it too, a broad smile filled Pike's face, that was the icing on the cake he needed.

A split second before they merged, Pike pulled back on the stick and shoved it to the right. Looking over his shoulder he saw that Packard was doing the same thing, only he was moving way to fast to make the turn. Pike began losing color in his vision and felt a little light-headed as the pressure of G-forces drained the blood from his head. He hated the odd sensation but he didn't have the luxury of a G-suit. With the pressure, he was beginning to feel every second of his age and he knew his body would give him hell to pay in the morning, but if he could just pull this off... he grit his teeth and continued to pull back on the stick. Pike came up and over the top of his loop and caught Packard halfway through his. Had this been a real fight, Pike would have raked the length of Packard's fuselage with gunfire, shooting straight into his canopy. As he was "shooting," Pike called out "guns, guns, guns" over the radio, simulating his firing. Pike then rolled the *Yankee Clipper* over and locked into a good firing position on the lieutenant's six and again called out "guns." He stayed within range for a solid three to four seconds, which is an eternity in aerial combat before the F-15s superior speed took over and he pulled out of gun range.

"I'm calling bingo fuel," Colonel Madison interrupted. "Fight's over."

"But Colonel," Packard protested.

"Negative, Lieutenant, it's time to return to base. If I'm getting low on fuel from just watching, you've got to be pushing it. My butt will be in a sling if anybody back at base finds out what we're doing out here, let alone if we run out of gas."

"Roger sir, forming up," Packard replied reluctantly.

Pike let out a sigh of relief as he joined up next to the colonel's plane. At forty-one, he was nowhere near being what you would call old, but pulling six-G turns in aerial combat was definitely a younger man's sport. "Thank you, gentlemen, I thoroughly enjoyed myself, though I think I'll be paying for it in the morning."

"Our pleasure, Mr. Pike, it's not often we get to fly in the same skies with a legendary war bird like yours," Madison replied.

"Mr. Pike...?" Packard began.

Oh no, here it comes, Pike thought, Packard's going to make all sorts of excuses for losing...

"...I just wanted to say thank you sir. You've taught me some valuable lessons today." Pike smiled and nodded his head slightly, *humility*, he thought, an even rarer commodity for a fighter pilot, this kid might just go places.

"You're welcome, Lieutenant."

"Keep 'em flying, Mr. Pike," Madison said. "Tower this is Black-jack Flight, we've identified the bogie as a private aircraft, we're coming home." Colonel Madison's plane banked smartly to the left followed by Packard's a split second later. Pike watched for a moment as the two F-15s pulled away, then he banked to the right.

CHAPTER FOUR

"Don't forget your lunch."

"Yes, dear," Albert Jenkins dutifully replied as he picked up the brown paper bag off the counter.

"And don't doddle tonight. Remember, the grandkids are coming over for dinner,"

"Yes, dear."

"Oh, and would you please take the garbage out with you? I forgot it last night."

"Yes, dear."

Martha Jenkins, Albert's wife of forty-one years, stopped wiping off the kitchen table and looked at her husband. "Are you listening to what I'm saying?" Putting her hands on her hips, "And if you answer 'yes, dear' one more time you'll be so far in the doghouse you'll be in the basement."

Jenkins walked over and gave his wife a hug and a peck on the cheek, then reached down and squeezed her lower cheek. Martha giggled and slapped him on the shoulder. "Dirty old man." Jenkins just smiled and cocked his head to one side and nodded slightly, said, "Yes, dear" and grabbed the sack of garbage as he went out the door.

"Morning, Albert."

"Morning, Steve." Jenkins greeted the branch manager as he let him in the front door. "Looks like it's going to be another hot one today."

"Not too hot, I hope," Steve Hertz replied, "My son's going up north for a football game today and you know those school busses don't have air conditioners. I wanted to go but somebody has to hold down the fort."

"No rest for the wicked, or for bank managers." Jenkins smiled. He turned to lock the door when he heard his name called. He looked up to see Mary Thomas running up the walk.

"Hey, Al!" Mary called out cheerfully. She was about the only one at the bank that called him Al, but he didn't mind.

"Hi, Mary, come on in." Jenkins smiled and swung the door open, bowing as he waved her in. Mary was his favorite teller. He'd never seen her down, always wearing a smile and the way she looked at life was so refreshing, especially from a young lady whose hair was blonde today but could change by the end of the week and who occasionally forgot to take out her nose ring. But his fondness for her was more than just her outlook on life. There was a personal side to it: she reminded him of his daughter. His Amanda would have been about three years older than Mary, if her life hadn't been taken from her.

"There's a new sushi bar that just opened down the street," Mary said cheerfully. "A bunch of us are going there for lunch, you wanna come?"

"No thanks," he said, shaking his head and chuckling a little. "I prefer my food cooked."

"Okay," she replied and got her cash drawer from the vault and prepared to open her window.

Jenkins opened the doors to the bank, then went to the back to bring out some coffee and cookies for the customers. When he returned, two men in old torn green Army jackets and tattered jeans were standing at the center island filling out deposit slips. One had dark greasy hair pulled back in a ponytail and the other had a shaved head with four or five earrings each running from his earlobe up through the cartilage. Neither looked like they had bathed in days.

He slowed a step as he approached, not liking what he was seeing. Nonchalantly, he put the coffee and cookies on the counter next to the men and sized them up the best he could without staring. He greeted them with a cheery "Good Morning." One ignored him completely while the other raised his head briefly and just grunted a sour "mornin'."

When he lifted his head, Jenkins noticed tiny beads of sweat on the man's forehead. It was warm outside, but not that warm. Jenkins felt his stomach twisting into a tangled mess of knots; he knew they were in serious trouble. Jenkins smiled and slowly turned around. "Mary, I forgot the napkins, I'll be back in a few!" he called out. He hoped that by telling these two guys why he was leaving it would keep them from panicking and give him time to trip the silent alarm.

He had taken three steps when he heard the front doors slam open. He turned to see two men come storming in the bank. One pulled out a handgun and the other carried a sawed off shotgun. They were shouting for everyone to get down. Jenkins quickly turned around, he had to get to the teller windows to send the alarm. He turned but stopped dead in his tracks, finding himself staring down the barrel of a gun.

"Going somewhere, old man?" the bald headed man said, snickering. He spun Jenkins around and shoved him toward the teller windows.

"For all you geniuses out there, this is a robbery!" the man with the shotgun yelled. He was wearing a long, black trench coat and had his hair oiled back, playing a very poor Neo wannabe from *The Matrix*. He took out pillowcases and tossed them to the man with the ponytail.

Ponytail went down the line and threw a pillowcase at the first two tellers but stopped when he got to Mary. He threw the last pillowcase to the end teller then turned to Mary and held it open. "Trick or Treat," he said with a slick smile.

Neo stood in front of the tellers and shouted, "Dump your cash drawers into the bags! Be smart and don't do anything stupid like give us any of your specially marked bills or be a hero and trip any silent alarms. Be smart and nobody gets hurt."

Jenkins was at the end of the counter and noticed that Ponytail was paying particular attention to Mary. He kept reaching across the counter and touching her hands as she emptied the drawer and each time she would swat them away like an annoying fly. *Good for you*, he thought; don't let the creep intimidate you.

"You sure are pretty. Maybe you and I could party a little, huh?" Ponytail said as he reached up and tried to touch Mary's hair.

She hit it away hard. "Buzz off, jerk."

Suddenly he reached out and grabbed her by the hair and nearly pulled her halfway across the countertop. She let out an involuntary yelp, just as much from surprise as from the pain. "Me and you is definitely going to do some partying." He shoved her back and turned, wearing a big, sadistic smile then he yelled to the man with the shotgun. "Hey boss, I like this one, can we keep her? I think she wants to play."

It was a defining moment for Albert Jenkins as he watched the drama unfolding before him. It opened up a floodgate of memories that swirled in his head like a cyclone. Thoughts of Martha, of Amanda when she was growing up, the fun they had… the last time he saw her alive. He bit his lip, fighting to contain the swelling emotions. He hadn't been there to save his Amanda, but he was here now and he would not let anything happen to Mary.

He knew it wouldn't bring his little girl back or even if it would help to relieve any of the pain. He also knew that he was projecting all those memories of Amanda onto Mary. The guilt and anguish came charging back like a wild animal, threatening to trample his heart again. But it also didn't change the fact that it was simply the right thing to do.

"Leave her alone," Jenkins said in a voice he couldn't believe was his own.

The smile faded from Ponytail's face as he looked at Jenkins, then stomped over and shoved his gun under his chin. "What did you say, old man?"

"I said leave her alone."

The gunman stared long and hard at Jenkins then burst out laughing. "Look at him, boss, the old man has the thousand yard stare. You tough guy, old man? Huh? You some kind of Rambo?" He laughed. "I think we're going to take her with us, you know, a 'sweet' hostage." He winked at Jenkins.

"You don't want to take a hostage," Jenkins said, amazed at himself for sounding so calm and cool. "She'll only slow you down and get in the way. Bank robbery is one thing but if you take a hostage the police are going to take it real personal. They won't stop until you're all caught... or dead."

Ponytail laughed again. "What is she, your little girlfriend?" Then his face turned cold again and shoved the gun harder into Jenkins' chin. "You want to die, old man? I said we're taking her. Keep it up and I'll send you straight to hell."

"I don't want to die and I'm not going to hell when I do die. Can you say the same? And you're still not taking her." Before Ponytail could reply, Jenkins turned to the man holding the shotgun. "Hey, boss man! Does this guy speak for everybody? Is he calling the shots here? Think about it, do you really want to make it personal and have the cops hound you to the ends of the earth over a girl?"

The gunman hit Jenkins across the face with the gun. "Oh don't you worry, old man, I intend to make it *real* personal." Jenkins staggered back with his lip bleeding but managed to stay on his feet.

"Enough talking now," Ponytail said, looking at Mary. "Get your sweet little butt over here and let's go. Do it quick and I might let your boyfriend here live."

"Leave her," Neo said.

"What?" No way!"

"I said leave her!" Neo shouted back. "The old man is right; we don't need her to slow us down. Besides, with as much money as we have, you can buy any woman you want."

"No! I want Rambo's girlfriend here and I'm taking her with us."

"Leave her or I'll leave you." Neo pumped the shotgun and fired a round into the side of the counter right next to his friend. "Your choice, man."

Ponytail stood there and shook with rage. He looked at Boss, then the hole in the wall, then back to Jenkins. Unable to contain his building rage any longer, he exploded like a volcano, letting out a huge prolonged yell, then turned to Jenkins and shot him in the chest.

"Let's go," Ponytail said as he grabbed the pillowcases full of money and headed for the door. Steve Hertz was standing at the other end of the counter and as Ponytail walked by, he shot him in the leg without even slowing down.

"Crazy idiot," Boss said, shaking his head. He whistled to the other two men and they all left.

Mary came running from behind the counter and knelt beside Jenkins and cradled his head in her arms, tears flowing.

"I'm one for two now." He coughed, seeing she was safe. "Tell my wife I'm going to be late for dinner."

CHAPTER FIVE

Pike throttled back and a brought the *Yankee Clipper* down to 8,000 feet and set the auto-pilot. He reached under his seat and grabbed a sandwich. His stomach was still a little queasy from the dogfight but he was hungry none the less. The roast beef was a little dry so he reached back under and grabbed a fruit drink pouch. He would have preferred a cold bottle of water or tall glass of milk, or better yet, a frosty mug of root beer, but none of those traveled well in his cramped cockpit.

With steely-eyed determination he took off the little straw and prepared to *try* and poke it through the tiny serving hole. He could pilot a fighter jet, decipher blueprints that would drive da Vinci mad and balance his checkbook at the end of the month, yet there were two things in life he couldn't do: figure out what made women tick and how to put the straw in a juice pouch without spilling it all over himself. After four failed attempts, which were two more than he usually tried, he reached into the shoulder pocket of his flight suit and pulled out a small Swiss Army Knife.

This was one of the more unusual of the Swiss knives; this one didn't have all the gizmos and gadgets: it actually had a blade that he could use. He'd learned from years of experience and dozens of dry cleaning bills just how to open one of these things without getting juice all over himself. He flipped out the blade, then carefully grabbed the top of the pouch with his left hand. With the skill of a surgeon, he inserted the blade into the pouch and began cutting.

The tab was removed and surgery was almost complete; all he had to do now was insert the straw and enjoy. Just as he was putting in the straw, the *Clipper* hit a pocket of rough air and bounced up and down harder than a Model T Ford on a washboard road. As he bounced, he accidentally squeezed the pouch, sending the straw shooting out like a missile and juice gushing out like a geyser. Some of the juice hit the top of the canopy then started "raining" down in tiny droplets, while more splattered on his flight suit, but the majority of it landed in his lap. Pike looked down and shook his head, hoping it would dry before he had to land and refuel. No amount of explaining would curb the snickers and laughs he would get as he climbed out of the cockpit if his suit were still wet. He ate his sandwich and downed what was left of the juice.

There were advantages to having your own private jet to fly in, but there were also disadvantages too, one being boredom. He hadn't quite figured out how to get a stewardess on board yet. He began tuning the radio to see if he could find anything interesting to listen to and help pass the time. He passed over two country western stations, one song was about getting out of prison and the other was about a dog and an old pickup truck. Next, he scanned across a soft rock station that almost put him to sleep on the spot.

Suddenly something up ahead caught his eye, so he decided to drop down and take a look. He leveled off at 5,000 feet and tipped his wing down as he did a fly over. There were two high school busses parked on the side of the road with four cars pulled in behind them. Several men were standing around the front of the lead bus while the drivers were working on changing a flat tire. Cheerleaders, football players and students were milling around the busses, cell phones in hand, no doubt relaying their harrowing plight to friends and families.

Pike brought the *Clipper* around for another pass, only this time he came in low and fast. He skimmed over the desert floor at about 500 feet and pushed the airspeed up to 400 knots. Every eye on the ground was watching as he roared by. Pike smiled to himself; this was one of those times when it was good to have your own jet. A couple of the football players raised their helmets and cheered as he went by while several of the cheerleaders shook their pompoms and did a quick cheer. As he streaked by the two drivers gave him a wave and he returned it with a quick salute and waggle of his wings. He smiled as he did a quick snap roll and then pulled up and out. Tom Cruise, eat your heart out.

The small adrenaline rush soon faded and he was back to channel surfing again. He found two rock stations, one classical, a talk show talking about the economy, what else? With nothing he really wanted to listen to, he was about to turn the radio off when the last station caught his ear.

"Breaking news. Police have just reported that the US Bank in Logandale has been robbed at gunpoint. One bank guard has been killed and another teller has also been shot and is in critical condition. Nevada Highway Patrol reports that the suspects are driving a dark green, late model Dodge Charger, and they are in a high-speed pursuit heading north on Highway 93. Suspects are armed and considered extremely dangerous. Anyone traveling north or south bound on Highway 93 between Ash Springs and Las Vegas should use extreme caution."

Pike frowned as an uneasy feeling crept into the cockpit with him. He had all the latest GPS navigational equipment but sometimes plain, good old-fashioned paper maps worked best. He unfolded one and quickly checked his location against his GPS, then turned the *Clipper* south and followed the road, hoping all the while that he was wrong. A few minutes later his worst fears were confirmed. In the distance he saw a trail of flashing lights following about a mile behind a dark sedan moving faster than a bat out of hell. They were on a collision course, heading straight for the stranded school busses. These criminals were desperate men who had already killed, Pike shuddered to think what would happen if they got their hands on a bus full of hostages.

There were only a few minutes before they would reach the kids; he had to do something, but what? If he were in his car, he would have hit the steering wheel out of frustration, since there was no wheel; he did the next best thing and slammed his fist against the side of his canopy. He pulled back up to 5,000 feet and swung back to the north, towards the buses. Time was running out, and he still didn't have any ideas of what he was going to do and he could only hit his canopy so many times. What could he do? It's not like he could dive down and strafe the bad guys… or could he?

Suddenly, the seed of a wild thought was sown. He knew he should have stopped and torn it out by the roots, but instead, he watered it with desperation and a plan soon began to flourish. Quickly he found the busses and surveyed the surrounding area. The vehicles were behind a small outcropping at the top of a slight rise. Pike banked hard around and saw the suspects coming up over a small hill. Soon they would drop down into a large, shallow draw. It was perfect.

He would probably lose his pilot's license for this but he couldn't stand by and do nothing. He pushed the throttle forward nearly to the stops and brought the *Yankee Clipper* out wide and flew down the middle of the draw, heading straight for the bandits' car. He concentrated as he flew down the draw, keeping a careful eye on the altimeter and air speed indicator as he put the plane in a shallow dive. For a moment he had visions of himself as William Holden in the movie *Bridges at Toko-Ri* or as the young Luke Skywalker as he focused on lining up on the car. He swore that if he heard the words "Use the Force, Luke," he was bailing out. The *Clipper* quickly gained speed and reached 600 miles an hour in a matter of seconds. He was down to 2,500 feet and still descending, still picking up speed.

The bank robbers had widened the distance between themselves and their pursuers to nearly a mile and a half now; timing would be everything. Pike continued to dive and was at 1,500 feet and pushing 725 miles an hour, just a little lower, just a little faster. At a half-mile out, he pushed the throttle to the stops and nudged the stick forward.

His hands were sweating and he could feel his heart racing, pounding out a beat that any punk-rock band would have trouble keeping up with. His mouth was dryer than the sands of the Nevada desert below and forget about even trying to describe how his stomach felt. Was this what it was like to go into real combat? Playing tag with the F-15s earlier had been fun and exciting, but nothing was really at stake, no lives to be saved or lost, only pride and egos, but this was different. Here, now, there was a very real threat, with the very real possibility of lives being lost, not only to the kids if they were taken hostage by the murderers, but to himself. One wrong move, one mistake at this speed and altitude and he wouldn't even have time to say "Oh crap" before he would plow into the desert floor.

Just before he reached the car, Pike took one last deep breath and leveled out at 500 feet and watched as his air speed reached 767 miles an hour. That's when it happened.

Slumbering dust and dirt particles now bolted up and swirled and mingled with leaves ripped from the desert plants. They formed a storm cloud that swarmed and engulfed the car in a chaotic mass. The windows on the bandits' car were shattered and the car jostled violently as if shaken by a giant unseen hand. It swerved off the road and the right front tire dug into the soft sand, flipping the car twice before it came to rest on its side. The sonic boom had lacerated the valley floor and the car as the silver F-86 Sabre streaked overhead, breaking the sound barrier.

Blowing out several deep breaths to calm himself, Pike gently pulled back on the stick with a shaky hand and circled the area. He felt such a rush that he felt like he didn't need the *Clipper* to fly right now. He felt like he had thrown the winning touchdown pass at the Super Bowl or hit a grand slam in the bottom of the ninth to win the game. Four Highway Patrol cruisers quickly surrounded the wrecked car and the troopers jumped out guns drawn and ready. The lead cruiser's windshield was shattered but was still intact; fortunately it had been far enough away from the sonic boom just to have it fractured and not blown it out completely. As he swung over the buses, Pike could see that some of the kids appeared scared but none seemed to be hurt. The slight roll of the draw and outcropping help shield the kids from the effects of the sound blast.

"*Yankee Clipper*, this is McCarran International, you are requested to change your flight plan and return here immediately."

Pike sighed, like he didn't know that was coming. No good deed goes unpunished, he thought, it was time to pay the piper now. "McCarran, this is *Yankee Clipper*, roger on your request, ETA in thirty minutes." Pike banked his Sabre around and passed over the swarm of police cars and the two news helicopters that were hovering over the scene. He circled one more time then pointed the *Clipper's* nose towards Las Vegas. At least he'd be there in time for the evening buffet, *if* he wasn't in jail.

CHAPTER SIX

The bright red helicopter with the flashy logo of a large number eight inside a diamond, and the catchy phrase "News You Can Trust," circled high overhead, swarming like locust with the other dozen or so news station helicopters. Below, twice that many number of boats of assorted sizes filled the crowded waters. You could tell who the big news stations were by the size of the yachts they had chartered to cover the event.

The big three major American news networks each had chartered large spacious yachts, sleek and modern with well-appointed interiors, projecting a sense of power, authority and believability when they flashed to their news anchors seated inside, surrounded by teak and polished brass.

The British and French networks, having a more classic sense of style, showed up with their own yachts. Older, traditional looking vessels with straight bowlines that parted the water rather than slashing at it like the stiletto bows of their American counterparts. But they too projected their own image of a regal, elegant time gone by when you could trust what you heard.

From there, the rest of the circling boats ranged in size, depending on the bank accounts of the news stations renting them. They varied from the family cabin cruiser to the weekend runabout and the YouTube amateur trying to make the next big viral video.

A few of the larger yachts came close to each other, each skipper displaying his seamanship in a show of one-upmanship. Not to be outdone, a few of the smaller speedboats intentionally soaked their neighbors in their wake, but all in all, it was an almost carnival-like atmosphere as everyone jockeyed for the best angle, the best shot to show their audience.

And at the center of this three-ring news circus was a huge iceberg, half a mile long and nearly that wide... being towed by ten oceangoing tugs.

A tanned and well-manicured hand picked up the remote off the podium and turned off the huge projection screen covering one wall of the conference room. Another button was pushed and the automatic shades silently began to rise, revealing a sweeping, panoramic view of the New York City skyline. The room had the look and feel of a lounge of a five star hotel rather than that of a corporate meeting room. Thirty-five wingback chairs surrounded the podium in a semi-circle; all crafted from the finest leather.

Each of the chairs had been pre-assigned by random selection. Nationally syndicated columnists or TV personalities seen by millions every day could find themselves sitting next to a reporter whose last story could have been on who attended the most resent Rotary Club meeting in Small Town, USA. Breaking the usual status quo like this was a practice that their host was well known for. He said he enjoyed the possibilities that it opened by defying the status quo. But despite their fame, or lack of it, every guest found on their chair a personalized press release and their favorite drink waiting for them on the solid oak cocktail tables that were nestled between the chairs. All the chairs were full, save one. The press release sat untouched in the chair and the frosted mug of root beer was getting warm.

As the lights and shades came up, so did the intensity and the anticipation in the room. All eyes shifted away from the screen and now concentrated on the man behind the podium. The room, the entire building, which he owned, reflected the presence of the man now standing before them. Physically, he was commanding, standing slightly less than six feet four inches. His dark brown hair was neatly trimmed, as was his Clark Gable mustache. By the age of 25, he had made his first million in technologies; by 35 he had branched out and diversified. He had oil investments in the Middle East, textile plants in the Far East, manufacturing facilities throughout Europe, and agricultural interests in South America, with his technology division based in the United States. At the ripe old age of 39, Nigel Cain had become one of the ten richest men in the world.

"Thank you all for coming," Cain said, his voice relaxed and friendly, yet projecting an air of authority and control. "That was the scene five years ago," he continued, pointing at the screen with the remote. "As you know, the purpose of moving the iceberg was to bring safe, affordable, clean water to impoverished third world countries whose populations have either outstripped their ability to provide fresh water for drinking and farming, or whose economies have been ravaged by drought."

Nearly every hand in the place rose like a classroom full of third graders, each one eager to have the teacher call on them first. Cain quickly scanned the room and picked a reporter sitting in the third row. The man was in his early forties, with graying hair that gave him an air of distinction. His glasses were five years out of style and out of habit, he pushed them up off the bridge of his nose before he raised his hand.

"Mr. Taylor, you have a question? For those of you who don't know, Mr. Taylor is from the St. Helens Chronicle, covering the news for us in the greater Portland metropolitan area in the great Pacific Northwest."

Taylor was in shock, surprised that Cain had actually chosen him over the famous news anchor that was sitting to his right, let alone knowing his name. Suddenly he felt very self-conscious as every eye in the room was on him. He cleared his throat and prayed his voice didn't crack as he asked his question.

"Yes, Mr. Cain." No cracks. "You said the purpose was to bring 'affordable' water to these countries. Isn't it true that you lost nearly ten million dollars on this venture with very little results?"

Cain smiled warmly and with a hint of satisfaction. It's the kind of smile you see on a gambler playing blackjack as the house stays on nineteen and he just drew a ten of diamonds for twenty. "Thank you, Mr. Taylor, I couldn't have asked for a better segue question even if I had written it myself." Light laughter floated around the room.

"Mr. Taylor, unlike a politician, I will answer your question directly." More chuckles. "To be precise, I lost 10.3 million dollars, and yes, less than fifteen percent of the iceberg's potential translated into usable water. But that was mostly a publicity stunt, meant to raise the public's awareness of the plight of third world countries and the devastating effects of droughts and the shifting weather patterns caused by global warming."

Cain paused for moment, his demeanor becoming more serious. "But now, this country, the greatest nation on the face of the earth, has begun to feel some of the very same effects of devastating droughts that our third world neighbors have felt. We have major reservoirs in several states drying up and already states are gearing up for the upcoming legal battles, preparing for the 'water wars' that will surely happen if we run out of water."

Cain placed both hands on the podium and leaned slightly forward, a wrinkle of concern creasing his tanned brow. Completely gone was the conversational language he had used earlier; he now spoke with more purpose and thought, as if each word spoken was more important than the last, building to a monumental truth. "What do think would happen to the economy of the United States if we ran out of water? Impossible you say?

"Devastating droughts have already hit the South, threatening millions in Georgia and Florida; reservoirs in upper New York State have dropped to record lows and in the west, the Sierra Nevada snowpack is melting faster than ever. The government reports that 36 states could face water shortages within the next five to seven years. Even if only a few states had to ration water, the economic turmoil would ripple through the entire country.

"And if the economy of this great country crumbles, so goes the entire world." Cain paused for a moment, letting the silence punctuate his point, looking slowly around the room. "Now I know I've painted a bleak picture, full of doom and gloom..." Cain paused and took a deep breath, then suddenly straightened up as he continued in a lighter tone, "...but I had to make some use of my Acting 101 class in college." Nervous smiles and laughter fell flat against the floor.

"But fear not, where there's a shadow, there's a light, where there's a will *and* technology, there is a way." With a nod of his head, the window blinds began to lower again and the lights dimmed. At the same time, six men came from behind the podium wheeling in a table that was fifteen feet long and five feet wide. It was draped with a white satin cloth that hung down to the floor, revealing nothing that was underneath.

"Many say that oil is the life blood of modern society and that oil, not love, is what makes the world go round. I'm certainly not going to argue the fact that oil and love are important things but let me put it to you this way. Man has survived centuries without oil but how long can he survive without water? Days, not centuries. Water is used not only for us to drink and bathe in but it grows the very food we eat, and it too, along with oil helps turns the wheels of industry.

"The United States uses more water than any other nation in the world. The average American uses about 100 gallons of water a day, compared to the average in India which is just 14 gallons—and the numbers go up from there. You're probably saying to yourself that you don't drink that much water... especially if there's a cold beer around." Just then someone in the back of the room yelled "Hear, Hear!" Everyone in the room laughed and Cain smiled as he continued. "That's right my friend, but did you know that it takes 1,500 gallons of water to produce just one barrel of beer? And that Big Mac or Whopper some of you will have for lunch today? One gallon of water to process it. But these numbers are only the beginning."

Cain now came around from the back of the podium and stood beside it, leaning on it with his left elbow, gesturing with his right hand. "Remember earlier, I said that water, not oil, is what makes the world go round? Well, it takes 1,851 gallons of water to refine that one barrel of oil. It takes over 39,000 gallons of water to make just one car and a staggering 62,000 gallons to make one ton of steel." Cain paused and picked up a glass of water and swirled the ice cubes around. The clinking sounds of the cubes filtered to the back of the room and the light refracted off the ice and the crystal glass, sending shards of light out, glittering like light bouncing off a disco ball. He took a big drink and let out a satisfying, "Ahhhh."

"Again, pardon me for my earlier theatrics, as I don't mean to cause alarm," he paused as he set the glass back down, "but the alarms have already sounded with the banners warning us of global warming." He stopped again and held up his hands in mock surrender. "Don't worry, this is not another speech about global warming, but the threat here is very real."

Cain stepped away from the podium and walked slowly back and forth as he continued to speak, like a preacher giving his Sunday morning sermon. "What you see before you is not *the* solution but just one of many. It will realize the dream that was begun five years ago with the first iceberg, to give developing and drought stricken countries a chance not only to help their people to survive but to overcome. And it will allow countries like ours to safeguard our own citizens and maintain our position of world leadership.

"Even as we speak," Cain continued as he stepped down from the podium and moved toward the covered table, "the prototype is being constructed and, in fact, is nearly complete." Cain grabbed the cloth and yanked it off with the flair of a magician revealing that he had just made his lovely assistant disappear. At the same moment, spotlights shown down, illuminating the case as if it were a great revelation from God Himself.

Cain quietly slipped back up to the podium while the crowd slowly gathered around the case. Cain enjoyed studying their faces as they gasped at the display. Most were duly impressed although they didn't fully realize or understand what they were looking at. A few faces were filled with wonder and he could see their minds racing. They too didn't fully comprehend but they had the idea, they got the concept. And a few, to his disappointment, actually looked bored. They were the same dull people who lived out their same dull lives day after day. He actually felt sorry for them; they were the people cursed with no imagination. Black and white is all they would ever understand.

The case contained a highly detailed ocean diorama, built by the finest model makers that Hollywood had to offer. In the center of the case was a huge oblong man-made iceberg. Buried deep within the block of ice were the hulls of four ships, equally spaced and connected together by steel beams. Running throughout the entire length and breadth of the block were a myriad of pipes, flowing from the ships like wires running out of an old fashioned switchboard. There were also mazes of tunnels carved out in the interior, making it look like a giant, elaborate ant farm.

The top of the iceberg was crowded with building of various sizes and shapes, all adorned with flashing neon lights. It looked like Cain had scooped up a city block from downtown Las Vegas and put it on top of the iceberg. One large ocean going tug was in the front towing it, with two more in the stern pushing.

When the initial buzz of excitement and conversation died down, Cain continued.

"I'll not bore you by throwing more facts and figures at you but I do need to touch on just a few of the highlights here. You'll find all the complete details and specific information inside your press binders." Cain walked around the display, gesturing passionately as he spoke. He wasn't just reciting facts, he was introducing his "baby" to the world, and spoke with almost the same fervor as a new father does while passing out cigars in the waiting room.

"The ice block is a 1,000 feet long, 100 feet high, and 100 feet deep. As you can see, buried within the ice are four support vessels. Each ship is 440 feet long, and in this day of reduce, reuse, recycle, all four ships are recycled WWII mothballed merchant ships, cleaned up and brought back to service.

"The elaborate piping system throughout the block has a two-fold purpose: one, during transport the pipes will circulate coolant to keep the block intact. And two, once it arrives at its destination, they will be used to help melt the ice. The entire system is self-contained. Once the ice starts to melt, it will be gathered and filtered in one of the ships which has a built-in processing station, making it safe to drink, then pumping it to shore. As the ice melts and the pipes become exposed, they will be dismantled and loaded back into another of the ships to be reused again and again.

"Once the tops of the ships are exposed, remaining chucks of ice will be loaded directly into the ship's melters and processed, giving us a 60-70% usage rate. And what does that 60-70% get you? About 42 million gallons of water. To break that down into more practical terms, at least for now and for our thirsty friend in the back there, that's enough to make 28,000 barrels of beer, and that's the whole plan in a nutshell."

CHAPTER SEVEN

...and here are several more reasons the Apollo moon landings in the 60s and 70s were a hoax. If debris from the Apollo missions was left on the Moon, then it would be visible today through powerful telescopes. However, no such debris can be seen. The Clementine probe that recently mapped the Moon's surface failed to show any Apollo artifacts left by Man during the missions. Where did the Moon Buggy and base of the LM go? And for that matter, why were blueprints and plans for the Lunar Module and Moon Buggy destroyed if this was one of history's greatest accomplishments?

Gabriel Pike pushed himself back from the small desk that was situated in the corner of his hotel room. He'd been reading for the past hour on his computer and he needed a break. He stood and stretched his muscles, which he could feel starting to tighten up, protesting his aerobatics earlier in the day. He wasn't looking forward to feeling their full wrath in the morning. As he stretched, he took a moment to look out at the view.

He was on the 28th floor of the Treasure Island. The night was clear and the dazzling lights of the casinos along the Strip blazed brightly, beckoning all to come visit Lady Luck and win their fortune. What most tourists didn't know was that Lady Luck had had already left town last night on the red-eye back to Pomona.

It was a warm night and the strip was crowed as usual. He watched as the crowds moved in packs between the blocks, governed by the traffic signals, followed by the inevitable stragglers who were heeding the Siren's call and were in too much of a hurry to lose their money to wait for the next light.

It was a nice view, certainly better than a jail cell, which was what he half expected after his little super-sonic stunt in the desert earlier that day. He sighed as he watched the lights of a Boeing 767 making its approach into McCarran and wondered if he would ever fly again. Thankfully his brush with the blues was cut short by a knock on the door.

Pike opened the door to see the smiling face of Tony Roberts. Tony was one of the interns who had been with Pike's engineering firm for about three months with one more year to go before he graduated from the University of Washington. He was a bright kid, tall with sandy blond hair and dimples that attracted girls like bees to honey when he smiled, which was most of the time. At 25, he was living the dream: he was single, in Las Vegas, *and* on a company expense account, a kid in a candy store with a pocket full of quarters.

"Howdy, boss," Tony beamed.

"Hey Tony, come on in."

Tony walked in and saw the laptop on the table. "What ya looking at there boss? Please don't tell me its porn, my whole image of you would be so shattered. I'd be scarred for life."

"Very funny. I was just relaxing a little."

Tony walked over and started reading. "More conspiracy stuff, huh? Let me guess: it was Dr. Pepper on the grassy knoll with a loaded widget... and he wasn't working alone because he was sponsored by a covert, black ops government agency, secretly working out of Area 51 using alien technology, right?"

"Oh, you read the post too, huh?" They both laughed.

"Come on, boss, everyone is waiting downstairs for you."

"Why? Are they giving me a going away wake before they ship me out to the big house?"

"You mean haven't seen the news?"

"No, I've been reading for the past couple of hours, why?

Tony shook his head and smiled as he led Pike out of his hotel room. "You really are more clever or lucky than you think you are."

As the elevator doors opened, Pike was immediately assaulted by a shock wave of sight and sound. Bleeps, chirps, buzzers and bells filled the cavernous main casino floor. Slot machines lined the floor like soldiers awaiting orders. The flashing lights and cheery sounds all helped to deaden the pain for the gamblers as the money went in but very little came out.

Though he wasn't much of a gambler, there was one thing he did miss. In the old days when the quarter was king, when you hit the jackpot, you heard the joyous sound of the quarters spewing out and clunking into the metal tray. With each clunk, you could hear and feel yourself getting richer and richer. The efficiency of modern business had taken over and now the machines spit out a little pieces of paper stating your winnings. No cascade of quarters to run your fingers through; just a slip of paper shot out, like the machine was sticking its tongue at you, being a sore loser.

Tony was in the lead as they pushed through the throngs of people toward the bar. Having lived in Las Vegas for a few years, Pike always enjoyed watching the people in the casinos, picking out the tourists from the locals. The tourists were usually overdressed, thinking they were high rollers, or they had the ever-present fanny pack and camera hanging around their neck.

Parting through the last wall of people, they entered the Mist Bar. Pike said a silent prayer of relief as they walked in and looked around. He was thankful that George hadn't picked a noisy sports bar with a bunch of beer chugging guys cheering at every point scored or arguing over who was the greatest player to ever play whichever game was on the television at the moment. He was also grateful that it wasn't a fern bar, where everyone was afraid to join in a conversation, usually dominated by one person— afraid to reveal to the rest of the world that they really didn't have a clue about the economy, global warming or what the latest Hollywood starlet was thinking when she wore that dress.

Instead, the Mist had a casual atmosphere, but like everything else in Vegas, it had a little glitz and glamour thrown in. Clustered around a group of overstuffed chairs at the side, Pike saw all the members of the firm. The owner George Talbot and his wife Marilyn were there, along with Nathaniel Grant, Arthur Dunmeyer, and K.D. Crooks, all partners like him. Halfway through the bar, Talbot spotted the pair and stood up and waved them over.

"You two are just in time," Talbot said as he grabbed and shook Pike's hand.

"In time for what?" Pike shouted over the noise in the bar.

"For the news, of course. Are you kidding?"

"He hasn't seen the news yet, Mr. Talbot," Tony said. "He was upstairs reading his conspiracy theory stuff, wearing a little hat made out of aluminum foil."

Talbot grinned from ear to ear. "Sit back and watch, Gabriel. You're a star."

The news came on the television and Talbot hollered at the bartender to turn it up.

"And our top story today, in what they are calling the 'Blast from the Past,' a vintage jet fighter flown by this man...." The screen switched from the news anchor to a picture of Pike, one that he thought looked worse than his driver's license picture. As soon as Pike's face flashed across the screen, everyone at the table whooped and hollered and cheered. Pike instantly felt his face turn red. "...Gabriel Pike, in a bit of quick thinking, averted certain disaster by derailing a car full of deadly bank robbers from two busloads of high school kids, by flying his Korean War era F-86 Sabre jet at supersonic speed and forcing the alleged bank robbers' car off the road, where police captured them moments later."

While the newscaster was speaking, the film showed the *Yankee Clipper* circling over the disabled bandits' car. In either in a bit of good film editing or sheer luck, the *Clipper* circled and then flew off into the sunset toward Las Vegas.

"Did you see that?" Dunmeyer shouted. "You're a hero, Gabe, a real life hero, man." Pike knew Arthur's enthusiasm was genuine but he also knew it was bolstered by the four beers he had already downed; still, he felt himself blushing again. For the next few minutes Talbot kept ordering more drinks and Pike was beginning to feel like a piñata from all the pats on the back he was receiving.

Pike looked at Grant and just rolled his eyes. Grant just smiled and tipped his glass, clearly enjoying his friend's predicament. Pike mouthed the words "I hate you," then got up and excused himself. He walked up to the bar and sat down.

"What'll you have?" the bartender asked as he walked up polishing a glass, but before Pike could answer, two girls came up behind him. They were about 25 years old and looked like they belonged to the local clubbing scene. One was wearing a black, low-cut cocktail dress and the other had on a white tank top and a mini-skirt with knee-high black leather boots.

"Hey," the girl in the cocktail dress said, "aren't you that hero pilot guy on the TV?"

Pike didn't think it was possible but he felt himself turning red once again.

"Yes."

"Cool." She opened her purse, took out a piece of paper, wrote something on it, then took Pike's hand and placed it inside, then the two girls walked away. As she walked away, she turned around and smiled seductively at him and whispered "call me," winked and disappeared into the crowd.

Pike was a little stunned as he looked at the piece of paper in his hand then to the bartender who was smiling. "This is Vegas. Enjoy your 15 minutes of fame. What'll you have?"

"Ahhh, ah… Diet Coke, please," Pike stammered out. He half expected someone to jump out and say he was on some kind of reality show, but thankfully no one did. The bartender returned with his drink and Pike started reaching for his wallet.

"Put your money away," the bartender said as he set down the drink down. "My neighbor's kid was on one of those buses you help save today. That was quick thinking on your part, and gutsy too. It's on the house; it ain't much, but it's my way of saying thank you."

"Well, thank you."

The bartender just nodded, then left to fill an order brought by one of the waitresses. Pike took a sip of his drink, trying to wrap his head around all the attention he was getting. He wasn't particularly shy, but having a complete stranger, and a beautiful one at that, just walk up to him and give him her phone number was not something he was used to.

"Hail to the King," Grant said as he placed his hand on Pike's shoulder and sat down on the barstool beside him.

"Not you too, Nate." Pike groaned.

"It's not every day I get to sit down next to—" He paused a moment in mock thought. "—how did Art put it, oh yeah, 'a real hero.'"

"Keep it up and guess who'll be getting all the bridge retrofit inspections for the next six months?"

"Okay, okay, but seriously, man, that was some piece of flying you did."

"I got lucky, that's all. I just hope the FAA doesn't pull my license."

Grant took a sip of his beer and set it down. "I don't think so. You've seen all the press; the media loves you. The FAA might slap

your hands in private and tell you never to do that again, but publicly there would be such an outcry if they took your license and I
don't think that's something they want to deal with."

"Maybe. I sure hope you're right." Pike took a sip of his diet Coke
and swished the ice around in this glass, it made a clinking sound,
almost like ones of the old poker machines paying out a jackpot, but
the ice also reminded him of something else.

"Have we heard anything from the Cain Corporation and the
final inspection of his iceberg? Since I missed the press conference I
wonder if we still have the contract?"

"I don't know; George hasn't said anything. It's probably a 50/50
bet either way. Big corporations don't like to be stood up and I'm
sure there are a dozen firms lined up just pounding on the door
ready to take our place."

"Thanks for cheering me up, old buddy."

A woman, about thirty with short blonde hair, wearing a two
piece pant suit, looking like she just stepped out of a business meeting sat down on the other side of Pike. She looked at Pike, gave him
a smile that you would greet any stranger with, then ordered a
drink. Then slowly she turned back to him and her eyes lit up as she
recognized him; suddenly the smile became a lot friendlier. "Aren't
you the pilot who saved all those kids today?"

"Yes, yes he is." Grant said, slapping Pike on the back. "Listen,
I've got to get back to the party." Then he leaned next to his friend
and whispered. "Remember, it's good to be King." Grant smiled at
the woman and then walked back to the table.

"Hi, I'm Linda, a pleasure to meet you," she said as she held out
her hand.

"Gabriel Pike." He shook her hand and he noticed she held on
just a little too long. They had been talking for a few minutes when
Pike suddenly felt a hand run across his shoulder, then felt the
warmth of someone's cheek brush up against his face and heard his

name whispered in his ear. Startled, Pike jumped and turned to see who it was.

"Geez, Marilyn, you scared me." Pike shook his head as he turned back around. What he didn't see was the look that Marilyn had given to Linda. It was the universal stare that one woman gives another, warning her to stay away or face the unpleasant consequences.

"It was nice talking to you, Gabriel, but I really have to run," Linda said abruptly.

"Okay; it was nice meeting you too," Pike replied, not knowing what he had said to upset her and have her leave so suddenly. He watched her leave then turned back to Marilyn. "I'll never understand you women. One second you're having a nice conversation and the next you'll suddenly get up and leave."

"Some women are just like that," Marilyn said shrugging her shoulders, and smiling to herself.

"You're quite the hot commodity right now, Gabe; every girl's dream. You know, the knight in shining armor," she said, placing her hand on his.

"Aircraft aluminum to be exact," he replied, trying to move his hand but unable to as Marilyn held it down, gently but firmly.

"You know, Gabe..." Marilyn started to say but was interrupted when K.D. walked up.

"Hey Gabe," she said as she sat down next to Pike on the other barstool. She leaned in front of Pike and looked at Marilyn. "Marilyn, your husband wants to talk to you back at the table."

"He does, does he?" Marilyn said coldly.

"Uh huh," K.D. replied nonchalantly, taking a drink and chewing on the ice.

Marilyn slid her hand off Pike's and turned slowly back toward the table, holding a steady glare on K.D. until the last possible moment.

Pike let out a long sigh. "Thanks, K.D., I owe you one."

"No problem," she replied, still chewing on her ice.

"I appreciate the help, but you had better watch your step. Marilyn doesn't take well to challenges."

"Well then I guess it's a good thing that I'm such a darn good engineer so you and George just *have* to keep me around or else you'd go out of business. But we all know why Marilyn won't let George fire you, and it's certainly not because of your engineering skills." K.D. smiled.

"Thanks a lot; what's the old saying, 'with friends like you, who need enemies?'"

"What can I say. We all have our talents."

Pike just smiled and shook his head. "Listen, can you do me one more favor?"

"Sure."

"Cover my retreat for me. I'm going to slip out, grab something to eat, and hide out in my room. I'm not quite ready for all this attention."

"Sure thing, Hot Shot."

"Thanks." He smiled at K.D. then got up and quietly slipped in with a group of businessmen leaving the bar. Once he got out into the lobby, he saw a little sandwich shop and tried to order a sandwich to go. But when the waiter recognized him, he asked him to stay right there and that he'd be right back. Wondering what was going on, Pike watched as the man scurried away and disappeared into the kitchen. A moment later, the manager, a short, round man of about fifty came out and said that his money was no good there, they he would take care of everything and not to worry and that his dinner would be delivered to his room in fifteen minutes. Pike tried to speak but the manager shooed him out of the restaurant like a grandmother chasing her grandkids out of the kitchen after she had just taken cookies out of the oven.

Slightly bewildered, Pike returned to his room and had just stepped out of the shower when he heard a knock on the door. At the door were two catering carts pushed by three waiters. With the trained skill of a professional sports team, the waiters set about transforming the hotel room into five-star restaurant with a table for one.

Two of the waiters took a fine, white linen cloth from under one of the carts, spread it over the table, then began setting the table using the shiniest sterling silver utensils Pike had ever seen. The other waiter began laying out a centerpiece for the table with brilliantly colored and exotic looking flowers that Pike thought only existed in magazines.

While the other two were setting the table, the third waiter worked on the food. As soon as the waiter removed the first of the round-topped silver platters, Pike's knees began to buckle. The smell of perfectly roasted prime rib escaped in a plume of steam when the lid was lifted and it filled the room like a low lying summer fog—light, barely viable, but unmistakably there.

The waiter lovingly placed the beef on the table then surrounded it with three small cups of horseradish sauce, mild, medium and "bring out the fire hose hot." He placed a baked potato that was flanked by an army of condiments next to the prime rib. Pike could feel his mouth starting to water and just when he thought it couldn't get any better, it did.

With the flair of a showman, the waiter took a smaller covered platter, whirled it around, then gently placed it on the table, and flipped off the cover to reveal a petite lobster tail worshiped by a congregation of bacon wrapped scallops.

Next the waiter placed another small covered platter to the back of the table. He lifted the lid just enough to reveal a chocolate cake drizzled with mint sauce. And just as quickly he put the lid back down, teasing him with its decadence, like a fan dancer teases, then strategically covers again.

Pike didn't know how long he had been staring at the food, when he suddenly realized he must look the fool. He started to say something but the headwaiter held up his hand.

"It is all taken care of Mr. Pike, compliments of the house, served with our thanks."

"Well thank you very much; hang on a second." He ducked into the bathroom to grab his wallet, hoping he had enough cash on hand to give these guys the tip they deserved. When he came back out, the door was just closing. He looked at the table and all the food. Maybe it *was* good to be King.

He took his time, wanting to savor and enjoy every bite and yes, enjoy a little of his fifteen minutes of fame as he knew the clock was ticking away. Satisfied, he stood and gazed out his window. He lived near Seattle, so the lights of the big city were nothing new to him, but the lights of Vegas were different from any other city on the planet. Here, not only were there more colors than a Sherwin-Williams paint store, they also moved.

They glittered, flashed, ran in lines, blinked on and off, popped with the sound of music; they were alive and gave life to the city. From space, he imagined that Vegas would look like some giant, undiscovered sea creature probing in the inky depths with its brightly colored tentacles scouring the dark ocean floor for food.

He enjoyed the pulsing lights for a few more minutes then closed the curtains and told the city good night. It had been a long day and he knew he would sleep well after the meal he had just devoured. He laid his clothes out for the next day and had just stripped down to his shorts and was preparing to climb into bed when he heard a knock on the door.

"What now?" he grumbled as he grabbed his robe and answered the door.

Marilyn Talbot stood at the door, eyeing Pike up and down.

"Looks like I'm just in time." She smiled seductively.

'"What do you want, Marilyn?" Pike said flatly. "I'm really tired and want to go to bed."

"Well don't let me stop you, why don't you open the door so I can come tuck you in?"

Pike sighed. "Marilyn, we've been through this before. I can't, we can't, you're my boss's wife for Pete's sake; besides, who says I'm alone in here?" He threw in as an afterthought.

Marilyn laughed. "That's a good one, Mr. Boy Scout. If you won't sleep with me, then why would you sleep with anyone else?"

"Marilyn?"

"Fine," she replied with a bit of frustration and anger in her voice. "George finally checked his voicemail and Nigel Cain's office called. They want you and the *Clipper* in New York by noon tomorrow."

"NOON?"

"Yup. George doesn't care how you do it or what time you have to get up and leave, he just wants you there. You know how important this contract is to him, to us?"

"Okay, okay. I've got a million things to do, not to mention trying to get a little sleep… alone."

"Alright." Marilyn ran her finger up and down Pike's cheek and around his lips then off his chin. "I'll leave you alone… for now." And in an instant, her mood changed from temptress to business executive. "Remember, twelve o'clock noon!" she said and walked away.

CHAPTER EIGHT

Nigel Cain walked with long purposeful strides, his Lucchese boots clicked on the polished marble hallway floor, pounding out a steady, strong beat. He didn't usually wear boots with his business suits but they had become a passion since visiting the factory in El Paso. Beside him, his personal assistant, Elizabeth Mallory, was matching him stride for stride even though she was a good eight inches shorter than he was.

Her brunette hair was pulled up into a business power bun held neatly in place by two ivory chopsticks crowned with gold caps. Her pantsuit didn't match, but rather complimented Cain's suit as they strode down the hallway from the conference room to the executive elevators. They both carried themselves as CEOs.

The walls of the hallway were lined with plaques and photographs of the company's history and achievements. There was the traditional first dollar bill earned, framed in gold and silver, set below a picture of a younger Cain standing under a sign of his first company, smiling at the camera. There were more photographs of him at numerous groundbreaking ceremonies from his factories throughout the world. Interspersed amongst these were various pictures of Cain with a variety of famous people.

In the center of the hall, in a section all to itself, was a series of black and white photographs. They showed the life of a young man in the early 1920s and '30s. Mallory knew they were pictures of Cain's grandfather but she knew very little of his early family history. There was one photograph that seemed extra special to Cain and he always slowed a step to look at it as he walked by. Today was different.

Cain paused and took the photograph off the wall and held it almost reverently. It was a small, tattered picture of a young man in a uniform sitting on the deck of ship with a blanket wrapped around him.

"Do you know who this is?" Cain asked.

"I assume it's your grandfather." Mallory replied.

Cain nodded his head. "Yes, it's my grandfather from my mother's side."

Mallory had never paid that much attention to the photograph before but now she stared at it intently. "You have his eyes." She said.

Cain smiled at the thought. "He's the reason for everything."

"I know, he laid the groundwork for the company in the early '20s."

Cain shook his head. "No, it's much more than that." He studied the picture for a moment longer, then gently hung it back on the wall. "I've never told the whole story about him, have I?"

Mallory tipped her head to one side. "The whole story, Nigel?"

"Yes, well soon..." Cain's voice tapered off as his mind began switching gears, exiting from memory lane and quickly moving into the express lane as he started walking again. "I noticed that seat number thirty-seven was empty."

"Yes sir," Mallory replied as she began to open her leather binder. But before she could reply, he continued.

"Gabriel Pike, I believe."

"Yes sir," she confirmed, looking at the guest roster. "He's from..."

"...from the Talbot engineering firm, out of Seattle. They were the firm contracted for the final safety inspection. Frosty mug of root beer for his beverage of choice if memory serves."

They reached the end of the corridor and Cain pushed the elevator button.

Mallory looked up at him, waiting for the door to open. "Nigel, if you already know all this information, why do you pay me to be your assistant?"

Cain smiled. "That's Executive Assistant..." The elevator chimed as it reached their floor and the door opened with a swift whoosh. Cain sidestepped and motioned with his hand for her to go first and then he followed. He pushed the lobby button and continued, "... and besides, you're kind of cute and make a good cup of coffee."

Anger and indignation shot out of her eyes. Her professional mantle was about to erupt with a 9.0 quake on the Wrath scale. She had a verbal broadside locked and loaded and ready to fire when Cain raised both hands, not in surrender but in exclamation.

"That's the fire I'm looking for. I haven't seen that passion in your eyes for a while..."

Mallory was caught completely off guard. First, because she couldn't believe the comment about the coffee, degrading her skills and worth as if making coffee was all she could do, but his follow-up remark was just as much a curve ball as the first.

Cain continued, "...that drive and self-confidence that used to be in your eyes that said that if I didn't hire you as my *executive* assistant, that I would be making the biggest mistake of my career, not to mention my life. For the past two months that flame of determination and excellence has been smoldering instead of burning brightly. Why?"

"I'm sorry, Nigel," Mallory said slowly, her shoulders slumping as if the emotional burdens she had been carrying had suddenly turned real, gaining a physical weight that pushed her down. "Tom is going through a difficult time right now. He's having trouble passing the bar exam and it still bothers him that I make more money than he does, though he will never admit that, and that in itself is a problem for me: his unwillingness to share his thoughts. I feel that we're drifting apart."

"Tom's a good guy, men are programmed to be the provider in the family and it doesn't sit well with him that he can't do that right now. Just give him a little time; as soon as he passes the bar and becomes a junior partner somewhere and starts raking in a six-figure income, he'll be fine. But if it would help, I can fire you so he'll be the top bread winner."

She hugged her day planner to her chest, giving a sarcastic smile. "Very funny...and thanks."

The elevator slowed to a stop and the doors whooshed open again, flooding the car with light. The first five floors of the front of the Cain Building were plate glass, allowing light to fill the cavernous lobby. The lobby itself was teeming with lush, exotic greenery that thrived on the sunlight. A two-story waterfall provided a soothing background noise as people hurried in and out of the building.

Cain nodded as they stepped out. "You're welcome, and where were we? Ah yes, the Talbot engineering firm. Did they call and say why Mr. Pike was not at the press conference?"

"No, sir, but..."

"All right then, I think we're going to have to replace them. I know that things happen but in this day and age, there is no reason they couldn't have called. I did want to go with the smaller firm, it gave more of a personal touch to the project, a bit more authenticity that the public would accept over a big city, high power firm, don't you agree?"

"Yes, sir, but..."

"When we get back to the office, go through my files and pick out the most pretentious firm we can find. You know, that one that has twenty-seven names in the title and each one sounds like they can walk on water."

"I don't think that would be a good idea, sir."

Now it was Cain's turn to stop in his tracks."

"Really? And can you tell me why not?"

Mallory looked around and spotted the security office. "I'll do better than that, sir, follow me." Cain was a little surprised but dutifully followed Mallory as she led them into the main security office. The man behind the reception desk was in his late twenties, square jaw, a short haircut, wearing a white shirt and tie with a black sports jacket, looking every bit the part of a corporate security person. His automatic reaction when someone came in the door was to stand and begin with the words "May I help…" But no further words managed to escape his lips when he saw who was walking through the door.

"Is Chief Anderson in?" Mallory asked as they walked in.

"Ah…no, ma'am," the young guard said, trying to regain his composure. He had never met Cain or Mallory before but everyone in the company knew who they were. When he was shaving this morning, he wasn't expecting to have a face to face meeting with God himself and his archangel. Suddenly he wished he had shaved a little closer; did he put deodorant on before he left home?

"Thank you," Mallory said. "We'll be in his office then." Mallory couldn't help the little smile that crossed her lips at the guard's reaction as they walked passed him and entered the office.

"What are we doing in here, Elizabeth?"

"I copied this earlier." Mallory sat down behind the desk and took out a DVD from her binder and inserted it into the computer. "This was all over the news earlier today, happened down in Vegas, but it's being picked up nationally." She pushed the button and played the news story about Pike stopping the bandits. "And look at this," Mallory said, pointing at the title on the screen. "They're calling it the 'Blast from the Past saves the day.'" She sat back looking smug. "What do you think? Still want to fire this guy?"

"That," Cain said, almost shouting, "is why you are my assistant!" The glow of his enthusiasm and excitement filled the small office as much as the light from the five story windows filled the lobby. "This is perfect; the media will eat this stuff up. I can see the headlines now. 'Blast from the past helps save the future.' We can have our picture taken in front of his plane, it'll be great. By this time tomorrow we'll be on the cover of every major newspaper in the country. This kind of PR just can't be bought." Cain reached down and popped the disk out of the computer.

"Come on, we've got to get back upstairs to the office and incorporate this guy into our final presentation."

Mallory took the disk from Cain and put it back into her binder. "We can't, we've got to get to the airport, you've got one more meeting with the Senate Transportation Committee to get the official green light for this project."

"But…"

"But I've got everything we need right here in my laptop. As soon as we get in the car, I'll make the calls. And by the way, that's *executive* assistant, sir." She beamed.

Cain just smiled as he followed her out of the security office.

"Welcome back, Elizabeth, that's the girl I've missed."

Mallory smiled to herself as they left the office and headed toward the front door, it felt good to be back in her groove. They passed through the large revolving doors and Cain stopped as soon as he saw the black stretch limousine parked at the curb waiting for them.

"I thought we were taking the town car?"

"You're flying out to meet with members of Congress, sir. With the public you need to be humble. With Congress you need to be intimidating."

"I guess you're right." He shrugged as they started walking down the steps toward the car, then he paused. "But why can't we do both?"

"What are you talking about?"

"Look there, over by the curb." Cain pointed. "Isn't that number seventeen, Mr. Taylor, and number thirty one, Ms. Jasper, from the conference?"

Mallory just looked up at her boss. "I'm not even going to bother to look them up, I'll just take your word for it since that was a rhetorical question anyway."

Cain chuckled. "Let's give them something to write about on their plane trip home. Let's see if they need a lift to the airport. They can tell all their readers back home how they rubbed elbows with this big wig in New York City and rode in a car that is more expensive than most of their homes.

"This should be interesting. Mr. Taylor and Ms. Jasper's lives have been rolling along, suddenly they hit a bump in the road and their paths cross here at the press conference, and now their paths will be changed even more by putting them with us in the limo. They will meet people they otherwise never would have. They will do things they haven't done before. How will this simple chance meeting change their lives? Or will it? Cause and effect, Elizabeth, cause and effect." Cain smiled.

"Mr. Taylor! Ms. Jasper!" Cain shouted and waved his hand at them. "Need a lift to the airport?" Cain then turned and whispered to Mallory. "Make sure our sources at AP pick up their stories from their local papers. Every little bit helps." He turned back to the two reporters and smiled as he held out his hand. "Might as well car pool it, don't you think?"

CHAPTER NINE

As the wheels of the *Yankee Clipper* touched down on the runway of JFK International, Gabriel Pike let out a long sigh of relief; it was good to be back on the ground again. He'd gotten up and left Las Vegas at 0-dark thirty and had the throttle all the way to the stops for the entire trip in order to arrive by noon as Marilyn had ordered. Though he'd stopped twice to refuel and to stretch his legs, they were still stiff and a little sore from the confines of his cockpit. Fortunately, there were no juice box stains to worry about.

The tower ordered him to taxi the entire length of the runway, then exit to the private hangars to his left at the end of the field. He felt a little self-conscious with his little plane taxing along this huge runway. He felt like he was being watched or was in a parade; but after what had just happened in Vegas, he was not about to question anyone or anything associated with the FAA.

Finally off the main runway and out from underneath the microscope, he moved down the taxiway toward the hangars. As he approached, he saw three mobile television trucks lined up in a row. All three had their telescoping antennas fully extended, looking like a giant claw of Wolverine of the X-Men, ready to swat down any plane that came close.

Surrounding the trucks was an army of reporters, he guessed somewhere between 35-40 strong. Some were just standing around talking to their cameraman, a few were still putting on makeup, but the majority were talking on their cell phones. Off to one side, sitting by itself, was a large black limousine. It wasn't the biggest he'd ever seen; after all, he had just come from Vegas where everything was big and gaudy, but this car was different. Pike could tell it was a Rolls Royce. It still had the recognizable classic square grill, but it, along with the rest of the timeless lines of the car, had been brushed-stroked with a modern design. It was still as stately and elegant as its predecessors and it still projected power and importance. The car was so polished that the finish seemed to swallow the light instead of reflecting it, making the car look even bigger and more powerful.

The car and the flock of reporters must be waiting for some kind of big shot or movie star to land in their private jet, Pike thought. He pulled his canopy back as he approached. Maybe he could catch a glimpse of whoever it was and tell the guys back at the office about it. As he got closer, one of the reporters turned, noticed him, and sounded the alarm like the British were coming. Suddenly the crowd, as if chained together, moved in one massive block of humanity and charged his plane.

Stunned with more fear than a junior high boy asking a girl out on his first date, Pike suddenly realized that *he* was the big shot they were waiting for. For a brief moment he thought about slamming his canopy shut and shoving the throttle to full military power and getting the hell out of Dodge.

Instead, he knew he had better shut the engine down, if these people were foolish enough to be waiting to see him, then they were foolish enough to stand behind a jet aircraft with its engine on. Leading the charge was an older man, perhaps in his late fifties to early sixties, running as fast as he could and still maintain his dignity. Next to him was a younger woman from a competitor station, gaining ground quickly. Pike couldn't hear what was being said, but by the man's red face, it wasn't a compliment on her hairstyle he was shouting. Either out of respect or intimidation, she fell back a step. Pike could also see that in the sprint, his toupee was starting to peel back like the lid on a sardine can.

For a moment, another thought flashed across his mind; he thought about kicking over the rudder and dousing the man with his jet wash. He could just imagine the pompous man bouncing down the tarmac in one direction and his toupee flying in another. He held the thought for just for a moment, then killed the engine, tapped the brakes and brought the *Yankee Clipper* to a stop just as the mob surrounded the plane.

He sat there for a moment, almost in a daze, overwhelmed by the crowd. Was this what it was like to be a rock star? Suddenly Pike was awakened from his stupor as one of the more ambitious reporters—or stupid ones, in his book—tried to climb onto the wing.

"Hey, what do you think you're doing?" Pike yelled as he tore off his helmet and jumped up on his seat. As soon as he stood up and left the sanctuary of the cockpit, the questions starting flying, hitting him like an artillery barrage. Leading the charge with a microphone in his right hand and using his practiced, TV baritone voice, the toupee man was bellowing out questions like a polite drill sergeant. Behind him and slightly to his left was the woman reporter who had followed him earlier. She too was trying to shout out her questions but every time she tried to speak, toupee man would ever so slightly elbow her in the ribs. To anyone in the crowd it would seem like normal jostling, but from his vantage point he could tell it was deliberate.

Cameras or no cameras, Pike was about to regret what he was going to say to the toupee man. But before he could make front-page news for all the wrong reasons, Pike noticed the crowd began to quiet. He looked up and recognized Nigel Cain. As he approached, his strides were casual yet confident, leaving no mistake in anyone's mind who was in charge. Cain was wearing a navy blue suit with

dark gray pinstripes and he was accompanied by an attractive brunette, equally well dressed. The closer he got, the more the crowd
began to move, as if Moses himself were parting the Red Sea.

By the time Cain had reached the *Clipper*, silence, as well as a nice
twenty-foot reporter-free buffer zone surrounded the plane. Cain
stood on the ground slightly in front of the cockpit with Pike above
him and to his left. Cain turned and faced the crowd and raised his
left hand pointing up to Pike.

"Ladies and gentlemen," Cain spoke in his polished corporate-
pitch voice. "May I present to you, the Blast from the Past, Mr.
Gabriel Pike."

Pike didn't realize it at the time, though he would be teased mercilessly for it later, saying he was posing, but he was standing with
one leg on the edge of the canopy with his helmet tucked under his
arm, wearing his flight suit and leather jacket. It was the perfect
publicity picture and just in time to make the cover of every evening
edition of every major newspaper in the country.

Pike stood on his high perch and watched as Cain worked the
crowd. Slowly Cain moved away from the plane, drawing the flock
of reports, which followed him like a gaggle of baby geese.

"Mr. Pike?"

Pike turned around and look down and saw the pretty brunette
was the one calling his name.

"Elisabeth Mallory, Mr. Cain's executive assistant. A pleasure to
meet you." She waited for him to climb down, then she extended
her hand.

"Hi. Gabriel Pike. Nice to meet you." He reached out and shook
her hand. He noticed that her grip was firm, yet not overpowering
or overcompensating. He liked that.

"If you'll just follow me, Mr. Pike, we'll get you out of this zoo."

"Please." He smiled and nodded, following her to a white Esca-
lade with dark tinted windows that appeared out of nowhere.

Pike was a little surprised when she climbed into the driver's side door instead of the back. Seeming to read his mind, she said, "I prefer driving myself." She put on her seat belt. "Besides, I hate press conferences; they are a necessary evil, but I still hate them. Some of the reporters are very good, but a lot of them are just vultures circling and waiting to pounce on their latest victims."

"Mr. Cain doesn't seem to mind," Pike replied as they drove past the crowd.

Mallory laughed. "Nigel loves it; he says he doesn't, but don't let that fool you. He's the ultimate lion tamer."

"Yeah, well thanks for saving me from the lions."

"I could tell you were a little out of your element back there."

"Just a little." Pike laughed. "So I assume we'll be leaving for the iceberg right away then?"

Mallory pulled onto an access road that skirted the airport and floored it.

"I can see why you like to drive," Pike said.

Mallory just smiled as they swerved around a lumbering fuel truck. "No, Mr. Pike, we'll be staying here in New York for two days before we leave."

"Gabe, please."

"Beth."

"Okay. Beth, if you don't mind my asking, a little over seven hours ago I was in Las Vegas. If we're not leaving for two days, then why the rush to get me here?"

"Image is everything, Mr. Pi... Gabe," Mallory corrected herself. "As you saw, Nigel knows how to work the press; he knows how important they can be. This project is controversial and the more positive press he can get out of it, the more support he can glean from Congress and other corporations.

"Your quick thinking in Nevada was the best thing that could have happened to this project. Right now you're the fair-haired wonder boy and the public loves you, and Nigel is going to take full advantage of that. Like it or not Gabe, you're a star."

Pike let out a sigh, still not comfortable being the flavor of the month.

"Don't worry, Gabe." Mallory smiled. "We'll try our best to keep the really hungry lions at bay. Oh, by the way, do you have one of these?" She reached into a bag beside her seat and pulled out a white scarf.

Pike got another pained look on his face as he held it up. "You want me to wear this? Don't you think this is a bit much?"

Mallory smiled again. "Like I said, image is everything. In today's world the guys who fly the fighter jets are pilots. You, however are different. You fly a vintage jet fighter and have been dubbed, 'The Blast from the Past.' The public likes to romanticize things, so in their minds, you are not a pilot; you are an aviator, and Nigel is going to use that. Today's pilots are all business that wears dull flight suits and bulky helmets with dark visors that cover their faces. On the other hand, in the public's mind, the dashing aviator wears snappy leather jackets, like the one you have on, and white scarves.

"People eat up nostalgia and that's what Nigel is going to do here. He's marrying the simpler, easier times of the past with the new technology of today to get the public to buy into it. Whether this works or not, and it will, the public will demand it, allowing Nigel to continue with his projects to help humanity. You should be grateful; Nigel wanted you to wear a leather helmet complete with goggles, but I talked him out of it."

"Thank you!"

"Don't mention it." She reached into her laptop case on the seat bag and pulled out a piece of paper. "Here's your itinerary for the day. We'll meet up with Nigel in twenty minutes or so and go from there."

Pike took the piece of paper and gave it a quick glance. "This is for the two days, right?"

Mallory shook her head. "That's just for today, I have tomorrow's schedule on my laptop."

"But I don't even see anytime here for lunch. I'm starved."

"Check under your seat."

Pike gave her a funny look then reached under his seat and pulled out a Styrofoam to-go box. He opened it to find a Reuben sandwich. It was still fresh as evidenced by a cloud of steam rolling out of the box. "It smells wonderful," Pike said, inhaling the steam.

"It's from Wolf's Delicatessen in Manhattan."

"No way," Pike replied, sounding like a schoolboy. "I've always wanted to go there."

"There's a cooler on the floor in the back with a bottle of root beer or water, your choice," Mallory replied, enjoying Pike's enthusiasm over a sandwich.

"But how did you... never mind." He took a bite and paused, it was the best Reuben he had ever had. "You didn't happen to..."

"Yes, I did," Mallory interrupted. "There's a container of potato salad along with a slice of cheesecake. I gained three pounds just looking at it," she kidded.

Pike's smile grew bigger than the Brooklyn Bridge. He savored several more bits then reluctantly stopped, used the second of his three napkins to wipe off his hands then picked up the itinerary. The joy of the moment began to fade as a scowl formed on his face and hardened the closer he examined the list.

"You're kidding, right? This is just for this afternoon? You don't even have time to think... What if I have to go to the bathroom? I don't see that scheduled here," he said with mild sarcasm.

"You're a pilot, there's a relief tube just to your right." Mallory looked at him and smirked. "Welcome to my world."

CHAPTER TEN

After a day that Pike could only describe as a blur, he was looking forward to getting some rest. As the limousine coasted to a stop, he looked out and saw that they certainly weren't in front of a Motel 6. His first clue was the set of red carpets cascading down from three sets of stairs that flowed out of the front of the building, with the center set flanked by highly polished gold railings. Four massive columns supported a regal balcony and grand canopy that covered the hotel entrance. Five huge flagpoles jutted out from the balcony like bowsprits from square-riggers of old.

The entrance was bathed in a soft glowing, almost golden light. Nestled between the canopy and the balcony were three stained glass panels, all glowing with the same soft lights as the entrance. The center panel was embedded with a crest showing two large P's back to back, symbolizing the regal aurora of The Plaza Hotel.

Any other time he would have been excited to be stopping at the famous Plaza. He would have loved to study the architecture and discover its history, but not tonight. Exhausted, he just sat there with his head leaning against the window, waiting for Cain to get out so they could take him to his hotel. When the doorman came and opened the door, it took him a moment to realize that Cain was still in the car. He looked over to find Cain and Mallory both looking at him and smiling.

"What?" Pike said, suddenly feeling self-conscious.

"You're here," Cain said, pointing. "This is your hotel."

Pike felt his chin hit the carpeted floor of the limousine. He expected Cain to be staying at the Plaza, not him. Cain read the confusion on Pike's face and continued.

"We can't have the toast of the town staying in just any hotel, can we? America wants her latest hero to be well taken care of."

Pike frowned; he still wasn't comfortable being called a hero, but right now he would take it if it meant being able to get some sleep. As he got out of the car, he bid Cain and Mallory good night. He thought it odd the way they looked at him, grinning, but at this point he didn't care. He was dead tired and all he wanted to do was take a hot shower, get something to eat, and then go to bed.

He watched the limo pull away from the curb and quickly disappear into traffic. He turned and walked up the center steps toward the hotel entrance. He reached for the door, but the doorman was quicker and had it open and waiting for him.

"Good evening, Mr. Pike," the doorman said, tipping this hat.

"Good evening," Pike replied, still a little uneasy that everyone seemed to know who he was, though he was beginning to get used to it by now.

He was getting his second wind now as the excitement began to overwhelm his fatigue. Stepping into the lobby, he was transported back to the golden days of the 1920s and '30s. With its glistening bronze fixtures and brightly colored carpets, Pike was in awe of the attention to detail, magnificent right down to the ornate elevator doors. He stood off to one side, out of the flow of traffic and just soaked it all in. He smiled; this sure beat the hotels that George set him up in for business trips.

He watched the ebb and flow of people as they moved about the hotel. After a while, it was easy to tell who were accustomed to the luxury, who expected it, who demanded it and who appreciated it.

He also enjoyed watching the reactions of the employees when they thought no one was looking. He caught several rolls of the eyes from the support staff trying to help a 20-something diva wannabe who thought she was all that and a bag of chips. He also observed a self-important man with a cell phone glued to his head that was getting upset because no one would help him. Forget the fact that he never once pried the phone away from his ear so he could tell anyone what he needed.

He watched the ever changing drama that was being played out before him for a few more minutes then walked up to the desk. "Hi, I'm Gabriel Pike. I'm…"

"Yes, good evening Mr. Pike, we've been expecting you. Everything has been taken care of. Your room has been prepared and your luggage has been brought from the airport. If there is anything we can do to make your stay with us more enjoyable, please don't hesitate to ask."

The desk manager was well dressed and in his mid-forties. He had dark, neatly trimmed hair with just enough gray in it to give him a distinguished look. He was everything Pike expected from a high profile, five–star hotel manager, except for his attitude. He wasn't snobby or boorish and didn't talk down to him because he wasn't rich or famous or because he really didn't belong there. He'd always heard about New Yorker's attitudes and was pleasantly surprised; but then he chuckled to himself, he hadn't ridden in a taxi yet either.

"James!" The manager called out, holding up the room key. "Take Mr. Pike to his suite, please."

The bellhop he'd been watching earlier came over and took the key. "Right away. If you will please follow me, Mr. Pike?"

As soon as they entered the elevator, the bellhop relaxed a bit.

"So, is this your first time in the Big Apple, Mr. Pike?"

Pike nodded his head. "Yes."

"Staying long?"

"No, it's what you call a whirlwind tour."

"Cool."

"What's your name again?"

"Jimmy."

Pike smiled. "You're pretty good at this aren't you Jimmy?"

"Good at what, sir?"

"Reading people."

"Sir?" he replied, slight hesitation floating in his voice.

"I watched you with that elderly couple earlier, helping them out with their luggage, very polite, very accommodating. I also saw you carrying the bags for that yuppie jet setter. You were attentive but pretty laid back. I heard them call you James, like the manager, and yet you introduced yourself to me as Jimmy. You figure I'm just some ordinary guy here on business so you give me the hometown boy act?"

Jimmy looked at Pike, sizing him up and deciding how to answer. "You're pretty observant, sir. Are you a cop?"

Pike smiled. "No, I'm an engineer. The devil is in the details, as they say. If you miss something, you lose out on a big tip; if I miss something, people could die."

"I bet you're a lot of fun at parties."

Pike chuckled, "Yeah, I tend to get a little over dramatic at times, but at least I don't have a pocket protector and wear my pants around my chest."

"You're okay, Mr. Pike." Jimmy smiled, "I've been doing this for about three years now and it's a pretty good gig. I've discovered that if you give people what they expect, as you have already guessed, I usually get a bigger tip. So with the rich snobs I play the good little servant and with regular people like you, I'm just the hometown boy struggling to make it in the big city."

"You're a pretty sharp kid and I doubt that you're struggling much."

Jimmy gave him a slick, knowing smile as the elevator stopped and the door opened on the 15th floor. He stepped aside and motioned for him to step through.

"Welcome to the hallowed halls," Jimmy said as he took the lead. "If only these walls could talk. I've seen so much stuff here it could keep a reality show going for ten years!"

"I bet you have." Pike smiled.

"Well, here we are, sir." Jimmy pulled the key-card out of his pocket and swiped it through the reader. "It's just your standard swipe card lock, sir," Jimmy said, handing it to Pike as he opened the door.

Pike was no country bumpkin fresh off the turnip truck, but when Jimmy opened the door to his room, he felt his jaw drop again and hit in the same spot as it had in the limousine.

Jimmy smiled to himself—he never tired of the look on people's faces when they saw one of the suites for the first time. "The master bedroom with a king bed is there," he said pointing, "and the second bedroom with a queen is over there. Your wet bar, microwave and refrigerator are there and of course you have your flat screens and internet along with butler service."

"Butler service?"

"Yes, sir."

"Who's staying here with me?" Pike asked in awe.

"That would be up to you, sir," Jimmy replied, doing his best to keep a straight face.

"I mean, this place is huge. It must be at least 1,200 square feet."

"Fifteen hundred, to be exact. It'll do in a pinch," Jimmy said, smiling.

"You could say that." Pike slowly recovered from his daze.

"You're a pretty sharp guy; I think you can find your way around." Out of habit, Jimmy reached into his coat pocket and pulled out a business card.

"They say that what happens in Vegas, stays in Vegas. The same is true here in New York. In my spiel, this is the part where I tell the lonely out-of-towner that if he wants to experience the more personal pleasures of the Big Apple to call the number on the back." Jimmy hesitated for a moment then put the card back in his pocket. "But you don't seem to be that kind of a guy."

Pike smiled and nodded his head in appreciation. "Big Apple? I've heard that term all my life but never really knew where the nickname came from. I know you probably get asked that a million times, but can you humor this lonely out-of-towner?"

Jimmy chucked. "You'd really be surprised how many times I *don't* get asked that question. But when I do, the answer I give usually depends and who's asking. If it's Marge and Homer Simpson fresh from Springfield, I usually tell them that it came from a famous turn of the century brothel whose madam was named Eve. That's not true of course but it adds a little bit of excitement to their trip here.

"In the real history lesson, the term is generally credited to a sportswriter named John Fitz Gerald in the 1920s. Short version is he was talking to a couple of stable hands who were taking their horse to New York, telling them they had better fatten it up or all they'd get from the apple was the core. It's also been associated with jazz musicians as the Big Apple being the biggest and best place to go." Jimmy headed toward the door and turned around when he reached it.

"If there is anything else you need, just call the front desk and I'll be right up."

"Thanks for the info, Jimmy," Pike said as he reached for his wallet.

Jimmy held up his hands. "No offense, Mr. Pike, but you couldn't afford the tip that usually comes with this room. Besides, it's all been taken care of. I don't know who you are or what you've done but you've got connections to some *very* wealthy people. My paycheck just doubled this week because of you, and I thank you for that. Now, maybe *I* can afford to eat here."

Jimmy opened the door and smiled. "Be sure to check out the balcony; it has a great view the skyline and overlooks Grand Army Plaza and the Pulitzer Fountain. It's kind of cool at night. Anyway, good night, Mr. Pike."

Pike stood and thought for a moment; how could Jimmy not know who he was? His picture had been plastered all over the newspapers and television—after all; he was "The Blast from the Past." He stopped for a moment, was he actually upset that someone in the known universe didn't know who *he* was? Pike shook his head; if he started believing all the hype about himself then he really was in trouble. Still, it was hard not to get caught up in all the rhetoric standing in the middle of this huge, opulent suite. He smiled, and resisted the urge to shout *hello* to see if he could hear an echo. Shaking his head at it all, he wondered if he should leave a trail of breadcrumbs as he headed toward the balcony.

Pike stepped out into the cool night and caught a whiff of salt air coming up from the harbor. It was the Atlantic Ocean, salt water just like the Pacific, but it smelled different. Without warning, a wave of homesickness washed over him. He wished he were back home in Seattle, at Pike Place Market, watching the flying fish, looking at the tourists, breathing the fresh salt air of the Pacific. Gazing at the fountain he suddenly thought, "What am I doing here?"

Leaving his melancholy mood outside, he found the bedroom and a king size bed that looked big enough to land the *Clipper* on. He also found a black tuxedo and a note attached. He frowned.

> *Gabe,*
> *The car will be back at 9:45 to pick you up.*
> *We're attending a last minute charity ball.*
> *No rest for the wicked, or the Blast from the Past.*
> *Sorry, Beth*

Pike glanced at his watch and muttered; that was just a little under an hour from now. Now he knew why they were smiling at him when he got out of the car.

After wandering a bit in his house-size suite, he finally stumbled upon the bathroom. The bathroom was huge (no surprise there, he thought), decorated with marble mosaic tile and 24-carat gold plated fixtures. He almost felt guilty using it, but use it he did as he took a quick shower then shaved.

He put on the tux and was surprised at how well it fit, like it was custom tailored. But then again, considering all he had been through today, he knew he really shouldn't be surprised at all. He stood in front of the mirror and thought he looked like James Bond. In his best British accent he said, "Pike... Gabriel Pike." He smiled at the thought of being the famous secret agent, then practiced the Bond walk from the opening credits where the secret agent walked across the screen then turned and fired his gun. After saving the world from the evil plans of SPECTRE and from the likes of Dr. No, Goldfinger, and Blofeld, he noticed the light on his phone was blinking.

The first message was from Marilyn, checking to see how the meeting went and if Cain needed any additional information. It was to the point and professional, a pleasant surprise from what he had expected from her. The next message was from Nate, saying he had seen him on the evening news and was wondering if the new Gabriel Pike action figure would be out in time for Christmas? "Ha ha." Pike said to himself, "Guess who gets to dangle under the Deception Pass Bridge and checking the supports when I get back?"

He tapped for the third message and was surprised to hear it was K.D. She asked how Mr. Hot Shot was doing and if his head was getting too big to fit through the door. She chatted about things around the office and warned him that she wasn't going to pick up the slack and do his work in addition while he was gone. K.D. told him about the dirty look Marilyn had given her when she asked her for his hotel number, then she laughed, saying that that look alone was worth the price of admission. He smiled too; he wished he could have seen that. She wished him well and told him to take care and that she'd see him when he got back.

Pike just sat on his bed holding the receiver in his hand trying to figure out what that was all about. He liked K.D. and they worked well together but he had never thought of her on anything more than a professional level. K.D.? Hmm, his mind started to wander. She was kind of cute and she was as smart as she was good looking… interesting. Suddenly the alarm on his watch beeped, bringing him back to the moment. 9:40. He had five minutes to get downstairs.

He hung up the phone, bounced up from the bed and headed toward the door. As he passed by the mirror, he gave himself one more Bond look, adjusted his bow tie and smiled. "Mr. Hot Shot!"

CHAPTER ELEVEN

"Thank you for seeing me at such a late hour, Senator."

"Nonsense, Nigel, nonsense. Please, come in." Senator Harlen "Pug" Williams smiled and waited for Cain to come to him, rising from behind a desk so large it must have taken an entire forest to build. Williams was a short man with a round face that matched his barrel-shaped body. He was in his early sixties but had the enthusiasm and step of a man in his forties. After shaking hands, Williams pointed to a chair for Cain.

"You remember Bobby Thornton, my aid?" Williams waved toward a young man in his late twenties, sitting behind a desk that was miniscule compared to Williams'. Thornton looked up and smiled at Cain but was cringing on the inside; he hated it when the Senator belittled him by calling him Bobby. "Bobby, would you fetch us some coffee, or perhaps Mr. Cain would like something a little stronger?" Williams said with a wink.

"Robert," Cain said, nodding to the aid. "And no, thank you, nothing for me. I have the children's charity banquet to attend tonight."

"Yes, that's right, I forgot about that. Wasn't I supposed to attend that?" Williams said looking to his aid.

"Yes, sir."

"Well, why didn't you remind me?" Irritation and impatience filled the Senator's voice.

"I tried to, sir, but…"

"Nonsense!" Williams blurted out. He leaned over the desk as if to whisper to Cain but spoke loud enough for Thornton to hear. "Like they say, good help is so hard to find. He's a good kid, got some political sense but just doesn't get it sometimes." Williams leaned back then spoke in a louder, commanding tone. "Go upstairs and lay out my tux and call Abigail and tell her I'll be spending the night here. I'll be too tired for the drive home after the banquet."

"Yes, sir," Thornton replied. "A pleasure to see you again, Mr. Cain." He stood and left the room. Cain could see the young man trying to disguise the fury building in his eyes. He wondered if he ever treated his employees that way. He looked back to the Senator, who either didn't see his assistant's anger or didn't care.

"I see your boy arrived in town today," Williams said, pointing to Pike's picture on the front page of the paper. "You really lucked out when you signed him on board."

Cain nodded. "I like to think that I make my own luck, but in this case I couldn't agree with you more."

"Is he going to be there tonight?"

"Yes, Elizabeth and I are picking him up." Cain could see a flash of wanderlust cross Williams' face at the mention of Mallory's name.

"Good. I'd like to get a few shots with him," Williams continued. "It never hurts to have your picture taken with a real-life hero."

"Always keep yourself in the public eye," Cain agreed.

"All right, down to business then. What brings you out to see me this late, Nigel?"

"Any trouble with the Senate Transportation Committee today? Is everything still a go for getting into the harbor?"

"All the wheels have been greased and doors open. Barring a major catastrophe or a flat out refusal by your boy to sign off, it'll be smooth sailing," Williams said with a big self-satisfying smile. When he smiled, his eyes nearly disappeared into the rolls of fat in his face, just one of the many reasons why he got the nickname of Pug.

"Excellent."

"You know," he said, leaning forward over his desk, "there was a lot of opposition to your project. Many feel this is just a grandstanding scheme for some hidden agenda of yours. Nobody trusts us politicians or the super wealthy."

"Not everyone has your foresight, Senator, not all can see the big picture the way you do. The public doesn't always know what's best for them, even when it's staring them in the face. That's why we need great leaders like you to guide them. The people of New York realize that and soon the entire nation will."

"You know," Williams said, with a smug look and equally smug tone, "there has been some talk of me running for the Presidency next year?"

Cain nodded, then leaned slightly forward as if giving more emphasis to his words. "When the nation sees your wisdom and forethought with this project, who but you could they turn to to lead them? You are not only the natural choice, you are the *only* choice!"

Williams leaned back in his chair, allowing his mind to wander for a moment, imagining himself being on Pennsylvania Avenue on a brisk, January inaugural morning.

"And of course," Cain almost whispered, planting a seed, "you'll have the full resources of Cain Industries to help you get there."

The Senator broke out in laughter. "You silver tongued devil, you're almost as good as me. It's a good thing you don't have any political ambitions."

"Who says I don't?" Cain replied coyly.

Williams paused for moment and looked at Cain, sizing up the statement, then both men burst out laughing. Williams shook his finger at Cain like he was reprimanding a wayward child.

"Well." Cain stood. "I must be going."

Williams stood to shake his hand. "I will see you there later. You know me, I have to arrive fashionably late to get the best press coverage." He smiled.

"Oh, you're still planning on being my guest on the iceberg aren't you?"

"Wouldn't miss it."

"Good," Cain replied and headed for the door. As he was leaving he heard Williams shouting. "BOBBY!!"

CHAPTER TWELVE

Pike had just stepped out the front door of the hotel and glanced down at his watch, 9:45 on the dot. As he looked up, he saw the same black limousine that he'd seen at the airport come gliding up to the curb. Before he had taken even three steps, the doorman was already there, holding the door open and tipping his hat, bidding him a good evening.

When he got in, Mallory was wearing a low cut designer dress that made her look like a Hollywood starlet. Cain looked like the all-powerful movie mogul.

"You look very handsome," Mallory said, "if a little uncomfortable."

"I clean up well, and yes, black tie affairs are not my strong suit, no pun intended."

"A glass of champagne to help fortify you against the perils of tonight?" Cain said, holding up a half full crystal flute.

Pike took the flute then held it in his hands. He hesitated for moment then spoke. "I don't drink, Mr. Cain, but then from what I've seen so far, I suspect you already knew that."

Cain smiled. "You guessed correctly, Mr. Pike. I like to know as much as possible about the people who work for me, especially those in the public spotlight. I have a lot of money but for a man in my position, there is one thing that is far more valuable than cold hard cash—public perception." Cain leaned back and took a sip of champagne and then explained.

"I could have the cure for cancer in the palm of my hand and be ready to give it away, but if the public perceives it as some kind of trick or a way for me to make a quick, dishonest buck, they'd fight me every step of the way, not only hurting themselves but everyone else as well.

"Take this champagne for instance," Cain said as he held it up. "I can take it, put it in a cheap bottle, mass produce it, advertise it as a 'party drink' and make money. Or, I can take the same champagne, put it in a nicer bottle, wrap it in a fancy label and advertise it for the 'discriminating, sophisticated palate,' charge only an arm for it instead of an arm and a leg, again perception of a good value, and make even more money. Why? Public perception is what drives the marketplace. If they perceive that it's a good value or good for them, they will accept it and embrace it. If not, no amount of PR in the world will change their mind.

"Right now, like it or not, you are the face of this venture. So even though I am doing a great service to humanity here by bringing them fresh water, if you were a fake or had a hidden agenda, John Q. Public would look right past all the good I'm trying to accomplish and focus on you. They would lose their vision of the big picture and all the benefits by clouding their minds with details that don't have anything to do with the project. All they would see is the wife beater or drug dealer and start to wonder if a guy like that is doing the final inspection, how safe can it really be? Why should we put our faith in you, Mr. Cain, when you have people like that working for you?

"But to answer the question you are really asking is, why did I offer it to you if I know you don't drink? I study humanity, the human condition, if you will." Cain put his glass down and leaned forward, clearly pleased to be talking about one of his favorite subjects.

"At first I used it as a strategy to get ahead in the business world. If I could read the other person during a negotiation then I held a huge advantage; I could either go in for the kill or cut my losses and move on. But after a while it became more than just a business tool. We are all creatures of habit, Mr. Pike. If you take away our routines, our habits we find comfort in, do we become different creatures? If you are out of your element, do you adapt and change to your new surroundings or do you hold steadfast to your old ways?"

"So you want to see if people's behaviors change with their circumstances?" Pike said, holding up the glass. "Are you talking about situational ethics? Are good people good only because they have to be in their circumstance or because they really are? Or are you more interested in a version of the chaos theory or butterfly effect?"

Mallory set down her glass and joined in the conversation. "Chaos? Let me tell you about what I know about the chaos theory. My wedding, oh my gosh. It was the hottest day of the year and all the flowers were starting to wilt. The caterer was there in plenty of time to set up... with the *wrong* food! So they had to rush back and get the right order and they had to set up during our vows. Nothing is more romantic than saying I love you punctuated by the sound of a ladle banging inside a steel pot. The wedding cake was stuck in traffic and by the time it arrived, it looked like the Leaning Tower of Pisa; and that's not all." She took another drink.

"One of my bridesmaids got frisky with one of the groomsmen the night before and she had hickeys all over her neck, and I mean ALL over. And to top it all off, I grabbed the wrong make-up; I thought I was putting on the waterproof mascara. Wrong! So when I started crying, my mascara ran all down my face and I looked like Alice Cooper."

Mallory punctuated the story with another drink, a big drink, reliving the *joy* of her wedding. Pike and Cain both looked at each other, then at Mallory, and then burst into laughter. Mallory shot both of them a hard stare and instantly a silence so profound filled the limousine, you could hear the proverbial pin drop.

She tried to keep a straight face but couldn't. The hard stare turned into a twinkle and all three exploded in laughter. "Chaos, yeah I know about your chaos theory," Mallory said, "but I've never heard about the butterfly effect."

"The basic idea is that seemingly small, unrelated events can have huge and dramatic effects on one another," Cain began. "The thought is, that as a butterfly flaps its wings, it's creating tiny changes in the atmosphere and that these tiny changes could ultimately alter the path of a tornado. The flapping of the wings is the spark that ignites the chain of events. So, if the butterfly hadn't have flapped its wings, the storm might not have moved or maybe not even existed at all."

"Or, in this case," Pike said as he raised his glass that started the whole conversation, "no spinning of the moral compass, no chaos or butterflies… simply good manners."

Cain smiled as raised his glass. "Touché."

CHAPTER THIRTEEN

"Prepare yourself." Mallory patted Pike on the knee as the limousine pulled in front of the hotel.

"Oh he'll do just fine," Cain said as they rolled to a stop and he popped open the door. Immediately he was assaulted by a barrage of reporters and flashbulbs. Cain turned and held out his hand and helped Mallory out; another wave of lighting erupted from the cameras.

Pike didn't want to move; he felt safe and protected in his little cocoon. Suddenly he had an odd thought. Is this what a baby feels like right before birth? Not wanting to leave the safety and comfort of the womb for the big unknown? In this case, he knew he definitely didn't want to walk toward the light. But life wouldn't wait, and in this case neither would Cain. Pike took a deep breath and emerged into his "new" life and once again night was turned into day by the flashes.

They were standing on the literal red carpet with gold stanchions on either side, linked with red velvet ropes that led from the car to the hotel entrance. Pike was paralyzed by the moment, trying to take it all in. Looking up, he could see three large grid works hanging from the front of the building right above the entrance, showcased by bright lights. Perched on the center of the foyer roof, welcoming all visitors, was a larger than life statue of a silver winged angel. Looking at it, he was reminded of a giant hood ornament. Above the angel in bright gold letters was the name of the hotel, Waldorf-Astoria.

While working and living the Seattle area, he was used to the big city but this was getting to be a bit too much to take in. Not only was he actually staying at the famous Plaza hotel, here he was standing on the red carpet, attending a charity event at the equally famous Waldorf-Astoria. The only thing his brain could relate this to was watching the Oscars on TV. Only he wasn't watching it, he was living it. He gazed over the vast sea of people, heads bobbing up and down like the tide, all struggling to get a glimpse of whoever the next limousine would disgorge, taking pictures or shouting out questions in hopes of being heard. As he stared at the sea of faces, it suddenly occurred to him, that there was not one person here he wouldn't consider beautiful, they all looked so perfect.

The men, all in their finely tailored suits and tuxedos, were dressed to the nines and the women were dressed up for each other as much as for the camera, clothed in exquisite evening gowns that he bet cost more than a year's salary for him. Even the reporters looked good in their tuxedos and low cut evening gowns. There was probably more silicon here than in Silicon Valley, Pike thought to himself.

"Breathe," Mallory said, taking Pike by the arm and gently urging him forward. Even though they were walking through the roped off section, the reporters were still pressing in, shoving the microphones in his face as if anything he had to say would be newsworthy.

Cain was leading the way, fielding questions and running interference. Pike felt like a running back picking his way through the defenders with the goal in sight. Just ten more feet and they would be at the revolving door, then home free. Just as he thought he might get through the line untouched, he was blindsided by an over anxious reporter who took the rope and stanchions with him as he leaned in and grabbed Pike by the arm.

Pike looked at him for moment and then the light of recognition turn on. The reporter smiled, pleased that Pike had recognized him. Pike recognized him all right… the toupee man!

"Mr. Pike, is this giant iceberg that Mr. Cain wants to bring into New York harbor really safe? Aren't there major environmental and safety issues here?"

You're about to have a major safety issue here, Pike wanted to say but didn't. "I don't know about the environmental issues," Pike replied flatly. "All I'm concerned about is the safety issues and from what I've seen so far, there shouldn't be any reason for concern. Now if you will excuse us." Pike pushed the microphone away with his left hand and guided Mallory through with his right, as they continued on and disappeared into the hotel.

When they were safely in the confines of the hotel, Mallory turned to Pike. "I know you don't like the press Gabe, but your answers shouldn't be so curt."

"On the contrary," Cain said as he joined them. "They're animals tonight." He straightened up his jacket.

Mallory looked at him. "You love it, Ringmaster."

Cain just smiled and nodded his head in acknowledgment. "As I was saying, Gabriel, your answer back there was perfect."

"And what do you mean by perfect?" Mallory asked. "How so? You've always said that we need the press and we have to woo them. Gabe's answer sounded more like wham, bam, thank you ma'am."

Pike stifled a chuckle as Cain continued. "The press expect schmoozing from you or I, not from Gabriel here. He gave the no-nonsense-down-to-business answer that an engineer would give. If he would have given the politically correct answer then they, the public, would begin to lose their trust in him and begin to doubt his authenticity and credibility."

Pike looked at Mallory and puffed up his chest a little and sported a small smirk.

"Don't let it go to your head," Mallory said, "you just got lucky this time."

"True enough, but I'd rather be lucky than good."

"Now, now children," Cain interjected. "I can't take you two anywhere."

"I'm hungry, let's go eat," Mallory said in mock indignation and started walking up the stairs. Cain and Pike followed but after a few steps, Pike slowed. As he ascended the stairs, the true elegance of the hotel began to be revealed. Hanging in the lobby was a massive chandelier surrounded on the wall by ten huge murals.

Reaching the top of the stairs, the room opened and Pike found himself standing on an eighteen-foot circular mosaic. He couldn't help but stare at his surroundings. He felt like a tourist gawking at the sites but the detail and craftsmanship were just too great to dismiss with a simple, passing glance.

"Living here, sometimes we take things for granted," Cain said, standing beside Pike.

"The architectural design and attention to detail is magnificent," Pike said.

"The murals and the mosaic are all the work of the renowned French artist Louis Rigal. It took him over a year to complete all the murals and there are over 148,000 pieces of marble in his famous *Wheel of Life* mosaic. The Waldorf was the largest hotel in the world when it opened in 1931. Come on. I want to show you the best part in the main lobby."

Main lobby? Pike thought. This isn't the main lobby? He followed Cain, wondering what could be better than this. Within a few moments, he had his answer. Standing before him in the center of the lobby was a nine-foot tall monster that weighed nearly two tons.

"This is amazing," Pike said in awe.

"It was built for the 1893 Chicago World's Fair by the Gold-smith Company of London and purchased by the Waldorf-Astoria as the focal point for the original hotel, where the Empire State building now stands. The eight-sided base has the likenesses of eight US Presidents and Queen Victoria, and is topped by the Statue of Liberty," Mallory rattled off.

"Wow, what times does the next tour start?" Pike joked.

Mallory smiled, "Sorry, I've been here over a dozen times playing tour guide, entertaining Nigel's guests."

"Yeah, I get that way too sometimes when I have friends from out of town and they all want to go to the Space Needle or my namesake, Pike Place Market."

"You know," Cain said, "I heard they were going to remove Queen Victoria's image from the clock and replace it with yours."

Pike shot Cain a dirty look then went back to examining the clock. He studied it for a few more minutes, then noticed the throngs of people moving in and out. "Is it always this busy in here?"

"It's probably busier than usual because of the banquet tonight," Mallory replied.

"Just how many people are attending?"

"About 1,500 or so."

"Fifteen hundred! Where are we eating, Madison Square Garden?" Pike said.

Cain looked at Mallory and they both smiled. "You ain't seen nothing yet."

Pike followed Cain and Mallory as they joined the stream of people moving toward the banquet room. They were stopped several times along the way by businessmen wanting an inside scoop, a Congressman's aid wanting to set up an appointment for his boss and a pair of women who discretely passed Cain a business card as they went by. It was easy to tell that they had more than business on their minds. Not breaking stride, Cain accepted the card then discreetly handed it to Mallory who just as discreetly torn it in half and tossed it in a waste can as they walked by.

Pike shook his head. This life style was so foreign to him; he felt small and insignificant in this high profile world of power and politics. He was a minnow swimming in a pond full of sharks and barracudas. He looked over at Cain and was glad he was swimming with the megalodon.

They approached a huge set of doors that was devouring people at an amazing rate. As they stepped through into a room so large, for a moment Pike really thought they were in The Garden. The room was 30 to 40 feet high and ornately decorated, filled with row after row of tables covered with gleaming white tablecloths, surrounded by simple, yet elegant low, round-back chairs. But the most amazing site was that the room was surrounded by balconies, jutting out from the walls, reminding him of the Galactic Senate room from *Star Wars: Attack of the Clones*. He half turned to Mallory, while still staring in wonderment at the room. "Okay, Beth, I'll take that tour lecture now please."

Mallory smiled. While she did tire of repeating the same thing over and over again, she never did get tired of the expression that first timers had when they saw the Grand Ballroom. "Soaring four stories high, it's the only two-tiered ballroom in New York City," Mallory recited her speech with a little more enthusiasm than usual, enjoying Pike's wonder. "It is the embodiment of grandeur and beauty as the Grand Ballroom is a re-creation of the Court Theatre in Versailles, a magnificent setting, where every occasion achieves greatness. The Grand Ballroom can accommodate as many as 1,500 guests with its unique rows of opera balconies."

"Boy, I'd hate to pay the electric bill for this place," Pike said.

"Spoken like the true, practical engineer that you are." Cain laughed.

Just then, Pike saw an usher dressed in a tuxedo that looked better than his come over to them. "Mr. Cain," he said, bowing his head slightly. "If you and your party would please follow me, I'll take you to your table."

As they followed, it seemed like someone greeted them from each table as they passed. Even in his short journey into this world of movers and shakers, Pike was beginning to be able to tell which greetings were sincere and which were purely self-motivated.

When they reached the table, there was already a man seated there and he rose as they approached. Mallory reached out and took his hands and gave him an affectionate kiss on the cheek. "Gabe, this is my husband Tom. Tom, Gabriel Pike." Pike held out his hand. "It's a pleasure to meet you."

"Likewise."

They all sat down, Pike next to Tom with Mallory in the middle and Cain on the other side.

With the initial shock worn off, Pike began to survey his surroundings. They were at a fundraiser for one of the local children's charities and there were more balloons floating around than the Macy's day parade and enough stuffed animals to fill Noah's Ark twice over. At the main entrance, they had passed two huge gumball machines towering eight feet above the floor, guarding the door like giant, multicolored sentinels.

The table centerpieces were a wide array of baseballs, footballs, ballerinas, cute animals, building blocks and generally a hodge-podge of anything related to children. Each one had a different theme and a price tag to be sold at the end of the evening. He thought about buying one for K.D. and mailing it back to her but decided against it for two reasons: first, if he sent her a present that was kid-themed, she might get the wrong idea, and second, the price tags. Even though he knew it was for a worthy cause, he decided he would rather make his car payment than buy a centerpiece. He would send K.D. a key chain of the Statue of Liberty instead.

"So tell me, Gabe, what do you think of New York so far?" Tom asked as everyone was being seated.

"Well to tell you the truth, I haven't seen that much of it, mostly just the insides of meeting halls and conference rooms."

Just then a scream filled the room, piercing the chatter like the whistle of a train piercing the silence in the middle of the night. All heads turned to see one of the waiters ripping a diamond necklace from one of the guests and race toward the door. Everyone was stunned, as nobody expected a robbery at such a glamorous affair. Cain and Pike both sprang to their feet but they were too far away to do anything; even an Olympic sprinter couldn't catch him from here.

Pike watched the man as he dashed down the side of the room. One elderly man stood and tried to stop him but was shoved down by the thief like a linebacker tearing through the secondary. As he watched the man run, for some strange reason Pike focused on the centerpieces and suddenly had an idea. He reached down and grabbed one of the baseballs from the centerpiece on the table in front of him. As he picked it up, he noticed it was autographed by Alex Rodriguez. He smiled. He never did like A-Rod much after he left the Mariners.

Pike threw the ball for all he was worth, like a centerfielder gunning down a greedy base runner trying to make it to home plate. The ball sailed by the thief's head and hit the giant gumball machine on the right side of the door. The glass shattered and thousands of tiny gumballs spilled onto the floor. When the would-be thief's feet hit the gumballs, he upended, his legs flying up in the air going in two separate directions. The whole scene looked like a stunt from a Hollywood movie. The thief landed hard with a loud thud, hitting his head in the floor and falling unconscious, the necklace still clutched in his hand.

The room was in stunned silence for a moment when it suddenly erupted in spontaneous applause at Pike's marksmanship. Within moments, security arrived and dragged the man off.

"I'm impressed," Mallory said, nodding in approval.

"Don't be," Pike replied, holding his arm. "I was aiming for him, not the gumball machine."

Cain roared with laughter. "I was kidding about putting your face on the clock earlier, but after that, I don't know," he said, patting Pike on the back. "Any doubts the public might have had about you being a one hit wonder have just been erased. You're now the real deal, Gabriel Pike."

Instantly Pike wished he hadn't thrown the ball.

CHAPTER FOURTEEN

Pike awoke with a start as his head banged against the side of the fuselage. He was still walking in the swirling mist, straddling the borderline with one foot in reality and the other still in sleep. It was that critical moment when he had a 50/50 chance of returning to his dream or waking up to face the challenges of the real world.

Suddenly his head banged against the wall a second time, shattering his dreamscape and propelling him into reality. He was disoriented for a brief moment, but thanks to the second jolt, his memories quickly returned.

One thing he didn't need reminding of was that he was tired. For the last two days he had been living in a haze, his fifteen minutes of fame had stretched into a good hour and a half. During that time he felt like he had been on the campaign trail, running for President of the United States. He'd been everywhere from press conferences held at Cain's corporate high rise to a meeting in front of City Hall. In fact, he thought he had even met the mayor, or was it the governor? For sure he had met a Senator, maybe? At this point he wasn't sure about all the names and faces that were jumbled into a heap in his brain. The one thing he was certain of was that he felt like he'd shaken hands with half of New York City and he'd smiled so much his cheeks hurt.

Oh, but how could he forget about the baseball? his memory teased. Someone at the event had a cell phone and had taken his picture just as he was throwing the ball. The headlines the next day read that the Yankees or Mets could sure use an arm like his in the bullpen next season.

Thankfully the campaign trail was over, as they left early the next morning with surprisingly little fanfare; at last they were finally heading out to the iceberg so he could do the job he'd been hired to do.

The first part of the journey had the usual Cain flair, flying in his private 747 that was more opulent than most five star hotels and so was the food. All of it looked like it had come from one of those reality-cooking shows and it tasted even better than it looked. It sure beat those little bags of peanuts on a commercial airliner or the juice pouches he had on the *Yankee Clipper*. But all the fame was beginning to have a bad side effect. The economy may be shrinking but his waistline sure wasn't. All the wonderful food was just too tempting to say no to. But he was confident that he would work it off once he started running all over the iceberg; at least that's what he kept telling himself.

The flight to Reykjavik, Iceland, had been quiet and uneventful— that is until they landed. They were met with a reception fit for a visiting head of state: it seems he had become an international celebrity by now. Cain said he had nothing to do with it but Pike knew better. Fortunately they were only in Reykjavik for one night.

And now here he was on the second part of the journey— again— traveling in typical Cain style. Pike didn't know how or where, but Cain had managed to get his hands on an old Sikorsky H-34 Choctaw helicopter. Inside it had been heavily modified to accommodate six people in great comfort and luxury, and all new avionics had been installed throughout. Cain had beautifully restored the outside, staying true to its vintage 1950s origin with polished aluminum finish and yellow bands wrapping around the rear boom, matching the colors of the *Yankee Clipper*.

Cain said it wouldn't be right to have the 'Blast from the Past' arriving on a sleek, modern helicopter. No, the swashbuckling hero needed to arrive on his own trusted steed. You have to give the public what they expect, he always said. Since the *Clipper* couldn't land on the iceberg, this was the next best thing. So here he was, wearing his leather jacket and yes, his white scarf, riding in a fifty-year-old-plus helicopter preparing to land on one of the most technologically advanced wonders of the world, just another day at the office.

Pike stood and stretched the best he could in the helicopter's small cabin. Though it was comfortable and well appointed, it was still small and he banged his head for a third time then plopped back down in his seat. Mallory got up from her seat on the other side of the cabin and sat beside him.

"Being short does have its advantages," she said.

Pike smiled as he rubbed his head.

"Would you like some coffee?"

"Yes, please."

Mallory got up and took the two steps to the front of the cabin and returned shortly with two cups of coffee and a sweet roll on a sterling silver platter.

"What, no stewardess on this flight?" Pike said jokingly.

"Actually, we had one, but she ate something in Reykjavik that disagreed with her so she couldn't make the flight; so we'll just have to make do." Mallory smiled, then handed Pike his coffee. "French Vanilla creamer and one sugar."

"You know more about me than if we were married." Pike shook his head as he took the coffee. "Kind of scary."

"Don't worry, Gabe, I don't know everything about you."

"Ah, good, you're awake," Cain said, coming down from the cockpit. "We're here."

Instantly a bolt of excitement shot through Pike like a child waking up on Christmas morning. Cain nodded his head to the left and

Pike nearly threw his cup down on the tray as he sprang up and rushed to the other side of the cabin. The sight was breathtaking.

Pike had seen all the drawings and the model Cain had painstakingly made, but none of those could hold a candle to the sight of the real thing. It was like watching the Seahawks on TV. He enjoyed the game, but there was no substitute for being at Qwest Field in person. Hearing the actual roar of the crowd, smelling the hot dogs and popcorn, *feeling* the excitement as it shot through the fans when the Hawks scored a touchdown. Television gave you the game, not the experience.

It was a glistening white block, floating in an ocean that was the deepest blue he had ever seen, adding all the more to the contrasts and richness of the colors. If you would have shown him this scene in a photograph he would swear that colors could not be this vivid and bright without being airbrushed; yet here they were.

Pike wiped the window with his sleeve for a third time as he pressed his face against the glass for a better view. Just like in the model, he saw the three tugs surrounding the massive block of ice, but as the helicopter circled, he saw something on the back corner of the iceberg that caught his eye.

"Is that the *Yankee Clipper* down there?" Pike asked, turning to Cain is disbelief.

Cain smiled, "Sure is."

"But how? Why?"

"The how was easy. Right after you landed, I called your boss and explained what I wanted to do and he loved the idea. I called in a favor from a General friend of mine at the Pentagon and the Army was kind enough to loan us a Chinook to haul her out here. The why, that's easy too. Can you think of a better way to inaugurate this project than to have you take off in your jet in the middle of New York harbor?"

"How am I going to do that? You didn't turn the *Clipper* into a Harrier did you? Concern laced Pike's question, afraid that Cain had modified his beloved plane.

Cain noticed the concerned look on his guest's face. "Relax, Gabriel. Again the solution is the blending of technologies. In the 1950s during the Cold War, military planners knew that airfields would be a prime target for the Soviets if war ever broke out. Test flights were conducted to determine the feasibility of launching aircraft without the use of conventional runways from mobile launchers: the experiments were called ZEL, or zero length launch. The concept was really pretty basic. They simply attached a rocket engine to the fuselage, pointed it into the air and launched it. After it was airborne the aircraft's own engine took over. We've modernized the system but being it's attached to The Blast from the Past's airplane." Cain smiled at Pike. "The equipment is as ascetically close to original looking as we could get it."

Pike nodded in approval, satisfied that his plane was still in one piece. He quickly fell back into his child-like wonder as he gazed back out the window. "Is that a pool down there?"

"Yes, warmed to a balmy 85 degrees. And at the stern, that green patch there is a driving range. Being at 25 plus feet above the ocean will make anyone's drive look like Tiger Woods'. Do you play golf, Gabriel?"

"When my dad retired, he took up golf in a big way and played for about ten or twelve years. I played with him occasionally, but the few times that I managed to hit the ball straight weren't enough to keep me playing. I figured why pay good money to chase a stupid little white ball around and get myself frustrated. How about you?"

"In the corporate world, the golf course is often used as the boardroom or the negotiation table so you could call it one of the job requirements. I can hold my own but at 6'4", I'd rather pick up a good game of hoops."

"Please take your seats, we're preparing to land," the pilot announced.

Cain sat down beside Mallory but Pike stayed where he was and continued staring out the window. They slowly descended and swung out wide and came in over the stern of the iceberg. "I've been out here over a dozen times during the construction yet I never get tired of looking at it," Cain said.

Pike was amazed at the small city Cain had constructed on top of the giant slab of ice. It looked like a miniaturized version of Las Vegas. The main casino building was fitted with mirrored plate glass that reflected the sky and ocean, giving an almost transparent look to the building. The gambling hall was also covered with the obligatory neon lights that flashed, blinked and pulsated. In front of the casino were the living quarters and office spaces, all decorated with splashes of color reminiscent of an art decor painting by one of the masters.

The most dominant feature of the skyline was the three-story monolith that rose from near the bow. It was white, with black stripes running around it, giving it the appearance of a New England lighthouse. It added all the more to the planned oddity and yet familiarity of this mini-Vegas, where on one intersection of its larger namesake, you have a medieval castle, across the street from an ancient pyramid that was kitty corner to a miniature replica of New York City.

As the chopper made its final approach, Pike could see the reporters standing under the palm trees. Palm trees on an iceberg, Pike thought, shaking his head. "I see the lions are here." Pike pointed. He recognized the young female reporter from the airport and a couple of other reporters from all the press conferences he'd attended during the last few days and then he saw his archenemy, Toupee Man.

"Isn't there anything more newsworthy for them to cover?" Instantly Pike cringed at his words. What Cain was doing with this iceberg truly was newsworthy; how conceited of him to automatically think they were here just to talk to the great Blast from the Past. They were here to talk to Cain about his amazing project.

"I'm sorry, Mr. Cain, I didn't mean…"

Cain smiled and raised his hand. "It's alright, Gabriel, I know what you meant. The press can be tiring but we need them on our side. And besides, they had better be here; I paid for all their airfares."

"You've come a long way in handling the press, Gabe," Mallory said. "But I know you're still uncomfortable with them. Don't worry, you'll still have to field a few questions but Nigel and I will handle the bulk of the interviews."

"About the interviews," Pike began, "I have an idea I would like to run by you later."

Cain looked at Pike, a coy smile coming to his face. "I don't know what you have in mind Gabriel, but from the look on your face, I like it."

Just then they felt a soft jolt as the wheels touched down. "We'll talk more on this later, but for now, it's show time," Cain said as he put on his practiced smile and threw open the door.

CHAPTER FIFTEEN

Pike felt his breath being sucked away as he stepped out of the helicopter, going from the warm, 75 degree heat of the cabin to the frigid 28 degree cold of the arctic air. The small crowd of reporters looked like a group of chain smokes as wisps of stream rose with each breath, creating their own fog bank.

Cain walked up to the small stage and podium that had been set up, and Mallory and Pike followed, standing off to his right. He waited until the last swoosh of the rotor blade stopped before he greeted the reporters.

"Thank you all for coming," he started out, "but then again, I suppose you had better be here since I paid for your tickets." Despite the cold, laughter filtered through the crowd. "I'll try and keep this brief and field just a few questions as I'm sure everyone is tired from their long journey. There will be plenty of time later to answer everyone's questions."

"Mr. Cain!" one reporter shouted out. "Now that you're standing on your dream that has finally become a reality, can you tell us how you feel?"

"I said I wanted to keep this short," Cain replied, smiling. He stood there, silent for a moment, taking a deep breath before he answered. "I have been very blessed and have had many milestones over the years, but I would have to say that this will be, no, this is my crowning achievement."

"Mr. Cain," another voice rang out. "We all know that the safety inspection on this project is just a formality. Isn't Mr. Pike's being here just another one of your famous publicity stunts?"

Pike was busy watching a pair of seagulls fighting over a small fish and not paying much attention to the questions until he heard his name being mentioned. He immediately snapped back to the moment and focused on the question and the person who asked it, Toupee Man. Pike wondered what he had ever done to the man for him to have such a grudge against him?

"I don't know?" Cain said, then turned and looked at Pike. "Gabriel, would you like to answer the question of why you are here?"

Pike reluctantly stepped up to the podium and faced the crowd of reporters. "Safety is never a just a matter of formality," he began, trying to keep his tone civil. He hated it when people took public safety for granted and thought that it was a given that everything was done right the first time and done with their best interests at heart. "There has been a lot of hard work put in by a lot of different people to make this project come to life. I don't just read the construction reports and take it as gospel and repeat everything word for word then rubber stamp it. It's my job is to make sure that all these separate components come together into one safe unit, not to take what someone else has said and just repeat it. A wise man once said 'trust but verify.' That, sir, is my job."

Pike knew he should have stopped there, but he just couldn't, then he looked directly at Toupee Man. "But I might ask you the same question sir, why are you here?" Pike tried, but he just couldn't keep a little sarcasm from slipping in. "Surely there are enough reporters here telling the same story that you don't need to be here too do, you?" Pike said, gesturing to the crowd. "Why do you need to tell *your* story? Aren't you just going to say the same thing everyone else does, repeating the same facts? No, sir," Pike said, shaking his head, "I suspect our jobs are very similar. We both see what's on the surface and then dig deeper to check to see if all the facts add up. At least that's what I do."

The only sound heard was that of the wind whistling around the helicopter blades. Pike knew he had pushed it and shouldn't have thrown in that last dig, but it felt so good. He thought he had actually heard Mallory gasp at his comment but he wasn't going to turn around to find out. He stood as steely as he could, facing the crowd. He would brass it out and hope he wasn't going home in the morning.

Suddenly a middle-aged woman wearing a bright blue ski parka called out, either feeling sorry for Pike and helping him out by breaking the awkward silence or else just taking advantage of it to call out her own question. "Mr. Cain, we heard rumors that Senator Williams will be accompanying you, all of us," she said waving at the crowd, "on this voyage and that there is speculation that he may be helping you with your own political ambitions?"

Cain smiled looking at the group of reporters and was about to speak when he stopped and looked over their heads. "Why don't you ask him yourself?" he said, pointing out over the horizon. "That's his chopper coming in now." As everyone turned to watch the helicopter circle the iceberg and prepare to land, Cain finished speaking.

"Thank you all once again for coming. We will be keeping you informed with regular updates. Now as the Senator lands, please give him your attention, you know how he loves a captive audience." The crowd's laughter was drowned out by the roar of the landing helicopter.

Cain, Mallory and Pike quietly slipped off the stage and entered the main building. As soon as they were inside, Mallory opened up on Pike. "What were you thinking, Gabe? Attacking a member of the press like that. Like it or not these people have a lot of influence that can either help us or hinder us on this project."

Pike hung his head low. "I'm sorry, Beth, Mr. Cain, but some-thing about that man just sticks in my craw." Pike let out a big sigh. "I'll make a public apology whenever you want, sir."

Cain looked at Pike with a solemn face, then suddenly burst out in a huge smile. "If I thought I could get away with it, I'd give you a big kiss right now."

In shock, Pike looked at Mallory who was just as surprised as he was. "My boy," Cain continued, "you've just done what I haven't been able to do for the last twenty years; put a member of the press in their place."

"But Nigel..." Mallory started to protest, but was stopped by a raised hand from Cain. "What you said put him in his place and I loved it, but please don't do it again. All the other reporters out there know he had that coming and they'll let it go this time, but if you attack one of their own again, even him, then they'll see you as a threat and start labeling you as an arrogant S.O.B who is full of himself. And that, is something I cannot afford."

Pike nodded his head. "Yes, sir."

"Now if you will excuse me," Cain said, "I'd better get back out there before the Senator says something that I will regret."

As soon as Cain left, Pike turned to Mallory. "Sorry, Beth, I didn't mean to embarrass you or Mr. Cain today."

Mallory just shook her head. "It's okay, but don't push your golden boy status. The press made you and they can break you just as fast."

Pike nodded his head. "Is there anything else on the official agenda for today? If there isn't, I'll go to my room and strap on my muzzle."

Mallory laughed, smiled. "No, that won't be necessary. The rest of the day is clear so you're free to wander around and do whatever. Enjoy yourself because playtime will be over as you start work tomorrow. It's time to start earning those big bucks."

"Thanks. I'll think I'll just get something to eat in my room and lay low and relax. I need to be bright eyed and bushy tailed for my first day on the job tomorrow."

"Good idea." Mallory said as she turned and started to walk away. "Let me know if you need anything else," she threw in over her shoulder as she rounded the corner.

After a little bit of wandering, Pike finally found his room. It wasn't the Plaza, but it would do; he smiled. It was a typical hotel room, a queen bed flanked by two dressers and a small, round table in the corner with a flat screen TV mounted on the wall. All in all it would suit his needs nicely.

He called room service and ordered a steak, put away his clothes and set up his laptop. While enjoying his steak, he did some research on his latest conspiracies on the Moon landings. After eating, he planned to lay down and rest his eyes then get back up and do some more surfing, but that never happened as the busy schedule of the past several days caught up with him and he never woke back up.

The phone rang with the intensity of a foghorn, shattering his sleep and dashing his dreams to pieces on the rocks of reality. Absently he reached over and picked it up and muttered a hello, or the closest thing to it he could manage.

"Good morning, Mr. Pike," the far too cheery voice on the other end of the line said. "Mr. Cain would like you to join him in his office in one hour for a working breakfast. Can I tell him you will attend?

Like I'm going to tell him no? Pike thought. "Yes, please tell Mr. Cain that I will be there."

"Thank you, sir. Your morning coffee and paper will be waiting for you on a cart outside your door. Someone will be there at 6:50 to show you the way to Mr. Cain's office. Have a pleasant day." And she hung up.

Pike rolled over and looked at the clock—6:01. He lay there for a moment and stretched. "I guess Mallory was right, the honeymoon is over, time to earn my pay," he said as he got out of bed and headed for the shower.

Feeling refreshed and awake after his shower, Pike wrapped his robe around him and opened his door. Just as the anonymous voice on the phone had promised, there was a small serving cart with a large, silver-domed platter and a folded newspaper beside it sitting right outside his door. He wheeled it into his room and when he removed the lid, he found a Starbucks grande black and white mocha, his favorite, and a single Krispy Kreme doughnut. He took a sip of his coffee and instantly felt a twinge of homesickness. After he got dressed, he still had a few minutes to kill before he had to meet Cain so he grabbed the doughnut and the newspaper and sat in the high-back leather chair next to the window.

He took another sip of coffee, a rather large bite of the doughnut and then opened the paper and immediately did a double take. It was the *Seattle Times*, but what really amazed him was that it carried today's date. Pike shook his head, took another sip of coffee, another bite and read the paper. It was remarkable the things you could do if you had the money.

Pike had just finished reading the comics when he heard a knock. He grabbed his coat and laptop and headed for the door. He was pleasantly surprised to see that Mallory was his escort.

"Good morning, Beth."

"Morning, Gabe. All ready to go?"

He gestured with his coat and laptop. "Lead the way."

They walked down the short hallway to the elevator which emptied into the casino. The lights, bells and whistles of this mini, floating Vegas were quiet now, all the one-armed bandits silent and the gaming tables empty.

There was a small restaurant/coffee shop that had a few people in it. Several looked like they were nursing hangovers and there was a couple in the corner who looked like they hadn't gone to bed yet. While the coffee shop may have been the cemetery, the Starbucks next to it was the wake. There were no living dead in there as most of the people were main-lining their caffeine, getting a jump on the day.

Half the tables were full, cups of coffee steaming and keyboards clicking as the reporters were filing their reports, snacking on biscotti and trying ever so subtly to peer over to see their neighbor's screen, checking out the competition and seeing if anyone knew more than they did.

That explains the coffee, Pike thought to himself as they walked by Starbucks, but how he got the paper was still a mystery.

They came to the end of the casino and stopped. "We have a little time," Mallory said, turning to Pike. "Nigel's office is in the bow; scenic route or expressway?

"Since we have the time, let's take the scenic route."

Mallory nodded and pointed to the right. They entered through a set of double doors, then went down a short hallway and opened another set of doors where Pike was struck with a sudden flash of vertigo. For moment, he thought he was going to fall off the edge of the iceberg.

The door opened to an enclosed walkway whose top and sides were made of clear Plexiglas. There were no metal or wooden railings to give a feel of security, just a clear openness creating the impression of walking off the face of the earth.

Pike stepped forward and looked through the glass with the wonder of a small child seeing an elephant or giraffe for the first time.

The morning was dull and overcast and the sky and sea blended together at the horizon, making it difficult to tell where one ended and the other began. With no point of reference, Pike almost felt like they were floating in space.

"Wow," Pike said after regaining his composure and balance. "When you said scenic route, you weren't kidding."

Mallory smiled. "Come on, we've got a ways to go and you don't want to be late for your first day on the job."

Pike smiled. "No, no, I don't." They walked quietly, enjoying the view for nearly 200 yards to the end of the walkway. They entered a small conference room that had chairs and tables to accommodate about thirty people.

"A short cut," Mallory said as they went through the conference room to the elevator on the other side. As soon as the door swooshed shut, Pike felt his stomach becoming queasy. Suddenly the reality and enormity of the job finally landed squarely on his shoulders. He loved personal challenges; he only hoped he was up to the task at hand. The elevator ended its short trip with a small jolt and as if that were his cue, Pike felt himself taking a deep breath.

When the doors opened, Pike found himself starring into a large, circular room. Instantly he knew where he was. He remembered seeing the tower and presumed it was some sort of enclosed radar or communications station. Now he knew it was none of the above, he was in the base of the lighthouse; this was Cain's private office.

Immediately he noticed the room was split into three levels. The main floor was the largest, covered with luxurious carpeting and comfortable couches and chairs strategically placed throughout, looking much like a sunken living room. This level was surrounded by a four foot high, six foot wide walkway that encircled it. Here the walls were covered with rich cherry and teak wood paneling and shelving, displaying artwork and many, many books. Cain's workstation was also on this level, discretely built into the wall. Jutting out and curving up alongside the wall was a wrought-iron staircase that lead to a walkway at the top of the room that was surrounded by white stanchions with guide ropes strung between, reminding Pike of the railing of some great ocean liner. It was all crowned with the rounded dome, painted a light, sky blue. Pike wouldn't have been surprised to see a reproduction of Michelangelo's Sistine Chapel on it. He did think it a bit odd to have an observation deck, with nothing to observe but the room below, but if this was Cain's only eccentricity, then he would consider himself lucky.

"Elizabeth, Gabriel, do come in." Cain greeted them with a genuine smile and an air of excitement in his voice. He got up from his desk and ushered them down to the main floor where a mini breakfast buffet had been set up. Cain sipped coffee and talked with Mallory while Pike filled his plate.

"This is where the rubber meets the road, as they say, Gabriel," Cain began. "This is a revolutionary, if not visionary, way to deal with the crisis that is looming so close on the horizon. This project will be bring much needed clean drinking water to those who need it the most, providing a stable and safe environment. Whether it's providing life-saving relief from a deadly drought in a third world country or shoring up the supplies to an industrial nation, I humbly believe this is the answer."

Cain paused for a moment, almost as if he were expecting applause, then his faced looked slightly embarrassed. "Forgive me, if you will, Gabriel; I get carried away at times. However, I won't apologize to Elizabeth," he said, smiling at his assistant. "She's used to my ranting by now."

"Given what I have seen, I really am impressed with the engineering feat you have accomplished here. This project is light years ahead of your first attempt at bringing safe drinking water by simply breaking off a hunk of ice and dragging it south. Yesterday after we arrived, I had a chance to look around and noticed that the ice on your berg here seems to be denser than regular ice. What process have you used?"

Cain smiled. "I hadn't really thought of this before but this is really rather ironic in two ways, I suppose." That statement made even Mallory pay attention, thinking she had heard all of this before.

"Being 'The Blast from the Past' you'll appreciate that the technology for this modern day project had its birth in the early days of WWII and that its inventor's name was also Pyke, spelled with a Y.

"As Elizabeth can well attest and as you have discovered a little through our earlier conversations, I enjoy the *what if* factors that can shape our lives without our even being aware of it. In one of my rare down times, I stumbled across a television program talking about secret weapons of WWII and how some of our modern day technology is based on those early designs. They talked about Germany's ideas for a death ray, which led to today's lasers. A sonic cannon using sound wave to bring down enemy aircraft; a variation of that same technology is used on cruise ships today as a non-lethal way to ward off pirates. All interesting stuff but it was a story about a man who wanted to build ships out of ice that piqued my interest. Who was this madman you ask? Geoffrey Nathaniel Pyke.

"Let's go back to the dark days of WWII." Cain was sitting down, but he leaned forward as he spoke, partly as if he were revealing a secret, partly like a camp counselor telling a ghost story around the campfire.

"Geoffrey Pyke has been described by some as, 'not a scientist, but a man of a vivid and uncontrollable imagination, and a totally uninhibited tongue,' and to call him eccentric would be an understatement. He would sometimes work from his bed, not wanting to waste time by getting up and getting dressed, and he would sometimes call military officials to his bedside for conferences." Cain paused and sipped some of his coffee, then continued.

"I'll spare you some of the more 'interesting' ideas he came up with to win the war, such as sending in Saint Bernards with flasks of brandy around their necks to get the German troops drunk. However, he did have one idea that did get quite a bit of attention.

"During the early years of WWII, German U-boats were wreaking havoc on Allied shipping and threatening to cut Britain off from the rest of the world. Pyke's idea was to create giant aircraft carriers to help hunt down the German U-boats and save England."

"What's so unique about that?" Pike asked.

"His idea was to make them out of ice."

"Ice?"

Cain smiled as he nodded his head. "His aircraft carrier, the *HMS Habbakuk*. He named it after a minor prophet in the Bible, whose name Pyke misspelled by the way. It had a hull 30 feet thick and was so large, at nearly half a mile long, it could handle all but the heaviest bombers the Allies had at the time. The entire ship was to be made from what was later to be called, pykrete, a mixture of water and wood pulp frozen solid. Pykrete was much stronger than normal ice, more stable, and melted a much slower rate.

"One of his greatest supporters was Lord Mountbatten, who was the head of Combined Operations. Mountbatten was so taken by the project that he burst into Churchill's bathroom and dropped a chunk of Pykrete into his hot bath to show how resistant it was to melting. I only hope Churchill wasn't in the tub at the time." Cain laughed.

"Later, at a secret Allied Chiefs of Staffs meeting, Mountbatten wanted to demonstrate the toughness of the pykrete, so he arranged for a demonstration. He had a block of regular ice brought in and to everyone's surprise, he took out his revolver and fired a round into the ice, shattering it to pieces. He then brought out a chunk of pykrete and fired another round, only this time, instead of penetrating or fracturing the ice, the bullet ricocheted and just missed hitting Fleet Admiral Ernest King.

"Having made his point, work proceeded on the project with a small prototype being built in a lake in Canada. The fact that it survived the hot summer was encouraging, but the high projected costs and the successful landing at Normandy doomed the project."

Cain stood and walked up the staircase, then motioned for Pike and Mallory to join him. When they reached the top and stepped onto the walkway, Cain turned to them. "That was Pyke's dream," he said, pointing to the display below. "This is my reality." Cain pushed a button on a small control panel and Pike heard and felt the drone of a several large electric motors.

Pike stood and marveled. Like a scene from a James Bond film, the panels of the dome began to fall away as if it were a giant orange peel. Instantly, light flooded the room as if the heavens had opened up. Pike wouldn't have been surprised to hear a choir at that moment singing the *Hallelujah* chorus.

Pike felt like he was on the top of Mount Everest. The sky had cleared and was now a dazzling blue as he swept from horizon to horizon with an unobstructed 360 degree view of it all. Not to be outdone by the cloudless blue sky, the ocean was a deep rich color that rolled in long, low swells.

In the front, he could see the tug churning white swatches of water as it struggled pulling this massive beast. As he walked around the observation deck he found himself staring at the floating city behind him.

"Just think," Cain continued, "what would have happened if we would have had technology like this in 2004 when the tsunami devastated the Indian Ocean? How many lives could have been saved in the earthquake that rocked Haiti in early 2010 by having fresh, clean drinking water available? How panic could have been avoided in the Japanese tsunami if they'd had fresh water and known they wouldn't run out?"

Cain stood on the observation walk and looked over his massive man-made iceberg and raised his hands as if in prayer and praise. "What Geoffrey Nathaniel Pyke first conceived of for death, destruction, and war, I have created to bring life, health, and peace."

That was a little over the top, Pike thought to himself as he stood watching Cain. He turned to look at Mallory and noticed she had a strange look on her face, not a readable expression like joy or sorrow but more of an echo, like she was thinking it but it hadn't gone all the way from her mind to her heart, then to her face. It was a strange look he just couldn't identify. She glanced at him and the echo quickly vanished, replaced by an embarrassed smile. "Nigel does get carried away at times," she said softly, almost reverently.

Tilting his head, Pike whispered back, "That he does."

Cain turned around, his winning smile filling his face. "Every great invention that has dared to step out of the box, so to speak, no matter how innovative or significant, has met with criticism, and my project is no exception," Cain said, as he trotted down the stairs and motioned for them to follow. "Because of the uniqueness and scope of my project, there are those who fear that it may be unsafe to bring into New York harbor. Can you believe that?" He shook his head, genuine hurt flooding his face. "I'm trying to save lives here."

Cain reached the main floor and continued on toward the elevator. "Like I said earlier, Gabriel, this is where the rubber meets the road. You are here to disprove the naysayers with a thorough safety inspection that will put their minds to rest."

They got in the elevator and Cain took a key out of his pocket, opened a small panel, pushed a button, then closed the panel again. The door shut and the elevator began to descend. "Don't want any reporters getting off on the wrong floor and wandering around, getting lost and turning into Popsicles, now to do we?" he said smiling.

"Anyway, I know that what I just said may sound like I am asking you to rubber stamp this project but I'm not. That's why I hired you, an independent firm, on the West coast even, with no ties to Cain Industries, to come out here to inspect this. I want everything on the up and up."

The elevator came to a smooth stop. When the door opened, Pike saw a group of three men talking. As soon as they saw it was Cain in the elevator, one of them started walking toward them. "This is where I leave you to your work. Elizabeth and I have work to do in a little warmer climate," Cain said, adding an exaggerated shiver. "That's Dean Miles, my chief engineer. He'll get you anything you need. If he doesn't, you just let me know."

"Thank you, sir," Pike replied as the door shut, swallowing Cain whole.

CHAPTER SIXTEEN

With the stealth not common for a man of his size, the intruder slipped quietly into the room. The woman had her back to him, facing the wall, watering some plants on the bookshelf. Perfect. He crept forward, slowly inching his way toward her. Just a few more feet and he would be upon her... he hoped.

"Hello, Senator Williams," Mallory said, her back still towards him. Disappointment at having been caught flashed across his face, which he quickly smothered as she turned around.

"Nigel will be here shortly. Please have a seat and I'll have some coffee brought in."

"That's just as well. This will give us a bit of a chance to get to know each other better," he said with a well-practiced, charming smile as he followed her back to her desk.

He sat on the corner of the desk as he continued to speak. "You've been with Nigel for a long time now, haven't you?"

Mallory nodded her head. "Nearly ten years," she replied with pride.

"So you two have been through a lot together?"

"Yes."

"So tell me, honestly, will this crazy idea of his work or does he have something else up his sleeve? Don't get me wrong, I admire Nigel, but I need to know if this horse will get out of the gate before I bet the farm on it."

"Oh, it will work, Senator. This isn't a long shot, this is the odds on, hands down sure winner you can bet the farm on." Mallory smiled as she spoke to the senator, but there was no warmth in her voice. She didn't like or trust the senator. She didn't like having to make a deal with the devil, so to speak, but there was nothing she could do about it, at least not at the moment. And what she hated the most was the way he looked at her. She wasn't new to this game and knew that boys will be boys, but the way he leered at her sometimes brought it down to a whole new level. The senator fancied himself as a ladies' man but his ugly grins, smug arrogance and not so subtle innuendos made her feel cheap, like she was an object to be used and thrown away and not a person. She hated him.

"We all know that Nigel has the financial means to make this project happen but like they say, money can't buy you love or congressional approval." Williams paused and thought about what he'd said. "Okay, maybe it can, but the point is, as powerful as Cain is, he still needs help in order to make this thing float."

"You have the political clout and connections to be nominated by your party to run for the presidency, and you're right of course, money can't buy you love or in this case, the money needed along the campaign trail," Mallory said coolly. "So I believe this is a win-win situation all the way around."

"Damn, girl!" Williams exclaimed, standing up. "You were made for politics. Come work for me!"

"Trying to steal my help, Pug?" Cain said, smiling as he walked into the room.

"I just might." He let his eyes linger over her then turned to Cain smiling. "She is a woman of considerable talents."

"You couldn't afford her, old friend; she is too high maintenance."

Mallory shot him a dirty look.

Just then Brad, the waiter from the Crystal Palace, brought in a serving tray with coffee, hot tea and an assortment of pastries. Cain grabbed a cup of tea and sat down at his desk. "What can I do for you, Pug?"

Williams leaned back in his chair and took a sip of coffee, drawing all the attention to himself, making them wait to hear what *he* had to say. "There are some potential benefits to this project, but also a lot of risks. While the benefits to third world and starving nations may be apparent, what can it offer industrialized nations such as the U.S.?"

Before Cain could answer, Williams took a sip of coffee then turned to Mallory. "Beth, *darling*, could you get me a little cream and sugar, please?"

Mallory remained calm and unaffected on the outside and even managed a polite smile, but inside she was about ready to explode. She knew the senator was testing her, that this was just one big game to him, but she was not about to give him the satisfaction of letting him know that she was the slightest bit irritated.

"Nigel, would you like something since I'm up?" Mallory said, making a point to serve him before Williams.

"Thank you, no," Cain replied, sitting back and watching the exchange.

"Senator?" Mallory said, standing over him with the service platter. "How would you like it— cream and sugar?" Throwing the ball back in his court.

Williams looked up at her and smiled, "Just set it down, thank you... *darlin'*," he threw in at the last moment, ending the volley.

Cain waited patiently for Williams to put the cream and sugar in his coffee before he began. "Let's get right to the backroom politics, shall we?" Cain said. Williams just smiled and nodded his head.

"Good; I'll be blunt then," Cain continued. "From the inception of this project you've been intrigued by it and have been enjoying the free publicity garnished from it, but now that the time is near, you're getting cold feet; should you stay and have your name associated with it or cut your losses and bail. And second, while you may have honest concerns about how it could help the U.S. economy, the real question going through your mind is, how or if it can help you get to the presidency? Stop me here anywhere along the line where I'm wrong."

Williams sat very noncommittally in his comfortable chair, sipping his coffee and not saying a word.

Cain continued. "In the short term, with your name on everybody's lips, can that be a bad thing with elections looming just over the horizon? Plus, think about the small economic boom this is bringing to New York. I've checked with the state's bureau of tourism and there's been a 35% spike for the city and a 23% increase for the state overall compared to this same time last year. I'm sure your PR boys can take those numbers and run with them. During the elections, you can spin those numbers again, taking credit for them saying you did it for New York and you can do it for the entire country too.

"In the long term, once you are elected, you'll be assured of a second term by being the President who saved the country. How? You will be at the forefront, the leader who is solving this nation's water shortage before it even happens. This," Cain said, waving his arms around the room, "all this is nothing but a big show, to get people's attention, to get them thinking about what is coming and what we can do now to avoid major rationing down the road. This is just a showboat. The real workhorses, if you will, will be smaller blocks towed directly to the cities in need, where nearly 100% of the iceberg can be converted into safe drinking water.

"Did I say affordable? Once stations are set up, a 16 ounce bottle of berg water will cost less than half that of its store bought competitor. In times of great need, it's cheap enough to be given away free and when there are just spot shortages, supplies can be brought in and sold to John Q. Public at a discount. The public will love you for this, and you can use the profits to supplement the bottles given away or whatever projects you need funded."

Cain moved from behind his desk and sat on its edge in front of Williams. "And this water supply is terrorist proof. For a determined terrorist, there are any number of ways to sabotage any major city's water supply. If that happens, bam! We, or should I say YOU, bring in a fleet of icebergs and the problem is solved. The terrorists can't hijack an iceberg and they can't sink it and they can't contaminate it. The only way to stop it would be to nuke it. And this same benevolence can be shared with other countries, creating unprecedented goodwill toward America, and towards you as its leader. Who knows, you may even become another Roosevelt and be elected to more than two terms."

Cain paused to let the idea sink in and to let Williams play with it a bit. He walked back around his desk and sat down and sipped his tea, enjoying the look on the Senator's face as visions of sugar plums, roaring crowds chanting his name, and a subservient House and Senate danced in his head.

"Pug?" Cain finally said after a few minutes.

"Yes?" Williams said, almost unwilling to let his dream go. "Ah yes," he said, clearing his throat, "you do make a very convincing argument but I learned at a very early age that there is no such thing as a free lunch. What more do you want from me?"

Cain shook his head. "Nothing more than what you're been doing already. Just keep running political interference against those who have no vision of the future and keep endorsing and touting the praises of the project."

Williams nodded his head slowly, considering every angle. "I've also learned that you don't get something for nothing, what's in this for you?"

"Complete and total world domination," Cain replied in a flat, mater-of-fact tone.

Williams just stared at his friend, not believing what he had just heard. He knew from experience that the super wealthy could be eccentric, but he never figured Cain to be one of those. Then, he saw a slight crack pierce Cain's lips and he stared to laugh, quickly followed by Cain. "Oh you had me there for second," Williams said between laughs. "Remind me never to play poker with you; that was one hell of a bluff."

After a few more bits of laughter, Williams looks back at Cain. "Seriously, Nigel, what are you getting out of all of this?"

Cain stood and held his arm up and Williams stood as well. Cain put his arm around the senator and led him to toward the door. "It doesn't really matter what I'm getting out of this, does it, so long as you get what you're hoping for?" Before Williams could answer, Cain continued. "No it doesn't, and as Beth pointed out earlier, this is a win-win for everyone."

By now they were standing at the door and Cain held out his hand. "Thanks for coming by and I'm glad we had this discussion and we're both on the same page. Now, if you will excuse me, I have some plans to make for taking over the world." Both men laughed as they shook hands and Cain skillfully led the senator out the door.

As soon as the door closed, Mallory spoke. "You'd better do something with him, Nigel," she said, grabbing a doughnut and biting it viciously in half, "*darlin',* or I will."

"I guess it's a good thing I showed up when I did then and came to the rescue," Cain replied.

Mallory shot him a dirty look. "I can take care of myself," she replied defiantly.

Cain laughed. "I showed up to rescue *him,* not you."

"Damn straight. I don't see how he and his ego fit on this chunk of ice. It's a wonder we haven't capsized yet."

"I know you don't like him, Elizabeth, but for now we need him."

"And he needs us. You know that as soon as he gets what he wants he'll drop you like a bad campaign promise."

"That's why we have to beat him to the punch."

"Did you say beat him?" Mallory's grin was sadistic.

Cain frowned. "Just be patient a little longer; don't worry, I'll tell you when the gloves can come off."

"Fine," Mallory replied like a spoiled child.

"I know Pug well enough to know that he has something else on his mind but he's too good at the game to tip his hand. See what you can find out from his aid Robert. There's already a little bit of animosity between them. Let's see if we can exploit that."

"Divide and conquer?"

"Exactly."

CHAPTER SEVENTEEN

"Mr. Pike, Dean Miles." Miles introduced himself as he walked up and stretched out his hand. Miles was a tall, rugged-looking man of about fifty with short wavy brown hair who looked more like a Texas oil wildcatter than an engineer. Pike caught himself. Here he was, an engineer himself, and he was putting the stereotype of the nerdy glasses and pocket protector on him. Pike introduced himself and both men shook hands; from his grip, Pike knew Miles was no nerd.

"Welcome to the ice planet Hoth." Miles smiled, holding up his hands, presenting the underground room. It was a huge cavern that was nearly as wide as the iceberg itself at eighty feet and almost as long at sixty. The room was well lit with banks of florescent lights that hung from the ten-foot high ceiling.

As Pike looked around, he noticed that there were stacks of lumber, pallets of supplies and other building equipment scattered around. The whole scene looked like any other construction job site except they were *inside* a huge iceberg floating toward New York City. He thought the walls would have been shinier since they were made of ice, reflecting light like a giant disco ball, but instead, they had a dull sheen. The two men stepped into a small trailer that acted as the office where Miles pulled out a set of blueprints.

"This is just an overview print," Miles said as he spread out the plans. "We have detailed plans for each level and you can see them anytime you like. We're here." Miles pointed to the plan. "And you have three main vertical tunnels, here, here, and here, that all connect to the Broadway tunnel here. It's the main and largest horizontal access tunnel that runs just above the ships. From there, we have two vertical tunnels each, running to the four ships encased in the ice. There is, of course, a honeycomb of service tunnels running throughout the iceberg. These shown here are just the main ones."

"The four ships here," Pike asked, "they're supposed to melt the ice once we arrive at our destination?"

Miles nodded. "The ships are old WWII mothballed liberty ships that Mr. Cain dug up from who knows where; they are all part of the big, reduce-reuse thing. The superstructures have been removed and they've been stripped of any asbestos and any another toxic material and are eco-friendly just in case there's an accident. All four still have their engines and supply all the power for the barge." Miles paused for a moment. "Ah, don't ever call the iceberg a barge in front of Mr. Cain, he doesn't like it. It really is a giant barge if you think about it, but he prefers not to think of it like that, not good PR he says."

"I'll want to take a closer look at all the specs later but right now I think I'd just like to take a look around. Can you give me the nickel tour?"

"Sure thing, but you'll need this first." Miles opened up a locker and tossed Pike a dark colored fur-lined parka.

They stepped out of the office and into an open ended freight elevator. Miles pulled a metal gate across the entrance and pushed the button.

Feeling the excitement grow, Pike watched as the sheer ice walls passed in front of them as they began to descend deeper into the berg. They reached bottom and emerged into a cavern a little smaller than the one they just left. Here, there were no pallets of equipment lying around; in fact, it was deserted except for two vehicles that resembled golf carts.

"I thought there'd be more people or equipment around," Pike said, stepping out of the elevator.

"Right now there's not a lot to do other than keeping an eye on the generators and fixing any coolant leaks we may find." They got into the cart and started down the tunnel. As they were driving, Pike noticed that there were two dozen three-inch pipes nestled in the ceiling with branches jutting out every twenty feet or so and disappearing into the walls. Seeing Pike looking up, Miles explained. "The pipes you see are for keeping the ice cold during transit and then we use them to melt the ice once we arrive. There's nearly forty miles of piping spider webbed throughout the barge, sorry, berg. This is the Broadway tunnel I mentioned earlier. It runs the entire length of the iceberg and is the only tunnel large enough to drive through, but there are dozens more just wide enough for a man to walk through that we use to inspect the pipes.

"Okay, here we are." Miles parked the cart in a small cutout that was just large enough to hold three of the small electric vehicles. The two men got out and walked down the short crystallized passageway and ended up in front of a metal tube that looked like a phone booth. Inside the tube, there were two sets of ladder rungs.

"This is one of four main tubes that go down to the ships," Miles said as he climbed onto a rung and began to go down. "There are four more escape ladders that go to the surface and four more that go up just above the waterline and end up on narrow shelves."

Pike peered down the tube and was a little surprised to see such a bright light at the end. "Follow the light." He chuckled to himself as he began to go down. They descended inside the dark tube for twenty feet, then suddenly came out the other end, like a swimmer broaching the surface of a lake, only backwards. Pike felt his fingers tighten their grip around the rungs of the ladder as he suddenly found himself suspended in mid-air.

The access tube they had been climbing down had ended but the ladder continued down another twenty feet to the deck of the ship below. He had gone from the close confines of a six-foot diameter tube and had emerged into a vast cavern that was nearly three football fields long and almost as wide. He could see all four ships, but it was odd not to see them floating in water. Instead, they were surrounded by fog, a solid, frozen fog.

"Enjoying the view?"

Pike looked down and saw Miles was on the deck looking up at him.

"Sorry." Pike apologized and climbed the rest of the way down. For some reason he took great comfort in the feel of the solid deck.

The two forward ships each had four large pipes coming up out of their decks, like giant smoke stacks that disappeared into the ice overhead. From the point where the pipes entered the ice, Pike could see smaller pipes branching out, like blood vessels breaking off the main artery, making the iceberg look like it had varicose veins.

Pike found himself gawking at everything like a little country boy on his first visit to the big city. Suddenly he was aware of Miles standing in the hatchway just looking at him. "We get that from everybody the first time they come down here," Miles said, smiling. "Come on, I'll show you the belly of the beast."

Pike followed the engineer through the hatch and narrow hallway where they descended three decks. Pike felt the butterflies swarming in his stomach . He'd seen lots of engineering projects over the years but ones like this came along only once in a lifetime. Suddenly he felt very small and humbled to be a part of something so grand and so important; he only hoped he was good enough.

He had felt a slight vibration when standing on the deck and heard a low rumble, like a stampeding herd of cattle far off in the distance. The lower he got into the bowels of the ship, the more pronounced both the noise and vibration became. The noise had now turned into a deep bass sound that rumbled in his stomach , the feeling that one gets when pulling up to a stop sign and hearing the blare from a teenager's radio three cars away.

As they reached the last hatch, Miles grabbed a hardhat and ear-muffs off the wall. "Safety first." He smiled as he handed them to Pike then put some on himself. For the second time in less than five minutes Pike found himself speechless and standing dumbfounded when Miles opened the hatch.

He didn't know quite what to expect, but he knew this wasn't it. All the bulkheads in the ship's hold had been removed, leaving one massive room. Pike envisioned the cargo hold to contain gigantic machines large enough to create their own weather patterns that would be surrounded by an array of smaller machines, filling every dark nook and cranny with pipes and wires. He thought he'd see endless panels full of dials and gauges attended by an army of men in white coats carrying clipboards.

He did find four gigantic machines lined up in rows that were attached to the huge funnels he'd seen sprouting up above the deck but that's where the similarities to his vision ended. The immense space of the ship's hold was still surprisingly spacious and there was very little clutter from smaller support machines. The room was well lit and not blast-furnace hot as he expected from all the heavy equipment.

"These are the generators that supply the refrigerant, keeping the berg cold. The other forward ship has an identical set up," Miles explained. "When the time comes for the meltdown, these two stations will convert from cooling to heating and begin thawing out the ice while the plants in the aft two ships begin processing the water and pumping it out."

"Very impressive," Pike said, staring at the massive machinery.

"Do you want to see the processing ships now?"

Pike shook his head slowly. "I would like to see them but what I think I should do now is go back to my room, study the specs and formulate an inspection plan and check-off list. I've got the Coast Guard regulations so there really shouldn't be a problem; the only snag we might run into is the sheer size of this thing."

"All the specs are on here. I thought you might want to see them." Miles handed Pike a thumb drive then continued: "I've got work to do here so I'll have one of my men take you back topside. If you need anything else, just let me know."

"Thanks," Pike replied as he shook Miles' hand. "I'll leave the coat back in the office."

"Keep it, you'll need it."

Pike nodded as he followed his guide back through the labyrinth.

CHAPTER EIGHTEEN

Williams was blowing steam like a locomotive as he stormed away from Cain's office. He was angry that Cain had outmaneuvered him by cleverly dismissing him before he was ready to go. He did have to admire him though, Cain was good. He just hoped the billionaire didn't get bored spending all his money and decide to run for office.

Williams chugged down the hallway and burst into his makeshift office. Thornton was sitting at his desk, surrounded by several stacks of papers.

"Senator?" Thornton said as his boss came storming in. "You've had three phone calls from Washington while you were gone."

"Not now, Bobby!" he shouted.

"But, sir…"

"He's up to something, I can smell it."

"Sir?"

"You don't get to a position like mine without developing a sixth sense about things like this."

"Who, sir?"

"Cain, Cain! Who else you idiot? Haven't you been paying attention?" Williams threw his hands up in the air out of frustration as he stared at his aid.

Thornton sat there quietly biting his lip and biding his time. Before he took this job, he'd heard all the stories from Capitol Hill about Williams and his reputation for chewing up interns and aids for breakfast and spitting them out before lunch, but he took the job anyway. He didn't need *a* job, he *wanted* this one. Despite what Williams thought, he had been paying attention and he did know what was going on. Williams had the experience and the connection and even if he was a Class A jerk, he was the one to learn from if he wanted to get anywhere in the political world.

"Of course, sir."

Williams transformed from the thundering locomotive to a caged animal, pacing back and forth in the office, tapping his chin, thinking as he walked. Thornton had seen his boss act like this before but not very often, so he knew something big was up. Thornton sat quietly as he watched his boss crisscross the room, talking to himself. Slowly the furious pacing began to subside to a gentle walk and Thornton knew he could talk now without disturbing the beast.

"How can I help, sir?"

"That's it," Williams said, snapping his fingers. "I'll work through channels on my end and I can have you play the end game with Beth."

"Beth?

"Beth Mallory, Cain's assistant. I want you to work that angle. I want you to get as much information out of her as possible. You know, one subordinate to another, that sort of thing, it may get her talking."

"Anything in particular you're looking for, sir?"

"I don't trust our benefactor as far as I can throw him. This iceberg thing has to be a cover for something else. No one goes through this much time and expense just to help their fellow man."

"That's a sad thought, sir," Thornton blurted out.

Williams looked at him with a disappointed scowl. "You've got a spark of potential, Robert, but don't let misguided, useless emotions make decisions for you. This is the real world here. Lead, follow or get out of the way. I intend to lead. If you want to sit in the big chair, you've got to make the tough calls. Politics is like a giant game of chess. You've got to know who to sacrifice and when in order to win the game. Sometimes you sacrifice people you just met, sometimes it's friends you've known for years; remember, the end justifies the means."

Williams looked long and hard at his aid. "Well, Bobby, are you a pawn or something bigger?"

"I'll take care of it," Thornton replied with a conviction that made Williams smile.

"Excellent, my boy, excellent. Now then, you said I missed some phone calls?"

"Yes, sir."

"Well let's get the mundane duties of running this country out of the way so we can get to the real fun and see what our friend Mr. Nigel Cain is really up to."

It was 6:30 by the time Pike realized he had worked through lunch and dinner, his growling stomach confirming that fact. Pouring over the plans, he had formulated a workable timetable that should allow for a thorough inspection and yet leave enough leeway to get into New York harbor on time. Pike was amazed at the simplicity of Cain's idea yet impressed with the complexity it took to bring it to life.

He stood and stretched then grabbed his coat and was heading out the door to grab a bite to eat when the phone rang.

"Hello?" he said, grabbing it just after the third ring.

"Hey, Gabe."

"K.D.!" Pike said excitedly.

"Have you done any work yet or are you still having caviar and oysters?"

"Ha ha, very funny. I've been studying the schematics for this place all day, besides, you know I don't like oysters. You should see this place, K.D., it is absolutely amazing." Pike spent the next several minutes describing the barge and the day's events.

He paused and finally took a breath. "Hey, what time is it there? Isn't there like a six hour time difference between here and there?" He glanced at his watch. "So what, it must be close to one in the morning there? How nice of you to stay up so late to call."

"Yeah, it's about one... in the afternoon, so don't flatter yourself, hot shot, I'm not losing any beauty sleep over you... and no wise crackers either."

"Yes, dear," Pike replied in mock obedience.

"But yes," she replied in a softer tone, "it's good to talk to you too."

"How's everything back at the office? Does everybody miss me?"

"Things are fine and everyone is jealous and hates you, though Nate is busy designing your new baseball action figure. You're wearing a Mariners uniform with a white scarf and a leather flying helmet. He wanted to have you wearing your leather flight jacket but I told him that was stupid."

"Well thank you for that."

"Yeah, besides everyone knows you could never throw a baseball with that thing on."

"I'm going to hang up now. And just for that I'm not going to give you that coffee mug I bought you in the airport gift shop at Reykjavik." They both laughed.

"Okay, I gotta go now. This call is on the company's dime and you know how Marilyn likes to watch her pennies."

"Well thanks for calling."

"No problem. Take care of yourself, hot shot, and don't slip on the ice."

Pike smiled as he hung up the phone. That's twice K.D. had called. After a couple of years working side by side, all of a sudden was a long distance romance shaping up? He'd definitely play this by ear but it was worth thinking about.

Even at this early hour, as Pike entered the casino, he was greeted by all the usual sound of the Vegas strip. The machines beeped and buzzed, the Keno numbers flashed across the screen and there were the occasional whoops and hollers from someone winning big. From the number of people playing and the stacks of chips sitting on the tables, it looked like Cain was winning back the airfares he paid to get these people here.

He was hungry and wanted to decompress a little after pouring over the schematics so he went past the small diner and entered the Crystal Palace. It was a first class restaurant where he hoped he could enjoy a quiet meal away from all the noise and glitz.

The Crystal Palace was decorated in a frosty winter theme with ice sculptures scattered about. The tables were made to look like chunks of ice supported by large pillars and were surrounded by glistening, crystallized chairs. The bar was a huge slab of acrylic ice, complete with frozen creatures captured inside. It reminded him of the ice hotel in the James Bond film *Die Another Day*.

When Pike walked in, he was disappointed to see that the place was packed and that he wasn't the only one with the idea of a quiet meal. He was just about to turn around and head back to the diner when he saw the maitre d' approach and call his name. "Mr. Pike, I have a table right this way, if you please?" He half expected him to have a stuffy French accent but instead, he had a pleasant, slight southwest drawl. He didn't question the special treatment as he nodded and gratefully followed. The maitre d' led him to a table that was in a semi-private room, thankfully quiet and with a magnificent view of the ocean. Apparently he still had a few seconds left on his fifteen minute fame clock.

He had just sat down when he heard a voice behind him. "Care for some company?" Pike turned around and saw Mallory standing there. "I was at the bar when I saw you come in."

He stood and pulled out her chair for her. "Please, I'm use to eating alone but I always enjoy good company whenever I can get it. Have you eaten yet?"

Mallory shook her head. "Not yet."

"Then please join me, my treat."

"Don't mind if I do."

After dinner was ordered, Mallory continued the conversation. "So how did your first day on the job go?"

Pike nodded. "It went very well. I studied all the schematics to get a basic layout and tomorrow I'll meet with Dean again to get the invoices to check on the building materials to see if everything meets environmental standards."

"Don't bother," Mallory said as the waiter brought the salad. "I'll save you a trip to the underworld. I have all the invoices and rec forms in my office as I did all the purchasing of materials for the barge."

Pike looked at her funny when she called the iceberg a barge. She read the expression on his face. "Don't worry, Gabe. I know Nigel doesn't like it being called a barge, but who do you think named it that in the first place?" She smiled.

Pike just smiled and shook his head as Mallory continued.

"I also have the lists of construction firms who have worked on the project and their background checks along with every state and federal license and permit needed. And I can answer any question Dean can, short of extreme engineer techno babble."

"Excellent. That will save me a lot of time and trouble and having to bundle up like Nanook of the North."

Just then the waiter came and delivered their dinner and the conversation lulled as they both concentrated on the meal. As Pike ate the last piece of his porterhouse steak, he let out a satisfied moan and pushed himself back from the table and ordered some coffee.

"I have a favor to ask of you and Mr. Cain."

"You know, it's okay to call him Nigel, he doesn't mind."

"I know, but it just feels uncomfortable."

"He can be a little intimidating but I've been with him so long he doesn't faze me any longer. Anyway, what's this favor?"

"You know I don't share the same affection for the news media as Mr. Cain does, but there is one reporter in particular that has ruffled my feathers."

"Oooo, revenge on the high seas, I like it. Brad?" Mallory called to the waiter. "Please bring me another glass of wine, we're going to be here a while."

CHAPTER NINETEEN

Pike arrived at Mallory's office the next morning at 9am sharp. He was greeted by Mallory who took him into a side conference room where he was met with four stacks of papers on the table that were large enough to be icebergs themselves.

"What's all this?" Pike asked.

"I knew you would want to do a thorough job so here are all the files we were talking about last night. I'll have some coffee and pastries brought in in a little while."

"I did ask for this, didn't I?"

"Yup," Mallory replied then closed the door behind her.

At 12:30, the door to the conference room opened and a blurry-eyed Pike stepped out.

"Well, look what the cat dragged in," Mallory joked as she was putting a file away in the cabinet.

"Remind me next time to just take your word for it that everything is in order," Pike said as he stretched. He threw his head side to side and rubbed the back of his neck. "One question—does Cain even know this thing exists?"

Mallory looked at him funny. "What do you mean?"

"You signed literally every piece of paper that had anything to do with this project. I found Cain's signature on only one piece of paper, the one authorizing you to oversee the construction of this place. Heck, you could have bought a villa in the south of France and Cain wouldn't have known. He must really trust you."

"Thank you, and he does. I've worked for Nigel for a long time but don't let that fool you. Even though you don't see Nigel's signature anywhere, you can bet he knew what was going on. And besides, I prefer the Australian outback to the French coast."

Pike tipped his head in thought and nodded slightly. "Yeah, you know what? I think I can see that. Anyway, I'm going to go to the diner and grab some lunch then go on deck to clear my head, do you wanna come?"

Mallory shook her head. "No, but thank you. I have a meeting with Nigel in half an hour concerning our conversation last night."

Pike lowered his head a bit, as if embarrassed. "I really appreciate it. I know it may seem childish and petty but the man irks me."

Mallory grew a big smile. "You are the great righter of wrongs," Mallory teased. "After I briefly ran your idea by Nigel, he instantly fell in love with it. We reviewed all the tapes we could find and we saw you were right. You know Nigel, he sees this as one of his cause and effects things he's so fond of. But remember, you have your part to do too. Be in Nigel's office at 3 this afternoon."

"You can count on it. Thanks again," Pike said as he left her office.

"This is Tabatha Amies reporting to you live from the Cain iceberg. Some call this floating deep freeze a modern miracle and hail it as an instrument that will save thousands of lives. Others call it a colossal waste of time and money, just another publicity stunt by a bored billionaire." The scene changed from the close up of the reporter to an outside view of the iceberg.

"This reporter has been granted an exclusive first time look into the bowels of this frozen beast. Later in the program I will have an exclusive interview with the visionary billionaire himself, Nigel Cain, and a rare chat with the man who has jumped to the forefront of the national media attention with his crime stopping prowess, Gabriel Pike, better known to millions as The Blast from the Past."

The view changed again to a stock shot of Cain in a business suit flashing to Pike standing in front of the *Yankee Clipper.*

"We'll begin tonight's segment with a press conference that took place earlier today on board Nigel Cain's iceberg." The image again changed to a view of a conference room crowded with reporters with Cain standing in the front behind a podium.

"Okay, here it comes," Mallory said, almost giggling like a teenager.

Cain, Mallory and Pike were in Cain's office sitting in front of the billionaire's 52 inch LCD big screen. Mallory was still in her business suit from the press conference but Cain had changed into a *Catalyst* T-shirt, a pair of faded Levi's and Converse tennis shoes. Pike was wearing his khaki pants and leather jacket from his interview. Mallory handed each of them a bowl of popcorn then she sat down at the end of the couch.

They were watching the special news report that had been recorded earlier that day. The screen went from the close up shot of the woman reporter to Cain standing at the podium in the room where Pike had spent the morning sifting through papers. Cain fielded several questions with the camera panning back and forth between Cain and the reporters asking the questions.

"It's right after this question," Mallory said with glee, tossing popcorn into her mouth. The camera went from Cain to a reporter sitting in the back row with his hand raised. When Cain called his name, the man stood slowly. Just as he did, a waiter walked by with a large silver platter containing wineglasses. The reporter's head hit the platter and the whole thing came tumbling down with a loud crash.

The camera zoomed in on the reporter who had a swirling combination of horror, anger, surprise and embarrassment etched on his face. At first, he stood there frozen with indecision, not knowing whether to ignore the disaster and continue on with his question or to simply get out of Dodge. The decision was made for him as Cain called out his name again. The reporter whirled back around and faced the podium. Putting on his best the show must go on face, he salvaged what dignity he had left then asked his question.

Pike burst out in laughter as did Mallory and Cain. "I'm sorry," Pike said, "That wasn't very nice but it sure was funny. That looked like a Chevy Chase and Dan Aykroyd scene from *Saturday Night Live.*"

"Oh it gets better," Cain replied. "Elizabeth, can you get me something to drink please?"

"Sure thing." Malory reached over and took the lid off the champagne cooler, but instead of a chilled bottle of expensive champagne, she pulled out a can of beer and tossed it to her boss. Pike just looked at Cain for a moment and thought how odd it seemed to see one of the richest men in the world in jeans and a T-shirt, looking like an everyday Joe drinking a beer.

The press conference continued as several more reporters asked questions. The same reporter in the back raised his hand again and Cain called on him. This time the man cautiously looked around before he stood. Satisfied he wasn't going to be ambushed, he stood and asked his question.

As he sat back down, the same waiter came walking behind him with a towel folded over his arm. Just as the reporter sat down, his head hit the waiter's arm. The downward motion caught his hair on the towel. The man sat down, but his hair, his toupee, stayed on the waiter's towel; for a moment it looked like the waiter was carrying a small cat.

The cameraman filming the news conference was the first to pick up on the bizarre accident and immediately zoomed in on the man's bald head. Suddenly the room erupted in laughter again. This time there was no saving face as Toupee Man shot out of his seat, grabbed his hair and stormed out of the room.

"I don't know what to say!" Pike managed to get out between bursts of laughter. He looked over and his companions were laughing hard as well.

"That was classic," Mallory said. She snorted when she said it, froze in embarrassment as she looked at Cain and Pike, then all three laughed even harder. Pike had been laughing so hard his side was beginning to hurt. Finally the laughter subsided As Mallory wiped tears from her eyes.

"Thanks Nigel." Pike said. "That was worth every minute of enduring my hardship as the Blast from the Past just to see that. I know it's mean of me but I hope everyone in America will see that."

"Don't worry, they will," Mallory said. "I uploaded it to YouTube and it's already gone viral."

"I'd like to shake that waiters hand if I could," Pike said.

Cain clicked the remote and turned off the TV. "Well you'd better hurry. Your Toupee Man, as you like to call him, demanded from his network that the man be fired for embarrassing him like that."

Suddenly the smile ran away from Pike's face and he felt his stomach twist. "No. Please don't tell me you fired him because of what I wanted?"

"I had to fire him to avert any suspicion from the network, but don't worry. He'll take a little vacation, paid of course, then go to work in one of my California spas."

Pike let out a sigh of relief. "That's good to know."

Mallory stood up and headed for the door. "I've got a couple of things to take care of then I'm going to give Tom a call."

"Thank you, Elizabeth," Cain said. "I'll see you in the morning, and give Tom my best."

"Thanks. Good night."

"If you will excuse me too, Mr. Cain, I need to finish up my reports from this morning. Tomorrow I'll start my hands-on inspection." Pike got up and had reached the door when Cain called him.

"Thank you, Gabriel."

"Sir?"

"Sometimes I forget."

"Forget what?"

"To have fun in life. I haven't laughed that hard in a long time."

"You're welcome," Pike said, nodding his head. "See you tomorrow."

CHAPTER TWENTY

Pike dotted the last "i" and crossed the last "t" then clicked the save button and pushed away from the desk, his report done. He yawned then stood and stretched and looked at his watch. He was tired but at 8:30, it was still too early for bed. He decided to take a walk and go up to the observation deck, take in the view, then come back and do a little conspiracy surfing.

The observation deck was a bubble sitting on top of the casino affording a 360 degree view of the floating palace. When he got there, he found the observation deck deserted except for one couple who were more interested in the view on the inside rather than the outside. As soon as they saw Pike, they acted like a couple of teenagers getting caught in the back seat of their father's car at makeout point. They straightened up their clothing and headed for the door, saying goodnight in passing, never looking him in the eye. He laughed to himself as they left; they were both in their forties.

Alone now, Pike watched as the sun hesitated on the horizon for a moment, then slowly began to sink. It cast out great rays of light, reflecting off the water as if trying to hold itself up, but the ocean would not be denied as it pulled the sun farther and farther into its depths. The last rays of light lashed out, hitting the iceberg and setting it ablaze in an orange hue as if lighting a signal fire so it could find its way back in the morning. The remaining flickers of light vanished as a dark, heavy night sky pushed the reluctant sun below the horizon.

"Beautiful, isn't it?"

Surprised, Pike turned around.

"Sorry, I didn't mean to startle you." The woman had shoulder-length blonde hair and was wearing a navy blue pantsuit that was business-like yet very stylish.

"Hi, Ms. Amies, I didn't know anyone else was up here, and yes it is." He turned back around as the last rays vanished. "I don't think I have ever watched a sunset from sea before."

"I have a couple of times, and it never gets old. The last time was from the deck of a navy frigate, I was doing a story on modern pirates. Trust me, the view this time is much more pleasant."

"You must lead an exciting life going all over the world on assignments."

"Trust me, it's not all glitz and glamour. It's a lot of hard work and the competition is ruthless out there. You have your major networks, local people, and anyone and everyone with a cell phone camera all scrambling to get the story. But when a gig like this one comes along, it makes it all worthwhile."

"Yeah, I bet the food on this trip is a little bit better than navy chow."

She smiled. "I just wanted to say thank you for what you did today but that it wasn't necessary.'

"All I did was give you an interview, nothing special about that."

She frowned at him. "I'm a reporter; it's my job to know things."

"Know things? Like what?" Pike asked, starting to feel like a kid with his hand in the cookie jar and hearing mom's footsteps.

"Things like it was you who arranged for me to have the exclusive interview with Mr. Cain and the first look inside this giant ice cube. And things like it was your idea to get back at the Toupee Man, as you call him, for the things he did to me. Thank you for the interview, but I can take care of myself and this in no way will get you any special privileges with me or a break on the way I cover the story, good or bad."

Pike was red-faced at being caught red-handed, embarrassed that the cat was now out of the bag. But there was something about her last statement that didn't sound right and then he realized what it was.

"Listen, Ms. Amies, I think there has been a misunderstanding here. None of this was set up to curry your favor, personal or professional. Call me a chauvinist pig, but I didn't do this for you or to get to you. I asked Mr. Cain to arrange something that would put Toupee Man in his place so to speak. I was tired of seeing him do whatever he wanted."

"Chauvinist pig?" she said, a small smile curving her lips.

"Sorry, a dated term. You probably don't know what it means."

"You're not that old and I'm not that young. I know what it means."

"I'm not doing too well here, am I?"

"It depends."

"I'm not trying to impress you so you'll feel obligated to me in anyway; I just hate pushy people who think they are better than everyone else, that's all." Pike paused and took a deep breath. "Can we move on to something else now... please?"

Amies stood and sized Pike up for a moment, deciding if he was telling the truth or just another really good liar. "I'm sorry, Mr. Pike. It's just that in my business, I hear every line there is. Everybody is always trying to get something, trying to get an angle. It's hard to take what someone says at face value."

"You're so young to be so jaded... wait, I forgot, you're not that young."

She smiled. "Okay, I deserve that one. So tell me, Mr. Pike, are you always in the habit of rescuing *young* damsels in distress?"

"Only if there are dragons to be slain." They both laughed.

"Well, Mr. Pike."

"Gabriel, please."

"Tabatha. Well, Gabriel, like I said, life as a correspondent is not all that it's cracked up to be. Like when you have a morning show to do, 3am comes far too early. Perhaps we can have dinner sometime if you can find the time between slaying dragons."

"I have an ogre scheduled in the morning and a small cyclops late afternoon, so I can't make any promises, but I think we can definitely work something out. Until then, fair maiden." Pike reached down and kissed her hand, then bowed low with a sweeping motion.

Tabatha curtsied, nodded in approval, then left. Pike watched her as she disappeared down the stairs. This could turn out to be an interesting trip after all. When this whole thing started with Toupee Man he had no idea it would lead to a date with a TV personality. He smiled to himself as he returned to his room. He wondered if this was one of Cain's butterfly effects.

CHAPTER TWENTY ONE

"Good morning, Dean," Pike said as he stepped into the office in the Hoth cave.

"Good morning Gabe. What can I do for you today?" Dean Miles replied with a smile.

"I went over all the plans and the ordering manifests, so with the paperwork out of the way I thought I'd start with the physical inspection."

Miles nodded. "Sounds good. Where would you like to start?"

Pike unslung the map tube that hung on his shoulder like a quiver and drew out a large schematic like an arrow and unrolled it on the work table. "I have to check from stem to stern so I thought I'd work on the outlying access and service tunnels first then work my way in."

"Mr. Cain is sure going to get his money's worth out of you," Miles said, smiling as he walked over to his desk. He opened the top drawer and pulled out an electronic notebook. "Here, take this."

Pike's eyes lit up like a Broadway marquee when he saw it. "This is cool. It looks kind of like an iPad only a little different and a bit bigger. How's that for a technical description from an engineer?"

Miles laughed. "It's a prototype, not yet released to the public. There are advantages to having the richest man in the world as your boss. It's got more apps than Carter has pills. Here, let me show you." Miles took it back and walked Pike through the simple set up routine. "And this is how you access the plans to the barge."

He tapped a few more icons and the plans for the iceberg came up. The first screen showed a two dimensional view of the plans like one would see looking down on a piece of paper. "Watch this," Miles said, "this is really cool." He tapped another icon and the screen switched to a three-dimensional side view. Pike's smile grew even bigger.

"And check this out." Miles tapped again and a small green dot appeared on the screen. "Your own personal GPS guide of the barge showing your exact location at any given time. And watch this." Miles typed in the word ENGINE ROOM ONE. As soon as he touched the enter key, a flashing red line appeared, emanating from the green dot, blinking through the different levels to show the most direct route.

"I gotta get me one of these things." Pike beamed.

"So I guess you don't want to take your paper maps with you then?"

Pike just frowned at him.

"I didn't think so," Miles said as he went back to his desk and picked up the phone. "Brian, would you come in here please?" Miles hung up then took a cell phone out of his desk drawer. "These are walkie-talkie phones." He said as he handed one to Pike. "Keep it with you at all times when you're below decks. I usually have the guys turn them in at the end of their shifts but I don't see you as a nine-to-five guy, so just keep it."

Just then the door opened and a young man about 22 walked in. He had short curly blond hair and bright, blue eyes that seemed to have a little apprehension in them. Pike thought he had the look of a kid being hauled into the principal's office.

"Gabriel Pike, this is Brian Centers. Brian, Gabriel Pike." Miles made the introductions. "Brian here is one of our best tunnel rats.

He can find his way around these tunnels in the dark; in fact, he has a couple of times. So even though you have the map, it never hurts to have a local guide."

"Glad to have the help," Pike said as he reached out his hand.

"Thank you, sir. When do you want to leave?"

"The sooner the better."

"Yes, sir. Give me a couple of minutes and I'll get us a cart." Centers turned and walked out the door.

"This is your baby," Pike said. "How long do you think it will take to check out all the service tunnels?"

Miles thought for a moment "Four, maybe five long days, if you really want to cover every inch of every tunnel, though I don't think that will really be necessary."

"Why's that?"

"Most of the tunnels are redundant in their features, just servicing the cooling/heating piping and ducting. If it's structural integrity you're worried about," Miles took the pad and pulled up and overall view of the barge, "as you can see, none of the tunnels are closer than ten feet to the outside. Obviously you can check anywhere you'd like but I might suggest that you start with the four main coolant/heat exchangers above the ships." Miles brought up another screen showing where the four relay stations were and the piping going out from them.

"Ready to go when you are, sir," Centers said as he popped his head in the door.

"Be right there." Pike replied looking at Centers then back to Miles. "Thanks Dean, I appreciate your advice." Pike shook his hand then left.

"Where to, sir?" Centers asked as Pike climbed into a modified golf cart.

"It's Gabe or Gabriel, which ever you prefer."

Centers relaxed a little. "Okay, Gabe, where would you like to go?"

"Let's head in the general direction of the bow, front or forward, whatever you call it on this thing."

Centers nodded and with a small fishtail on the ice, they entered the main tunnel.

"How long have you been on board?" Pike asked.

"Almost since the beginning."

"So you really do know your way around this tub then?"

"Oh yes, sir," Centers replied, a prideful smile on his face. "I helped lay nearly every foot of pipe on this thing."

Pike nodded his head. "Good. Then where would you suggest I start?"

"Start? What are you looking for?"

"Mr. Cain has me doing the final safety inspection for the Coast Guard so we can get approval to bring the barge into New York harbor."

"Where did Mr. Miles tell you to go?"

Pike smiled and shook his head. "I know where he suggested. I want to know where would *you* suggest?"

Centers thought for a moment then stopped the cart. "May I see the pad please?"

"Are you looking at the safety of the structural integrity of the barge or the mechanical?"

"Both."

"Okay. For the mechanical, I would start here." He brought up a screen showing the four-coolant/heat exchangers. Pike was just about to say that that was where Miles suggested when Centers took his finger and ran it across the screen, moving past the exchangers to another set of relays.

"What are these?" Pike asked, staring at the screen.

"These are the secondaries for the juice."

"Juice?"

"Sorry, that's what we call the mix we pump through the piping. The juice flows up from the ships to these four main exchanges.

From here they are sent, under pressure, to the next set of relays and so on. Each set of relays increases the pressure so the juice can reach the outer pipes." Centers flipped through the screens showing the pipes branching out, going from the primary to the secondary to the sub relays, giving Pike an overall view of the piping network. Then he scrolled back to the secondary relays.

"Like I said, I would start here because this is where the most initial pressure will come from, shooting out the juice to all the sub-relays."

"What would happen if one or more of these secondary relays failed?"

"It's hard to say. In theory, nothing. There are back up systems in place to take over in case of a failure. In theory, the juice would stop flowing and eventually that section of the barge would begin to melt. But that shouldn't be a problem because of the extremely slow rate of melting; a brand new pump could be flown in and installed before any appreciable ice would be lost. I suppose at the other end of the scale the worst case scenario would be that one or more lines would rupture and they couldn't turn off the main pump for what-ever reason, then the back flow would flood the cavern. The barge wouldn't sink, but Mr. Cain would be out a whole lot of money. This is new technology and such a departure from established engi-neering, so who really knows?"

"Okay," Pike said, thinking for a moment. "You said you would start here at the secondary relays for any mechanical safety issues. Where would you go then for any structural concerns?"

"Here." Centers brought up another screen. The screen came to life showing the front half of the iceberg with two spots glowing red. He tapped again and the view zoomed in and turned into a digital 3D animation. The view pierced through the layers of ice and emerged in the cavern housing the four ships. The animation circled around two large towers that rose from the decks of the two lead ships then disappeared into the ice.

"I saw these towers yesterday. What are they?" Pike asked.

"Those are the towing bridal support towers. They support the harness that's used to hook up to the cable the tug pulls the barge with," Centers replied.

Pike nodded. "Yeah, I can see where they'd be subject to a lot of stress." Pike thought for a moment then checked the pad again. "Stress testing the load factors should be relatively easy so we'll come back to the towers. Let's check out the relays first."

"You got it," Centers said. "Right this way."

CHAPTER TWENTY TWO

Pike fell on his bed exhausted, not even bothering to take off his parka. He lay there not wanting to move but as much as his muscles told him to relax, his stomach was ordering him up. He decided to compromise, stay in and order room service.

He had just mustered the energy to sit up and was gathering more strength to actually get off the bed and take a shower when the phone rang. He didn't know why, but he half expected, half hoped that it was K.D.

"Hello?"

"Hi Gabe, it's me, Tabatha."

"Oh... hi."

"It sounds like you're disappointed. Were you expecting someone else?"

"No, no, it's not that, it's just that I'm really tired. I spent the whole day running all over this thing doing my inspection."

"Sounds interesting. Have you eaten yet? Nothing like a good hot meal to bring you back to life. You can tell me all about your adventure over dinner."

"Well I was just going to get something from room service."

"You hero types do work fast, don't you? Inviting me to your room for dinner after we only just met."

"No, no, that's not what I meant." Pike felt himself getting flustered and embarrassed. "What I meant was…" Pike stopped in mid-sentence when he heard laughter on the other end.

"It's okay Gabe, I was only teasing."

"Whew, you had me going there for a minute."

"Good; well, unless you throw me out, I'll be over in half an hour."

"Why don't you make it forty-five minutes; I have to take a quick shower."

"In that case, I'll be over in ten."

There was dead silence on the phone. Pike didn't know what to say. Finally after what seemed like an hour all he could come up with was "Ahhh…"

Suddenly more laughter filled Pike's earpiece. "I'll see you in forty-five minutes," then she hung up.

He hung up the phone and suddenly felt like he was in junior high again. Well, at least he wasn't tired anymore and actually looked forward to spending a little more time with the lady reporter.

Thirty minutes later he heard a knock on the door. "You're early …" he started to say but stopped when he saw it was two waiters with serving carts.

"Early, sir?" One of the waiters asked.

"Never mind. There must be some mistake, I haven't ordered anything yet."

"Yes, sir." He replied as he took out a folded piece of paper and handed it to him. The note read: *Sorry, I took the liberty of ordering, see you in a few minutes. Tabatha.*

"Sir?" The waiter asked, looking into the room

"Yes, please come in." The waiter nodded as they rolled the two carts in. The first one was covered with silver dome-topped food servers and the second had all their dishes and silverware.

"Where would you like us to set up sir?"

"Don't worry about it. I'll take it from here." He started to reach into his pocket for their tip. "It's all taken care of sir. Enjoy your meal." With that, both waiters smiled and left.

Pike noticed that there was a bottle of wine and two glasses sitting on one of the carts. She must not be much of a reporter, he thought, otherwise she would know that I don't drink. Pike's stomach was shouting praises as heavenly aromas were beginning to escape from their silver cages. Was it impolite to peek and see what she had ordered? Should he wait for her? He decided, or should he say his stomach decided, that it would be okay to take a peek since she was the one who ordered it. He lifted the lid on the closest platter and saw a beautiful porterhouse steak, still sizzling.

Suddenly he heard a knock on the door and quickly put the lid back. A twinge of nervousness shot through his body. What was he going to do if she was in a slinky black cocktail dress with the top cut down to there and the hemline way up to here? He took a deep breath, held it for a moment, blew it out slowly, then opened the door.

"I'm sorry to disturb you sir, but this was left off the cart." The waiter said, holding a pitcher of iced tea.

"Please." Pike motioned for him to come in. The waiter quickly came in, set the pitcher down then left. You're losing it, Gabriel, he said to himself. Just then there was another knock on the door. He opened the door wondering what the waiter had forgotten this time. Instead, he was standing face to face with Tabatha Amies.

"Well there's a look I don't get every day," she said.

It took Pike a second to snap out of his surprise. "Sorry. It's just that… never mind, please come in." There was no slinky cocktail dress as she was wearing blue jeans, a white button down blouse with a jean jacket over it. He wasn't sure if he was relived or disappointed.

"What's for dinner? It sure smells good," Pike said.

"You didn't look."

"No, that would be rude, not waiting for my guest." He paused for a second, "Okay, yes I did; curiosity and the aroma got the better of me."

"It's okay; I won't report you to the manners police."

"Good, because I'm starved. Allow me to set the table." Yesterday's newspaper was spread out over the small table in the corner by the window. With a sweeping motion of his hand, he sent all the papers flying into the corner onto the floor. Tabatha did nothing to hide the curiosity that flooded her face as she watched her host going about his business. Pike disappeared into the bathroom and returned a moment later with two hand towels and laid them on the table as place mats. "Don't worry, they're clean." He smiled, then walked over and took her by the hand. "If you please, madam." and seated her at the table.

He served the food, consisting of salad, dinner rolls and a steak for each of them. When he was done, he stood back for a moment, tapping his chin, thinking.

"That's it!" he said, snapping his fingers. He walked over to the desk and entered a few commands on to his laptop then grabbed it and brought it over to the table. He set it down and opened it up to a scene of a fireplace burning brightly.

"I thought this was appropriate, being as we're floating on a giant chunk of ice." Pike smiled.

"You're good." She laughed. "Now all we need is some good music."

"I'd serenade you, but since you said *good* music..." He reached over and pushed another key. Violin and cello chamber music began playing.

Tabatha sat up a little bit, tilting her head to one side, listening intently. "I know that!" she said excitedly. "That's Haydn's Opus 20, the 'Sun' quartet. I played that when I was in college. How did you know?"

Pike smiled. "I may not be a reporter, but I do know how to use the internet. You're a famous person so it was easy to find information about you. By the way, I think you would have won the talent contest you entered if you hadn't had that wardrobe malfunction."

Suddenly her face was flush with embarrassment, and then she reached over and hit him on the arm. "I was four years old!"

"You know," Pike said between a bite of salad, quickly changing the subject, "Haydn is generally credited with creating the modern form of chamber music as we know it."

"My music instructor often told us that. He was a great fan of Haydn."

"Yes, but it was Beethoven who transformed chamber music, raising it to a new plane, don't you think? Both in terms of its content and in terms of the technical demands it made on its performers and its audiences?"

"That's true, although I prefer the depth and variety that Mozart brought to his compositions. I liked the way he brought an independent role for the string instruments to chamber music, how he used them to counter the piano."

Pike nodded his head in approval as he ate a large piece of steak. Tabatha looked at him for a moment then a suspicious smile began forming on her face. "You really don't have a clue about what I'm talking about do you?"

Pike stopped in mid-chew, looking like the cat with the canary caught in his mouth. He grunted as he shrugged his shoulders and shook his head. "I read it on the internet right before you got here," he told her sheepishly.

She studied him for an instant then burst out in laughter. "You are an interesting man, Gabriel Pike."

"Thank you," he said, tilting his head to one side. "This is a fine Bordeaux, would you like some?" He popped the cork, let the bottle breathe, and then poured her a glass. He set the wine bottle down then poured his iced tea into the other wineglass. "A toast."

"And to what are we drinking?"

"To the power of the internet. To Haydn, wardrobe malfunctions and crackling fires," he said looking at the computer screen. "And to new friendships." He finished, smiling back at her. Their glasses clinked, the music played, the fire crackled as they sipped their drinks and stared into each other's eyes. Magic was floating about the room... right until the phone rang and brought it down in flames.

"Excuse me, please." Pike apologized as he got up to answer the phone. "Hello?" he said, trying his best to hide the frustration in his voice.

"Well, hello to you too."

"K.D.!" Pike could do nothing to cover the surprise in his voice. He was happy to hear from her, yet he also felt embarrassed.

"You don't seem too happy to hear from me. Am I interrupting anything?"

"Well, yes. I mean, no. I was just having dinner... with a friend."

"Oh, sorry. I'll call back later. Talk to you soon."

"Okay, thanks, bye." He stood there for a second, not quite knowing what to think. He was glad to hear from her yet he felt guilty because he had another woman in his room, yet he knew he shouldn't feel that way because there was nothing between them, or him and Tabatha. And yet he was a little disappointed at the same time because of the way she seemed to take it all in stride, considering it no big deal.

He turned back around to find Tabatha looking at him with a sly look on her face. "That was K.D... Crooks, just a co-worker, from the office, back home in Seattle."

"I see," was her simple reply.

Pike sat back down and began eating again. He had taken two bites of his steak when he realized that Tabatha was just looking at him, reading him like book. "May I ask you a question, Gabe?"

"Sure," he answered almost hesitantly.

"Why do you look guilty of committing some great crime against humanity?"

"I do?"

"Yes, you do. Let me ask you another question. Is she your girlfriend?

"No."

"Does she think she is?"

"No."

"Do *you* think she is?"

"No."

"Have you slept with her?"

"NO!"

"Do you feel guilty sitting here with me?"

Pike paused for a moment. "After the phone call… a little, I guess."

"Why?"

Pike shook his head and threw his hands up in the air. "That's just it, I don't know why. K.D. and I don't have a past and you and I just met. So I have no reason whatsoever to feel guilty about anything."

"And yet you do."

"Yeah," he replied, letting out a long sigh.

Tabatha laughed, but it wasn't a mocking laugh. "Like I said, Gabriel Pike, you are an interesting man."

CHAPTER TWENTY THREE

"Thanks for letting me take a look around, Captain."

"My pleasure, Mr. Pike," replied Captain Daniel Gregory. Gregory was a fit man in his mid-fifties with salt and pepper hair and a neatly trimmed matching beard. He projected an air of confidence and experience that immediately set Pike's mind at ease.

Pike was standing on the Command Bridge of the iceberg, looking out the huge glass windows affording a beautiful view of the ocean; only today, the view was not so magnificent. The sky was a mass of solid, dull gray clouds. The sea was running in long, fifteen foot rolling swells, topped with white peaks, before a strong, unrelenting wind.

He had enjoyed his unexpected dinner with Tabatha last night but the evening was cut short because the network executives back in New York paged her and wanted to go over some upcoming events. After their goodnights and the hard day he'd had, bed was the most appealing option so he would have a fresh start on the new day.

Three hundred yards in front of them, he could see the lead tug straining on her towline as she struggled with her monstrous load in the rough seas. On the bridge, he could hardly feel the iceberg slowly rise and fall but looking at the tug was a different story. He watched as another tug off to their left would climb up the front of one wave then slide down the backside, her bow sending out huge sheets of spray as she landed in the bottom of the trough and then the whole process would start all over again.

He was mesmerized as he watched the struggle between man and nature when he suddenly jumped back, startled as a sheet of water shot up over the front of the iceberg and smashed against the windows. Embarrassed, Pike quickly looked around to see if he was the only one caught off guard. He was, but no one said anything.

"How high up are we, Captain?" Pike asked.

"We have a free board of nearly thirty feet in calm seas, less when it's stormy," he replied with a smile.

"So I see."

"Not to worry, Mr. Pike, we're perfectly safe up here."

He looked back at the tug just as it plunged deep into another wave. "I'm not so much worried about us as I am about them," he said pointing to the tugs, "they seem so small."

"The sea can be cruel and unforgiving, but I wouldn't worry too much about them either though. Those are the newest Crowley boats out there, built especially to handle weather like this. They're not so tiny either. Each is 146 feet long and 44 feet wide, plus they have over 10,000 horsepower to help them battle the waves. Now compare that to the Mayflower that crossed the Atlantic with the pilgrims on board, she was just 90 feet long with a 25 foot beam and she only had sails for power, so I think they can handle themselves. That's the *Rachel B.* out there in front, skippered by Captain Pat Bair, one of the best." Gregory said, pointing out the window. "Our escort to port is the *Cheri B.* and we have a trailer at the stern, the *Alyssa B.* They may get tossed around a bit by this weather, but they'll be fine."

Not sure if it was the weather or just the power of suggestion, but Pike was feeling slightly woozy so he decided he'd seen of enough of the outside view and thought it best to concentrate on the inside.

Other than the helm and a radarscope, he didn't recognize much of anything else that would tell him he was on the bridge of a ship. There were literally dozens of computer screens, consoles and workstations whose purpose he couldn't even begin to guess. The whole room looked more like mission control for a space shuttle launch than the bridge of a ship.

"Captain," Pike said, being careful to keep his eyes from wandering to the tossing waves, "as you know, I've been tasked with doing the final safety inspection before entering New York harbor. From a maritime point of view, how does this thing stack up against, say a super tanker of similar size?"

"We are much the same as any large ship. Even without the tug we can move and steer ourselves with the four ships underneath us, though it wouldn't be pretty or fast." He walked over to a large computer screen that showed a miniature top view of the iceberg. "Now this is something that other ships don't have." He tapped a command and over a dozen readouts popped up all over the iceberg.

"What are those?" Pike asked.

"Stress points. Notice how the numbers are all in green and fluctuate as the ship rolls? This gives us a good indication of how well she's handling the seas and we can make course adjustments as needed."

"I noticed that up here," he said, pointing to the screen, "at the support towers for the tow cable, some of the indicators flashed amber every once in a while."

The captain nodded. "Yes. We measure four different levels of stress: green, amber, yellow and red. As you have guessed, green means everything is within normal parameters. Amber indicates stress and fatigue levels rising in certain areas but well within safety limits. Yellow indicates a potential problem. If the sensor stays yellow, then an appropriate action plan needs to be formulated. If a sensor flashes red occasionally, it is time for concern but don't head for the lifeboats yet. If it stays red, then structural failure is imminent and action must be taken immediately. In this case, I would expect to see a few amber lights and maybe an occasional flashing yellow, all depending on the severity of the weather. Not to worry, Mr. Pike, everything is under control."

Just then another wall of water shot up in front of the window accompanied by a loud whack as the wave smacked against the bow of the ice berg. Pike jumped again but not nearly as much as at the first wave. He quickly glanced around the room and thought he caught a couple of raised eyebrows from the crew.

"What are these blue areas?" Pike was pointing at four small blues squares at each of the corners of the iceberg.

"Those are the anchors."

"Anchors? I don't remember seeing any anchors when we flew in?"

The captain smiled. "That's the whole point, it was designed that way. Mr. Cain didn't want such necessary evils as anchors distracting from the beauty of the iceberg so they're hidden. Each anchor room is buried five feet under the main deck and is encased by a one-foot thick wall of ice at the entrance. When the anchor is released, it will easily shatter the wall as it plummets to the ocean. It should look quite spectacular when they punch through the ice."

"Captain?" A crewman at the far end of the bridge called out. "Barometric pressure is at 28.91 and dropping fast and winds steady at 55 knots with gusts up to 80."

"Radar?"

"We have a cloud mass forming and coming down out of the north, sir."

"A storm brewing, Captain?" Pike asked.

The captain nodded. "Yes" was his simple answer. He gazed out the window, staring silently at the wind-tossed sea, watching, waiting, and listening intently as if it were speaking to him. The sea answered him in a not so still voice as another wave smashed against the berg, sending up another wall of water. This time Pike felt a small jerk as the towline between the tug and the iceberg had gone slack then tightened with the push of the wave. He looked down just in time to see nearly half the sensors on the towing support structure flash with an amber glow.

"Thompson," the Captain said quietly, "get me Mr. Cain on the phone please."

Suddenly Pike felt his stomach twisting into a knot, and it wasn't from seasickness. The captain turned to Pike, seeing the concern on his face. "No need for worry, Mr. Pike. As a precaution, I'm informing Mr. Cain that we're setting a new course, heading south to try to get us away from this storm. After all, it wouldn't do to have Mr. Cain's guests getting seasick, now would it?"

"That certainly would be some mess to clean up, huh?"

"Exactly." The captain smiled as he placed his hand on Pike's shoulder. "A favor if you would, Mr. Pike."

"Sure."

"Most of the people on board have never been at sea before, let alone in a storm. They tend to immediately think the worst and visions of the *Poseidon Adventure* or *Titanic* jump to the forefront of their minds. So if you could mingle with the guests, telling them you've been on the bridge and talked to me and reassure them that everything will be all right, it will help calm their nerves greatly. They'll believe it coming from you because they know you and trust you. Get them to the gaming tables so they'll forget their seasickness and this nasty weather."

"Sure thing, Captain, I'll do my best." As Pike walked off the bridge, the captain turned to his radio operator. "Thompson, get me Dean Miles on the horn please."

"Sir?"

"That's right, David, I need you to re-check the safety pins on all four anchor bridles," Dean Miles said.

"But Mr. Miles, I set those pins myself, they're okay, besides I'm off in half an hour and it'll take at least two to check them."

"I know David, but we're in for some bad weather and we need to make sure."

"But, sir..."

"David," Miles said in a stern voice, losing patience. "I need those pins checked now!"

David turned off his walkie-talkie and stormed off down the passageway, his smoldering anger melting ice with each step. "David do this, David do that, David we need this over here, David we need that moved over there. You would think I'm the only one on this whole stupid barge who could do anything. Bad weather, huh! This thing is as big as an aircraft carrier and they're afraid of a few waves. Hello!" he said as he hit the wall with his hands. "This thing is made of ice. Have you ever seen ice sink? Corporate idiots. They're sipping wine and eating HOT food while I'm down here freezing my butt off so that someone *up there* could say that *they* took care of it."

David Towers continued muttering to himself as he grabbed the rung of the first of three two-story service ladders he'd have to climb in order to check the safety pins. "You should have stayed in school, but nooOOOooooo. At 20 years old, you were too smart for school, you didn't want to be tied down, you wanted some adventure before you turned old and gray. You happy now, Einstein?" His question to himself bounced off empty walls as he reached the top level. He paused for a moment, bending over as he caught his breath. "The hours suck but at least the pay isn't bad," he said, consoling himself.

Straightening up, he entered the forward port side anchor room and immediately his breath was taken away by the frigid temperature. With no air circulating, as in the tunnels, the room held the cold like a deep freeze. Stepping back, he caught his breath, spewed out a few more choice words for corporate America then stepped in and flipped on the light switch.

He walked over to the anchor and grabbed the safety pin that held the locking mechanism, holding the anchor in its cradle. He jerked on it several times and it didn't move. "See, I told you!" He shouted out loud to no one in particular.

Towers stood for a moment and looked out the front wall. Being only a foot thick, light filtered through it, casting a strange view of the outside world. From here too, he could feel the barge swaying back and forth with the rhythm of the storm waves. As he stood there watching, the front wall would grow darker for an instant then lighten up again. It took him a moment to realize what was happening; it was getting darker and lighter because the waves were splashing that high on the side of the barge.

He looked at his watch. He was supposed to be off in fifteen minutes, he would never make it. He closed the door and headed to the starboard anchor room; he didn't give it a second thought or realize that the waves were reaching 25 feet up the side of the iceberg.

He found the starboard bow anchor secure just as he had the port, and as he descended the three stories to start his journey aft, he felt his frustration growing on the inside as fast as the storm was growing on the outside. He wasn't sure if it was just because he was hungry or because the weather was getting to him, but his stomach was getting upset, adding all the more to his sour mood.

Reaching the aft starboard anchor he found everything just as it should be, just as he knew it would be. Halfway up the ladder to the stern port anchor room, and an hour into overtime, his walkie beeped.

"Dave, are you done yet? The food is cold and the beer is getting warm. You need to get up here, man, we have the place all to ourselves." Towers looked up the shaft as if he could see his friend talking. He also heard laughter in the background and the clanging of a glass. They were up there having fun and he was stuck down here in the deep freeze. He sighed out of frustration; he could almost feel the warm air. "Yeah, man, I'm so done here. I'll be there in a few."

Screw this, he said to himself as he switched off his walkie. The stupid pin is set just like the others were. He was halfway to the top and for a brief moment he thought about just going the rest of the way up and finishing the job, but then an image of his friends eating and drinking without him flashed through his mind, sending him straight down the ladder.

If he had taken just five more minutes, he would have seen that the pin in the starboard anchor was not in position like the others. It hadn't been properly set in the first place and the swaying and rocking motion of the iceberg from the storm had loosened it even more; it was on the verge of falling out.

CHAPTER TWENTY FOUR

When Pike entered the casino, he knew the captain had been right. The place was deserted. The gaming tables were empty and the dealers were all standing together talking, as were the cocktail waitresses huddled by the bar. The slot machines still called out cheerily with their bright lights and happy chirps and beeps, but no one was there to listen.

He walked into the Crystal Palace and as he expected, found everyone standing by the windows, staring out at the storm. Tabatha was the first one to see him.

"How's everyone doing?" Pike asked as she came over.

"A lot of people are worried, though they're trying to not show it."

"Being a reporter, you picked up on that, huh?"

"Very funny," she replied as she hit him in the shoulder.

"I deserved that," he said, rubbing his shoulder. "But seriously, what about you?"

She looked up at him and debated whether to tell the truth or play the tough, street wise reporter. "To be honest, I'm a little scared. A couple of times..." Tabatha was interrupted by a startled shriek coming from someone standing by the window. They both turned to see spray shooting up over the side of the railing and splashing against the window. "...We've seen that happen." She continued: "And it seems like the waves are getting bigger and splashing over the railing more often. I think everyone would be more comfortable if they had a steel ship under their feet instead of floating on something you put in your drink."

"I just came from the bridge and the captain doesn't seem concerned."

"Yeah, well, neither did the captain of the *Titanic*."

Pike frowned and gave her a dirty look. "Anyway, we're turning south to try to skirt the storm."

"If everything is all right as the captain says, why are we changing course?"

"What, once a reporter always a reporter? Can't you take anything at face value?"

"Sorry, but it comes with the territory."

Pike frowned again. "Anyway, I need your help in distracting these people from the storm. The more they stare at the crashing waves, the more their imagination will run away with them and the more frightened they'll become."

"Amen to that," Tabatha replied, watching as another wave crashed over the railing.

"Everyone, can I have your attention please?" Pike shouted. He not only wanted to get their minds off the storm but to get them away from the plate glass windows in case they shattered. A few people turned, but most ignored him, still concentrating on the weather outside. Suddenly Pike thought his eardrums would rupture from the loud whistle that came from right behind him. Instantly everyone turned around. Pike turned and looked at Tabatha who was wearing a big smile.

"What?" she said innocently. "You said you wanted my help."

"Yeah, I may need your help finding an ear doctor after that."

"Ever try hailing a cab in New York?" She smiled.

Pike turned back to the crowd who was now paying attention, thanks to Tabatha's whistle. "I've just come from the bridge and the captain has assured me that everything is going to be okay."

"Those waves look pretty damn big to me!" one man shouted.

"Yeah, and I don't remember seeing any life boats on this giant ice cube!" another shouted. A low murmur started to spread through the crowd like a deadly mist.

"Where's Cain? Why isn't he here?"

"He's probably long gone by now. Flew the coop in that fancy helicopter of his."

"We're perfectly safe, nothing is going to happen." Pike tried to reassure them but hysteria already had a firm grip on them with one hand and was reaching up to choke out the last thoughts of reason with the other. He was losing them and he had to act fast. He was about to find out how good a poker player he was.

"Mr. Cain is still on board, and in fact he sent me down here," he lied. "You all know what a gracious host Mr. Cain is and while he can do a lot of things, he can't control the weather. Yet." There was a small nervous chuckle or two but not the tension breaker he was hoping for. "So to make up for this inconvenience, Mr. Cain will credit everyone's account in the casino for five hundred dollars. He wants you to have fun and this is his way of making up for the bad weather."

This caught the attention of over half the people but there were still a few holdouts. "Hey, would the Blast from the Past lie?" He held up his hands and put on his cheesiest smile. More laughter, almost there. "Tabatha, is this right?"

"Yes, yes, it is," she joined in.

"There, you see? She's a reporter, and we all know that reporters don't stretch the truth." Laughter now filled the room; hysteria's grip broken as they all started leaving the restaurant and heading back to the casino.

"Thanks for the backup back there," Pike said as the last of the crowd shuffled by.

"You were pretty quick on your feet back there. Mr. Cain never said he'd give everyone five hundred bucks, did he?"

Pike sighed then shook his head. "No, but one problem at a time for now. I still need your help."

"Sure."

"I need you to go out and play the gracious host for me. Keep everybody playing; keep their minds off the storm. Can you do that for me?"

"Sure, I can help the Blast from the Past, but it will cost you."

"Like what?"

"I don't know yet, but I'll think of something." She smiled and walked into the casino.

Pike immediately turned to close the curtains over the windows. As he was walking, he noticed a glass of water on one of the tables. The water in the glass was slowly swaying back and forth; the storm was getting worse.

After closing all the curtains, he found the maître d' who wasn't too happy when Pike told him to close off that part of the restaurant that faced the ocean. After Pike threw Cain's name around a few times, the maître d' reluctantly agreed.

Pike walked back into the casino, happy to find things almost back to normal. A few people were leaving, obviously seasick by the way they were holding the stomachs and their hands over their mouths. He looked around and found Tabatha standing at a roulette table, cheering the players on. She looked up and smiled and waved at him.

Just then the elevator door opened and Cain and Mallory stepped out. They were greeted almost like the Second Coming, everyone stopping in mid-bet and rushing over to them. Cain greeted them like a politician on the campaign trail, smiling and shaking their hands. As they gathered around, he settled their nerves by telling them that everything was fine and that there was no need for concern. He expounded on the safety of the iceberg and the experience of the crew.

After several minutes of mingling with his guests, Cain came over to Pike who was sitting on one of the stools in Starbucks. "Mr. Cain," Pike began solemnly, "I believe I may owe you some money."

"Close to twenty grand, I believe."

"Ouch." Pike flinched. "I wanted to get the people away from the windows and their minds off the storm as quickly as possible. Sorry, sir, it was the best I could come up with on such short notice."

"And a fine solution it was, Gabriel," Cain said, a smile finally breaking. "You accomplished your mission with flying colors. I would expect nothing less from the Blast from the Past, although I think they would have been just as happy with a hundred apiece." He chuckled.

"I guess there goes my paycheck for the trip."

"Nonsense. Best PR money I've spent in a long time."

"Sir?"

"They say money can't buy love, but in this case it can buy a lot of good will," Mallory answered, seeing the puzzled look on Pike's face. "You defused the situation and got their minds off the storm and when this whole thing blows over, all they'll remember is that it was a little windy outside and how much fun they had playing on Nigel's money."

"Glad to be of service," Pike replied, shrugging his shoulders.

"The offer you extended to the others also applies to you, Gabriel. Grab a stack of chips and go have some fun."

Pike thought about it for a moment then nodded his head. "You know what? I think I might just take you up on that."

"Good man." Cain slapped Pike on the back.

"You know, Nigel, it would push some fears away and boost confidence if you stayed and played awhile yourself," Mallory said.

"You are probably right. Maybe I can win back some of my money that Gabriel spent."

"Good man." Mallory slapped Cain on the back.

"Very funny. Now go grab us both a stack of chips and meet me at the craps table."

"You know what the only thing better than spending Tom's money is?"

"What?"

"Spending yours." She laughed.

"Like I said, very funny. Now go get the chips," Cain said, pointing his finger at the cashier's cage like his was ordering his puppy out of the room. As he watched her walk away, his phone rang. As he talked he smiled and waved at people. Mallory looked at Cain when she came back with the chips and instantly knew something was wrong.

She smiled as she handed him the chips, keeping up appearances. "What's wrong?" she said under her breath as they walked toward the craps table, still smiling.

"We may have a slight problem. I want you to mingle around then work your way over to Gabriel. Tell him the captain would like to see him on the bridge but not to leave right away. He needs to be discrete when he leaves and not to cause suspicion and undo everything he's accomplished here."

"Of course," Mallory said, laughing, playing her part. Cain smiled and walked over to the craps table and was immediately swallowed by the crowd of gamblers. Mallory wandered over to the blackjack tables and quickly lost two hands then made her way over to Pike who was playing a slot machine with Tabatha Amies seated next to him.

"Gabe, can I talk to you for a moment?"

"Sure. All I'm doing here is giving Mr. Cain his money back anyway."

She pulled him aside and explained the situation.

"But what about Tabatha? I'm sure her spider senses are already on alert by the fact that you pulled me aside."

"I'll worry about her. Just make your rounds then quietly leave."

"Okay," Pike agreed, nodding his head.

Mallory turned back to the reporter. "Tabatha, there's something I'd like to talk to you about." Pike stood back and could see the wheels turning in Tabatha's head as her eyes darted back and forth between him and Mallory. She could smell a story but wasn't quite sure if the bigger story was to stay with him or go with Mallory. She fell back on the reporter's first rule, always follow the source. She kissed Pike on the cheek then turned to Mallory: "I'm all ears."

Pike left the casino after five long minutes of acting. He had taken the elevator down to the Hoth cave and was just jumping onto one of the carts when Miles came out of the office.

"Hi, Gabe, in here please."

"What's up?" Pike said as they entered Miles' office. "Mr. Cain said there was some sort of problem and wanted me on the bridge."

"You need to see this before you go up there," Miles replied, worry lines burrowed deep into his forehead. He flipped open his laptop and brought up a screen similar to the control panel he saw on the bridge. He recognized the screen showing the four anchor positions. Three were blue with the aft port anchor flashing red.

"The safety pin that secures the anchor to its cradle has fallen out and we can't get it back in."

"Okay, what does that mean?"

"The pin is used to keep the launch mechanism for the anchor frozen. In theory, with it gone, nothing should happen as the weight of the anchor should hold it on the cradle. But without the pin, in these heavy seas, it's possible the anchor could slide off."

"What's the worst case scenario if this happens?"

"The anchors as you know are sealed in their rooms. The outside wall is only a foot thick. If the anchor breaks free and slides forward, it will punch through the ice like it was a wet paper a bag."

"Can you bring up the schematics please?"

"Sure thing." Miles tapped a few keys and brought up a 3D view of the anchor room, with the view slowly circling around the anchor. "See, that's where the pin is supposed to be." He pointed to an area highlighted in red.

"Okay, expand it out a bit."

Miles expanded the view that now showed the entire back half of the iceberg with a view of the starboard anchor as well.

"What's this here?" Pike said pointing to the center of the screen.

"Those are the winches for the anchors. Each anchor has its own winch, but for efficiency we housed them together."

"And these?"

"Support beams running out from the winch housing to each anchor room. They're used to strengthen and disperse the load when we raise the anchor."

"May I?" Pike asked as he took the laptop. Pike brought up a cut away view of the stern showing steel beams running vertically from the two ships buried below to the anchor rooms.

"This girder work is attached to the housing floor plate and then secured to the deck of the ships, correct?"

Miles nodded his head. "Yes, again for support, since it's very difficult to secure something as large and heavy as anchors to justice."

"Just how heavy are these anchors?" Pike asked, worry lines now beginning to form on his face.

"These aren't anchors to your twenty-five foot Bayliner here. This barge is as big as an aircraft carrier and so are its anchors. Each anchor weighs close to 60,000 pounds and there are about 200 links per chain, weighing in at 360 pounds per link."

Pike's frown grew deeper. "Does your laptop have modeling software?"

"Yeah, give me a second."

"How deep of water are we in?" Pike asked while Miles was setting up the program.

"About 12,000 feet or so. I could get you the exact depth if you need it."

"What is the length of the anchor chain?"

"Six hundred feet."

"Here." Miles gave the laptop to Pike. Pike took over and started typing like a madman, muttering numbers as he went. Every once in a while, Pike would shake his head then mutter some more, but all the while his fingers never left the keyboard.

After five minutes of furious typing, he turned the laptop around for Miles to see. The worry lines that had formed earlier were now etched like the Grand Canyon on his face.

"What is this?" Miles asked.

"It's a computer model, projecting what will happen if the port anchor slips off its cradle and falls into the ocean."

Pike pushed the button and the screen came up showing a line drawing of the barge. It zoomed in to where the port anchor was then it showed it dropping. It showed the anchor in free fall and when it reached the end of its chain, it yanked the winches free, pulling the cross-support beam that ran from the housing plate down to the ship, acting like a giant meat cleaver, slicing off the stern of the iceberg, pulled by the enormous weight of the anchors.

"What just happened here?" Miles asked, staring blankly at the screen.

"That's the worst case scenario if the anchor breaks loose and falls. The winches are designed to lift the anchors, not lower them. They have no brakes. When it goes, it goes. When the chain reaches the end, it's not stopping. The housing and winch platforms weren't designed to stop 35 tons of free falling steel. So when the starboard anchor goes, it will yank both winches out of their housings and probably drag the starboard anchor with it. It will literally rip the stern off the barge."

"Wow," was all Miles could say.

"Can we cut the chain?"

"No." Miles shook his head. "We don't have the proper equipment on board to cut through that thickness of steel."

"Can we weld the anchor onto the cradle?"

Again, Miles shook his head. "There's not enough surface area that would make the weld strong enough to hold against the tension."

"All right, let's get up to the anchor room to see what we can see," Pike said.

"Right. Follow me."

By now, Pike was used to seeing his breath panting out like stream from a locomotive in the ice passageways and he was familiar with climbing the ladders in the confines of the missile silo tubes that connected the decks; what he wasn't used to was the amount of physical labor it took. He *thought* he was in shape until he took this job.

"You know you guys could have put a few more elevators in this thing," Pike said, gasping for breath after climbing up the last set of ladders.

"You know, you're not the first person to say that." Miles smiled. "Come on." Pike followed Miles as they entered through a plain wooden door into the anchor room.

Stepping into the room, Miles turned on the light and Pike stopped dead in his tracks; he was amazed at the sheer size of the anchor itself and awed by the two foot size links of the chain that held it. The anchor was lying at an angle on the cradle, but even then, it was still taller than he was. In amazement, he slowly walked around to the front and gawked at the two flukes that were big enough to use as a bed, and marveled that it was well over six feet at the base. It looked to be every bit the 35 tons Miles said it was.

"Here," Miles said, calling Pike over to the other side. "This is where the pin was supposed to be. As you can see, the anchor has shifted just enough that we can't get it back in."

Pike nodded as he examined the anchor and cradle. Just then the iceberg rolled enough to the left that he had to reach out and grab the chain to steady himself. At the same moment, they heard the groaning of metal. Both men instantly jumped back from the anchor and a split second later there was a loud snap. Pike felt his heart stop as he stood in horror and watched as the front half of the anchor slipped off the cradle and fell onto the ice floor with a dull thud.

Large fissures spiraled out in the ice from the point of impact like streaks of lighting. Pike and Miles stared at each other, just waiting for the floor to give way at any second or for the anchor to slide the rest of the way off its cradle and mow them down like a runaway freight train.

Barely breathing, Pike carefully slid under the taunt chain and moved gingerly back to the door and stood by Miles.

"What are we going to do?" Miles whispered, afraid the sound of his voice would crack the ice.

"I don't know," Pike whispered back. "I'm trying to think."

The ship rolled again, leaning even farther this time and with another sickening thud, the anchor slid the rest of the way off the cradle and gently nudged the front panel of ice, creating another spiraling art display. Pike held his breath as he saw cracks forming and shooting up the wall. It was horrifyingly beautifully to watch as the fissures formed. Some shot out like lightning bolts while other slowly crawled up the wall like slithering snakes in sand. Even with the storm raging outside, he would never forget the hideous sound the crackling ice made. As the anchor slid forward and kissed the wall, he prayed that the foot thick piece of ice was enough to keep the 35 ton monster at bay.

"Think, think, think," Pike said out loud. 'What's below us?"

Miles nervously fumbled with his computer pad as he took it out of its case. "Nothing," he reported. "It's solid ice all the way down to the keel except for piping carrying the juice."

"Okay, no help there. How about above us?" Pike asked, never taking his eyes off the anchor. He watched with morbid fascination as one large fissure ran straight up the middle, then split out like a T, eight feet up and stopped two feet short of either edge.

Miles brought up another screen then showed it to Pike. "There's not much on the stern. You've got the golf tee, the swimming pool and sunbathing area."

Sunbathing area on an iceberg? Pike frowned at how ridiculous that sounded as he forced himself to take his eyes off the wall and look at the pad. He started to turn back and stare at the wall when something caught his eye. "What's this here? Is that what I think it is?"

"That's your plane if that's what you mean."

Pike grabbed the pad and stared at it. "Is this the exact location of the plane? Is it is sitting directly above us?"

"Yes."

"And the pool? This is its correct location?"

Miles nodded his head.

"How thick is the ice above us?"

"Five feet." Miles could hear the growing excitement in Pike's voice. "What is it? What are you thinking?"

"I can't tell you yet. You'd think I'm crazy. Come on, we need to get up on deck," he said as he rushed out the door.

CHAPTER TWENTY FIVE

Stepping out of the health spa onto the sundeck, Pike felt like he had been transported into another world. Gone was the relative quiet, peace and warmth of the indoors. He suddenly felt like he was living in a *National Geographic* special as he trudged forward, assaulted by blasts of arctic air hurled at him by eighty mile an hour winds.

Gone were the sounds of civilization, the beeps and bells of the casino, the sound of people talking, the humming and clattering of mechanical things. The only sound now was the raw roar of nature.

The gale howled as it whipped across the deck, taking everything with it that wasn't fastened down. In its anger, the wind sent the snow flying sideways, flashing by like tracer bullets, reflecting the light from the building. It also chopped mercilessly at the ocean, making it bleed white spray as it severed the tops off the waves.

Pike shivered as he leaned into the wind, bracing himself against its wrath, taking careful, measured steps that led him to the swimming pool. Nearly exhausted from his short battle with nature, he leaned against a palm tree and stared at the pool. How odd, he thought; it reminded him of a miniature version of the ocean, reflecting its anger and turmoil, spilling over its sides. Looking around, he saw that everything else on the deck was covered either in snow or a thin layer of ice with small drifts forming around the few deck chairs that hadn't blown away.

With the white blanket of snow, it looked like a Christmas scene, but not a cheery one surrounded by friends and family. This was a dark Christmas, one with no joy. The first Christmas with your children gone, with your loved one serving overseas or the first time there is no present under the tree from them because they're gone. The tree is still there, the lights are still on but the smiles are strained and empty.

Between the gusts of snow, Pike saw the one shiny ornament from that tree, the one thing that might bring them all hope and the reason he was out there: the *Yankee Clipper*. Pike slowly made his way over to the plane. Twice, he nearly fell as the wind and waves conspired against him, a classic one-two punch rolling the iceberg and hitting him with heavy gusts.

Reaching the plane, he walked around it, inspecting it and the surrounding area. He tugged on the tie-down straps, checked the wheel chocks on the launch platform, then brushed the snow and ice away and inspected the launch controls. Satisfied that she was weathering the storm, he unzipped his jacket and pulled out his c-pad, tugged his gloves off with his teeth then tapped in a few commands. He surveyed the area, getting his bearings, checked the pad, then nodded and quickly retreated to the warmth and safety of the spa.

"Are you sure this is going to work?" Miles asked.

Pike took off his fur-lined parka and stamped his feet, and rubbed his hands together, trying to warm up. Cain and Mallory walked up and Mallory handed Pike a cup of coffee. "Thanks," he said as he just held the cup for a moment, enjoying the heat and letting it warm up his cold fingers. He took a sip and smiled. "It's even a mocha."

"Gabriel?" Cain said.

"Sorry, this warm cup feels so good, and yes, it will work." He took another quick sip. "It has to work."

"Your idea is really, crazy you know," Mallory said, skeptical of the whole thing.

"I know, but what other choice do we have? I've talked to the captain and the storm will get worse before it gets better. The anchor has already slipped off its cradle and is resting against the front wall; it's not a matter of *if* it will crash through, it's a question of *when*."

Pike took out the c-pad and all three crowded around it as he brought up a 3D view of the stern of the iceberg. "See here, this is the anchor room, and right above it is the *Clipper*. The *Clipper* is lined up in a perfect position right over the anchor room. We use the jet engine to melt through the roof, pump the water from the pool into the anchor room, crank up the A/C units in this section and freeze the water in the room, thus freezing the anchor in place. Problem solved."

"Why do you have to melt the ice? Why not just pump the water directly from the pool?" Mallory asked.

"We already thought of that," Miles replied. "We simply don't have enough hosing to reach from the pool to the anchor room."

Mallory shook her head. "I think all three of you are crazy for even thinking this idea will work." Just then the iceberg rolled to the right and hung there for what seemed like an hour before it righted itself. "I still think it's crazy," Mallory said, a lot less conviction in her voice.

"Oh ye of little faith," Cain said optimistically. "I like it! What do you need, Gabriel?"

"I need you to get all the drinking ice we have on board. When we start to fill the room, I want to dump the ice in. It will help freeze the water quicker."

"Anything else?"

"Nope, that should do it."

"Dean, I need you to get a crew together and seal the anchor room as soon as soon as possible."

"You got it."

"Mr. Cain," Pike said, turning to his boss, "while all this is going on I need you to do what you do best: keep these people calm and use this situation to our advantage. Questions anyone? Good. Let's get to work then. We don't have much time."

Mallory shook her head again. "And I thought some of *your* ideas were crazy," she said, looking at Cain.

"You're standing on the craziest one," he shouted as she walked away.

CHAPTER TWENTY SIX

"Okay, is everything ready?" Pike was standing in the spa area with his parka on, ready to go back outside. In front of him were Cain, Mallory, and Miles, surrounded by a work crew of ten or twelve.

"Miles?"

"We've already sealed off the anchor room and I've got two crews standing by so as soon as you melt through, we can start pumping. It should take about half an hour or so to fill the room and another three to set up hard."

"Good. Beth?"

"We've had the ice making machine cranked up and by the time you're ready we should have about 600 pounds to dump in."

"Excellent, that will really help. Mr. Cain?"

"I'm not hiding anything from our passengers, hoping that things don't go wrong. I've told everyone what's happened and what we're doing to solve this problem and I've moved everyone to the front of the iceberg. Besides," Cain smiled, "with a boatload of reporters I don't think I could have kept it a secret even if I tried." Everyone laughed nervously, easing the tension a little. "I also have both escort tugs standing by... just in case."

"Thank you all very much," Pike said. "I'm guessing it will take about twenty minutes to melt through five feet of ice, so everyone can wait here where it's warm and dry; everyone except you, Dean. I'll need your help out there."

"I've got it, Dean. You can stay here," Cain said.

"Sir?" Miles said.

"My berg, my mess. I'll help clean it up." Cain replied.

"It's pretty nasty out there, Mr. Cain," Pike said.

"I may be rich, but I'm not a pampered pansy."

Pike nodded. "Well, alright then, let's get this show on the road." Pike pulled up his hood and headed for the door. "That's a pretty old looking parka you have there." He said as he watched Cain put it on. "I'd of thought you'd have the latest in hi-tech outerwear."

"I do, but this belonged to my great-grandfather and it brought him good luck, so I'm hoping it will do the same for me."

Pike nodded. "I hope so too."

He grabbed the stepladder he would need to climb into the cockpit and stepped out the door. Two steps out, he gasped as his breath was taken away by the cold. The temperature had dropped to 25 degrees and falling, but the wind was now at a steady 50 knots, putting the wind chill factor at -16. He could appreciate the sentiment of Cain using his great-grandfather's parka but he was sure glad he was using the latest in modern cold weather gear.

"Okay, when we get there," Pike shouted above the roar of the wind, "and after I get in the plane, you'll have to adjust the angle of the launcher, setting it as high as you can to put the engine as close to the ice as possible."

Cain nodded, and they continued their trek across the frozen wasteland of the sundeck. Pike was cold in his modern, triple stitched, triple layer insulated waterproof parka, so he could only imagine that Cain must be freezing in his 100 year old coat, but to his credit, Cain didn't complain.

Reaching the *Yankee Clipper*, Pike took the ladder and jammed it into the snow like he was planting his flag on Mount Everest. He looked at Cain who gave him an enthusiastic thumbs up then turned and started climbing. He had just stepped onto the second rung when a gust of wind swirled underneath him and sent both him and the ladder flying. Pike landed hard on his side with his left foot twisted in the rungs.

"Are you all right, Gabriel?" Cain shouted over the wind as he reached down and freed Pike's foot.

Pike cringed in pain as Cain removed the ladder. "Yeah, I think so," he replied as Cain helped him to his feet. He tentatively put pressure on it and stifled a cry of pain.

"You are a terrible liar, Gabriel. Remind me to invite you to my next poker game."

"I'm afraid the kind of stakes you play for, I couldn't even afford the ante." Pike took a few more steps, trying to walk it out but he didn't have the time or the room to do that. At least the cold helped deaden the pain. "Help me back to the plane, please. And if you don't mind, I'll have you hold the ladder this time."

"I thought you might." Cain set the ladder up again and helped steady Pike as he hobbled back to the plane. Pike gingerly put his hurt foot on the rung and instantly felt a bolt of pain shoot up his leg. He bit his lip and willed himself the rest of the way up.

He didn't think it was broken but it sure hurt like it was. He could remember hurting himself like this only one other time. He was fourteen or fifteen and playing Babe Ruth baseball. He was stealing second base and slid in to beat the throw but started his slide a little too late. His foot landed on the edge of the base and twisted. He was hoping for a solid cast so he could get more sympathy but all he ended up with was the kind that you took on and off. What he wouldn't do for that cast right now.

Pike grabbed the edge of the canopy and yanked on it three times before he could break it free. Reaching the top rung, he tumbled rather than climbed into the cockpit. It was a welcome relief when he finally got inside and pulled the canopy closed. Not only because he could rest his ankle but also because it got him out of the vicious wind. The wind buffeting the canopy reminded him of the sound the air made as it rushed passed during flight. He sat there for a moment, just enjoying the peace and quiet.

Suddenly he realized that Cain was still outside waiting for him. Quickly he turned and gave him the thumbs up. With a jerk that reminded him of the start of a roller coaster ride, the *Yankee Clipper's* nose slowly began to rise. When the plane stopped, Pike looked down to Cain who signaled that that was as far as it would go. Pike nodded then turned his attention to starting the plane.

Pike was worried that because of the bitter cold, he would have trouble starting the *Clipper*, but such was not the case. After going through his preflight checklist, much to his surprise and delight, the turbine turned over and picked up speed and soon was running at idling speed.

He increased the throttle as much as he dared, trying to find the happy medium between using enough power to melt the ice quickly and not using so much it would rip the plane off its tie downs. With everything fine-tuned, all he had to do now was wait and that shouldn't take long as he figured the heat from the exhaust was somewhere around 1,200 degrees.

It was a little unnerving, Pike thought, to be perched fifteen feet above the pitching deck of an iceberg that was swaying more than the hips of a belly dancer. Several times when the berg was rolling, he could see over his right wing and look straight down and see nothing but angry water below. Just like when he was on the bridge, he concentrated on the inside of his cockpit, doing his best to ignore the world outside.

It was warm in the cockpit and with the swaying motion of the iceberg and the steady whine of his engine, he was having a hard time keeping his eyes open. He didn't know if he had actually been asleep for a while or just nodded off but he was quickly wakened by a loud thump. His head snapped up, his eyes wide open. He felt embarrassed, like he had fallen asleep in church and he looked around to see if anyone had noticed. They had. The thump that woke him was a well-thrown snowball slamming against his canopy. He looked through the slush and saw Cain standing a few feet away with another snowball in his hand.

Pike quickly got out his walkie. "Sorry, boss," he said sheepishly.

"It looks like we've melted through to the anchor room," Cain replied, ignoring Pike's sleeping habits.

"Very good sir. Dean, do you copy?"

"Right here, Gabe."

"You heard Mr. Cain; we're through the roof now. I'll shut the engine down and you can go ahead and send the crews out and have them get started."

"Will do."

Pike turned off the ignition and as the engine wound down, he saw the first of the two five man teams rushing out of the spa building like a team of fire fighters. Each team carried a six-inch flex hose and were going to run it from the swimming pool and drain it through the two foot hole that he had just created to the anchor room below.

Pike waited for Cain to lower the *Clipper*, then cracked open the canopy and immediately all the warm air that had been in his cocoon was sucked away by the vicious storm. Carefully he put his foot onto the top rung of the ladder, testing his ankle; it was still tender and sore but feeling better. He shivered as he descended the ladder, the wind buffeting him vindictively, as if it were making up for lost time, angry at him for hiding in the plane.

Once on the deck, Pike dropped to his hands and knees and crawled over and peered into the hole. Taking a flashlight, he was pleased to see that there was already about six inches of water sloshing around on the floor. He was also pleased to see that the anchor hadn't shifted any more during the rising seas.

"Out of the way, coming through." Pike was surprised at hearing the familiar voice of Mallory booming over the roar of the wind. He turned to see her, followed by three others, each carrying large bags over their shoulders, like strange looking Santa clones. She dropped her bag by the hole and stepped aside while the others opened their bags and began pouring the ice inside.

"How come in this great plan of yours I'm hauling fifty pound bags of ice around and you get to sit in the warm cockpit of your plane?"

"Because it's my plan." Mallory could see the smile underneath Pike's parka. "Why are you out here?" Pike asked. "Your crew should be doing this."

"Like Nigel said, he may be rich but he's not a pansy. Well I'm not rich, and I'm not a pansy either. I can do my fair share."

"Fair enough," Pike said as he watched the others pour in their ice. "You know how to catch a polar bear, don't you?"

Mallory looked at him and shook her head. "I know I shouldn't ask, but how?"

"You kick him in the ice hole."

Mallory groaned. "That was bad, I mean, really bad. I hope your plan works better than your jokes."

Pike just looked at her and grinned. "Here, let me help."

Mallory was stooped over while Pike knelt on the ice beside the hole and began untying the string of the laundry bag turned ice carrier. He shifted several times trying to maintain his balance on the rolling deck. They were somewhat sheltered kneeling behind the *Yankee Clipper,* but the wind still managed to rip at their clothing like the frenzied crowd at a concert trying to get a piece of their favorite rock star.

However, nothing could protect them from the sheer power of the raging sea. As the night had progressed, so had the anger and churning of the ocean. The swells had continued to grow and even though the iceberg was 1,000 feet long and weighed over 100,000 tons, Mother Nature was not impressed.

What started out as a slight, barely noticeable gentle swaying of the iceberg, had quickly escalated into long, sweeping rolls that had sent dishes sliding off tables and laptops landing in the laps of their users. Walking had become difficult, making everyone look like staggering drunks, as they tried but failed to walk in a straight line.

Pike had almost emptied his bag when a cross wave hit the side of the iceberg, pitching it up on its side. So violent was this assault that the man behind Pike holding a bag of ice lost his balance. He tumbled to his left, but held on to the bag as it fell off his shoulder and it swung him around like an athlete throwing the hammer at an Olympic track and field meet.

The bag hit Pike on the shoulder, smacking him down hard onto the deck and plowing into Mallory like an out of control car at a demolition derby. She landed with a sickening thud on her back that could be heard even above the wind, then she slid feet first into the void.

Pike's eyes filled with horror as he watched her slide in. It was surreal, like watching a horror movie, only he wasn't watching it, he was living it. He managed to roll over and reach out his left hand and grab her sleeve. For a fleeting moment he thought he had her, but her momentum tore her from his grip, and she was gone; swallowed whole like Jonah.

Pike scrambled over to the side of the hole and shouted into the darkness. "Beth! Can you hear me? Are you all right?" He heard a low moan which was a good sign; it meant she was conscious and alive. "Don't worry, Beth! I'm going to get you out!"

He grabbed his flashlight and shined it down into the abyss, hesitating for a moment, afraid of what he might see. The beam pierced the darkness and shone on Mallory like a spotlight. He was relieved to see that she was leaning against the shank of the anchor in thigh deep water. She had fallen feet first and the angle of the shank had helped break her fall as she slid down it, much like a ski jumper landing on a steep slope.

But he was not happy to see that her feet had landed at the base of the anchor and were resting against the thin wall that held the anchor in place. If the anchor shifted, it could pin her to the wall making a rescue almost impossible or worse yet, it could break the ice wall and plummet to the ocean below, taking Mallory with it.

"You wanna get that out of my eyes?" Mallory said weakly, shielding her face from the light.

"Are you okay?" Pike asked.

"I-I don't know. My back is sore and I don't think I can feel my legs."

He was glad she couldn't see his deep frown. Not feeling her legs was not a good sign. He could hear the trembling in her voice and see her shaking from the cold and he prayed her loss of feeling was just from the numbing ice and not from a back injury. In either case, he had to get her out of there in a hurry.

Just then he heard a loud crack and he shined the light just in time to see a five foot fissure streaking up the front wall. The light reflected off the fracture making it look like a lightning bolt. He tried to turn the light off but he wasn't quick enough; Mallory saw it too.

"Gabe! Get me out of here!" The sheer terror in her voice was enough to freeze his heart.

"Don't worry, Beth. We'll have you out of there in a jiffy." He hoped his voice conveyed more confidence than he felt. "Hang on, Beth, I'm going to get some help. I'll be right back.'"

"Don't leave ,Gabe! Don't leave me here all alone. Gabe?" Now his heart was melting, hearing the desperation in her voice.

"It's okay, Beth, I'm here," he shouted back. He looked around quickly and was relieved to see Miles inching his way toward him.

Pike reached back and pulled Miles up to him and handed him the flashlight. "Dean is here, Beth!" He waited for a moment then called again. Still no answer. His heart was racing now and panic was the driver. "Beth!" He shouted so loud it hurt his throat.

"I'm here," was the simple reply.

Pike turned to Miles. "Whatever you do, keep her talking. Hypothermia is setting in and if she falls asleep, she could slide off the anchor and drown or simply not wake up at all."

Miles nodded his head. "Hey, Mallory, remember the other day..."

Pike stood and looked around frantically. He had no idea what he was going to do; he only knew he had to do it quickly. Suddenly he saw Centers and Cain and he waved them both over.

"I was inside, what happened?" Cain asked.

"Mallory felt into the hole."

Concern creased Cain's forehead. "Is she okay?"

"She is for now, but we haven't much time."

"What do you need? Name it and you got it," Cain replied. Cain's voice was calm on the outside but Pike could hear the underlying emotions.

As Cain was talking Pike noticed the *Yankee Clipper* behind him. He was almost ignoring Cain as a plan was taking shape in his mind. "Rope. Can you get me some rope?" he blurted out, looking at Centers.

"Yeah," Centers shouted above the howling wind, "but it's down on the ships. It'll take me about ten minutes to get it. Why don't we just use the ladder there?"

"It's not tall enough. Remember, the ice is five feet thick and the ceiling is another eight feet and this is only a six foot stepladder. Now go!" Pike shouted and patted Centers on the shoulder as he turned to leave.

"What do you want me to do?" Cain asked.

"We don't have ten minutes. Help me with the ladder." They both grabbed the ladder and put it up beside the *Yankee Clipper*.

"What are we doing?" Cain asked.

"Hold it steady, I've got to get something out of the cockpit."

Cain nodded, and then held the ladder, burying his chin into his chest, trying to protect himself against the harsh winds. Pike steadied himself on the first rung, then shot up the ladder like a rocket on rails. Reaching the top, he pulled back the canopy and leaned in, his feet dangling in the air as he searched. After a few moments, Cain heard a muffled "Yes!" then Pike climbed back down.

"What have you got?" Cain asked, anxious to see what Pike thought was so important.

"This." He grinned, holding up two rolls of duct tape.

Cain looked in amazement. "Duct tape? You're kidding me, right? Do you always carry duct tape with you?"

Pike nodded his head. "I'm an engineer. I never leave home without it. Come on, we have to hurry. Beth could be dead in ten minutes if we don't do anything."

Cain nodded his head. "Okay, what do we do?"

"Here," Pike said as he handed one of the rolls to Cain and began to unroll his. "Press the two pieces of tape together to create a single strand."

"How much do we need?"

"Enough to loop over the tail of the *Clipper*."

"What?"

"Yeah, I know. Just do it."

The two men began unpeeling their respective rolls of tape and carefully pressing them together making one single strand. They continued to pay out the tape until they had a piece about twenty feet long, then Pike took out his Swiss Army knife and cut them.

"Now what?" Cain asked.

"Adjust the sled and point the nose of the *Clipper* back up as high as it will go."

"This just keeps getting better and better," Cain said, shaking his head as he readjusted the launch sled. Pike waited impatiently as the nose of his fighter went up and the tail went down. With a clunk, the plane stopped and Cain signaled that that was as far as it went.

"Okay!" Pike yelled. "Get over on the other side of the tail and catch this when I throw it." Cain nodded and waited on the other side of the plane like an outfielder waiting for a fly ball. On the first attempt, Pike hit the tail and the tape bounced back, almost hitting him on the head. On the second toss, his aim was better but a gust of wind caught the tape and blew it back, nearly ripping it out of his hands. Frustrated, Pike took a deep breath and waited for what he thought was a lull in the wind and threw them again. This time everything went according to plan and Cain caught the roll.

"We've got to hurry," Pike said. "Let's finish splicing these two rolls together then tie it off on the tail."

"I get it," Cain said, as they both worked as fast as their frozen fingers would allow them. "By wrapping the tape around the tail, we're going to use it as an anchor to lower someone down to get Elizabeth."

"Partly right," Pike replied as they came to the end of the rolls. He threw the one cardboard center away but kept the other and wrapped the tape around it, placed it on the deck then put his foot in the middle of the hole and pulled as hard as he could, testing its strength. "That should do," he said, satisfied that it would hold him. "My dad always taught me, work smarter, not harder. "We're going to use the tail as an anchor alright, but I'm going to let the sled do the work and use it as a crane to pull me and Beth up. When you lower the nose, the tail will go up and hopefully lift us out."

"Very clever, Gabriel."

Pike nodded modestly then picked up the ladder and dragged it over to the hole.

"How's she doing?" Pike asked as he and Cain crawled up beside Miles.

"I can't get her to answer me anymore," Miles replied, panic and frustration filling his voice.

Pike grabbed the ladder and shoved it across the opening. "You two, sit here on the edge with your feet on the ladder and lower me down. When I signal I've got her, raise us up with the sled."

Pike crawled gingerly out onto the ladder until he was sitting directly over the center of the hole. He slipped his foot into the cardboard ring like a stirrup and with some trepidation, eased himself over the edge and nodded for them to lower him down. As more and more of his weight was transferred from the ladder to his tape-rope, he could feel it stretching and for a fleeting moment he wished that he had waited for the rope, but he knew deep down inside that Beth couldn't wait. With a deep breath and a leap of faith, he let go of the ladder, placing all his weight onto the tape.

It stretched even more, but it held. He gave them a shaky thumbs up and they started to lower him down. It was a strange sensation as he began descending. Almost immediately he noticed how quiet it had gotten. The howling wind had turned to a mere whisper as he traveled through the five foot thick ceiling and reached the inside of the anchor room itself. He also felt like he was floating, not just suspended like some giant piñata.

Because he was hanging from the tape, gone was nearly all the swaying and pitching motion of the iceberg. It was almost like he was in a dream as he gently swayed back and forth in the dark, but he knew this dream would turn into a nightmare if he couldn't get to Mallory in time.

He was almost enjoying his ride when all of a sudden he felt his stomach press against the top of his throat as the rope slipped and fell two feet. He felt the stirrup stretch under the sudden surge of his weight and he held his breath as he expected it to snap, sending him plummeting onto the anchor.

"Are you okay?" Pike heard Cain shouting.

"Yeah, what happened?"

"Sorry about that, a gust of wind caught us and knocked us sideways and the tape slipped."

"Okay, hang on." Pike took out his flashlight and had a look around. He was suspended about five feet above the floor and could see that Mallory was still lying on the anchor. A thin layer of ice had already formed on the surface of the water which was a good sign showing that their plan was working but a bad sign for Mallory because she was submerged nearly up to her waist in the bone chilling water. She stared at him with wide open eyes in a death stare but he could still see a spark of life in them. "Hang on, Beth, I'm going to get you out of here," he said trying to reassure her. He thought he saw a faint smile but he couldn't tell because her teeth were chattering and her whole body was shaking uncontrollably.

"Okay, lower me down another four feet, that should do it!" Pike shouted back up the hole.

"We can't, you are at the end of your rope, literally," Cain replied.

Great, Pike muttered to himself, *why can't anything ever be simple?* He grabbed the tape-rope with both hands and gently pulled himself up to get his foot out of the stirrup. He took a deep breath and tried to psych himself up; he was not looking forward to dropping down into freezing water. He looked at Mallory again and noticed that her eye lids were getting very heavy. If she fell asleep now, she would not wake up. That was all the motivation he needed as he let go of the rope.

He let out an involuntary gasp as he hit the frigid water. The shock was much greater than he had anticipated as his legs felt like they were being stabbed over and over again by a million angry seamstresses. He steadied himself with the rope for a second while his legs went completely numb, then sloshed over to Mallory. "Come on, Beth, time to get out of here."

He grabbed her legs and swung them down to the floor then reached out and grabbed her in a bear hug. She was as limp as a rag doll and he was having a hard time getting hold of her because of their bulky jackets. Finally he managed to get his arms around her and as he held her, he reached into his pocket and pulled out a half roll of tape. His teeth were starting to chatter now as he took the tape and reached around behind her and started taping the two of them together.

He carefully stood supporting both their weights. The one good benefit of the cold water was that he couldn't feel the pain in his ankle anymore. With the ice cover broken, small waves now sloshed through the room as the iceberg was tossed by the storm, adding all the more to his difficulties. He steadied himself against the mini tidal waves. If he slipped and fell now, they both would drown. He felt like a sumo wrestler as he picked up one foot then placed it down as he dragged her to the dangling rope. After four squat-steps, he placed his left arm through the loop and grabbed his left elbow with his right hand. He prayed that he had the strength to hold on, supporting not only his weight but Mallory's too.

"Miles? Can you hear me?" Pike shouted.

"Right here, Gabe."

"Tell Nigel to bring us up, slowly."

"Will do, stand by."

Almost immediately, Pike could feel the tension start as the sled began pulling them up. For a moment, he felt the pressure and saw the tape stretch but they weren't moving. The tape kept stretching and he thought for sure it was going to break, but then he felt his arm rise and his feet leave the floor. Slowly, they steadily rose toward the light. Their feet cleared the water and they were now suspended between heaven and earth as they ascended through the five foot thick ice ceiling. Everything was white and Pike felt like he was floating through a cloud.

They were about a foot from the top of the entrance when they stopped moving. The sled must be level Pike thought. The next thing he knew, he felt three sets of strong hands grabbed him and pulled them the rest of the way up. They plopped down hard on the ice with Mallory landing on top of him. Her limp head snapped forward, hitting him in the nose, causing it to bleed.

"Get these two into the Jacuzzi!" Pike heard Cain yell. Quickly, the two Siamese twins were separated and Mallory was carried off by two men and Pike limped along with the help from Miles. When Pike stepped through the door and felt the heat from the spa, he felt like he had just stepped into the middle of the Sahara desert.

Mallory was seated on the floor propped up against a chair. The men had her jacket off but had stopped, hesitant and confused on just how much clothing they should remove. Pike would have laughed at their predicament if he weren't so cold.

"Just leave her, I'll take care of her," Pike said, staring at the shorter of the two men, "You go get us some hot tea and something to eat. And you," he turned to the other, "you go find Tabatha Amies and bring her here, please," Both men nodded and quickly left, clearly happy to be relieved of their awkward situation.

"Dean, would you go and get us plenty of towels please and then make sure they're still pumping water into the room. We aren't out of the woods yet."

"Sure thing, Gabe," Miles replied.

Pike took off his jacket and walked over and grabbed Mallory and dragged her to the side of the Jacuzzi. He slid his feet in, shoes and all, then slowly lowered himself the rest of the way in. It felt scalding hot and every part of his body started tingling as he began to thaw. He reached up and dragged Mallory in, clothes and all and held her by his side, keeping her head above water. Slowly she began to stir as the warmth spread throughout her body.

"So this is how you got this gig, huh? Hot tubbing with the boss' assistant," Tabatha Amies said, walking in the door.

"Very funny. I need your help here."

She thought about teasing Pike some more but from his worn look decided against it. "What can I do?" she simply said.

"As soon as I get out of here, I'll need you to help Beth change and get her back to her room."

"Okay, not a problem."

Miles came in and dropped off the towels then went back outside. Shortly after he left, the tea and food arrived. Feeling like a thawed out pork chop, Pike got out of the hot tub and wrapped a towel around his shoulders, then drank some tea. By now Mallory was awake and greedily took some tea from Tabatha. She looked around and sized up the situation.

"I take it you were the one who got me out?" she said, looking at Pike.

Pike tipped his teacup to her. "My pleasure."

"Gabe." They turned to see Miles coming toward them. "Mr. Cain would like to see you on the bridge."

Pike frowned, not liking the urgency in Miles' voice. "Did he say what he wanted?"

Miles shook his head. "No, just that he wanted you there as soon as possible."

"Okay," Pike said wearily. "Tell him I'll be there as soon as I can. Obviously I have to change first. Tell Mr. Cain I should there in about twenty minutes to half an hour."

"No problem."

"How's it going out there?" Pike asked as he stood, putting down his tea.

"Great! The room is almost full and it's already freezing... as you well know." He smiled at Mallory and Pike. "Everything seems to be going according to plan and barring anything unforeseen, the anchor should be frozen solid in place within two hours."

"Good to hear, please keep me posted." Pike nodded to all and walked out, leaving a trail of waterlogged shoe prints.

CHAPTER TWENTY SEVEN

The bow of the tug boat pitched down like a roller coaster as it rode down the backside of the wave, smashing straight into the base of the next. The water rolled up and over the bow, swallowing the ship, washing over the bridge like a submerging submarine. For a moment, all was quiet, no sound of the howling wind in the rigging, no crashing of the waves against the steel hull, just a hushed silence as the bridge was smothered in a blanket of water.

Abject horror filled the eyes of the young deckhand as he watched the ocean consume his ship. He was a sailor experienced in coastal waters but he was a last minute replacement in the crew and this was his first open ocean run. His eyes darted back and forth between the captain and first officer, looking for signs of whether or not he should be grabbing his rosary beads.

Captain Patrick Bair sat in his chair, timing his sips of coffee between the swells. He looked alert yet not overly concerned that his ship was becoming a submarine. Bair had cut his teeth pulling log booms and pushing sawdust barges on the Columbia River, then turned pilot, bringing cargo ships from the mouth of the great river up to the docks in Portland, Oregon.

The First Officer, Matt Beasley, seemed as equally uncon-cerned about their plight; he was huddled over the radarscope, nibbling at a tuna fish sandwich. He too came from the Pacific

Northwest working on tugs and skippering the ferries that criss-crossed Puget Sound.

Suddenly, like a car crashing through a brick wall, the *Rachel B.* broke through the wave. Free of their cocoon of water, they were instantly assaulted by a barrage of sounds, reassuring them that they were still alive and afloat.

Bair glanced over at his first officer and they shared a smile at the crewman's expense. "Mr. Palmer," Bair said, "why don't you go down to the galley and help Mr. Clemens with some sandwiches? The crew's been on station for quite a while now. The weather's too rough to cook anything but they'll still be hungry nonetheless and a cold sandwich is better than nothing."

"Yes sir, right away." Just as Palmer reached the hatch, the ship lurched, like a dog pulling on its chain trying to chase the neighborhood cat.

"Sir?" Palmer said, spinning around, looking at the captain, fear once again filling his eyes.

"It's all right, Palmer," Bair said reassuringly. "That's just the soft brake working, everything is going to be just fine. Now go below and help Mr. Clemens with the sandwiches." The soft brake was a setting used on the towing winch that acted like a buffer, allowing the cable to slip a little so it wouldn't break from the tension in rough seas, much like the drag setting on a fishing reel.

"Yes, sir," Palmer said hesitantly, then disappeared down the ladder.

Bair turned to Beasley. "It's getting worse."

Beasley nodded. "We can't make fast enough headway to outrun this thing. The storm front is filling my entire screen and it's dropping down out of the north fast." Bair felt himself being nudged forward in his chair as the *Rachel B.* staggered again.

"We can't take much more of this," Bair continued. "The waves are too large and unpredictable; they're pushing us back then shoving us forward making the tow cable go slack, then snapping it back. If the soft brake fails, we could be in some serious trouble. It'll rip the spindle off our deck, tear the towing bridle off the barge, or snap the cable."

"Not a very good selection to choose from." Beasley frowned.

Just then the tug jerked so hard Bair was nearly thrown out of his seat and Beasley ended up on the floor next to his tuna fish sandwich.

"That was the soft brake; it's gone!" Bair shouted. "You've got the bridge, Matt, I'm going aft to see how bad it is." The captain of the *Rachel B.* dashed out the rear hatch and scrambled down the back stairs. Twice he had to stop and hold onto the railings as the tug lurched again and rolled hard to port in the heavy seas. At last he was on the main deck and ready to go outside.

"What took you so long?" Al Painter, the ship's engineer, said with a crooked smile. Painter was on the low side of his fifties with a narrow face that was always wearing a smile. He had nearly as many years at sea as his captain but was getting ready to retire to his gentleman's ranch, as he liked to call it, in Oregon. Rather than the grand scale of ribbons of white wooden fences surrounding his palatial estate, his gentlemen's ranch was more along the lines of ten acres, a large barn and a couple of horses.

Both men were looking at the winch assembly out the porthole on the stern door hatch when it was smothered and disappeared as a three-foot high wall of water washed across the deck.

"You really want to go out there?" Painter asked.

Bair shook his head. "No, but I don't think we have a choice. I think the soft brake is gone and we have to see if we can fix it."

"I'll tell you exactly what's wrong. That!" Painter said, point out the porthole. In the distance between the washes of spray and the low, swirling clouds, they could see the bulky outline of the iceberg. "We don't have the right kind of foul weather gear to be towing that thing in a storm like this. That giant ice cube out there is going to rip our stern off if we're not careful."

"That's why I have you, Scotty."

Painter frowned; he hated it when Bair compared him to the miracle working engineer from *Star Trek*. Bair reached into his back pocket and pulled out his wallet then flipped it open.

"Beam me up, there's no intelligent life here." Both men laughed.

Painter sighed. "The teeth of the slip gears have probably been torn off by the sheer weight of that brute out there."

"Can you fix it?"

Painter smiled. "Why do you think they call me the miracle worker?"

Ten minutes later both men were standing by the hatch with their survival suits on.

"Are you ready for this?" Bair asked.

"No, but let's go anyway." Painter picked up his tool bag as Bair placed one hand on the handle and looked at Painter, who gave him a tentative nod. Timing between the pitching swells, Bair opened the door and both men quickly stepped out and snapped themselves to the safety line.

Stepping from the relative calm of the cabin onto the deck was like moving from sanity and plunging into chaos. Sensing their presence, the wind swirled and howled around them like an angry banshee chasing its tail. The ocean, not to be outdone, assaulted the two men, alternating between pelting them with spray that felt like it was fired from a shotgun to rolls of water that pounded at their legs like a linebacker sacking a quarterback.

Driven by purpose, they ignored the raging elements as best they could as they carefully inched their way along the deckhouse toward the winch on the stern of the tug. Suddenly, the *Rachel B.* was slammed on her starboard side by a massive wave that pushed the stout vessel hard over to port. The men quickly found themselves submerged up to their waists in foaming, freezing water and watched as the port side of the tug was engulfed in water.

Gripping tightly to the rail, Bair stayed on his feet. As the swirling waters subsided, he stole a quick glance back to make sure his engineer was all right. He saw Painter wearing a grim smile on his face, then heard him shout above the wind, "This is fun." Bair just shook his head then turned back around.

They finally reached the end of the deckhouse where they faced the most dangerous part of their trip: crossing the twenty feet of open deck to reach the winch.

"I'll go first!" Bair shouted above the roar of the wind. "When I signal, you run to me as fast as you can."

"No argument there," Painter replied.

Bair stood like a statue staring at the ocean, reading, interpreting, looking for a sign of when he could cross. After nearly a minute of waiting, Painter was just about to ask his captain if he had fallen asleep, when suddenly Bair sprinted across a level deck and easily made it to the winch.

Now it was Painter's turn as he waited at the corner of the deckhouse staring intently at his captain, like a base runner looking for his coach's signal to steal second base. After only twenty seconds, Bair gave the signal and Painter dashed to second base, minus the slide.

Bair's relief at the two of them making it safely across the open deck was short lived as he looked forward and shuddered, seeing a massive wall of water looming in front of them.

"Hang on!" he managed to shout just as the bow of the tug dipped down into the trough. The *Rachel B.* plunged into the base of the wave, then clawed up the other side and pushed her way through the wave halfway up. The bow split the swell in half, sending rivers of water running down both sides of the superstructure.

Bair looped his arm around the winch housing just before the water swept his feet out from under him. He felt his shoulder pop from the strain but managed to keep his grip. "Al, you okay?" he shouted as he spit out a mouth full of water. When he didn't hear a ready answer from his engineer, he desperately looked around, only to find an empty deck. "Al!" Helplessness washed over him as real as any storm wave.

"What's all the shouting about?" Painter said, stepping out from behind the winch.

"I thought you were washed overboard," he replied, his knees suddenly feeling weak from the relief. "That wave nearly got me."

"When I saw the wave, I moved in behind the winch for protection. Us engineers are smart that way." He smiled.

"Yeah, how smart are you going to be when I have you inspect the bilges?" Bair shot back. "I'm going to check the deck bolts on the winch to see if there's any damage there. Get that access panel off and let's find out if the soft break can be fixed."

Painter nodded and ducking under the tow cable and disappeared around to the other side. Bair stooped down and examined the first of four two-inch bolts that held the winch to the deck. As best as he could tell under the conditions, it looked like the deck plating had a slight bow to it and was starting to buckle under the strain.

He heard it first, the moaning of metal against metal as the tension stretched the winch and tow cable to its design limits as the stern began to rise. He heard it, then felt it as a rogue wave came over the stern of the tug, pushing it away from the berg, yanking the *Rachel B.* to a standstill. The sudden jerk staggered him to one knee and he had just managed to get one hand on the housing bar when the rest of the wave came rolling over the stern.

He held on through the initial crest of the wave, but the continual flow of thousands of gallons of water ripped his hand away and carried him off like a piece of driftwood. He tried to call out to Painter but his voice was drowned out as he was submerged in the deluge. Bair was slammed into the deckhouse and when the water subsided, he was left sitting on the deck, leaning against the wall like rag doll carefully placed there by its owner. Ignoring the pain from the beating he had taken being dragged across the deck, he staggered to his feet and yelled for Painter. Bair half expected his friend to poke his head around the corner and make some smart aleck engineer remark, but the only reply he got was the mocking howl from the wind.

"A-L-A-N!" he shouted again, but still there was no reply. Frantically he searched for any sign of his friend when his eyes suddenly focused on Painter's safety cable leading over the side of the tug. Bair ran to the railing and began hauling in the safety line as fast as he could pull it.

"No, no, no," Bair kept saying, over and over, his words building in a crescendo as he was pulling. The line was coming up too easily; there no weight to it like there should be if there was a man attached to it. Suddenly his spirit burned brighter as he caught a flash of orange from Painter's survival suit. But in an instant, his bright rays of hope were devoured by the black hole of despair; the safety line popped out of the water and landed on the deck with only a torn piece of the suit.

The suit had torn at the section where the safety line attached to the belt. Bair stood up and scanned the turbulent waters, searching for any sign of his friend as he called his name. He knew with a torn suit that his friend was in serious trouble. With the suit, it would not only keep him afloat, acting as a one-man raft but it would also protect him from the freezing water. In these conditions, Bair knew the suit would insulate him from the frigid water for eight to ten hours, but with a hole in it he would be exposed and have minutes, not hours, to live before hypothermia would set in and he would die.

Bair started for the hatch but was knocked down by another wave and washed along the deck like seaweed. Between swells, he was finally able to make it to the deckhouse and get in. He dashed up the stairs, still in his survival suit, barking out orders as he charged through the hatch.

"Get me the *Alyssa B.* and the *Cheri B.* on the horn. Tell them we have a man overboard and to get over here to look for him now!"

Beasley looked at Bair as they both understood. There was precious little time before the rescue mission turned into a recovery mission. Beasley had just grabbed the microphone when the *Rachel B.* lurched abruptly. Beasley was thrown down, and as he fell, he was still holding onto the microphone and he yanked the cord out of the radio.

With a calm voice, Bair looked at his first officer, "Matt, grab a walkie and raise the other two tugs with our distress call, then see if you can raise the iceberg so I can apprise them of our situation." Bair then turned to the crewman manning the helm. "I'll take the wheel, Jeff, go get another cord so we can fix the radio, then find Palmer and tell him to bring us some coffee. Lots of it."

CHAPTER TWENTY EIGHT

Thirty minutes later and feeling one hundred percent better, Pike stepped on to the bridge, flexing his fingers, still getting his feeling back.

"How's it going back there?" Cain asked as Pike entered the doorway.

"Good, sir. The door seal is holding and the room should be filled by now and it should be frozen solid in an hour or two."

"How's Elizabeth doing?"

"Beth will be fine. Tabatha... Ms. Amies is helping her back to her cabin."

"And you?"

"I'm okay. I imagine I'll be a little stiff and sore in the morning, but it's nothing I can't handle.

"Good," Cain said, nodding. "Come here and take a look at this, will you?"

Pike walked up to the console where Cain was standing. It was the sensor board for the towing assembly he'd seen earlier. It looked like a massive bank of traffic lights with all its flashing yellow and red lights.

"We've got trouble." Cain said as he explained the situation with the *Rachel B's* missing crewman and the damaged soft brake. Pike stood there for a moment, staring out the window at the lights of the *Rachel B.* and thinking.

"Can I talk to their captain?" Pike asked.

"Go ahead," Captain Gregory said. "I've put it on speaker."

"Thanks." Pike nodded. "Captain Bair, this is Gabriel Pike. I wish we could have met under better circumstances. I'm sorry to hear about your missing man."

"Thank you, Mr. Pike."

"Please, call me Gabe."

"Pat."

"I'm an engineer, but I don't have much background in naval engineering, so help me out here. I understand that the problem is that what you call the soft brake is broken and that it acts as a buffer, if you will, to reduce the tension between the tow line, the tug and the iceberg in rough weather?"

"Basically, yes."

"And it can't be fixed?"

"We were working on it..."

Pike could hear Bair's voice tighten with emotion.

"...when we lost Al."

"So forgive my ignorance, why don't we either release the cable or just maintain slack in the line so neither one of us gets torn apart?"

"If we release the cable it would be darn near impossible to hook it back up at sea, even in perfect weather. We could push the iceberg into port but it would mean at least a week's delay in arrival time. Second, and more importantly, if we cut the cable or backed off we would lose steerage and the iceberg would be running free before the storm. That thing is not built to handle seas like this. The waves from this storm are large enough that if the iceberg got turned sideways in the troughs, the waves could capsize it."

Pike thought for a moment, his mind turning things over. "So at this point it's not really about how fast we go, it's about keeping the bow straight, pointed into the waves?"

"Yes, that's right."

"Okay, and our problem right now is that there is no buffer between the two of us and we keep pulling against each other?"

"Yes."

"Kind of like a light bulb, it's either on or off?"

Bair thought about it for a couple of seconds. "Yeah, I suppose you could put it that way."

"So what we need between us is a dimmer switch? Something to take up the slack slowly instead of all at once?"

Again, Bair had to think about it. "That's kind of a strange way to think about it but I guess you could compare it that way."

"How far away are you?"

"About five hundred yards."

"How much cable do you have?"

"Our spool has 7,500 feet of six inch cable."

"How much does all that weigh?"

"The cable itself weighs probably weighs three to four tons and..." Pike could tell that the captain was beginning to follow his train of thought, which was a good thing because if the captain picked up on it then it must have some chance of working. "...if we pay all the cable out, the cable itself will act as a soft brake. The cable will sink at least 200 feet and the weight and depth of the cable moving through the water will put less strain on both the winch and the towing bridle on the barge. We won't be making much headway but at least we'll have steerage and keep the bow into the waves and the tension on both vessels will be greatly reduced. Brilliant, Gabe."

"In theory it sounds good, when can we put it to the test?"

"Right now," Bair replied. 'We can make all the adjustments from here in the wheelhouse. I want to pay the cable out slowly, so it should take about ten minutes to deploy the entire cable. Once that's done, we'll see if it works. I'll let you know when we're done. *Rachel B.* out."

Almost immediately, most of the red sensor warning lights went to yellow and amber but the true test as Captain Bair had pointed out was when all the cable was all the way out and they were towing again.

"I certainly am getting my money's worth out of hiring you, Gabriel," Cain said, smiling. "I wish all my employees multitasked as well as you do."

"Yeah, it's amazing what you can do when your neck is on the line."

"Very true." Cain nodded.

"Now Beth is the amazing employee," Pike said. "I don't think it falls under her job description to be pouring fifty pound bags of ice down a twelve foot deep hole in the middle of a raging storm."

"Actually it does. It falls under 'and all other related duties.'"

Pike looked at Cain and they both burst out laughing. "You are a hard man, Mr. Cain. No wonder you rule the world."

Cain smiled, "Not yet, but I'm working on it."

"This is the *Rachel B.*, do you copy?"

"Go ahead, Captain Bair," Cain said.

"We've paid out all the cable except for two layers that I'm keeping for reserve. Our ride over here has smoothed out greatly and we're still maintaining a forward movement of three knots. How are things on your end?"

Cain and Pike studied the board for a moment. "All the sensors are looking good," Cain replied. "Barring anything unforeseen, we should be okay. We'll keep you posted if things change."

"Likewise. *Rachel B.* out."

"Looks like a happy ending," Cain said.

"Not for all of us." Pike said, looking out the window, search lights slashing at the water as the other two tugs searched for the missing crewman.

"I'm going to go and check on Elizabeth," Cain said quietly.

"I think I'll check in with Dean and make sure things are still on track in the anchor room," Pike replied with equal reserve. Neither man really wanted to think or mention that someone had died. Pike could tell by the expression Cain wore that he felt he was somehow responsible. Logically he knew he wasn't, but right now that didn't seem to matter.

"We'll meet in an hour or so in the Crystal Palace," Cain said. "You go ahead, I'll be along shortly."

Pike nodded and turned to leave. Just as he was going through the door he looked back and saw Cain rubbing the back of his neck then run his hand through his hair, clearly feeling the agony of the lost sailor. Right now he wouldn't trade places with Cain for all the money in the world.

CHAPTER TWENTY NINE

"Is everyone okay?" Pike asked as he walked up. Cain and Mallory were sitting alone at a table in the Crystal Palace, nursing their coffee. They were staring out the window, exhausted by the night. The seas had calmed, turning from angry, foaming white crests, into long, rolling swells. The clouds too had lost their ominous, dark countenance and were beginning to lighten as the new day began pushing back the night.

Pike immediately noticed that Cain looked a lot happier than when he had last left him on the bridge. Cain spoke before Pike had a chance to ask what happened.

"About twenty minute after you left, the *Rachel B.* called and said that one of the other tugs had found the missing sailor. Alive!"

"That's great!" Pike said.

"Yes it is," Cain beamed. "Seems that only the outer shell of his survival suit had torn so he was still somewhat protected. It had a built-in light and transponder so they were able to find him in time."

"I can't believe they were able to pick him up in such heavy seas," Pike replied.

"Speaking of heavy seas," Mallory said, "you would have thought we were at a Martian convention last night from all the green-faced people. I've never seen so many seasick people in my life. I passed a few of the more hardy ones outside at Starbucks on my way here. I guess the rest are still in their rooms sleeping, which is where I should be."

"Thanks, Elizabeth," Cain said as he reached over and patted her hand. "You performed above and beyond the call of duty last night. Go back to your room and get some rest."

"Does that mean I can take the day off?"

"We need to do a damage assessment, but it will wait until two this afternoon."

"Gee thanks," she said with a weary smile, "I am going to charge you overtime, you know."

Cain chuckled. "Fair enough. Now go get some rest." Mallory started to get up, then paused. "I was going to ask you earlier, that coat looks awfully familiar. Didn't I see one very similar to that in one of the pictures of your grandfather back at the office?"

Cain slowly nodded his head.

"You always said you'd tell me the whole story behind that coat and your grandfather, now is as good a time as any."

Pike watched with great curiosity as Cain's expression and nearly his entire countenance slowly began to change. He had been laughing only moments before, but now the smile seemed a hundred years ago. His look was not one of sadness but more of a reverence, or perhaps a longing. Pike could see that Cain was trying to decide what, if anything to say and what words he could possibly use to describe the way he felt.

Cain began to speak slowly, testing each word to see if it would come out. He took a deep breath, then blew it out slowly. "What I'm about to tell you... I have not shared with anyone else. Anyone. And after hearing me out, you will either think me a fool, or a crazy liar, or perhaps both."

Pike and Mallory looked at each other, both reflecting the same curiosity and bewilderment at what Cain was telling them. "Elizabeth, you know my grandfather, Thayer Lehmann, was a German immigrant who came over to this country around 1920." Mallory looked at her boss and nodded her head.

"Yes, well what you don't know is how he got here. Does the date April 14th, 1912 mean anything to either of you?"

Pike nodded his head. "Yeah, that's the date the *Titanic* struck the iceberg and sank."

Mallory's eye popped open wide. "Your grandfather was on the *Titanic*?"

"In a way."

Mallory looked at her boss in total confusion now. "In a way? What does that mean?"

"Grandpa Thayer wasn't on the Titanic; he helped sink it."

"Sink it!" Pike and Mallory exclaimed in unison.

"I know, I know," Cain said, holding up his hands. "Let me finish before you call in the guys with the straight jacket."

"Sorry," Pike said, "but you did throw us a mighty big curveball there."

"I understand," Cain said, nodding understandingly. "Back in 1912, Thayer and his brother, Damien, joined the *Kaiserliche* Marine, the Imperial German Navy, in search of adventure where they volunteered for the fledgling *Underseeboot* service."

"The what?" Mallory asked.

"U-boats," Pike said. "Submarines."

She nodded her head knowingly.

"Even in 1912," Cain continued, "rumors of war and unrest plagued the royal families of Europe. The potential of the U-boat had not been realized as a weapon yet so instead of preparing it for combat, it was used as a reconnaissance vehicle. The boat Thayer and his brother were on was testing a new form of camouflage to use to spy on enemy shipping."

"And it was disguised as an iceberg?" Pike said.

Cain nodded. "Exactly, Gabriel, very good. Grandpa Thayer was up on deck as a lookout when the accident occurred. The *Titanic* was passing close to the sub when something happened to the steering and the sub ran into the side of the great passenger liner. The forward dive plane of the submarine punctured the hull and tore a huge gash down the side of the ship. He was thrown clear and ended up floating on a patch of real ice. The only thing that saved his life was this jacket. The dark blue color stood out like a sore thumb against the white of the ice and he was spotted and rescued.

"Afraid of what might happen if he told his rescuers that a German submarine, not pack ice, was responsible for the sinking of the *Titanic*, he decided to keep quiet. Grandpa Thayer knew he would never get another opportunity like this to come to America, and there really wasn't anything left for him back home with his brother dead, so he kept to himself and he just disappeared after he landed in New York."

Cain shifted silently in his chair and hung his head low, like a nervous defendant in a courtroom, waiting anxiously for the jury to reconvene, waiting to see if they believed his story or not.

Both Mallory and Pike looked at each other, not knowing what to say. It was Pike who broke the stunned silence. "Wow. And no one else knows about this?"

Cain shook his head. "No one knows and there would be no point in bringing out the truth."

Pike nodded his head slowly in agreement. "Let sleeping dogs lie."

"Exactly."

"Nigel, I had no idea," Mallory said, putting her hand on his arm. Pike watched as a sense of relief washed over Cain, knowing that she believed him.

"I don't know why," Cain continued, "but I feel better now that I've told someone."

Mallory started to smile but a huge yawn stifled her in mid-grin. "Don't take this wrong," Cain said, "but you look like you've been rode hard and put up wet. Now go get some rest. And make it three o'clock and not two."

Mallory got up and slowly walked away. "Thanks, but I'm still charging you overtime," she said over her shoulder as she left the restaurant.

Cain took a sip of coffee and turned to Pike. "How are you doing there Mr. MacGyver? That was a pretty slick trick you did back there with the duct tape and using the plane as a crane."

"I wish I were as smart as him." Pike grinned. "But I'm doing okay, nothing that a few hours of shuteye won't fix. I'll get some sleep then start inspecting the damaged areas of the berg." Pike took his coffee cup and wrapped his hands around it, letting it warm up his stiff fingers. "I just hope this little storm won't keep us from entering the harbor.

A worry line shot across Cain's forehead. "Why would it? We're still afloat and in one piece, thanks to you, so I don't see how any of this could upset our schedule?"

Pike nodded his head. "I agree. There shouldn't be a problem, but that's what you're paying me for, to make sure there isn't one."

"Of course." Cain's expression lightened a bit. "I'll leave you to your work as I know you have a lot to do, as do I."

"I'll check in this afternoon with a preliminary report."

Pike watched as Cain got up and left with strong, purposeful steps. Doesn't the man ever get tired? Pike said to himself. He was just about to get up himself when he heard a voice behind him.

"There you are."

He turned to see Tabatha Amies.

"Hi. You're either up really early," she paused for a moment as she saw his face then continued, "or up really late, and now that I think of it, definitely up really late."

"Thanks a lot," Pike replied with a mock scowl on his face.

"When can we talk, Mr. Hero?"

Pike cringed at the word: *hero*. He thought about correcting her but he was just too tired. "Talk about what?"

"Part of the deal in helping Beth keep everything quiet and calm was that I'd get an exclusive interview with you on what happened and how you fixed it."

"Okay, but not now. I'm really tired and I need to grab some sleep then start inspecting any damage we might have suffered during the storm. Maybe we can talk over dinner tonight?"

"Sounds good," she replied, "call me at six, that is if you aren't not too busy saving the world." Getting in the last dig, she got up and left before he could reply.

He smiled as he watched her leave, then got up himself and went to his room where he collapsed on the bed and fell asleep without even taking his clothes off.

Pike awoke with a start. He sprang up in bed, disoriented, not sure where he was. He had a nagging thought tugging at the back of his mind that he had neglected something very important that he was supposed to. He sat still for a moment, letting the fog of sleep slowly dissipate. Suddenly it hit him harder than a plate of bad sushi. He was supposed to be inspecting the storm's damage to the barge. He looked around his room, it was dark. Had he slept all day and into the night? He whirled around to look at the clock: 2:00. He had slept until two in the morning! He had missed his inspection, missed his date with Tabatha and would probably be missing his job after this.

"Great! Just great," he said out loud as he plopped back down on the bed. As he lay there wondering what he was going to do, he noticed a crack of light running down the side of the curtain. Was there a ship passing by? He got up and threw open the curtains and suddenly felt like Dracula, throwing up his arms to protect himself from the penetrating rays of the sun. He shook his head; it was two in the afternoon. He'd been asleep only for a few hours. He felt very stupid at the moment, then suddenly stopped in mid-thought: his *date* with Tabatha? Was he going on a date? It was an interview, right? Just an interview? He took a deep breath and let it out slowly. He was not only feeling stupid, but now also confused.

He grabbed some clean clothes and was on his way to the shower when his phone rang. "Hello?"

"Hey, Hot Shot."

"K.D.! How are you?"

"The question is, how are *you*? We saw the news last night and it showed the storm and pictures of the iceberg and waves rolling over it. It looked pretty rough. Are you okay?"

For the next several minutes, Pike explained everything that had happed with the anchor chain and the towing braces and how they had fixed it and how he was getting ready to inspect the damage and she filled him in with everything that was happening back at the office.

"I hate to say this K.D., I've enjoyed talking to you and am really glad you called, but I gotta run."

"I know, me too."

"Speaking of which, it sounds like you already are. Are you on a plane? I can hear a constant rumbling in the background."

"Yes, I am, and that's why I have to go too. Some of us have to work for a living. I'll see you later."

"Okay, it was great talking to you. Bye."

As he hung up the phone, he suddenly realized how much he missed home... and talking to her, but a quick glance at his watch told him he didn't have time to be homesick. If he took a shower and hurried, and didn't run into any major problems, he could inspect the anchor room and the towing assembly and still meet Tabatha on time. Tabatha. He sighed, suddenly feeling guilty again for some reason.

CHAPTER THIRTY

Pike stepped out onto the pool deck. The breeze was still brisk, a steady ten knot stream but its coolness was tempered by the rays of the sun. He took a deep breath and closed his eyes, facing the sun and enjoying its warmth. It was a far cry from the way it was last night. The sky was now clear and a brilliant shade of blue. The *Yankee Clipper* was perched on the corner of the iceberg like a giant weather vane, her silver skin gleaming in the sun's rays.

Directly behind the plane was a group of ten people in a circle, looking like a football huddle or a group singing around a campfire. At first he couldn't figure out what they were doing, then it occurred to him: they were staring in the hole he had burned in the ice last night.

He flipped up his hood and zipped it all the way up with just his eyes showing in hopes that no one would recognize him. He walked over to the *Clipper*, checking her for damage and was pleased to find that she had weathered the storm just fine. Coming around from the far side of the plane, he walked over to the hole and looked down. The edge tapered down about a foot and ended in a three-foot crater, looking like someone had punched through the ice with a giant sledge hammer.

The ice in the anchor room had frozen clear, so the anchor could clearly be seen leaning up against the outside wall. Its massive size was magnified even more by the ice, adding to the rumors of the danger they had all been in and elevating his feat last night to near Herculean proportions. Satisfied that there were no problems, he turned and went back inside to check the anchor room from below.

"Hi, Mr. Pike." Pike heard his name called as he climbed up the last rungs of the ladder, popping his head up just outside the anchor room like the groundhog, Punxsutawney Phil. He reached up and Brian Centers helped him the rest of the way.

"Hi, Brian, and call me Gabe, remember?" Pike replied as he stepped onto the ice. "Have you seen Dean? I told him I was heading up this way."

Centers nodded. "Mr. Miles is down on the ships, checking things out there, so he sent me up here to help you."

"Good. Let's go take a look." They walked over to the anchor room door and Pike began to examine it. "The seals look like they held well with minimal leaking." Pike kneeled down and pointed to the bottom of the door where water froze while seeping out. He examined the rest of the door and then stood. "Looks good here, Brian. But since we have the time, I'd like to see if we can find a way to secure the anchor chain."

"Why?" Centers asked.

"There's still a very slight possibility that the block of ice in the anchor room could slip out like an ice cube popping out of a tray. No use taking chances if we don't have to."

Centers nodded his head. "I'll talk to Mr. Miles about it right away."

"Great. Now let's get up to the bridge and check in with the captain and see what else we need to take a look at."

Pike stood on the bridge, staring at the control screen for the towing bridle. Most of the screen was green but several stress points held at steady amber and two points on the left bridle flashed red intermittently. Still not good, he thought, but a far cry better than it was last night.

"Is there any way to relieve the stress on these two points?" Pike asked the captain.

Captain Gregory shook his head. "I've talked to the captain of the *Rachel B.* and we both agree there's nothing more we can do until the seas calm a bit more. Once they do, we'll bring in the other two tugs on the stern and they can push, relieving some of the burden on the bridle."

Pike nodded. "Is there any way to either shore up or separate the towing towers so that if one side goes, it won't yank the other out and rip off the front of the berg?"

"I don't know, Mr. Pike, that's not my field of expertise."

"How far out are we from New York Harbor?"

"Two to three days, depending on how much speed we can maintain."

Pike frowned. "That's not very much time to recheck everything considering all the damage we took." Pike studied the screen for a moment longer, and then turned to Centers. "Can you take me here?" he said, pointing to the first of the flashing red censors.

Centers shook his head. "That's buried behind five feet of ice."

Pike frowned. "How about this one?" He was pointing to the other red light.

"Ten feet."

"You're full of good news. How about here? The bases of the support towers are on the decks of the ships, right?"

Centers smiled and nodded his head, "That I can do."

"Then lead on, Macduff," Pike said.

"Macduff?" Centers asked with a puzzled look on his face.

"I'll explain on the way. Captain, does Mr. Cain know about all this?"

Gregory tried to stifle a yawn but wasn't very successful. "Sorry, it's been a long night," he said, taking a sip of his coffee. "Mr. Cain was here earlier this morning and knows the entire situation."

"All right, Captain, and thank you. If he calls, please let him know where I'm going."

"Will do."

Pike and Centers left the bridge and headed for the elevator to take them down to the ship decks. "Who is Macduff?" Centers asked as they walked along.

Pike smiled. "Kind of a hobby of mine, quotes and where they come from. 'Lead on, Macduff' is actually a misquote. It's a line from Shakespeare's *Macbeth*. The real line is 'Lay on, Mcaduff.' It's a fight scene where Macduff tells Macbeth to give it his best shot as they fight to the death. I've tried to find out why it's so misquoted but I can't find an answer anywhere."

"Interesting. Got any more?" Centers asked as they reached the elevator and waited for the door to open.

Pike thought for a moment. "Sure. Have you heard the expression 'Cut to the chase?'"

Centers nodded as the doors opened and they entered.

"Back in the beginnings of the film industry during silent movies, the chase scene was usually the most exciting part of a film. People didn't like watching all the boring stuff, so they wanted the producers to cut, or edit, the film to the best part, usually the chase scene... thus 'Cut to the chase.' Or as we use it today, it means get to the point."

The doors of the elevator opened and deposited them on the forward ship, on the port side. The cavernous chamber was humming with activity, as work crews were scurrying about the decks and disappearing in the access tunnels like worker ants attending their queen. Pike stood and marveled at the sight. Even though he had seen it before, it still amazed him, not only the size of the cavern but the sheer size of Cain's project. Pike followed Centers as they walked toward the bow and the first towing support tower.

They reached the base of the two foot diameter steel pole where Pike began examining it closely.

The eight bolts that held the tower to the deck were all in place and the deck level, with no signs of stress or buckling. The shaft revealed no fractures and ran straight and true as it disappeared into the ice ceiling. The ice around the shaft where the two met was also solid, swallowing the pipe whole, showing no signs of cracking or splintering, which was also another very good sign.

Pike and Centers crossed the catwalk that linked the two ships to reach the other support tower. He knew he would find problems there, since it was this tower that was glowing with the steady amber and flashing red lights on the service screen. He just hoped it wasn't too badly damaged.

From ten feet away, he could tell his hopes were sunk. The steel decking at the base of the tower was bulging slightly in places, showing where the stress had pulled on the tower. One deck bolt was sheared off completely and two more were twisted. There were also telltale streaks at the base of the pole, indicating stress fractures. Above, it looked like a giant hand had shaken the shaft, chipping and cracking the ice at the top where it joined the pole, routing out a six inch space between them.

"That's not good," Pike said, straining his neck. "If we have another storm, this shaft will either twist itself out of the deck or cause a stress fracture in the ice that could split this section in two, or both." Pike glanced at his watch. "Do me favor will you? Find Miles and see if he knows about the problem with this shaft and find out what other problems he's come across in his travels. As long as the weather holds, I don't think we're in any immediate danger but we still have a lot of checking to do before we can pass muster and enter New York harbor."

"Pass muster, now that one I have heard before." Centers smiled.

Pike chuckled. "Thanks, Brian. I would like to meet with you and Dean in his office tomorrow morning, say 8:30?"

"I'll take care of it."

"Great." Pike looked at his watch again. "I gotta run. See you in the morning." He bounded back across the catwalk and vanished into the elevator.

CHAPTER THIRTY ONE

Pike slowed to catch his breath as he entered the casino; he didn't want to be panting or appear over eager when he sat down with Tabatha. He looked around at the busy, brightly lit room that was nearly full of happy gamblers. Gone were any signs of the struggles from the previous night's storm. Now, their biggest concern was whether to keep the money Cain had given them the night before or to simply blow it all since it was free.

He moved past the row of slots and the craps tables toward the restaurant. He had on a navy blue sports coat, light blue button down shirt and khaki pants. He thought about wearing a tie but decided against it, wanting to keep their dinner and interview casual. Walking past the Crystal Palace's entrance, he grabbed a flower from one of the arrangements to give to Tabatha. He'd seen them do that in the movies and had always wanted to do it himself. Now he sort of wished he had worn his James Bond tuxedo.

He was met at the door by the maître d' who greeted him by name and escorted him to his table. He wouldn't admit it, but he was getting used to all the special attention and he knew he would miss it a little when he got back home. As soon as he saw Tabatha, he *knew* he should have worn the tuxedo. She was wearing a dark blue evening gown that accented her pearl necklace and matching earrings. She wore her hair down to her shoulders.

"Wow, you look beautiful," Pike said as he sat down. "Sorry I'm late."

Tabatha smiled. "That's alright. I know you had a lot of work to do down below."

"How did you..." he started to say, then stopped. "I know: you're a reporter."

She smiled and tipped her wine glass at him. "That's right." She took a sip then set it down. "Is that for me?" she said pointing at the flower. "Or did you just pick up a snack to eat later?"

"Oh yes. Sorry," Pike replied, feeling his face flush. Just as he started to hand it to her, the maître d' walked up with a small vase, filled with greenery. He took the flower and placed it in the vase then set in on the table in front of them. When Tabatha wasn't looking, Pike mouthed a thank you to him and the maître d' replied with a slight tilt of his head and a quick wink.

"Since you already know what I did today, there's no need for an interview. Have you ordered for us already as well?"

"As a matter of fact, yes."

"Ah, I see; a modern woman. Confident, self-assured, one knows what she wants and how to get it, yet not afraid to show that she's still a woman," he said, complimenting her on her dress. "Let's see how good you really are. Appetizers?"

"Calamari."

"Good choice. Soup?"

"New England clam chowder."

"A seafood theme going here. Salad?"

"None. Need to save room for the main course."

"Which is?"

"Southern fried chicken, mashed potatoes with gravy and corn on the cob."

"Bold, unpredicted. So simple a choice for a floating five star restaurant." Pike nodded his head slowly, thinking. "I like it. Now for the crucial choice. Dessert?"

A sly smile crept to her lips. "The basics are always the best. A simple, double chocolate fudge cake topped with vanilla ice cream."

Pike held his hands out in submission and lowered his head. "I bow to the master."

"Now there's an interesting picture."

Pike spun around faster than a turnstile in a New York subway. "K.D.?" He stood, nearly knocking his chair over as he did.

"Am I interrupting?"

"No. What? How?" he stammered. "I don't understand. How did you get here? I mean, I know you got here by helicopter," Pike rambled, "but what are you doing here?" Pike nervously realized he was stuck between a rock and a hard place and all the while not understanding why he felt like this. He hadn't done anything wrong, but then, in his forty-some years of life, one thing he had learned was that when it came to women, you didn't necessarily have to do anything wrong to get into trouble.

K.D. looked at her coworker and could tell by the confusion in his eyes that his answer was sincere but a quick glance at the woman in the stunning blue dress said that she *was* interrupting. Suddenly she felt confused herself. Seeing Gabe standing there all flustered was amusing, but there was something more to it now. She had always liked Gabe, as a friend, but seeing him with this other woman, something changed. It took her a moment before she realized that she was jealous. Jealous? How could that be? Was it that she wanted him now simply for the fact that he was with someone else? Was the old saying really true: you don't appreciate what you have until it's gone? Her world was beginning to reel and it wasn't because the iceberg was being tossed by the waves either.

Pike took a deep breath and was just starting to gain some measure of composure when he saw Marilyn walk in. She walked by K.D. as if she didn't exist and gave Pike a long, warm hug and kiss on the left cheek, which was on the side facing Tabatha. As Marilyn kissed his cheek, she looked over and stared at Tabatha and then slid up the side of his face and nibbled on his ear.

"You really hate him, don't you?" Mallory said to Cain. They were in the back of the restaurant watching the scene unfold. "Bet you never saw this coming with your butterfly thing."

"I had no idea," Cain replied, spellbound.

"Yeah, sure."

"This is better than any soap opera. Poor Gabriel, stuck in the middle of three woman. I wish I had the power to read minds because I would give half my fortune to know what's going through his head right now."

Suddenly Cain felt Mallory grip his arm. "What?"

"Oh no; she's not."

"Not what?"

"She's going to, I don't believe it."

"Who's doing what? Tell me?" Cain half pleaded, half demanded. Just then they saw Pike jump.

"What was that?" Cain asked. "What did she do to him?"

"When she kissed Gabe on the cheek, she looked over at the reporter then took a nibble on his ear. She just pissed on the lawn, marking her territory."

"Really? You saw all that?"

"Watch and learn," Mallory replied. "See his coworker there, I think her name is K.D. Crooks. Did you see the way she walked up to Pike and Tabatha? Very calm, very casual, but look at her now. She is standing stiff legged and her arms are almost glued to her side because she doesn't know what to do. She's always liked Gabe as a friend but thought nothing more of it until now. Seeing him with Tabatha, especially dressed like that has made her suddenly rethink things and she's confused. We always tend to want what we can't have. It's like when a woman is trying to decide which dress to buy in the store, the red one or the blue one. She likes them both but can't make up her mind until someone comes along and grabs the red one. All of a sudden she wants the red one because she can't have it.

"Take our reporter friend there. She is interested in our boy but she's not quite sure if it's personal or just to get a good story. She's done her homework and knows that Gabe doesn't sleep around so she's trying to catch him off guard by hitting him with her best shot right out of the gate with her slinky blue dress, just to make sure. And Marilyn Talbot, the boss's wife, well, she's just a plain old man killer. She's just in it for the challenge and thrill of the hunt. She'll chew him up and spit him out then step on what's left of him as she walks out the door."

Cain looked at Mallory in amazement. "In just these few minutes, you read all that? Wow, I am truly impressed. I see I'm going to have to bring you with me to board meetings more often."

"Trust me, women understand these things."

"Maybe women do, but poor Gabriel is clueless in Seattle right now."

"You know you really should go over there and rescue him."

"Not a chance," Cain said with a mischievous laugh. "He's the Blast from the Past; let's see how he gets out of this situation. Oh look, I think the reporter is going to get up. This is about to get real interesting."

"Gabe won't do you any good if he's dead." Mallory shook her head. "If you want anything done right, you have to do it yourself."

"Uh oh." Cain said, looking at his assistant. "I've seen that look before so I don't want to be anywhere near here when you know what hits the fan. Besides, being in my office gives me plausible deniability when the police arrive for the dead body." He smiled. "After the dust settles, bring what's left of our boy to my office please."

Mallory didn't even acknowledge her boss as she started walking forward.

Pike jumped when Marilyn gently bit his ear, more startled than anything else. He pulled her away to ask her what she was doing, but as he did, he saw that she wasn't even paying attention to him; she was looking at Tabatha. He glanced at K.D., but by the lost look on her face, he could tell she wouldn't be any help either. What was going on? He wanted to scream. Then he saw a familiar face coming toward him, it was Mallory; at last someone to help... or was she?

Even from a distance and through the low lights, he could see that something wasn't right. Her walk was different. Usually she moved with strong, confident steps, even when she didn't have someplace to be. Sauntering was the only word he could think of to describe the way she was walking, her hips gently swaying with each step. But the real change came when she came into the light.

As her body moved, her head remained still, her eyes focused like laser beams, locked on target, and he was the target. She wore a look that he had never seen before, one of controlled fury and passion. As she drew closer, Pike felt his chin hit the floor harder than the 30 ton anchor they'd just wrestled with. He felt the urge to swallow but discovered his mouth was too dry.

They say that clothes make the man or woman, but in this case, clothing had nothing to do with the tension. All she was wearing was a simple pullover sweater and jeans. She projected an air of beauty, confidence, and sexiness that was so hot he would not have had to use the *Clipper* to melt through the ice last night. At any moment he wouldn't have been surprised if music would have start playing and a spotlight shone on her as she walked. As she moved, he half expected every light bulb in the place to explode from all the electricity in the room.

Mallory slipped past K.D. and with one quick glance kept Tabatha in her seat. Seductively she slipped between Pike and Marilyn and took his arm then shot her a look that left no doubt who was in charge. "I'll take it from here, honey," she said in a sickly sweet voice.

As she led him toward the door, she slowly leaned up and whispered in his ear. "Close your mouth, Gabe." He silently obeyed as they walked out of the room, every eye in the place focused on them; the legend of Gabriel Pike soaring to new heights with each step "Breathe, Gabe." Slowly his deer-in-the-headlight look began to fade.

"What just happened in there?" Pike asked, sounding like a man just coming out of a coma.

"And I thought my life was complicated." Mallory laughed, leading Pike toward the elevator. "Nigel wants to see you in his office right away."

"I'm having dinner with a friend then K.D. shows up out of nowhere. I start feeling like an idiot, then Marilyn appears and throws gasoline on the fire and then you stroll up." His head began to clear and he stopped Mallory at the elevator. "Am I in trouble?"

Mallory laughed. "Let's see here. You have three women interested in you all at the same time: a coworker, the bosses' wife and a news reporter. And they all show up at the same time. Gee, what could possibly go wrong?"

Pike shook his head. "No, I mean with Cain. Why are K.D. and Marilyn here? Did I do something wrong?"

"Your intern Tony Roberts is here too. And Nigel will explain everything to you."

"Thank you for back there. I don't know what I would have done."

"I'm sure you would have figured something out." Mallory smiled.

"Thanks for the vote of confidence but I'm not so sure. When it comes to women and matters of the heart, the Blast from the Past usually fizzles out. Maybe that's why I'm still single."

"Or maybe the right girl for you hasn't come along yet."

Pike smiled. "You sound like my mother now."

"Well maybe your mom is right. Tom and I were lucky. We found each other without having to go through a lot of the dating crap out there."

"Yeah, you are lucky. I'll see what Cain wants and if I get done early enough maybe I'll swing by and see K.D."

Mallory shook her head. "I don't think I'd do that tonight if I were you. I think she's going to need a little time. Just call it woman's intuition."

"I won't argue with that. I'll see you in the morning then... I hope," he said and headed off towards Cain's office.

K.D. sat down on her bed and felt like crying, but she refused to. What made her even more furious was the fact that she really wasn't sure why she wanted to cry. She had been looking forward to coming out here, working on this project, and yes, working with Gabe; but now... now she was beginning to regret the whole thing. What had happened there in the restaurant? Did she have feelings for Gabe and it took the proverbial slap in the face to make her realize it? Maybe her feelings for him ran deeper than she wanted to admit.

But let's face it, she told herself as she lay down and stared at the ceiling, what chance did she have with Gabe now? Maybe back in Seattle before all this started, but not now that he was famous and living in a whole other world, one that she barely belonged in anymore. How could she compete, even if she wanted to? She laughed out loud. She was honest enough with herself to know that she did, though she still wasn't quite sure why. Marilyn? She knew she could handle her, and besides, she wasn't a real threat. She only wanted one thing and she would never get it; even if she did, she would quickly move on. But the other two were a different story.

She wasn't sure, but she thought she recognized the girl in the blue dress from television. How could she go up against a celebrity? And that blue dress? K.D. got up and looked at herself in the full-length mirror. She knew she wasn't the prettiest woman in the world but she also knew she was not that bad looking. She'd turned

a few heads in her time, but posing in front of the mirror, she wondered if those days were gone.

She tried to imagine herself wearing the blue dress but didn't like
the way she looked so she went to her suitcase to find some real
clothes. The more she dug, the more frustrated she became. She sat
down on the edge of the bed in defeat. All she had to wear were
jeans, flannel shirts and frumpy old work boots, nothing to compete
against a slinky blue dress. She didn't even have a pretty nightgown,
just an old oversized Mariners t-shirt. She could feel the tears welling
inside but refused to let the dam burst.

She stood and began pacing back and forth, still clutching a hand-
ful of flannel shirts. And that other woman, the one who is supposed
to be her boss, Beth Mallory. What was her problem? She walked
right passed her as if she wasn't even there. *Why is everyone always
ignoring me?* K.D. threw the shirts across the room in frustration and
plopped down on the bed, no longer able to keep her tears in check.

She replayed the whole thing over and over again in her mind:
Marilyn walking past her, *ignoring* her and focusing on little Miss
Blue Dress and biting Gabe on the ear. She picked up one of her
boots and let it fly across the room, making a very satisfying crash as
it hit the dresser.

And that Beth woman, how unprofessional. Waltzing right up,
ignoring me *again*. And how dare she shoot me a little wink as she
strolled by with Gabe on her arm. But despite the tears, a small smile
managed to find its way onto her face.

It was kind of funny the way she kept Miss Blue Dress down with
just a stare, and the look she handed Marilyn was priceless. She sure
put her in her place. But she was still furious because of the way she
ignored her, not even thinking she was a threat.

Suddenly she stopped in mid sob. *She ignored me because she didn't
think I was a threat.* That was it! This Beth chick wasn't slamming
her, she was telling the other two that Gabe was out of bounds, but

she didn't tell her that! Beth wasn't an evil vixen but more like a silent partner.

With renewed confidence, she stood in front of the mirror again, posing with her flannel shirts. "Yeah, you'd be lucky to get any of this, Gabriel Pike," she laughed. K.D. whirled around the room like a giddy schoolgirl, striking pose after pose, the weight of the world falling off her shoulders.

CHAPTER THIRTY TWO

Pike was disappointed that he'd missed his fried chicken dinner but was grateful that he had escaped with his life. He'd grabbed a candy bar from a vending machine and had just finished it when he reached Cain's office.

"Mr. Cain?" he called out as he stuck his head inside the office.

"Up here, Gabriel."

The office was dimly lit but he could see Cain silhouetted against the night sky on the observation deck. Waiting a moment for his eyes to adjust, Pike climbed the stairs and was soon standing next to Cain. The view was spectacular. With the sun beginning to set, it created a cascading hue of blues in the twilight skies. The iceberg glistened brightly in spots, reflecting the colorful lights of the casino while it almost glowed in others, soaking up the last light of the sun and reflecting it back.

Cain was standing with his back to Pike, his hands behind his back as he surveyed his creation before him. "This is my crowning glory, Gabriel," Cain said, still beholding his wonder.

"I'm surprised to see K.D., Tony and Marilyn here. Am I in trouble, sir? Are you not satisfied with my work?

"That's what I like about you, Gabriel," Cain said as he turned to face Pike, "always thinking like an engineer, straight and to the point. Like I said, this project is my crowning glory, probably the one thing in this life I will be remembered for and to answer your question directly: no, I am not unhappy with your work."

Pike felt himself grow two inches, the weight of uncertainty lifted off his shoulders. "However," Cain continued, "having said that, I won't let anything interfere with that dream either; that's why I brought in your associates. The storm caused damaged I wasn't anticipating and everything must continue on schedule. If we're late entering New York harbor it creates a domino effect, one canceled meeting cancels another and so on, snowballing into a marketing and PR blizzard that can't be stopped. You are still in charge, and K.D. and your intern Tony will report directly to you."

"Okay," Pike said, nodding his head in agreement, "but why bring in Marilyn? She's not an engineer."

"From here on out, Mallory and I are going to become very busy and won't have the luxury of talking to you as much as we have in the past. Ms. Talbot will be the liaison between us." Cain's expression suddenly turned serious as he looked Pike directly in the eye. "Up until now, I have given you pretty much free rein in how you conduct your inspection and that's not going to change, but I do expect results, Gabriel. Nothing must slow us down and we have to stay on schedule. Do I make myself clear?"

"Yes sir."

Cain's statement was said with such authority and finality that there wasn't room for any other answer.

"Thank you. The last few days have been trying and the upcoming ones are likely to be worse. I know you would probably like to see your friends but I would suggest you get some rest tonight instead."

"Wise counsel, sir."

Cain smiled, lightening up the mood a bit. "You can still talk to me any time, Gabriel, but I would appreciate it if the everyday dealings went through Ms. Talbot. Good night." Cain said, turning back around and staring out the window.

Pike was wired by the time he got back to his room. Part of his brain was saying that Cain was right in bringing in K.D. and Tony, but part of him was a little upset and disappointed that Cain thought he needed help. He turned on his laptop and started going over the damage reports that Centers had sent him earlier and started formulating an inspection schedule. But he was having trouble concentrating as his mind kept drifting off to what happened at the restaurant and what would later be called the Faceoff at the O.K. Corral. He was wrestling with his thoughts and emotions about Tabatha and K.D. and how he was feeling guilty; like he was cheating but logically he wasn't since he had no commitment to either. But he also knew that logic and emotions seldom went hand in hand.

He sent K.D. and Tony a copy of his work files in an e-mail and set up a meeting at eight in the morning in the conference room in Mallory's office. He knew his mind was too cluttered to think straight now and he needed to decompress. He shut down the work file and decided it was time to relax and delve into his world of conspiracy theories.

Since they were in the middle of the Atlantic Ocean and on a giant iceberg, it seemed only fitting that he start his conspiracy quest to see what the world had to say about the sinking of the *Titanic,* especially after Cain's revelation. While he believed Cain, or at least believed that Cain thought it was the truth, he wanted to see if there was any supporting evidence to back up his story. He soon found out that it wasn't a tragedy that just happened on its own; as with all good conspiracy theories, there were always unseen forces working on their own agendas.

After reading a few minutes, Pike was surprised to find out that the great ship did not sink because of icebergs or poor seamanship. The *Titanic* fell victim to the Curse of the Mummy! Pike smiled to himself as he read; he loved these urban legends.

The Egyptian Princess of Amen Ra lived around 1050 B.C. When she died, she was laid to rest in an ornate wooden coffin and buried deep in a vault at the city Luxor on the banks of the Nile. She lay undisturbed for over 800 years until she was unearthed sometime in the 1880s by four English explorers who drew lots to see who would buy the coffin; that's when the trouble began. Of the original four men, one man wandered into the desert, never to be seen again, another had his arm amputated, the third lost his life, and the fourth suffered a severe illness and lost his job. And that was only the beginning.

Calamity and bad luck continued to follow the owners of the coffin until it was reportedly sold to an American investor who wanted to bring it back to the States but knew the coffin wouldn't be loaded on board the *Titanic* because of its cursed reputation, so he smuggled it on the ship under a car chassis that he was transporting to America. He kept his mummy a secret right up until the day before the ship sank when he was overheard bragging about it to other passengers.

Wow, Pike thought, hell hath no fury like a woman scorned. He laughed, the whole story sounded like it would make a great Halloween movie, Jason versus the Mummy; or in this case, being it's at the bottom of the Atlantic, Jaws versus the Mummy.

This one looks interesting he said as he opened another link and began reading. The *Titanic* had a sister ship, the *Olympic*, which seemed to draw bad luck, including running aground and colliding with the *HMS Hawke*. The owners of the ships, the White Star Line, couldn't afford to pay for the costly repairs to the ship, so a scheme was hatched to switch the ships' names and sink the *Olympic*, posing as the *Titanic*, to collect the insurance money.

Captain Smith was to scuttle the ship at a predetermined location where there would "happen" to be several other vessels in the area to pick up passengers from the sinking ship since the White Star Line wanted no loss of life. It was even proposed that the *Titanic* didn't strike an iceberg at all but actually ran into one of the rescue ships drifting with its lights off. Unfortunately the *Titanic* was mortally wounded a day before the supposed accident, left with no rendezvous.

Pike paused for a moment while he considered that theory. It had a ring of truth that would tend to support Cain's story; insurance fraud was nothing new, even a hundred years ago, he thought. Was Cain's grandfather involved with the plot or merely an innocent bystander?

Interesting.

Pike scrolled down a few more screens and found a few more theories, one suggesting that there was a fire in the coal bunkers that inadvertently led to the sinking while another said the expansion joints failed and led the ship to sink quicker with great loss of life.

He yawned. It was getting late and he knew he had a long, difficult day ahead. He was just about to turn off computer and go to bed when another theory caught his eye.

As he began reading, the whole story began unfolding like a Dan Brown novel. The Jesuits were responsible for sinking the *Titanic*.

The Jesuits had been around since the late 1500s and were confessors to the European rich, and defended the Pope and Catholicism throughout the world. Theorists argued that the Jesuits were founded so the order could establish greater financial wealth and thus influence business and governments around the world. Furthermore, the sinking of the *Titanic* was a direct plot by the Jesuits as a means to an end: the creation of the Federal Reserve Board.

Pike stopped right there and grabbed a root beer out of the mini fridge and threw a bag of popcorn in the small microwave. This was going to be good.

According the article, in 1910, seven men met on Jekyll Island off the coast of Georgia to discuss plans to form the Federal Reserve Bank. At the meeting were representatives from the financial empires of the Rockefellers, JP Morgan, and the Rothschilds, who were the banking agents for the Jesuits and held the key to the wealth of the Catholic Church.

Their goal in creating the Federal Reserve was to be able to not only influence the regulation of both private and governmental financial institutions in the United Stated but also to exercise that same control all over the world. But they knew there would be opposition in many forms but the most prominent three were Benjamin Guggenheim, Isidor Strauss and, probably the richest man in the world at the time, John Jacob Astor. All three had to be killed and in such a way as to not arouse any suspicion whatsoever; the sinking of the *Titanic* was the perfect solution.

Pike snacked on his popcorn and lost all track of time as he read through the supporting details. This is interesting, he thought. This theory had the captain of the *Titanic*, Edward Smith, as a major conspirator. Reportedly, Smith was a Jesuit and would do anything for the Order and for God's will. His job was to sink the ship, insuring the plans of the Jesuits would succeed.

In December of 1913, about a year and eight months after the sinking, the Federal Reserve was put in place as part of the Federal Reserve Act. It is believed by some that the Federal Reserve and the Jesuits were responsible for funding the United States, Russia and Germany during the First World War.

Pike glanced at his watch. It was nearly midnight. He would have to spend some more time on this theory later. He enjoyed the political mystery and intrigue and there was just enough evidence to put this conspiracy within the realm of possibility. He smiled, but then again, that's what a good conspiracy theory was all about.

Reluctantly, he turned off his computer. He was very tired, but the Curse of the Mummy story had been entertaining and the Jesuits' conspiracy was intriguing, igniting his imagination and both had helped to clear his head and put things back into perspective. He fell asleep with figures hiding in the shadow, visions of the *Titanic* sailing through ice filled waters and of mummies going bump in the night.

Pike was still sleepy from last night's foray into the secret world of conspiracies but he was also a little nervous as he walked to his first meeting with K.D. and Marilyn after the Faceoff at the O.K. Corral last night. He decided the best course of action was to pretend it never happened and just conduct business as usual. Feeling the butterflies fluttering in his stomach he rounded the corner and entered the room. He was relieved to see that he was the first to arrive, which was the way he liked it. He poured himself a cup of coffee but passed on the doughnuts that Mallory had left for them. As he was getting set up, Tony was the first to arrive. Pike could tell by the expression on his face that he wanted to ask him about last night but he didn't give him the opportunity.

Next Marilyn came in, greeted them both, poured herself some coffee then sat down. Pike waited in anticipation for K.D. to show up and he didn't have long to wait. As she entered, their eyes locked for a moment but he couldn't get a read on what she was thinking. She smiled pleasantly and greeted everyone, grabbed a doughnut and some coffee, then sat down. Good, Pike said to himself; this might be easier than he thought.

"We've got a lot of work to do," Pike said, opening up the meeting. "Have you all had a chance to look at the files I sent last night and familiarize yourselves with what we're facing here?" he said, looking at K.D. and Tony. Both nodded their heads.

"Good. Our major concern is the towing towers, especially the starboard side tower. K.D., I'd like you and Tony to take an in-depth look at the stress points and the fractures in the base anchors for the towers and come up with a recommendation. I'll check out the relays for the juice and test their integrity. We'll meet back here at one for a working lunch, compare notes, and go from there. Marilyn, I'm afraid I won't have much for you to do until then."

"Not a problem."

Just then they heard a knock on the door. "Everyone, this is Brian Centers. I've asked him to play tour guide for you until you get your bearings. This place can be a little overwhelming at times." Centers smiled and waved.

"Any questions?" When none were asked, he ended the meeting and everyone got up.

"I'll be right there," K.D. said to Tony, then turned to Pike. Here it comes, he thought, the moment of truth. "Nate wanted me to give you this," she said as she reached into her laptop case and pulled out a small package.

"What's this?" He asked.

K.D. shrugged her shoulders. "I don't know. All he would say is that you'll need this."

"Okay, thanks."

"Tony or I will call you if we have any problems," she said as she rounded the corner on her way out.

"Well now," Pike said out loud to himself as she disappeared. "That was interesting." He quickly gathered his things and headed back to his room to change and get to work; so much for making a mountain out of a mole hill, he thought.

Half an hour later, Pike was in the Hoth cave and had formulated a plan with Miles to inspect the juice relay stations. Leaving the meeting, he decided to walk down the long tunnel instead of taking the cart. The air was cold and had a stale taste to it but he enjoyed the walk nonetheless. After a few minutes of walking, he was beginning to feel that he really was on the Planet Hoth on the far side of the galaxy. He hadn't seen a soul since he left the office area. The solitude was a little unnerving but welcome just the same as it was a good chance to focus on his inspection and try to forget how much more complicated his life had become in the last 24 hours.

He came to the first of the main relay stations and opened up the control panel then took out the c-pad Miles had given him and tried to bring up the schematics. Come on, hot shot, concentrate... Hot Shot... he sighed.

"Do you believe this place?" Tony Roberts said, standing on the deck of the number three ship. Like a six year old on their first visit to Disneyland, he was staring in wonder at the marvels of the huge cavern housing the support ships.

"Now I know what Jonah must have felt like," K.D. replied.

"Who?"

"Didn't you ever go to Sunday school? Never mind," she said, shaking her head.

"If you will follow me," Centers said, "the support towers Gabe wants you to look at are up here."

Tony and K.D. followed Centers toward the bow. As they were walking, Tony continued. "Boy, what I wouldn't give to be in Gabe's shoes right now."

"Why?"

"Come on, are you kidding? He's famous, a celebrity. He can get anything he wants." Tony paused. "Well, you are too, kind of, sort of, after last night."

She stopped and grabbed Tony by the arm and swung him around. "What are you talking about?"

"Here, let me show you." He pulled out his iPhone and began searching the web. "Yeah, you're all over the internet. Some sites are calling you the mystery woman because no one knows who you are. But on YouTube, you're GB3."

"I'm what? GB3?"

Suddenly Tony looked embarrassed. "I didn't call you that, the guys on the videos did."

"What is a GB3?"

He hesitated a moment, "Remember, I'm only the messenger here."

"What does it mean, Tony?" she asked sharply.

He hesitated for a moment but a stern look from K.D. made him continue. "Gabe's Babes; you're number 3"

"That happened less than twelve hours ago and it's already all over the internet? How? Why?"

"The how is simple; we're on a boat full of reporters who are bored with nothing else to do. The why is because you're associated with Gabe, and right now he's the hottest thing around, especially after he saved the ship, or iceberg or whatever you call this thing." He showed her several different videos of what happened in the restaurant last night. K.D. started pacing back and forth as she watched the videos, shaking her head and mumbling. "Oh come on, they're calling me fat, that I'm not as slender as GB 1 or 2."

"You're not fat," Tony said sheepishly. "Remember, they say the camera adds ten pounds."

"Great! Just great!" She continued: "I'm plastered all over the web and what am I wearing? I'm wearing jeans and an old sweater, that's what! And look at what the other two are wearing. I'm going to kill him," K.D. ranted. "I'm just going to kill him."

"Who? The guy who posted it on YouTube?

"No, Mr. Blast from the Past himself."

"You're right; after you kill him you can put him on ice," Tony said, smiling and holding his hands up displaying the room.

She stopped and looked at Tony with a strange expression then burst out laughing. "Okay, maybe I was a little over the top there."

"Just a little." Tony held up his thumb and forefinger.

They looked around and saw that Centers had discretely moved to the bow of the ship and was waiting for them to catch up. K.D. waved and the two of them started walking again. "So you think I can make some money from this celebrity thing, huh?" she asked.

"Oh yeah, I heard they're going to have this reality show…"

"Shut up, Tony."

"Yes, ma'am."

"Here are the supports that Gabe wanted me to show you. This is the starboard and that's the port. There's a catwalk over there to get to the other side." Centers pointed to the right then reached into his coat and pulled out a small notebook computer and handed it to K.D. "I've downloaded all the schematics and pertinent information on here for you. The boss just called so I have to go, but here," Centered pulled a walkie-talkie and handed it to Tony, "you can reach me on this anytime."

"Okay, thanks," K.D. said. She turned around and leaned back, following the tower all the way until it disappeared into the ceiling. "All right then," she said as she turned on the notebook, "we're here," showing Tony on the screen, "and you're going to be here," she said, pointing to the support anchors below the deck.

"Ah come on, even out here I still get the crap jobs?" Tony whined.

K.D. looked at him and took her finger and pointed at herself first and then to him. "Partner in the firm, intern at the firm. Besides, don't mess with the GB3 or you'll be 1DB."

He looked at her, not understanding.

"One Dead Boy." She smirked. "Now get moving."

"Yes, ma'am," Tony replied, his head hanging down in defeat as he started below deck.

CHAPTER THIRTY THREE

Mallory looked up from her desk when she heard the light tap on her office door; it was her secretary, Cindy. "Senator Williams' aid, Robert Thornton, is here and would like to speak with you."

"Thank you, Cindy. Send him in in ten minutes please."

She nodded and closed the door behind her on her way out. *I wonder what he wants*, Mallory thought to herself. She actually had the time to see Thornton right now but it was always best to make people wait, reminding them that they were the one who wanted to see you, a trick she had learned from her boss. Whatever it was, it couldn't be good. *Old Pug is up to something*, she thought, *and he's probably using Thornton to try to pump information from me, hoping I'll be all buddy-buddy with his little minion.* She smirked, loving the challenge, divide and conquer.

Just before Cindy let him in, she positioned herself by the coffee-pot. Hearing his knock, she stifled a smile as she poured a cup of coffee. Show time!

"Hi, Bobby," she said warmly, "I was just having some coffee, can I pour you a cup?" *Let's test this boy right out of the gate and see what he's got. I know he hates to be called Bobby so if he corrects me, he has at least a little self-respect and if he doesn't then he's a little puppy dog with his tail between his legs and I'll chew him up and spit him out.*

"Hi Elizabeth, thank you for seeing me. I know how busy you are, and yes, some coffee would be nice," *He's polite but...* "and I prefer Robert." *Good boy.*

"Not at all, now what I can do for you, Robert?"

"Well, Elizabeth..."

"Please, call me Beth." Lower his defenses with familiarity.

"Beth, as you know, I work for Senator Williams, and the senator has a great many interests..."

Let's see how this boy does under pressure, how well he thinks on his feet when he can't use his practiced scripted.

"Well, Robert," she interrupted, "as you said, my time is valuable, so why not skip the political double speak and tell me the real reason you're here?"

Thornton released a small sigh. "Putting it plain and simple, my boss doesn't trust your boss and he wants me to try and find out what Mr. Cain is up to through you."

An admission? A frontal assault made to lower my defenses to get me to trust him? Perhaps Bobby here is not so simple and innocent after all. This could be interesting.

"What doesn't he trust? Doesn't he think the entire project is real?" Mallory asked.

"What the senator doesn't trust are Mr. Cain's motivations and his ultimate intentions."

"His ultimate intentions? You're kidding right? Pug doesn't believe that Nigel wants to bring fresh water to millions and ease pain and suffering around the world?"

"That he believes, but what he doesn't trust are his ulterior motives."

"Ulterior motives? What ulterior motives? That's ridiculous."

Thornton sighed. "It's bad enough that the senator treats me like an idiot and if you can't or don't want to help me then fine, but please, at least show me a little common decency and respect. I know how the game is played; I am not a fool"

Interesting. So he isn't a total lap dog for the senator. Is he show-ing he's brave by speaking out or trying to play the sympathy card? Let's see just how loyal he is.

"I'm sorry, you're right. I've heard old Pug Williams can be a tough S.O.B. If he's as bad as they say, then why do you stay with him?"

"Does Mr. Cain always do everything the way you want? Have you two never had cross words?"

I think this boy really could be a player, throwing back the ques-tion, hmmm.

Mallory shook her head. "Of course we have our disagree-ments but we argue from the standpoint of mutual respect, not master/minion. I don't think you can say the same."

"No, no, I can't. There are times I want to tell him he can take this job and shove it where the sun don't shine but then I know that would defeat the purpose."

"What purpose?"

"He is crafty, sneaky, kind when he wants to be and manages to get things done when others falter. He can kiss the babies at the supermarket and hang a political enemy out to dry in the same afternoon. I've seen him take 'campaign funds' from big business and then turn around and rake them over the coals in the media to help a lowly widow get her dead husband's pension.

"Agree or disagree with his style or personality, he is still one of the greatest, pure politicians to ever live. If you want to be the best, you have to learn from the best."

Mallory leaned back in her chair and considered this. Well, well, this boy is ambitious and seems to have a good sense of how things work. In a few years he could be a real contender on Capitol Hill. I'll nibble a little to see what more I can get out of him.

"Okay, just what is it that Pug is worried about? Why does he see Nigel as threat?" she asked in a softer, more conciliatory tone to lighten the mood and put Thornton more at ease.

"The senator knows that a man like Mr. Cain doesn't sink tens of millions of dollars into a project without expecting some sort of return. Mr. Cain has more money than he could possibly ever use, so his pay off must not be financial. So the only profit from this venture would be goodwill and the only place that goodwill is marketable is in the political arena."

"So you think Nigel has political ambitions?"

"It makes sense."

"Your boss doesn't keep you very well informed, does he?"

Thornton had a puzzled look on his face. "What do you mean?"

"Williams himself has talked to Nigel about throwing his hat into the political arena. Your boss wants the presidency and if he gets it, he wanted Nigel to be one of his cabinet appointees."

Thornton looked stunned.

"I can tell by the look on your face that Williams hasn't bothered to tell you any of this?"

"Honestly, no."

"Pug knows all this. He's either ridiculing you by sending you here on a fool's errand or he really has no idea and is sending you on a fishing expedition and hopes you'll get lucky. I have no idea either what he is suspicious of. I'll talk to Nigel if you want, to see if he has any thoughts."

Thornton's face was a mixture of anger at his boss and gratitude to Mallory for her help. "Thank you, Beth, I appreciate it."

"No problem, and if you pick up anything from Pug, you let me know too."

Thornton nodded as he got up. "Yeah, sure thing," he replied. His mind was racing a hundred miles an hour and he didn't like the direction it was heading.

CHAPTER THIRTY FOUR

All the service lights on the main relay panel were green, indicating that all was well, but being who he was, Pike didn't take many things at face value. He didn't know if it was some psychological things that the shrinks could trace back to his childhood and blame his mother for, or if it was his study and training as an engineer that caused him to be nit picky (as K.D. would say), he preferred to think of it as being precise. Or maybe, he mused, after all his studies into the world of conspiracies, things were never as they seemed.

Whatever the reason, he accessed the flow charts for the starboard relay pump and traced the flow of all the lines and everything was fine, as indicated on the control panel. Next he opened up the port relay panel and it too showed a driver's dream of all green lights. Undaunted, he checked the flows of the first three lines and all was well; however, the last line showed a slight increase in pressure. Not a major concern, he thought to himself; it could be anything as simple as a faulty sensor to as serious as a clog somewhere down the line. He would have to trace the line from here to the secondary relay and farther if necessary. The secondary relay pump was on the same level as the main but farther out toward the edge of the iceberg. Pike left the large, spacious corridor for the confines of one of the service passageways. It was four feet wide and barely high enough for him to stand upright, with the ceiling and sides covered with conduit and piping.

Reaching the relay, it opened up into a room not much bigger than a walk-in closet. Again, he accessed the control panel and discovered that there was still back pressure but it wasn't from this station. Then where? He really didn't want to have to trace the line to its final distribution point when suddenly it hit him. He bet the problem was related to the way they had taxed the system to freeze the water in the anchor room.

He headed toward the anchor room, inspecting the piping as he went. After several minutes of walking, he spotted something odd on the wall just ahead. The normally pristine white wall had a green stain on it that looked like mold. When he got closer, he could see that it wasn't mold but a stain from a leak. During the storm, the stress on the iceberg from the wind and tossing ocean must have caused several of the fittings to rupture, causing leaks.

Like antifreeze dripping from the radiator of a car, several green patches lined the passageway, making the walls look like they'd been vandalized. Though the leaks were not significant, he made notes of their locations to give to Miles when he got back. He also noticed that it seemed just a tad warmer in the passage. He would have to talk to Miles to see if it was just because he was in an enclosed space or if it had anything to do with the juice.

He reached the end of the passage and climbed up the ladders to the same level as the anchor room. According the schematics on his c-pad, this passage should parallel the side of the berg, zigzag near the anchor room, then open out into the main corridor.

Coming to the end of the corridor he turned left, then stopped dead in his tracks as he looked up. The entire passageway was covered in green. It looked like a scene from a Hollywood horror film with green stains covering the ceiling and floor with small streams of slime oozing down the walls. As if the sight alone were not enough, he realized it was now noticeably warmer. He wouldn't be taking his shirt off, but it felt about ten degrees warmer in the passageway.

He carefully followed the main piping and found where it fed into the anchor room. About three feet up from the floor, he found a T-joint that split the pipe that sent coolant wrapping around the room. He could see that when they filled the room with water and it froze, it had expanded just enough to kink the joints in several of the lines and he found a four foot section that had nearly been pinched in two.

Being in all this ice and eerie frozen wasteland brought the movie *The Thing* to mind. He looked around, then continued walking slowly. He felt silly as he let out an almost inaudible sigh of relief when he came into the main corridor in front of the anchor room.

He went over and began examining the anchor room door again, making sure that the leaking coolant hadn't affected the stability of the ice or the seal. Suddenly he stopped and turned around, thinking he had heard something. He stood for a moment, listening intently, but heard nothing more than his own imagination getting the better of him. He turned back around but suddenly heard the noise again, only this time he knew it was real and it was getting closer.

It wasn't the monster from the movie, but something nearly as bad, a flock of reporters, all armed with cameras and microphones. A camera crew and five other reporters were following Cain and Williams as they walked. Pike saw that Tabatha was among the reporters, along with Toupee Man.

"Gabriel!" Cain said, as he saw Pike standing there. "I see you are hard at it, making sure everything is ready for our grand entrance into New York harbor." Cain was talking as much to the cameras as he was to Pike. Pike smiled and held out his hand as Cain approached, thinking that now would not be the best time to tell him about the leak.

"You remember Senator Williams?" Cain said as the short, round man bullied his way in front of the pair.

"Of course," Pike lied. With that answer, Pike realized that he was getting used to being the Blast from the Past and was fitting into the role, knowing what to say and what not to say; at that moment he wasn't sure if that was good or not.

"Fine work you did the last night," Williams said, shaking Pike's hand and posing for the cameras in one fluid motion, a skill he had honed to perfection during his many years on the campaign trail.

"Thank you, sir," Pike replied, remembering to smile.

"We're filming a short documentary about the iceberg," Williams began. "You know, showing the folks back home that I really am working out here and not working on my suntan." He winked. Everyone laughed appropriately at the senator's joke. "Bobby, why don't you take everyone and head over to the other anchor room? I want everyone to see what a Cracker Jack job our boy here did," Williams said, putting his arm around Pike. Thornton nodded and gathered his flock of reporters. The lights went off, and the cameras dropped as the group went back the other way. As soon as everyone was gone, Williams reached into his coat pocket and pulled out a cigarette. "It's not that you didn't do a great job," Williams said, turning to Pike, "it's just that I was dying for a smoke."

"You really shouldn't smoke down here, Pug," Cain said. "It's not the kind of image you want to portray."

"Nonsense," Williams replied as he took out his lighter and flicked it. "And besides, why do you think I sent them away?"

"Sorry, Pug, but I really must insist you put it out," Cain said in a stricter tone.

Pike had never heard Cain talk in such a stern voice before. It not only caught his attention, but the senator's as well. Williams stared at Cain. Pike could see the anger flashing in Williams' eyes, not used to anyone talking to him like that. Pike wanted to melt into the wall. He didn't want to be anywhere near ground zero when World War III started between two of the most powerful men in the world. Just as he thought the power struggle was about to escalate, Williams' expression changed.

"When in Rome, do as the Romans do," Williams said. "This is your dinghy." Williams took a deep drag out of defiance then flicked the burning cigarette down the passageway Pike had just come from.

"Thank you," Cain replied, his tone softened but still firm.

"Nice seeing you again," Williams said, turning to Pike. "We'll have to get together after all this hullabaloo is over." He nodded to Pike and turned to walk with Cain but before they took a step both men stopped. "What's that sound?"

Pike listened and at first it sounded like someone had left a window open and you could hear the ocean outside. But then he felt a slight draft leaving the room as if a giant dragon had just taken a huge breath and sucked out all the air.

Then the dragon breathed.

Pike turned and looking down the dark passageway, he saw a light like that of a train coming out of a tunnel and he heard what he could only describe as the sound of rushing wind.

Horrified, Pike suddenly realized what was happening, as the expression on his face must have shown. He remembered seeing Cain and Williams looking at him with a have-you-lost-your-mind look. He also remembered shouting something, diving towards them, a blinding flash of light and a searing wave of heat, then nothing.

When he opened his eyes again, his vision was blurry and had slowed down to one blink at a time and his hearing was muffled, like his ears were stuffed with cotton. He felt hot and cold at the same time and couldn't figure out why. Off in the distance, he thought he could make out the sounds of shouting but it sounded like it was coming from the far side of the Moon.

As the fog began to lift, he realized that he was lying face down on the floor. How did he get on the floor in the first place? Slowly he raised up to one elbow and looked to his left where he saw a man lying next to him, he thought it was Cain but wasn't sure. Propping himself up on his other elbow, he turned to his right and saw another man lying on the ground. He was wearing the same jacket that the senator had on only it was on fire. ON FIRE!

In the blink of an eye, as if someone had flicked on a switch, Pike's senses were back to normal and then some. He thought that he could actually feel the adrenaline shooting through his veins like water through a fire hose.

Pike saw that Williams' back and his left pant leg was on fire. Pike got to his knees and started patting the flames out. By now, the reporters had poured back into the room, having heard the explosion, cameras blazing. Tabatha and Toupee Man rushed over to where Williams lay.

Instinct took over and Pike would later regret it as much as he did throwing the baseball. Being unsuccessful at putting the flames out with his hands, he reached up and tore the toupee off the reporter's head and began using the hairpiece to beat the flames into submission. Despite the severity and chaos of the situation, Pike heard Tabatha stifle a giggle when he grabbed the toupee. He had not intending to embarrass the man; he just wanted to put the flames out.

"What the hell are you doing?" Williams grumbled as Pike was beating on him. The senator rolled over and was about to let more colorful expletives fly when he saw the cameras pointing at him. His expression immediately changed from anger to a well-practiced look of unknowing innocence. "What happened?" he asked. This time it was not an act, sincere confusion was in his voice."

"Sorry, senator," Pike said as he helped him sit up, "but you were on fire."

"I am pretty hot," he said, winking into the camera. "I've heard of a celebrity roast, but this is ridiculous." Williams smiled as laughter flooded the room. Being the consummate opportunist, the senator played the wounded warrior to the cameras for all it was worth as he had several of the reporters help him to his feet. As Williams was getting up, Pike saw the senator cast a concealed scowl toward Cain. At first he thought the senator's eyes were full of anger but decided it must have been pain from having just been knocked to the floor.

As the entourage made its way back to the elevator with Williams recounting the harrowing events, Pike helped Cain to his feet. "What was that?" Cain asked as he brushed himself off.

"I was hoping you could tell me."

Cain gave Pike a puzzled look.

"Just before you arrived, I came through the passageway that just blew up. I discovered several ruptures in the piping and coolant was leaking all over that walls. Is that stuff flammable?"

"Not that I know of, but Elizabeth would be the final authority on that. Why didn't you tell me about the leaks?"

"I just now discovered them and besides, I didn't think it would be a good time to say we might have problems in front of all the reporters."

Cain smiled and nodded his head. "Yeah, good call."

"I'll let Miles know all about this and we'll see what we can come up with," Pike said.

"No, let Miles know what happened here but I don't want you bogged down on this. You need to carry on with the rest of your inspection. We can't afford any delays. Besides, Miles is a good man, he can handle it."

"You're the boss."

"And as the boss I'd like to tell you to take the rest of the day off, but I can't. However, I can tell you to take a long lunch and clean up a bit before you get back at it. There'll be plenty of time to rest once we're in port."

Pike nodded his head. "Understood. You think that maybe after dinner tonight the senator would want to have peaches flambeau for dessert?"

Cain looked at Pike, smiled, and just shook his head, then his face went serious. "And by the way, thank you."

Pike nodded as Cain turned and left.

CHAPTER THIRTY FIVE

"Are you all right?" Mallory almost shouted as she barged into Cain's office. Cain was sitting at his desk wearing a large bathrobe with a towel around his neck and a cognac in his hand.

"I'm fine, Elizabeth, thank you. Our boy saved the day again."

"What happened?"

"Pug was smoking when he knew he shouldn't be, and tossed a lit cigarette down one of the passageways and there was an explosion. Gabriel found leaking juice and thinks that's what caused it."

"Impossible."

Cain shrugged his shoulders. "That's what he thinks."

"Was anyone hurt? Any damage?"

"Thankfully no to both questions. Miles sent me a preliminary report and the damage is only superficial. However, I think we may have another problem."

Mallory cocked her head to one side. "How's that?"

"First, tell me about your meeting with Thornton."

"It was very interesting. The kid's got ambition and he could go places if he can survive working for Pug. If I ever complain about working for you again, slap me silly. Pug abuses that boy so badly. I think Robert is sincere, but I don't fully trust him either, but I think we'll be able to work with him."

Mallory moved a chair to the side of Cain's desk and sat down. "Pug is uneasy about something and Thornton says that the senator doesn't trust you but Thornton doesn't know why, and I believe him. But then he didn't know you and Pug had talked about any politics either so Pug's playing things pretty close to the vest."

"I agree; something has got Pug really spooked. Physically he's fine and he played well into the cameras this morning, but I know the senator and something is sure eating at him."

"Do you think that whatever his problem is has him worried enough to withdraw his backing for this project?" Mallory asked, concern filling her brown eyes.

Cain shook his head. "I honestly don't know. Pug is a very ambitious man and you know he wants the presidency, but he also knows that if he tries to leave us high and dry he can expect the same from us."

"Does he think he's strong enough without your help to make it on his own?"

"He's egotistical but not stupid. If he does pull out you know he thinks he's got a better plan. Do you think that Thornton can be of any help?"

Mallory shook her head. "He's got smarts but I think that Williams either hasn't told him yet or doesn't trust him enough to keep such a huge secret."

Cain sighed. "You're probably right. I'd better have a talk with him myself to see if I can figure out what's got him so jittery."

Mallory shook her head again. "He's not going to tell you anything, he thinks you're part of the problem, he thinks you *are* the problem. You'd better let me handle him."

"I don't like it. We both know that when it comes to you, he has a one-track mind."

"Thank you, Nigel, but we both also know I can take care of myself."

Cain chuckled. "That I do. But I still don't like it."

"Good, then it's settled."

Cain just frowned at his headstrong assistant. "If you'll excuse me," Cain said, pointing to his robe, "I have to get dressed."

Mallory nodded and headed for the door, then stopped halfway. "I know this is off the subject, but I have to know if it's true or not."

"What's that?"

"Did Gabe really tear the toupee off Wright's head and use it to put out the fire on the senator?"

Cain smiled. "I didn't actually see him tear it off but I would have given half my Fortune 500 companies to have seen the look on his face. By the time I came around, it looked like a singed Brillo pad hanging limp in Gabriel's hand."

"Poor Wright, he'll never live this one down." Cain heard Mallory laughing all the way down the hall.

"Okay, thank you." Pike hung up the phone and got up off his bed and walked over to the table. He pushed his computer and work papers off to one side to make room for his dinner. After what happened last night in the Crystal Palace, and his fiery rescue today, he was tired and wanted to avoid all the well-wishers and questions about what happened, so he thought it wise to lay low and eat in his room. He didn't really mind, as it would give him a chance to rest up and to do a little more research on the *Titanic* while he ate.

He had just finished clearing the table when he heard a knock on the door. Wow, that was fast service, he thought. He opened the door but instead of dinner, he was surprised to see K.D. standing there. She was wearing a Seattle Mariners hooded sweatshirt, jeans and tennis shoes.

"K.D.?"

"I was in the neighborhood and thought I'd stop by. I'm not interrupting anything, am I?"

"No, no, of course not. I'm sorry, please come in." He stepped aside to let her in, feeling a little excited and awkward at the same time.

"Nice place," she said, looking around.

"It's not the Plaza, but it'll do."

K.D. smiled politely, but he could see that she was a bit uncomfortable too.

"Have you eaten yet?" she asked.

"No, I just ordered something from room service. You know, dining in, catching up on a little paper work."

"Work?" She frowned. "Probably lone gunman stuff."

Pike smiled. "You know me and my conspiracy theories all too well."

"Well, since you haven't eaten yet, I brought you some dessert then," she said as she handed him a small package.

"What's this?" He said as he took it and unwrapped it.

"Oh it's nothing. I just made a batch of brownies before I left and brought a few with me."

Pike's eyes lit up. "Nothing? Are these the same ones you brought to the office party last Christmas?"

"Yes."

"The ones with the chocolate chips and the frosting?"

"Yes, "she said again, becoming a little embarrassed.

"These aren't nothing! These are only the best brownies I've ever had in my life." He held them in his hands as if they were a holy relic. After gazing at them for a moment, he carefully placed them on the table. "Would you like to stay? I can call and get whatever you'd like."

"No, that's okay, I really should be going."

"Are you sure? You know you're more than welcome to stay." Pike felt the awkwardness leaving the more he talked to her.

"No, I'd better go." He could hear the hesitation in her voice and wanted to ask her to stay but decided not to push it after all that had happened.

"Okay, I understand." For a split second he saw disappointment flash across her eyes with the speed of a lightning bolt because he *didn't* push it. If it were physically possible he would have kicked himself in the butt for being so stupid.

As she started to leave, she glanced over and saw the package that she had delivered earlier from their co-worker, Nathaniel Grant.

"What did Nate send you?"

"Oh, that; I forgot all about it. Come on, I'll open it now. Please, sit down, I insist." Good save, he thought to himself as she sat down at the table. He quickly cut away the wrapper with his knife and opened up the shoebox and found a note inside.

> Hey Gabe
> I know that crime fighting can be a tough job, so here are a few things to make your life as a super-hero easier.
> Nate, your faithful sidekick.

"Funny, Nate, very funny," Pike said, shaking his head.

"Let's see what's in here," K.D. said, smiling. It was good to see her smiling again, Pike thought. The first thing he took out of the box was a mask and a pair of glasses with another note attached.

> Every super-hero needs to protect his identity, so you have a mask like Zorro's or a pair of glasses like Clark Kent's to keep people from seeing who you really are.

Pike and K.D. both grinned as they took out the next item. A gold rope that looked like it was a pull cord from some fancy draperies and a pair of two inch wide gaudy bracelets that somehow managed to survive the disco age.

Wonder Woman is on vacation so she loaned these to me. The bracelets will deflect bullets and laser beams and once you capture the bad guy you can tie him up in the cord. It's unbreakable and it makes whoever is tied up in it tell the truth.

Pike held up the cord. "Boy I sure could have used this thing on the guy I bought that used Jet Ski from." They looked in the box and there were two items left, a key and a pair of handcuffs.

The key is to Wonder Woman's invisible air plane that they tell me is parked on the roof. I think it's faster than the Clipper *so be careful. And last but not least, if all else fails, you can use these good old-fashioned handcuffs.*

PS, I would have sent your tights but they weren't back from the cleaners yet.

"Nate has way too much time on his hands," Pike said, smiling as he shook his head.

"Hey, he's your sidekick," K.D. shot back.

Just then they heard a knock.

"That must be my dinner," Pike said as he went to the door. When he opened it, instead of finding the waiter with his grilled club sandwich and onion rings, he was surprised to see Tabatha Amies standing in the doorway. She was wearing a low-cut cashmere sweater and black leather pants that were so tight they looked like they had been painted on.

"Hi Gabe, I just came by to…" Tabatha stopped in mid-sentence when she saw K.D. sitting at the table. "Oh, I didn't see you had company," she completed her sentence then casually pushed her way in. "I hope I'm interrupting something," she said snidely, looking directly at K.D..

"Hi, Tabatha," Pike said tentatively, not sure where the evening was going. "I just ordered some dinner." He was hoping Tabatha would take the hint and leave.

"It looks like you started with dessert first," she said, seeing the brownies.

"K.D. made those for me, would you like one?" Trying to defuse the situation unsuccessfully.

"How nice, she can bake." Before anyone could say anything, she continued: "Oh look, and party favors too." Tabatha said, pulling the handcuffs and gold cord out of the box. "My, my, Gabe, is there another side of you I don't know about?" She looked at Pike, then turned to K.D. and winked.

Pike could see that things were spiraling out of control. K.D. was getting upset and embarrassed and he didn't know what to do. Suddenly there was another knock on the door and he felt like a punch-drunk fighter saved by the bell. He opened the door just enough to see the corner of the serving cart then he turned back to Tabatha and K.D.

"Food's here!" he said, continuing to open the door. He was puzzled by the looks on their faces as the door swung open; K.D.'s expression was one of dread while Tabatha's lips almost curled into a snarl. He couldn't understand their reaction to a simple food cart until he turned around and saw that Marilyn was the one pushing the cart.

"I saw the server outside and told him I'd take it from here," Marilyn said. "I see that you started with the appetizers," she continued, looking at Tabatha and K.D. "You can send them home because the main course is here."

Pike could see the events of last night repeating themselves all over again like a bad dream. He felt helpless as the women jockeyed for position.

"Yeah, for the main course if he wants tough leftovers," K.D. said.

K.D.'s statement shut everything down for a moment, stunning them all; no one expected her to say something like that, especially Marilyn.

Pike didn't know if was a full moon or what because he didn't know why everyone was acting so crazy, but what he did know was that he knew a lynching when he saw one and for some reason, they were stringing up the rope for K.D., and he'd had enough. But before he could circle the wagons around her, there was another knock on the door. Pike rolled his eyes; could this night get any worse? He was grateful for the short reprieve but swore that if it was Mallory at the door, he was going to jump overboard. Pike opened the door and was relieved to see that it was Tony Roberts.

"Hi Gabe, I was wondering..." Tony started to say then slowed down as he saw the room full of women. "...if you wanted to go out for a drink and see what was happening, but it looks like you've got all the action you can handle right here." K.D. was holding the rope, Tabatha twirling the handcuffs and Marilyn standing to one side.

Pike just frowned at him. "K.D., would you like to go for a walk?" He said it more as a statement than a questions and she stood right away. "Whoever is the last one out, please turn off the lights." Pike and K.D. left, slamming the door.

"Come on," he said as he half pulled her down the hallway, "I'm hungry; let's get something to eat." When they reached the end of the hall, she touched him on the shoulder.

"Thanks Gabe, but I'm not really in the mood to eat right now."

"I'm sorry, K.D."

"Don't worry about it; I know it's not your fault."

"But it is my fault. Everybody thinks I'm this big superhero."

"Not a superhero, just an ordinary one." She reached up and gently gave him a small kiss on the cheek. "I'm going back to my room. See you in the morning." She walked down the corridor to her room then turned and looked at him as she rounded the corner. "Thanks again, Hot Shot." And then she disappeared.

Pike rubbed the bridge of his nose out of frustration then headed toward the casino. The bright lights and cheery noise did little to lift his mood, which was bordering between anger, frustration, and self-pity. Surprisingly he was still hungry but he decided to skip the Crystal Palace and all its crowds and instead went into the diner. He wasn't sure if it was anger that fueled his appetite but he devoured his French Dip sandwich like a castaway rescued from a deserted island.

His stomach was settled but his mind was still restless so he decided to go up to the observation lounge. When he arrived, he was happy to find that he had the entire room to himself. He stepped over to the bay windows and examined their little moving island. He saw the *Yankee Clipper* perched on the stern, lit up with spotlights like a trophy on display. Next, he followed the stern to the left, passed the drained pool that looked like a giant sand trap next to the driving range and passed the brightly lit pavilion; that too was deserted.

His vision followed up through the colorful casino lights, sweeping to the bow of the berg to Cain's monolithic tower to the bobbing lights marking the locations of the attending tugs. This man-made monstrosity was huge by man's standard, but as he stared out past the tugs to the open ocean, he was overwhelmed by its vastness. Suddenly he felt incredibly small and his petty problems were terribly insignificant in the grand scheme of things. He was just getting a perspective on things when he felt two hands gently caress his shoulders and he heard his name whispered low and sexy.

At first he jumped because it startled him then, he shook his head and slowly turned around. "Listen I don't know what…" He stopped in mid-sentence as his eyes flew open wide seeing who was there.

"Beth!"

Silently she briefly looked into his eyes, then burst out laughing.

"Large, man-made ice berg, $81.3 million dollars. Three tugs and crew to tow it, $1.9 million dollars. The look on your face just then, priceless."

Pike just stood there speechless, not sure what was going on.

"Sorry, Gabe," Mallory continued, "but I heard what happened in your room and I just couldn't resist."

Pike blinked his eyes. "You already heard what happened down in my room, less than an hour ago?"

Mallory smiled. "It's a small iceberg full of busybodies; besides, it's my job to know everything that happens on this tub."

"I know, but still."

"Are you all right? Is all this Love Boat drama going to affect you or your inspection schedule?"

Pike shook his head. "No, it is a little distracting I'll admit, but I can handle it, It's K.D. I'm worried about."

Mallory smiled. "I heard what she said to Marilyn. I think she can handle things by herself, but if it will make you feel any better, I can talk to her if you'd like."

"That would be great, thanks."

"No problem. I have it on good authority that your room is clear now so I suggest you go back and get some sleep. Nigel is expecting a full report in the morning."

"Okay. Thanks again." Pike smiled, and returned to his room.

CHAPTER THIRTY SIX

K.D. jumped when she heard the knock on the door. She'd been lying on her bed, half-thinking, half-dozing. Part of her wanted it to be Gabe so they could talk, but another part was hoping it wasn't him because she was afraid to talk to him. With some hesitation, she got up and answered the door. When she opened the door, neither part was happy.

"Hello, K.D.," Tabatha Amies said, "may I come in?" She pushed her way in without waiting for her to answer.

"What do you want?" K.D. asked, her voice barely civil.

"We need to have little talk, you and I."

"Really, about what?"

"About Gabriel."

"What about him?"

"Oh come on now, K.D., don't play dumb with me, you know we both want Gabe." Tabatha walked over to the table and flipped open the box that had the brownies in it. "How sweet." She said, her voice dripping with sarcasm. "I suppose you make a pretty mean meatloaf too? Trying the old ploy of the way to a man's heart is through his stomach ?"

"And your version: his heart is through his pants?" K.D. shot back.

"Ohhhh," Tabatha replied, as she pretended to pull an imaginary arrow out of her heart. "Nice one, but you're still no match for me. I lead an exciting life, I've traveled all over the world, covered important stories and met dozens of world leaders; can you say the same? What can you offer him, hmm? Exciting nights of Scrabble, Saturday afternoons at the local market watching them throw fish, or visiting the local strawberry festival?"

Tabatha walked over to the closet and began thumbing through the clothes. "These flannel shirts and sweats are attractive; did you pick them up on sale at Wal-Mart?" She spun around and faced her. "Come on, K.D., face it, there was a time when you might have had a chance with Gabe but you didn't take it. The Gabe you once knew is gone. He's no longer the hometown boy; he's an international celebrity now. He's outgrown that old life style and he's outgrown you."

Sticks and stones may break my bones but words will never hurt me is the biggest lie we tell our children, K.D. thought as she heard Tabatha's words. They cut deeper into her heart than any surgeon's blade ever could, especially if she was right. Had Gabe outgrown his old life, outgrown her?

Tabatha could tell she struck a nerve by the expression on K.D.'s face. "If you really care about him, then step aside and let him go."

"Do you love him?" K.D. asked quietly.

"Do you *love* him or are you like so many women who are just in love with the idea of being in love?" Tabatha walked over and sat down at the table and grabbed one of the brownies.

"Although all this drama makes great press, I prefer to keep things a little more quiet. Bow out gracefully now and there will be no harm, no foul. If you continue with your silly pipe dream that you actually think you have a chance with Gabe, I'll be forced to take other measures."

"Take other measures? Are you threatening me?" K.D. glared at her.

Tabatha smiled. "Let's just say that as a reporter I have certain skills and ways of bringing things to light that most people want to stay buried."

"Like what?" K.D. scowled.

"If you want to play hardball, like when you were caught stealing as a teenager."

"I was thirteen and I didn't steal anything. The friend I was with put a pair of shorts in my bag when I wasn't looking. Besides, there was never any police report or charges filed."

"True, but that doesn't matter. Headlines will read 'Girlfriend of the Blast from the Past was Involved in a Teenage Shoplifting Ring.' Because of his association with Mr. Cain, Gabe will be forced to distance himself from you, causing all the more pain, and publicity, I might add."

Up until that point, K.D. was seriously considering Tabatha's words, how she might be right and how it might be best for Gabe if she quietly went away. But not now, she thought, I won't be challenged, I won't be threatened and I won't be told what to do. K.D.'s anger had just gone from simmer to the boiling point. Her adrenaline had kicked in and the fight or flight mode had taken over, and she wasn't going anywhere. She was about to explode when it suddenly came to her.

Her eyes narrowed as she looked at Tabatha. "Why are you doing this?"

"Why?" Tabatha shook her head in disbelief. "You're kidding, right? Are you that dense?"

"No, I mean, why are you going through all this trouble to try and intimidate me, to get me 'to quietly step aside,' as you put it? If you think you are so much better than me then why bother? If you're so confident then why not just go full speed ahead and blow me out of the water?"

"What are you talking about?" Tabatha asked, a hint of hesitation in her voice.

"That's it," K.D. smiled. "You're not doing this just to be nice, to save me the embarrassment of losing and you're not thinking of Gabe and it's not even because you're unsure of yourself; it because you're unsure of Gabe. You've never met anyone like him before and when he didn't immediately fall under your spell, you had your doubts so you're trying to get me out of the picture to hedge your bet. You are not used to losing and it scares you."

"What? That's crazy."

"Is it?"

"Listen, little Ms. Betty Crocker and her brownies..."

"No, you listen to me, you..." K.D. interrupted Tabatha but was interrupted herself by a knock on the door. She glared at Tabatha then angrily reached for the door. If it was Marilyn trying to throw her two cents worth in then she was dead where she stood. K.D. threw open the door and was surprised to see Mallory standing there. For the time being she held her fire, not knowing if she was friend or foe.

"Hi, K.D.," she said, then looked passed her to Amies. "Hi Tabatha, I'm glad you're here. Mr. Cain is holding a press conference tomorrow afternoon. I slipped an advanced copy of the press release under your door and I thought you might want to look at it."

Tabatha was caught off guard by Mallory's statement. She wasn't finished with K.D. yet but her reporter instincts took over and she was excited to have a scoop before anyone else did.

"Ah, thanks, Beth," Tabatha replied, "I'll get right on it." She smiled at Mallory as she walked by but shot K.D. a dirty look as she closed the door.

K.D. took in a deep breath then let it out slowly. "Thanks, it seems like you're making a habit of rescuing me."

Mallory chuckled, "From the look on your face when you opened the door, it didn't look like you were the one who was going to need the rescuing."

"Yeah, well thanks nonetheless."

"Let me guess," Mallory continued, "Tabatha was here to warn you off Gabe, that she had staked her claim and that you weren't good enough for him?"

K.D. plopped down in the chair. "You guessed it. She basically said that I had my chance and that Gabe was now out of my league and for me to quietly step aside if I really cared for him. She even threatened me if I didn't back off."

"Well do you?

"Do I what?" K.D. replied.

"Do you really care for him?"

K.D. sighed. "I've been giving that a lot of thought lately. Gabe has become a whole new person and it's kind of exciting to be with someone like that, to get to know him all over again and be a part of a whole new world, but you know what? I knew him before he was this famous superhero and I liked him even then." She paused and thought for a moment. "So I guess to answer your question, yes, I really do care for him."

"Then what are you going to do about it?" Mallory asked, picking up a brownie.

K.D. shot up from her chair and began pacing like an expectant father. "That's just it; I don't know what to do. I'm no Pollyanna, but I don't know how to compete against women like Tabatha or even Marilyn for that matter."

"Don't worry about Marilyn; she's not a real threat. She doesn't want Gabe, she just wants to have him then move on. If not, Gabe would have slept with her a long time ago."

"Okay, what about Tabatha then?"

"She is definitely the one you have to contend with."

"Yeah, but how? She's younger than me, makes more money, and has a better, more exciting job that has taken her all over the world. It's a little tough for a local girl born in Lake Stevens, Washington to compete with that."

Mallory smiled. "Most men are dumb and don't know what they want or have even when it's standing right in front of them." She paused and licked the brownie off her finger. "These are really good. If I were Gabe, I'd marry you. I'd be fat and happy. Anyway, I don't know Gabe as well as you do, but from what I've seen he's not going to be thrown by a little cleavage and a tight, short dress. Again, if that were the case, he could have had much better looking women than you already with all the exposure he's gotten. Sorry, no offense."

She smiled,."None taken."

"Still though, he is a man, and men don't always think with the right organ." Mallory got up and walked over to the closet and looked through her clothes. She turned when she heard K.D. sigh. "What's wrong?"

"Sorry, it just seems like everyone is interested in what I wear."

"Tabatha went through your clothes?"

K.D. nodded.

"Well, the old saying is true; clothes do make the man, or the woman. You have to throw the man a bone here you know. Everything you have here is very functional but not very stylish."

"I know, but what am I supposed to do? In my work, a lot of the time I'm crawling under houses or swinging from rafters looking for structural defects—not exactly the place for high heels."

"You may be doing a man's job but it doesn't mean you have to look like one. Sometimes, yes, you do have to put on coveralls and go spelunking around, but not always. You need to think outside the box a little, stop being an engineer and start being a woman; you can do both. You don't have to have everything hanging out to get noticed."

"How?"

"Think about what you're going to be doing and dress accordingly."

"I have been."

Mallory smiled and shook her head. "No, again, think like both a woman and an engineer. For example, what are you doing here, what is the environment you're in? It's cold but not very messy.

Instead of bundling up like Quinn the Eskimo in a bulky fur-lined parka, how about a nice ski jumpsuit? It's warm, comfortable, and functional and most important in this case, it's stylish. It can show that you're still a woman doing a man's job."

She nodded her head slowly as a smile began to brighten her face. "I like it."

"And so will he. I trust Gabe will make the right choice here. He may just need a little push, that's all."

"Thank you, Beth," K.D. said as she gave her a hug. "All great advice, but as big as this place is, there's still no mall here."

Mallory gave K.D. a knowing smile. "You just leave that to me."

After Mallory left, K.D. felt as giddy as a schoolgirl, excited and terrified at the same time, her mind going ten different directions at once. She sat down and grabbed a brownie and had it halfway to her mouth then stopped and put it back. She couldn't fit into that snow bunny outfit if she kept eating these things.

CHAPTER THIRTY SEVEN

Pike was seated at the table in the conference room with his laptop open, a cup of coffee and snacking on an apple fritter. Marilyn was the first to arrive and like the day before, she was all business. She greeted him politely and began to set up for the meeting. The same routine was followed as Tony arrived and K.D. walked in shortly thereafter.

As soon as he saw her, he knew something was different but he couldn't put his finger on it. She had the same laptop, hair looked the same, same flannel... that was it! She wasn't wearing her usual cargo pants and flannel shirt and work boots.

She was wearing a light blue button down blouse covered with a dark blue blazer with dark slacks and black leather shoes. It was K.D., only different, and he liked the difference.

As soon as everyone was settled in, Pike began. "Marilyn, we'll start with you. Do you have anything for us?"

"Nothing new here, it's just like work back home; we have a deadline to meet. I've been going over the events and arrival schedules with Beth and things are pretty tight with not a lot of leeway for delays. Until I get a report from you guys, that's all I've got. Oh, I almost forgot. Arthur's oldest son Luke and his wife Ashley just had their first baby, a little girl and they named her Lucy Ann."

"Everybody doing okay?" K.D. asked.

Marilyn nodded her head. "Baby and mother are doing fine but we're not sure about Arthur, he says he's too young to be a grandpa."

Pike was happy for Art but he had real mixed emotions about kids. He'd seen families before, the shared smiles that he knew love and being together brought, but he also knew children were huge time consumers and honestly he didn't know if he was too selfish to be a good parent.

He stole a quick glance at K.D. and she had that maternal look all over her that women get whenever someone mentions newborns. She looked at him and smiled and he quickly looked away. Her look scared the bejeebers out of him and yet…

"Thanks, Marilyn," Pike quickly said, letting his mind run from places it didn't need to go… right now. "K.D., what do you and Tony have?"

"Nothing good, I'm afraid." She tapped a key on her computer and sent a file to Marilyn and Gabe. "From a structural standpoint, the starboard towing tower is in good shape. A little stress and fatigue is visible at the base and at the connection point to the tow cable itself but otherwise it passes just fine. The port tower, however, is a completely different story."

She sent another attachment to everyone and waited for them to open it. "As you can see in the first six pictures, there is significant buckling, not only on the deck plating but also to the sub supports below deck. In pics six and seven, you can see that the housing around the tower where it joins the ceiling is no longer flush but has routed out a two inch wide ring between itself and the ice, adding to its instability. The main support arm attached to the towing bridle is actually bent. In my opinion, under ideal conditions in calm, enclosed waters, this would be very marginal at best, but in the open ocean, this is a disaster waiting to happen."

"Thanks K.D.," Pike said with a solemn face. "I'm afraid my report is not that much better."

"Sorry we're late," Cain said as he and Mallory entered the room.

Pike looked up in surprise. "Mr. Cain, Beth, what are you doing here?"

Cain grabbed a cup of coffee for himself and Mallory while she sat down next to Marilyn and set up her laptop. "We wanted to hear what your findings were from your inspection."

"This is just the preliminary, raw data, sir," Pike explained. "We haven't had time to come to any conclusions or make any recommendations yet."

Cain sipped his coffee and waved his hand, dismissing Pike's concerns. "Time is growing short so why waste it reading a report when I can get it firsthand. There's no time to form a committee to discuss options. The clock is ticking so we need to be able to take action now if we have to."

"Yes, sir, you're the boss." Pike continued, "To bring you up to speed, in a nutshell, K.D. reports that the port towing tower assembly is shot and unstable. In her words, a disaster waiting to happen." Pike noticed that neither Cain nor Mallory showed much reaction to the potentially bad news.

"As I was about to say, my findings aren't much better. As everyone is aware by now, there was an explosion in one of the access tunnels near the port anchor room. Fortunately, no one was seriously hurt and damage was negligible. Just before the explosion I found several large areas of the corridors covered with leaking juice."

"Juice?" Tony asked.

"Sorry, juice is the nickname for the heating/coolant fluid circulated throughout the iceberg. Juice is not supposed to be flammable so the burning cigarette that Senator Williams threw should not have ignited it. I've talked with Dean Miles and I've asked him for samples of the juice at both the main circulation point and at a random location to make sure nothing has been added to the mixture to make it flammable."

Cain's calm demeanor suddenly shattered. "What do you mean, added to the mixture? Are you saying the explosion was deliberate, that it was an act of sabotage?"

"I'm not saying anything yet, Mr. Cain; like I said, this is all raw data."

"Still," Cain continued, "that seems like a pretty big leap for just raw data."

"I'm just kicking ideas around sir. It could also be an accidental mixing, something caused by the stress from the storm. Or it could have nothing to do with the juice at all, but maybe something site specific to the construction in that corridor. Until we know for sure, I think caution is advisable."

Cain nodded his head in agreement. "I agree, but what form does caution take shape for you?"

That was the $64,000 question, Pike thought. He knew he had better choose his next words wisely. "As Chief Inspector, it is my responsibility to determine whether or not this project poses a threat to public safety. As we have seen, there are clearly issues of concern here; however, I am not ready to delay the project at this time. I also want it clearly understood that I will delay entry of the iceberg into New York harbor for as long as necessary if I deem the danger great enough."

"All right then," Cain said as he nodded to Mallory and she began shutting down her computer. "Thank you all for your hard work and I look forward to reading your report in depth and for your recommendations. Gabriel, please give your final draft to Marilyn and Elizabeth and I will go over it with her, being she's the liaison here."

Cain stood with Mallory by his side. "Any questions?" With none asked, they both disappeared.

As they left, Pike was having a hard time reading Cain's expression. He couldn't tell if he was upset or if he accepted his judgment.

But being unreadable, Pike figured, was how Cain got to be where he was. Still it made him feel a little uncomfortable not knowing where he stood with his boss.

As soon as Cain and Mallory left, Pike ordered another pot of coffee; it was going to be a long meeting.

"What's your gut reaction? Do you think Gabriel will postpone entry?" Cain asked Mallory as the two of them walked toward his office.

"Gabe is a good man and dedicated to his job. Whatever decision he makes, I'm sure he thinks it will be in the best interests of the public, but not necessarily in ours. Gabe has come a long way in understanding things outside his slide rule world but he still doesn't grasp the real big picture and what you are trying to accomplish here."

Cain reluctantly nodded and sighed. "I'm afraid you're right. I'm going to go talk to Miles and see what the status is on the repairs to the towing tower. What are you going to do?"

"Oh, I'm going to have much more fun than you are. I'm going to pay a visit to our favorite senator and try and talk a little sense into him. If I can find out what's bothering him then maybe I can reassure him. Then maybe he could talk some sense into Gabe."

"Keep me posted, and be careful. Pug's been acting a little strange lately, but with this whole explosion thing, it might just have pushed him over the edge."

"If I'm not back in an hour, send in the Marines. He'll need them."

CHAPTER THIRTY EIGHT

"Come in." Thornton said, hearing a knock on the door.

"Hi, Robert," Mallory said, stepping through the door.

"Hey, Beth, good to see you," Thornton said as he stepped out from behind his desk to shake her hand. "What brings you here?"

"After our conversation yesterday, I wanted to talk to Pug myself to see if we can straighten this whole thing out and put his mind at ease."

"Bobby!" Williams yelled as he stepped out of his office. As soon as he saw Mallory, his entire demeanor changed. "Well, well, to what do I owe the distinct pleasure of your company Ms. Mallory?"

"I came by to see how you were doing after the explosion and thought we could discuss a few things."

"By all means, please come in," Williams said, stepping aside and motioning her to come into his office. As she walked by, he turned to his aid. "Bobby, make sure we are not disturbed." As Williams disappeared into the office, Thornton could have sworn he saw a leer flash across his boss's face.

"Please sit down," Williams said, pointing to a large plush chair. As she sat down he went over to the bar and poured each of them a brandy.

"Your concern for my wellbeing overwhelms me," Williams said. "I didn't know you care so much."

Mallory felt her stomach churning as Williams flattered himself by thinking that she actually cared about him. "Senators often get roasted on Capitol Hill, though not quite so literally. I just wanted to make sure you weren't too well done."

"Well you can poke me with a fork but this old bird ain't done yet." He laughed. "Now as much as I would like to think that you really did come here to check up on my health, we both know that's only partly true. Now tell me, Beth, what really brings you to my lair?"

Mallory took a sip of her drink. "That's what I like about you, Senator, you always have good liquor and you're always straight and to the point."

Williams smiled and raised his glass.

"What's bothering you, Pug?" Mallory continued. "Why did you send Robert on that fishing expedition? If you have any concerns, why not just talk to Nigel or myself in person?"

"Bobby's an idiot."

Mallory shook her head. "You should give him a little more credit than you do; he's not as incompetent as you think."

"Thank you, Dr. Phil."

Mallory frowned. "Okay Pug, what gives?"

Williams put his drink down and leaned back in his chair, crossing his legs. "I don't think this is working for me anymore."

Mallory tilted her head, "What isn't working?"

"This!" He said waving his arms around, "This monstrosity Cain has created. I'm not buying his 'help for humanity' crap any longer."

"What *are* you talking about?"

"You and Cain are up to something here and I don't want to be a part of it. In fact, if you or your boy Pike try to sign off on this thing and cover up all the things wrong with this giant ice cube, I'll launch an immediate investigation and have this thing sitting outside the harbor so long that by the time the dust settles, you'll be able to bring it into port in a wine glass."

"Why are you doing this, Pug? What has gotten into you?"

Williams rose out of his chair, his face burning red with anger. "What's gotten into me? That's a good one! The question is what's gotten into you? Why did you and Cain try to kill me?"

"Try to kill you?" Mallory stared at the senator in disbelief.

"Don't play coy with me. You tried to kill me in the tunnel and make it look like an accident with that 'unexplained' explosion."

"No one tried to kill you, Pug," Mallory said, shaking her head. "If you remember, Nigel was standing right next to you and Gabe saved you both."

"Your boy just missed when he dove, accidentally taking me with him when he tackled Cain."

"Just listen to yourself, you're as bad as Gabe is with all his conspiracy theories. We have no reason to kill you, you're our partner. We're all working together for a common goal."

"Are we?" Williams said cynically.

"Yes, we are. Could Cain accomplish his goals without you? Yes he could, but it would be much more difficult and time consuming without your help. But more than that, you both share a political view, a view of the future and how this country should be run. How it should be back at the forefront as a world leader. You are both great men and together you can accomplish great things."

"And a chicken in every pot," he said sarcastically. "But you see, I too can achieve my goals without Cain's help, though as you said, it will take more time, effort, and yes, money. But the glory I obtain will be mine and mine alone. I won't have to answer to anyone else or fear anyone trying to pull my strings."

"No one is trying to kill you or to undermine your political objectives, Pug. We are all on the same side here.."

"I know that you believe in Nigel and in his work, and it would be a great shame for him to be humiliated like this. I want to believe you, Beth, I really do," Williams said as he moved closer and sat down on the corner of the desk, his voice taking on a more conciliatory tone. "I need assurances, Beth, that this isn't just a game that your boss is playing."

"I can assure you, Senator, that this is no game, that Nigel is sincere in his beliefs and goals."

"Can you assure me?" Williams said, as he put his hand on her shoulder. "Can you show me *your* sincerity?"

Mallory slowly stood and placed her hands on Williams' shoulders and looked into his eyes. "I guess there is only one way," she whispered softly.

The lustful smile beginning to form on Williams' face never matured but was replaced in an instant with a look of horrible pain as Mallory's right knee smashed into his groin. Before he could collapse in pain to the floor, Mallory shoved him back so hard he hit the chair and both he and it went flying over backwards. She walked around to the other side of the desk and placed her knee against his throat.

"Now you listen to me you arrogant, pompous little ass," she said in a calm but assertive voice. "How dare you think you can stand in the way of Nigel's greatness or question the worthiness or sincerity of his dreams? And how dare you think that I would lower myself to sleep with you if you promised to protect Nigel when we both know you had no intention of following through on that promise?"

Williams struggled to speak but Mallory just drove her knee harder into his throat. "No one was trying to kill you in the tunnel, you idiot, it *was* an accident. Now listen and listen to me good. You will continue on just as you have been in supporting Nigel and his projects and he will continue to support you. And don't you even think for one moment that you can double-cross me. I have so much dirt on you that I can grow enough food in it to feed your home state of New York. And after the media wolves have torn you apart and your wife has left you and your life lies in ruins, I'll start all over again."

She stood and immediately Williams rolled over and started coughing. "Life can continue happily along or you can follow your own delusions of grandeur and face the very unpleasant conse-quences." On her way out she grabbed her brandy. "Thanks for the drink, Pug, I enjoyed our little talk. We'll have to do it again some time." She finished the rest of it then set the glass down, and calmly walked out of the room.

CHAPTER THIRTY NINE

"This is either a really late lunch or a really early dinner," Pike said as he sat down.

"I don't care what you call it, I'm starved," K.D. replied.

The pair was seated in the Crystal Palace overlooking the ocean. They watched the *Alyssa B.* as she gently rose and fell, riding the slow moving swells, followed by a squadron of seagulls.

"You look, ah, different today," Pike said, sipping his water.

"Different how? Different good or different bad?" Slight misgiving floated in her voice.

"Oh, different good, definitely good."

She smiled shyly.

"Hello, Mr. Pike, Miss," the waiter said as he came up.

"Hi, Brad, I think I'll have the fish-n-chips and a root beer please. K.D?"

"I'll just have a small chicken salad please."

Brad nodded and left.

"What do you think Marilyn will do?"

"What do you mean?" Pike asked.

"I mean with our recommendations. Do you think she'll take them for what they are and recommend we hold off on entering the harbor until the safety issues can be addressed or will she whitewash our findings?"

"We're engineers, that's our world. Marilyn isn't, but she knows enough to see that we're right. However, there are political ramifications here that I don't think we understand but she does; that's more her world. To us it's black and white; to her, she can see some grey."

The food arrived and the conversation waned as they both began eating. After several bites, K.D. continued: "Let me ask you this, Gabe: while we discovered major safety issues, do you really think them significant enough and a great enough threat to public safety to keep the iceberg out of the harbor? Couldn't you let Cain have his day then fix the issues later?"

Pike put down his piece of cod and sighed. "I've been giving that a lot of thought lately. We've all heard the expression, 'if this law or this feature can save just one life, then it's worth it.' My question is: is it? It sounds good but in reality it is seldom the rule, and more often than not, the exception. You've seen the statue of Lady Justice, a scale in one hand and a sword in the other?"

K.D. nodded.

"Our jobs are like that statue, a balancing act. We weigh the value of the dollar against the value of public safety. Sometimes the scales are heavily weighted one way or the other, making our jobs easier. Other times the scales are nearly balanced, making our decisions very difficult. At that point we have to become Vegas bookies, trying to determine the odds as best we can to justify our decision."

"Wow, I was just looking for a basic yes or no answer." She smiled.

Pike laughed. "I know I tend to over think things at times, my only flaw in an otherwise perfect personality," he added, smiling and looking at K.D., who just rolled her eyes. "But seriously, you and I both know that if the iceberg is allowed in the harbor, it's not moving, they won't tow it back out for repairs. The biggest danger is not letting it into the harbor, it's allowing it to stay.

"When the meltdown process starts, that's when the danger magnifies. Without proper bracing, once the ice starts to melt I can almost guarantee you that the towing towers will collapse. What if a commuter ferry or a service barge is too close when a tower falls? What would happen to a work crew inside the berg if the anchor pops out, dragging tons of steel chain behind it? But the biggest unknown to me is what caused the explosion? Everyone from Miles to Mallory to Cain himself has assured me that the juice being pumped through this thing like blood is not the cause. Then what is?

"But at the end of the day, if something does go wrong, it's my name on the report. I will be blamed if something happens, if someone dies. Saying I protested it being brought in will only go so far in court... and with my conscience, I'll have to fight tooth and nail to absolve either one if I feel that strongly about it."

"Do you?"

"Despite what Mallory and Cain think, I really do see the big picture here, and surprisingly, I'm leaning toward letting it in IF they can provide me with a reasonable explanation for what caused the explosion and their assurances that it won't happen again. That is the deal breaker for me."

Pike laid his napkin down and moved his plate away, having lost his appetite. "I'm sorry K.D., this was supposed to be a light, old-friends-catching-up lunch and here I am burdening you with my woes."

"It's okay," K.D. said, as she placed her hand on his.

"Thanks." They held hands, and for a moment everything seemed to disappear around them, until Brad came back with their dessert. Embarrassed, they both pulled back their hands. As she did, K.D.'s bracelet snagged on her napkin, tipping over her water glass. In her rush to get out of the way of the flowing water, she tugged on the tablecloth, knocking over the candle.

"I'm sorry, I'm such a klutz," she apologized.

"Nonsense," Pike replied as he reached over to the next table and grabbed another napkin to help clean up the spill. When he turned back to the table, the candle had fallen over and the flame was resting on one of the ice cubes that had spilled out of K.D.'s drink, but instead of putting out the flame, the ice cube itself was actually burning. He studied it for a second then quickly put it out, then grabbed it and wrapped it in the napkin then shoved it into his pocket. Neither K.D. nor Brad had seen it.

"Where did you get these ice cubes?" Pike questioned the waiter.

"Sir?"

"I said, where did you get the ice cubes?" Pike's tone was so harsh it caught K.D.'s attention.

"Gabe? What's wrong?" She questioned.

"Brad, the ice cubes?"

Concern filled the young waiter's eyes, not sure if he was in trouble but he answered anyway. "We used up all the regular ice filling the hole during the storm and the icemaker broke. The guests were complaining about not having any ice so I've been chipping it out of one of the service tunnels near the food locker. No one's complained," he quickly threw in, hoping it would keep him out of trouble.

Pike dashed out of the restaurant, leaving a confused waiter and an even more confused friend behind.

Cain was standing on his observation level watching a lone seagull soaring around the tower, surfing the air currents.

"Becoming Jonathon Livingston Seagull, are we?"

Cain turned around and smiled. "I would, but I've seen what they eat," he said to Mallory. She went over and poured herself a drink as Cain came down the stairs. "I see you're still in one piece, I'll tell the Marines to stand down."

Mallory poured a second glass and handed it to Cain. "How did your talk with the senator go?" he asked. "Did you set his mind at ease?"

"We are all on the same page now and he has a clear view of what our expectations are."

"Excellent. You are my best negotiator, Elizabeth, always choosing the right words at the right time."

"Thank you, I do try to look out for your best interests."

Just then they heard the door slam against the wall as Pike came rushing through like a linebacker going after the quarterback.

"I think we have a major problem on our hands," Pike shouted, trying to catch his breath.

"Calm down, Gabriel. What are you talking about?" Cain said as he went over and guided Pike to a chair.

"It wasn't the juice; it's something in the ice itself."

"You're not making any sense, Gabe," Mallory said, leaning down beside him. "Start from the beginning."

Pike took two more deep breaths then recounted the events at dinner, the spill, the candle, the burning ice and where it came from. He ended by taking the napkin out of his pocket and unwrapping it, revealing what turned out to be a wet spot and a piece of ice about the size of a tooth.

Cain took the tiny shard and placed it on a coaster and tried to light it. They all watched expectantly but instead of igniting the chunk, the flame simply melted it.

"I know what I saw," Pike said. "The piece here is probably too small to burn. But don't you see? It wasn't the juice that was flammable; there is something in the ice itself that burns!"

"So you're telling me that this entire iceberg is made of, well, ice that can catch fire?" Mallory said, her voice heavy with skepticism.

"This isn't regular ice, remember? It's a blend of water, wood fibers and whatever else you put in it to strengthen it and retard melting. There must be something in the mixture that when combined is flammable. Until we find out what that is, we don't dare sail into New York harbor or any other harbor for that matter. In an enclosed harbor setting do you know what would happen if the entire iceberg caught on fire or exploded? The damage would be catastrophic."

"Aren't you overreacting just a little here?" Mallory asked. "We don't even know what we have here yet and you already have half of New York going up in a ball of fire."

"That's the point! We don't know what we have here. We're two days out. I'm sorry, but if we can't come up with an explanation and a solution to the burning ice, I'm afraid I can't approve the entrance to the harbor. I know there is a lot at stake here, Mr. Cain, I really do, but I think you would agree that the safety of thousands of people is more important than meeting a deadline."

"Are you serious, Gabe?" Mallory said, anger replacing the skepticism in her voice. "I don't understand. We can't and won't shut down this immensely important project just because you had a Moses at the burning bush experience."

"Mallory, please," Cain said looking at his assistant. "I believe Gabriel here is sincere in his belief that there may be a hidden danger built into the iceberg but," he looked at Pike, "I'm not entirely convinced of it either. We still have time to investigate further and gather our facts to make an informed decision when the time comes.

"Now then, did K.D. or Brad see the ice burning or does anyone else know about this?"

Pike shook his head. "I don't think so. I think they were too busy cleaning up the table to notice and I took off in such a hurry I didn't have time to relay my suspicions."

Cain nodded his head, "Good, let's keep it that way. We don't need to raise any suspicion or create a panic until we have all the facts. Agreed?"

Both Mallory and Pike nodded their heads.

"Excellent. Elizabeth and I will start the ball rolling on our end."

"What am I going to tell K.D.? She must think I'm nuts from the way I ran out of there."

"Just tell her you got back to back pages, one from me and one from Nigel, and you were confused. She'll believe that," Mallory said.

Pike frowned at her. "Thanks a lot."

Mallory just winked at him.

"Now, now, children, play nice," Cain interjected.

"Seriously, I wouldn't say anything at all." Mallory continued, "In fact, I don't think you should see her for the rest of the day. Don't you have some work to do or is this just the Love Boat? Don't worry," her tone softened a bit, "I'll tell her I'm being a slave driver and that you haven't earned time off for good behavior yet."

"Understood. I'll keep you posted," Pike said as he turned and left.

Mallory couldn't help smiling; he looked like a dejected puppy.

As Pike left, Cain turned to his assistant. "I'm going to go talk to Miles to see what he has to say about all this. You?"

"The clock is running, I'm going to talk to Marilyn to see if she has any insights into all of this, see if there was anything in their reports from this morning. I'll check in with you later."

Cain nodded as he went out the door and Mallory headed toward the phone on the desk.

CHAPTER FORTY

"Beth, hold up a second," Robert Thornton called out. Mallory was walking down the outside walkway but not paying attention to the beautiful scenery; her mind was on other things.

"Hi, Robert," she replied, barely breaking stride.

"I need to talk you," he said as he ran the last few steps to catch up to her.

"Can this wait? I have an important meeting to get to."

"It's about the senator."

Something in the tone of his voice made her stop and for the first time she looked at him and saw the worry and concern on his face.

"What about the senator?" she asked cautiously.

Thornton shook his head. "I don't know what happened between you two in the office or what you talked about, but when I came back he was furious. I have never seen him that angry before. He had kicked over his chair and was pacing back and forth like a raging bull. His face was so flush with anger that I thought he was going to have a heart attack.

"As he was pacing, he kept muttering something like, they can't do this to me, who do they think they are, stuff like that. He told me to call a press conference for first thing in the morning, then he ordered me out. When I tried to talk to him, to ask him what was wrong, he swore at me with words I never heard before and if I hadn't left that second, I think he would have come over and physically kicked me out."

"What time did you call the press conference for?"

"At 9am. He's going to use his pull and have it interrupt regularly scheduled programming."

"It's okay," Mallory said, placing her hand on his shoulder, "you did the right thing by telling me."

"What's going on, Beth? I've never seen him like this before and quite frankly, it scares me a little."

"Don't worry. You know Pug when he goes off on one of his tangents. By tonight he'll be yelling at you for calling the press conference, telling you you shouldn't have listened to him when he's upset. I'll have Nigel talk to him later tonight and get this whole thing ironed out. In the meantime, I suggest you lay low and keep this under your hat for now. When this all blows over, the less anyone knows the less embarrassment there will be to go around."

"Thanks, Beth, I really appreciate your help and advice."

She smiled at him. "We underlings have to stick together."

He nodded and turned and left. As soon as he had turned, the smile on Mallory's face vanished. "Tick tock," she said to herself as she continued to her office.

Mallory was at her desk working on her computer when she heard a knock and her secretary stuck her head in and told her that Marilyn was here. "Thanks, Cindy, send her in in five minutes please."

Mallory was still at her keyboard when Marilyn was brought in. Mallory motioned for her to sit down but continued to work. Again, she was setting the tone for the meeting by making her wait.

"Thanks for coming, Marilyn. We have a lot to discuss, so if you don't mind, I'll get right to it."

"By all means," Marilyn replied.

"You know Gabe pretty well, though not as much as you'd like to. Once he has his mind made up, can he be swayed to change it?"

Marilyn thought the phrasing of Mallory's question was a little strange but ignored its implications and answered the question. "It depends. He can be a little stubborn at times but he's generally open to any suggestions. But if he's passionate about his ideas at the time and he *knows* he's right, then no amount of talking can dissuade him."

"I bet you'd like to know a little more about his passion," Mallory said conversationally then continued right on. "So having read his report and knowing him personally, if he decided not to sign off on the project to allow the berg into New York, no amount of logic would change his mind?"

Marilyn felt herself growing angry at Mallory's questions and her innuendoes about her and Gabe. Still, she bit her tongue knowing the importance of the contract with Mr. Cain. She shook her head. "I'm afraid that once his mind is made up and he sees it as a righteous cause, then nothing can change it."

"Too bad he doesn't have his mind on you."

Contract or not contract, she'd had enough. "What's this all about?" Marilyn said, proud of herself for keeping most of the anger out of her voice. "What's with the double meanings and what does my relationship with Gabe have to do with this project?

Mallory leaned back in her chair looking Marilyn straight in the eye. "What I'm trying to do is to get into the mind of one of my employees, to understand their thought processes on how they make their decisions. Take you, for example: you are a very beautiful and desirable woman, every sailor's dream, yet time and again, Gabe has spurned your advances. And now it looks like K.D. is going to succeed where you've failed. They had lunch together today, you know. Don't get me wrong; K.D. is not a bad looking woman, but come on, she's not even in the same league as you.

"When this is all over and you get back to your office, are you going to fire her because of your pride or will you keep her because she's a good engineer? So, Marilyn, how does it make you feel that she won and you lost?"

Mallory could see that Marilyn wanted to explode but to her credit she channeled her anger. "I didn't lose anything. I can't help it if Gabe made the wrong choice. Besides, I don't want to marry him so how could I lose, that's not the goal here. And to answer your question, I'll fire her within the first week we get back, citing the company's policy of not dating coworkers."

"So you'd get rid of the competition."

Marilyn laughed smugly. "What competition? Does that answer your question about my mindset?" She smirked.

"Well it answers one of them but we have one more key item on my agenda to discuss." Mallory leaned forward and slid a piece of paper across the desk in front of Marilyn then held up her finger to suspend the conversation, then called her secretary on the intercom. "Cindy, would you bring us some sandwiches and coffee? We're going to be here a while."

"What's this?" Marilyn asked.

"It's the sign-off sheet for the iceberg inspection."

CHAPTER FORTY ONE

"Tick-tock," Mallory said as she walked into Cain's office, looking at her watch.

"What was that?" Cain asked.

"Nothing," Mallory muttered as she walked by and started rummaging through her desk.

"Is everything okay?"

"It will be soon enough."

Cain was puzzled by her response, but didn't pursue it.

"Listen, Nigel," Mallory continued," if you don't mind, I need you to wine and dine Gabe tonight, work that old Cain charm on him to see if we can do this the easy way and have him sign off on the inspection."

"I'm good." Cain smiled. "But I don't think that even I can persuade Gabriel to sign."

"We'll you at least need to try. Ah, here it is," Mallory said, taking a small card out of her desk and shoving it into her pocket.

"You've got that look," Cain said, looking at his assistant suspiciously. "I've seen it before; you've got something up your sleeve." Mallory just looked at him and smiled. "What time would you like me to work this miracle?"

"You know me all too well," she said innocently. "If everything goes according to plan, between six and seven-thirty should do fine."

"Do I even want to know?"

"Do you?"

Cain thought about it for a moment. "Not really."

"Good choice. If anything changes, I'll let you know." She smiled and turned, disappearing out the door.

"Tick-tock," he said quietly as he watched her leave.

Robert Thornton looked up in surprise and suddenly grew very nervous as he saw Mallory walking through the office door.

"What are you doing here?" he asked.

"Is the senator in?"

"Yes, but you can't go in there. He's finally calmed down and he's stopped yelling and throwing things."

"I'll be in there less than a minute."

"But..." Thornton started to protest but Mallory shoved him aside and went in, locking the door behind her. When Williams saw her, his eyes sprung open, first in fear then in rage. He started to reach for something on his desk to throw at her but there was nothing left. Before he could utter a sound, she spoke.

"I'm sorry, Senator Williams, for my actions earlier today; there is no excuse for my behavior other than my passion for my work, something I'm sure you can understand. I come waving a white flag and I bear a peace offering." She paused to read his expression. He was still angry but he was still Pug Williams, so the gesture of a peace offering held him at bay for the moment.

Mallory slowly walked over to the desk and laid down a room cardkey. "I have someone who would like to meet you. She is a *very* big fan. She also understands the meaning of discretion and knows that there may never be another opportunity like this for her to be able to see you and spend time with you. She's also asked me to tell you that she is a little shy about all this and not to be alarmed when you enter the room and find it dark.

"This is a small iceberg, so timing is critical in order to assure discretion for both parties. Please arrive promptly at seven."

"Who is it?"

Mallory smiled coyly. "I'm not going to tell you, though you could find out if you really wanted to, but then that would spoil the anticipation, wouldn't it? Trust me, you won't be disappointed. And, to anticipate your next question, no this is not a trap or a set up. The offer is genuine and she is real."

She bowed slightly as she backed toward the door. "Again, my apologies and I hope this will mend some of the fences I tore down." Mallory left the office and walked passed a stunned Thornton who expected World War III to start. After Mallory left, he rushed into the office half expecting to see the senator lying on the floor in a pool of blood. Instead, he was sitting quietly at his desk wearing a strange smile.

CHAPTER FORTY TWO

"Thanks for asking me out for drinks." K.D. said, sitting at the bar in the Crystal Palace, sipping on a rum and coke. She was looking down through the acrylic ice counter top of the bar at a prehistoric fish frozen in the ice. It was about two feet long with tiny eyes and an extended jaw with razor sharp protruding teeth and a tail like an eel. She smiled to herself. She didn't know why, but it reminded her of her high school drama teacher.

"The boys aren't the only ones who need to unwind after a tough day at the office," Mallory replied.

"Here, here!" K.D. said as they raised their glasses in a toast.

"This must be a little bit different work than you're used to back home."

"You can say that again. We don't get many exciting projects, though we did do a little work on the implosions of the Kingdome and then some work on Qwest and Safeco Field."

"Oh, I almost forgot, I've arranged a little surprise."

"Really?" K.D. replied, not trying to hide her excitement. "What is it?"

"It's not a what, but a who, and I don't think you'll be disappointed." She winked. "Schedules are tight and there are more snooping eyes and ears on the barge than at grandma's quilting bee, so timing is everything." Mallory looked at her watch. "It's six now.

We'll hang out here for another twenty minutes, then you head back to your place and be there at exactly 6:30."

"This is kind of exciting." K.D. said.

"Here, let me freshen up our drinks, I'll be right back." Mallory grabbed both their glasses and headed toward the bar. She looked backed and smiled at K.D. who was in her own little world, thinking about what the evening had in store for her. The bartender refilled their drinks, and while no one was looking, Mallory took a small vial out of her pocket and poured it into K.D.'s drink.

Mallory glanced at her watch as she returned to the table and handed K.D. her drink. "Bottoms up."

K.D. was feeling woozy and a little light headed when she reached her door. With her head spinning, it took her three tries to swipe her keycard though the lock. With the door open, she staggered into the room like a drunken sailor on leave. She couldn't understand why she was feeling this way; she knew she hadn't had that much to drink. She saw a flash of movement out of the corner of her eye and started to call out Gabe's name. She wanted to apologize to him for being this way, for ruining his surprise, but she never got the chance. The last thing she saw wasn't Gabe's face, but a dark blur swing toward her head, then a sharp pain in her temple. Then darkness.

Marilyn Talbot strategically placed the brass candleholder she had just hit K.D. with on the floor beside the bed.

"Pick her up and throw her on the bed," she said.

Tony Roberts felt like throwing up as he looked down at his lifeless coworker. "I-I didn't sign up for this," he said, his voice trembling.

Marilyn calmly walked over to him then shoved him hard, pinning his neck against the wall with her left forearm and grabbing his crotch in a death grip with the other.

"Listen, lover boy, you were all hot to trot when the lights were down low; now it's time to pay the piper. You're in this now just as deep as I am and I can't do this alone."

She loosened her grip, going from terminator to temptress. "Listen, Tony we're making a lot of money here, a lot of money. Just think of the freedom we'll have with this money, think of all the things we can do together." She leaned forward and kissed him hard and passionately, but even while kissing him she knew it was a lie; she was already getting bored with him.

Tony struggled as he dragged K.D.'s body to the bed, then picked her up and tossed her on it. He straightened up and rubbed his lower back. "They make this look so easy on television." Marilyn ignored his comment and tossed him a small package.

"What's this?"

"Pantyhose. Lay her out on the bed and tie one hand with it to the bed post, then rip open her blouse."

"What?" he nearly shouted. "I can't do that."

"You're pathetic," Marilyn said as she shoved him out of the way and ripped the shirt. "Now tie up her hand, you idiot." She shoved him in the chest then went back over to the table and pulled a small vial out of her bag and hid it under the cloth napkin that was sitting beside a bottle of champagne and two glasses.

"What is that?" Tony asked, seeing her hide the vial.

"It's GHB. It's a date rape drug; that's why we're doing all this. The wine, tying her up, the torn blouse, we're making this look like a plan that went horribly wrong. Now hurry up, we don't have much time."

Marilyn walked over and laid one of the chairs at the table over on its side then tipped over one of the lamps beside the bed. She looked at it for a moment then decided to stomp on it, breaking it into pieces. She stepped back and studied the room for a moment, like an artist studying her canvas. Putting on the finishing touch, she filled one of the champagne glasses half full, then knocked it over.

Satisfied, she began looking in her bag, and then patted her pockets, "Do you have the knife?" She asked.

Tony nodded, then reached into his pocket and pulled out a red Swiss Army Knife. "Who are we setting up?" he asked.

Marilyn grinned wickedly. "The man who owns that knife."

Senator Harlen "Pug" Williams walked confidently but quietly down the hallway, his mind overflowing with curiosity and lust. Mallory was right, the thrill and mystery of the unknown heightened his anticipation, but this wasn't his first rodeo and he was no fool by taking Mallory's peace offering at face value.

Although he had Bobby do most of the work on the computer, he was pretty handy with the keyboard, a fact that he liked to keep to himself, and with a little digging he was able to verify the name on the cardkey. As he opened the file and checked the registration, he was surprised at who it was. At first, he had thought it might have been a bored socialite or even that young blonde reporter, Tab, Tabby, whatever her name was, but it wasn't.

Looking at her registration picture she was not the kind of woman who usually did things like this, but sometimes the quiet ones were the most passionate. The more he looked at her picture, the more his lust grew and best of all, he knew Mallory had not set him up, that this was the real deal. After all, she wouldn't want to expose their little rendezvous and risk tarnishing the reputation of their golden boy.

As he casually strolled, he had several well-practiced, polished, and believable reasons why he was walking alone in this part of the barge at this time of night. As he rounded the corner he saw the door and his heart skipped a beat. Would the encounter be met with wild abandon, would it take on the form of shy flirting or would he have to woo her and overcome any hesitation or second thoughts? Oh, the thrill of the hunt!

He came to the door and looked at his watch: seven on the dot. If nothing else, he was a punctual man. With a lustful grin, he opened the door and quickly stepped through, closing it behind him. As promised, the lights were off and he stood there for a moment, letting his eyes adjust to the darkness. "Hello?" he said quietly.

"I'm over here." He heard the sound of a soft, feminine voice calling him. With eager anticipation, he took one step forward then felt a powerful hand grasp his mouth and pull his head back. Before he had time to react, he felt a sharp pain penetrate his chest, then another and another. He felt the hands release their grip and he crumpled to the floor.

As he lay there gasping for breath, he knew he was dying. The last thoughts he had were not of his wife or family but of disappointment because he would never become president and he died wondering who would fill his vacant seat in the senate.

Marilyn turned on the lights and looked at the senator lying on the floor. She bent down and ruffled his hair, untucked his shirt a little and undid his belt buckle. Then she stood in front of the senator's body, held up the knife and dropped it. "That should do it."

She looked over at Tony. "You don't look as queasy this time. Easier second time around, lover?"

"Not easier, just different because I didn't know him."

"Yeah, well you can drown your sorrows while baking in the sun on the deck of a 150 foot yacht floating in the blue-green waters of the Mediterranean."

A slow smile crept to Tony's face. "I wanna drive."

Marilyn reached up and patted him on the cheek, "Of course you can. Now let's double check the room and get out of here. I have to get back to my room and call George; I want to check on my cats, I think Bubbles has worms."

CHAPTER FORTY THREE

Pike was feeling good about himself as he walked down the hall. Professionally, his career was probably shot. He had just said no to the richest man in the world and he had no doubts that if he wanted to, Cain could ruin him. But he was also grateful to Cain for helping him realize that money can't buy everything, especially integrity, self-esteem, self-respect, and a clear conscience knowing that he did the right thing for the right reason.

On the flip side, his personal life was looking better and better. He had also discovered that while you could go through life alone, what was the point? People were what mattered, not the almighty dollar. Easy to say now while he still had two nickels to rub together but a principle he knew was true. He wasn't afraid anymore.

He took a deep breath as he stood outside K.D.'s door. He didn't know if she felt the same way but there was only one way to find out. With fear, hope, dread, and a thousand and one other emotions, he knocked.

As he did, the door popped ajar. He stuck his head in and knocked again, calling her name. The room was dark so he flipped on the light. Nothing in the world, in the universe, could have prepared him for what he saw. He was stunned and frozen in place. K.D. was lying on the bed, one hand tied to the bedpost and her shirt ripped open. The room was a shambles and Senator Williams was on the floor, floating in a pool of blood.

His eyes were seeing, but his mind was having a hard time comprehending the message they were sending his brain. Pike felt emotions surging inside him. He didn't know if they were fear, anger or revenge, but they burst through like a lightning bolt, freeing him from his frozen indecision.

He leaped over the senator's body and rushed to K.D.'s side. He was hoping she was just unconscious but when he touched her face, her head fell to one side, revealing a blood soaked pillow and the entire side of her head covered and caked with dried blood.

"No, no, no," he heard himself saying over and over. At least he thought the voice was his, it sounded so faint and far away, so lost. "What had happened here? Who did this to you, K.D.? Who?" His eyes drifted over to the Senator on the floor. "Did you do this to her or did you try to save her and they killed you too?" He didn't know if he should hate the man or be grateful to him. It added all the more to his confusion. Right now he desperately wanted to hate someone but he didn't know who to channel his hatred towards.

As he looked at the body of the senator sprawled out on the floor, something caught his eye. He tried to move but his legs suddenly felt like they were made of lead and weighed a thousand pounds each. Feeling more like a machine than a man, he managed to move one foot in front of the other until he was standing in front of the familiar object. He bent down and picked it up. It was a Swiss Army Knife, *his* Swiss Army Knife. He had had it this morning. How did it end up here?

Quiet down now please." Mallory was flanked by two reporters and their film and sound crews. They were moving down one of the hallways in the guest quarters section of the iceberg. Mallory continued. "As much as he's been in the news lately, Gabriel Pike is still a man of mystery to many of your viewers and they want to know more about the man behind the leather jacket. Package it however you want, but as promised here's an inside look at what Gabe does on his off time. As some of you may have heard, there's romance brewing in our hero's life."

The group of reporters followed Mallory around the corner and entered the hallway that led to K.D.'s room. "We're in luck," Mallory whispered, "the door's open and the lights are on." The two groups quietly made their way to either side of the door. Mallory silently giggled as she held her finger up to her lips and pointed at the door. As soon as the groups were ready, Mallory pushed it open and stepped through. "Hi Gabe and K.D.," she said in a loud voice, "I hope you two are decent because you have…"

Mallory stopped speaking in mid-sentence then let out a horrific scream when she saw Pike standing over Williams' body with the knife in his hand. Both film crews rushed in and began filming the grizzly scene.

Pike looked up at Mallory after she screamed. "Help me…" His voice was faint and sorrowful.

"What did you do?" Pike heard a voice scream.

Pike looked over to the reporter who asked the question, "Tabatha, is that you?" Pike was still in a daze when he heard another man standing in front of the camera speaking.

"We don't have all the facts yet but it appears that the popular figure, Gabriel Pike, also known to millions as the Blast from the Past, has killed Senator Harlen Williams, in an apparent fit of jealous rage in a lover's triangle gone horribly, horribly wrong."

"WHAT!" Pike shouted. The reporter making the newscast may not be responsible for K.D.'s death but Pike now had someone to focus at least part of his anger on.

"How dare you? How dare you make a statement like that? I didn't kill anyone. You call yourself a reporter? You walk into a room and make a snap judgment like that in five seconds?"

The reporter signaled to his cameraman to keep rolling, then he turned around to face Pike. Pike's eyes grew wide when he saw that it was the Toupee Man, Peter Wright.

"Hey buddy, I'm not the one standing over a dead body with the murder weapon in my hand and it wasn't my girlfriend playing stuff the ballot box with the senator."

"Why you son of a…" Pike said, taking a step forward.

"GABE!" Mallory shouted. "Stop! Just stop and put the knife down please! We can talk about this."

Suddenly Pike realized what all this must really look like with him standing with a knife in his hand then moving toward the Toupee Man with it. With a huge sigh, he set the knife down and raised his hands. "I know what this must look like but I didn't kill anyone and K.D. was not sleeping with the senator," he said, glaring directly at Wright.

"Okay, everyone. Let's just all take a deep breath here and take a step back." Mallory said. "Gabe, I've called Nigel and he's sending a couple of the crew to escort you back to his office until we can get this whole thing sorted out. Are you okay with that?"

"Yes! Yes, yes! I want to know what happened here more than any of you."

"Yeah, right."

Pike heard Toupee Man mutter under his breath, which really wasn't that quiet. He knew he was baiting him and it was all he could do not to rip the man's head off. "Yes I do," he replied as calmly as he could.

"Good. Ah, here they are now." Just then, two crewmembers Pike didn't recognize came in the door, one carrying a length of rope.

Pike looked at Mallory and shook his head in disappointment. "Is that really necessary?"

She looked at Pike and saw the hurt in his eyes. "No, but don't make me regret it, Gabe." She nodded, and the rope disappeared into the man's pocket.

"Thank you." Pike walked toward the door and everyone gave him a wide berth as he approached, all except Toupee, who stood where he was, making a statement to Pike by making him walk around him.

CHAPTER FORTY FOUR

"I like you Gabriel, I really do and I would do anything for you but even with all my money there's not a lot I can do when a news camera shows you standing over the dead body of a US Senator with a knife in your hand," Cain said, sitting behind his desk in his office.

"But I didn't kill him. Don't you believe me?" Pike pleaded.

Mallory shook her head. "It doesn't matter what we believe. What matters is what the evidence says."

"Remember when we first met?" Cain said. "I told you that we needed the public on our side, that to them, perception was everything? That's why we molded you into the Blast from the Past. So they would believe in and support this project. It was a bonus, a very nice bonus that you happened to live up to your billing."

"And the public perception of you now is that of a fallen hero," Mallory added. "We found a vial of GHB, a date-rape drug, on the table. It would appear that the senator used it on K.D., she resisted, he got carried away and killed her. You walked in on him, went insane with anger and killed him with your knife. I'm sorry, Gabe," Mallory said shaking her head sadly, "but the evidence is overwhelming."

"But I didn't do it."

You keep saying that," Mallory replied, "but what you say doesn't make any difference."

"As I said earlier," Cain continued, "I really do like you but unfortunately you are just too good at your job. Although I really don't think you can claim all the credit for your discovery because the chain of events that led us to this moment are a direct result of a butterfly effect."

Mallory rolled her eyes. "You and your butterfly effect."

Cain just frowned at Mallory, then continued. "Who would have thought that the simple act of spilling a glass of water would lead to the premature deaths of so many people?"

"Discovery? What discovery did I make and who else is dead?" Pike pleaded, more confused than ever.

Cain smiled at Pike as he walked by slowly. He was smiling because at an early age he had learned that the old saying "knowledge is power" was true, and right now he held all the power because he had knowledge that Pike wanted so desperately. He stepped up to the bar where he took a silver martini shaker out of the refrigerator, took off the lid, and set it on the counter. Next, he grabbed a martini glass and poured four ice cubes into it.

"I think the term, hidden in plain sight, best fits this situation," Cain said, all the while, still smiling like the Cheshire cat. With glass in hand, he walked over and stood in front of the massive model of the iceberg he had used at his corporate headquarters when he first revealed his master plan to the press.

"Hidden in plain sight," he said making a grand sweeping motion over the model. "It's all around us." Cain enjoyed the confused look on Pike's face.

"What's all around us? What's hidden in plain sight?" Pike cried out in frustration.

Cain reached into his coat pocket and pulled out a cigarette lighter. He set the martini glass on top of the display case, then held the open flame from the lighter onto the top ice cube. To Pike's astonishment, the ice cube sprouted a tiny flame like a candle on top of a birthday cake.

Pike slowly stood and walked over and gazed at the burning ice cube much the same way Moses must have stared at the burning bush. "That's exactly what happened in the restaurant," Pike said, dumfounded.

"Amazing, isn't it?" Cain circled behind Pike, enjoying his bewilderment. "It's called methane hydrate."

"Methane? You mean like in swamp gas?"

"Yes," Cain said as he went back to the bar. "Methane hydrate, simply put, is methane gas trapped in water or ice. The methane is released when it warms up or the pressure on the ice is reduced. Frozen methane hydrate can contain 170 times its own volume of methane gas."

Pike thought for a moment, digesting what Cain had said, then he snapped his fingers. "That's it! That's what caused the explosion. There must be methane in the ice in the tunnel and when the cooling pipes ruptured, the ice melted just enough to release the vapors and Williams' cigarette ignited it."

Cain smiled and looked at Mallory. "I told you he was good."

Pike shook his head, "But why put such a dangerous and combustible gas into a project that would put it into such close proximity to a large population? Was it part of the process to keep the ice from melting? Surely you knew the dangers? If this entire iceberg were constructed with the methane hydrate, the potential for the level of destruction would be unimaginable. If it were to explode in New York harbor, the blast radius..." Pike's words trailed off as he began to realize the implications of what he was saying. He suddenly felt sick to his stomach. "So all this is..."

"A giant floating bomb," Cain said, finishing Pike's sentence.

"But how, why?"

"The *how* is a little complicated but being an engineer, I'm sure you'll appreciate how complex yet simple the idea is. Methane gas has great potential as a natural source for power and we discovered a huge deposit of the methane hydrate while doing exploratory drilling on the ocean floor.

"Methane hydrate is nothing new. President Clinton signed the Methane Hydrate Research and Development Act to help industry exploit the energy source. The original concept was to construct an iceberg of methane and float it to the States and process the methane there, but Legal was quick to point out that no city government, let alone the Coast Guard, would allow such a potentially dangerous and lethal cargo into any US port. It wouldn't be cost effective to build a processing plant on site, so plans were shelved."

Cain picked up the glass with the burning ice cube in it and swirled the cubes around. Instantly the other cubes caught fire and turned the glass into a mini bonfire. "In business, I have learned never to close the door on any project completely and to always look for options and opportunities. When I saw the television program about World War II I told you about when we first met, I instantly saw the potential.

"The entire structure of the iceberg is permeated with the methane hydrate. The center of the berg was purposely hollowed out to allow tens of thousands of cubic feet of the gas to accumulate until the time of detonation. As you guessed earlier, with a few simple additives, the juice will become extremely volatile, acting as an accelerant. The force of the explosion will level nearly everything within a one mile radius of ground zero while hundreds of secondary fires will be started by the falling debris and still burning chunks of ice."

Cain walked over and sat down in a leather recliner. "That's the *how*; the *why* is equally simple. This country is sick, Gabriel, and has been for quite some time. I'm tired of seeing this great nation tear itself apart with self-serving, mindless bickering; we have lost our focus. I'm also tired of seeing two-bit thugs who rose to power in third rate nations through murder and intimidation threaten us with blatant terrorism, all in the guise of religious intolerance.

"Even with all my money, there's only so much weight I can throw around outside the political arena. In order to do any good, any real good, I have to cut the cancer out from the inside."

"So you're a rich terrorist who wants to be elected so you can be a rich *and* crooked terrorist."

"Nigel is not a terrorist," Mallory spat out, "he's a patriot."

"I haven't looked it up in the dictionary lately, but I'm pretty sure that killing thousands of your own countrymen isn't considered being a patriot," Pike replied.

Mallory started to get up and Pike had the distinct feeling she was going to slap him, or worse, but a raised hand from Cain stopped her. Cain got up and walked back over to the bar, taking his time to defuse the situation a little. He reached for a bottle and a small brandy snifter and filled it halfway. He swished the amber liquid around in the glass then inhaled it deeply, a smile beginning on his face that blossomed into a full smile after he took a sip.

"Louis Royer Preference VSOP Cognac. Delicious. I'd offer you some but then again you don't drink. Pity really. Did you know the word Brandy is a Dutch word meaning 'burnt wine' because they boiled it to distill it?" Another whiff, another sip and another smile. "Even though the finest brandies in the world come from the Cognac region in France, I bet you didn't know that it has its origins in the Middle East starting sometime in the seventh or eighth centuries?"

"Oh, I'm sorry, I was wrong before," Pike said snidely, "I should have said you are a rich, crooked and *well-educated* terrorist." He looked over at Mallory and he could see that she was seething with anger but Cain calmly kept her at bay. "Okay, I understand you want political power, but how is destroying New York going to accomplish that? It's been tried once before and it didn't work then. Can't you just run for office like everybody else?"

"What happened in 2001 was the work of madmen; their only goal was senseless destruction."

"And you don't call this senseless destruction?" Pike nearly shouted.

Gain shook his head. "You lack vision, Gabriel," Cain continued. "The perfect example of what I'm trying to accomplish can be found in your own home town of Seattle. The Seahawks play in Qwest Field, a beautiful new stadium, but in order for it to have been built; the old Kingdome had to come down first. A lot of people didn't want to see the Kingdome go, but in the end, I think everyone would agree that the new Qwest field is a much better facility all the way around. Being an engineer you understand the need to raze the past in order to build the future.

"Great adversity or challenge brings this country together like nothing else can. You're a student of history. The attack on Pearl Harbor galvanized this nation like nothing else in history ever has. The modern equivalent to Pearl Harbor was the Twin Towers. In times of catastrophe, people look for heroes. Case in point: The name of Rudy W. Giuliani, the mayor of New York City at the time, skyrocketed to the forefront of national attention for his handling of the crisis both during and after the bombing. If you remember, he became so popular that he ran for president of the United States."

"So you want to become the president of the United States?"

"Eventually, yes. But like any complex plan, it will take time."

Pike shook his head. "But why would the people support you when it was your iceberg that caused all the misery and damage in the first place?"

"It will be my iceberg, but not my fault. What day is it?"

"It's the 10th."

"And tomorrow is…"

"September 11th."

"Exactly! That's why I needed to stay on such a tight time schedule. When the iceberg blows up in New York harbor on September 11th, everyone is automatically going to assume it was a terrorist attack. In this country, New York has become the symbol for terrorist attacks with the World Trade Center bombing in 1993 and then Twin Tower attack in 2001. But more importantly, it has become the symbol of defiance and freedom and the resolve of the American people against such attacks.

"I will use that justifiable pride when I convey my sorrows to the people of New York, ashamed that my vessel, which was meant to bringing hope, instead brought death and destruction, I will then publicly commit my personal fortune to rebuilding the city.

"Contrary to what you may believe, this is not some quick-fix plan hatched by a madman in a moment of outrage or indignation. I have been laying the ground work for this event for years. I have established an elaborate and extensive infrastructure all designed not only to consolidate my grip on power but to quickly bring the resources together to rebuild the city bigger and better than ever. In gratitude, the people will elect me to continue to lead them as governor, and from there I'll parlay my good will and experience and take the presidency. Once I'm in the Oval Office, with my new political clout and financial resources, I'll be able to weed out the corruption and rebuild and focus this country on issues that really matter, establishing the U.S. once again as the world leader. First New York... then the country... and then I'll rule the world!" He shouted, building to a crescendo, then bursting out in loud, deep laughter. Then he abruptly stopped and smiled as he looked at Pike.

"Sorry, Gabriel, I just couldn't resist."

Pike just shook his head. "But what does K.D., the senator or even me have to do with all this? Why kill them? How could they possibly be involved with your grand, twisted scheme to be president?"

"Their deaths are actually your fault," Mallory said, taking pleasure in her words.

"My fault?" The words stung as they came out of his mouth.

"You can actually blame all this on Nigel's damn butterfly theory," Mallory continued, "which he has done nothing but gloat about nonstop since it happened."

Pike just shook his head, not understanding but suddenly feeling guilty to think that he might somehow really be responsible for K.D.'s death.

"You were right on the edge of signing off on the safety inspection, then your stupid girlfriend tipped over that glass of water and that set the whole thing in motion. Once you knew there might be a fire danger, we knew your moral compass would be set and there would be no changing your course. For the public legitimacy of the project, we still needed the safety inspection signed off, so we had to discredit you so we could get a replacement signature with no questions asked. Marilyn and your little intern friend were more than willing to help.

"So, as you can see, Mr. High and Mighty, it really was your fault that she died because of your self-rightness and unwillingness to bend from your principals." Mallory calmly got up and walked over and slapped Pike hard in the face. "That's for calling Nigel a terrorist." She stared at him intently for a moment, then quickly turned around and poured herself a brandy.

She took a drink, held it in her hand and thought for a moment. "You know, it's kind of funny. You have high moral standards and convictions, and yet here you are, all but convicted of a heinous crime, and on the other hand, Marilyn, who has the morals of... well, you know, Marilyn is walking around free as a bird with tons of cash. Pretty screwed up world, huh, Gabe?"

"Marilyn helped you?" Pike asked in disbelief.

Mallory laughed. "She was more than willing to sell you out. In fact, she not only signed the inspection document allowing us to enter the harbor, but for a little extra cash, she was also willing to kill K.D. and the senator for us."

"Marilyn killed K.D.?" Pike said quietly.

"As I said earlier, since we knew you wouldn't sign we had to find a way to discredit you. Senator Williams was also becoming a liability and suddenly the opportunity to kill two birds with one stone presented itself, so we took it. Pug is a known womanizer so it was easy to set up the fake date rape scenario and to have you stumble across it. Pictures are worth a thousand words so the icing on the cake was having the news cameras there to catch you red handed. By the way, thank you for picking up the knife when you did. I couldn't have scripted it better myself."

"The film crews were in on it too? Tabatha?"

"Makes for a great conspiracy theory, huh? Hell hath no fury like a woman scorned, or a man with his toupee torn off." Mallory shook her head. "They weren't in on the original set up but being reporters, they were more than willing to help spread the news story once they saw what had happened."

Mallory sat back down in her chair, still nursing her brandy. "You should be proud, Gabe; your love triangle story preempted the President and his economic summit. 'The Blast from the Past Just Crashed!' Kind of catchy, don't you think? The newspapers love it."

"You'll never get away with it," Pike said.

Mallory and Cain looked at each other and burst out laughing.

"That's so cliché!" Cain roared. "I expected much better from you."

"Sorry." Pike shrugged his shoulders. "You'll understand if I'm not at the top of my game right now."

Just then the phone rang and Cain answered. He talked for a few moments then hung up. "That was Captain Gregory. He informs me that we should make landfall by the early morning hours and be anchored in the harbor by mid-morning. Allowing for all the fanfare, speeches and what not, everyone should be disembarked by 1pm, leaving the berg empty so the meltdown sequence can begin. It will take approximately three hours for enough vapors to build, filling the hold and all the tunnels. Detonation is set for 4pm, right before the afternoon commute, insuring maximum effect."

"You mean maximum carnage," Pike said flatly. "When are you going to kill me?"

"Again, straight to the point," Cain said smiling, "I really will miss you, Gabriel. I truly wish things would have worked out differently for you and me. To answer your question, you are a clever man and I can't take the chance of you escaping and causing any more trouble. I'd have you killed now, which is what I should do but I can't, you are still The Blast from the Past, so it must be done in the proper time and the proper way without raising any suspicions. For now, you'll be led from here to a holding area where later tonight, after things have settled down a bit, you will be shot while 'trying to escape.' Don't worry, I promise it will be quick and painless."

"Gee thanks," he replied sarcastically, "but don't you think that my being shot will raise a few questions?"

Cain shrugged his shoulders. "Possibly, but after the explosion, who's really going to care what happened to a murderer?"

"Can I go now?" Pike said standing up rather quickly. "I'm getting a headache." He noticed that when he stood, Mallory jumped a little. "What's the matter, Beth, a little nervous?"

"Goodbye, Gabe," was her simple reply.

CHAPTER FORTY FIVE

A moment later, a man dressed as a deckhand appeared in the door-way. Though he was dressed in overalls, Pike could tell by the way he carried himself that he was security through and through. Pike was a little miffed that Cain didn't think him enough of a physical threat to bring more than one guard. As they passed Cain's desk, he simply nodded to him as he left.

Once outside in the hallway, Pike thought about jumping the guy and trying to escape. He had never been in a fight before in his entire life but desperate times called for desperate measures. He quickly decided, however, that that was a bad idea. This man was profes-sionally trained and knew how to handle himself in situations like this. But looking into his eyes Pike could see more than a trained professional, he saw cruelty and malice that went beyond his train-ing. So in the end, he would still be a prisoner, only he would be beaten and battered.

They left the main corridor and came to a small service elevator that he didn't remember seeing on the schematics. They descended two floors then got off and followed several more small passage-ways. They passed several rat ladders and came to a small ice room next to an escape hatch.

During his tour, Miles had shown him the ladders and hatches. The ladders were used to travel between decks and were supposed to be used by the men who worked deep within the bowels of the ship as escape routes in case there was trouble. That's why they were called rat ladders, for the rats leaving the sinking ship.

The escape hatches were large, trashcan lid sized holes in the ice high above the waterline and were less than a foot thick. Beside each hatch were a sledgehammer and several lifejackets. In an emergency, the escaping crewmember would take the sledgehammer, smash a hole through the ice and escape.

The guard opened the door and, without even saying a word, shoved him into the dark room. Pike landed hard on the floor, hitting his shoulder and left knee. He lay there for a second, not letting his keeper provoke him. After a few moments, the guard just grunted and closed the door, disappointed that Pike didn't get up and fight.

Pike stood up and felt his way to the door and found the light switch. He turned it on and surveyed his new and probably last home. It appeared to be some sort of storage room that was hastily converted into a brig. Fortunately the entire room was lined with the same, one-inch thick corkboard panels used in all the ice rooms, so he knew he wouldn't freeze to death, not that he would be around that long to get the chance. There was a pile of canvas and plastic work tarps in the corner along with a bucket and mop, a stepladder, and an emergency flashlight plugged into the wall. In the center of the room was a single, bent metal chair that had his parka on it; how nice, Pike thought, Cain didn't want him to catch his death of cold before he shot him.

He quickly pulled on the jacket and sat down in the chair to appraise his situation. His first thought was to have a well-deserved pity party. After all, just a week ago his biggest concern was whether or not he would lose his pilot's license. Now he was in a life and death struggle with a madman who wanted to take over the world. Yeah, he deserved a pity party all right. He wondered if you served tea and crumpets with a party like that. He smiled to himself, and shook his head no; he didn't have time for self-indulgence.

Looking around he began to think if he could use anything in the storage room to help him escape. Sitting in the middle of the giant ice ship, he wondered if Geoffrey Pyke, Cain's inspiration, would be proud to see his dream had come true in Cain's monstrosity.

Suddenly Pike had an idea and he shot out of the chair as if it were electrified. He started pacing, talking quietly to himself as he brainstormed. Normally when he had a problem to solve, he would write out all the pros and cons of the idea. It helped him make more sense of the situation if he could actually see what his options were. But with no pen and paper at hand, pacing back and forth like an expectant father in a waiting room would have to do. Cain's inspiration had come from a man involved in WWII and so did his: the famous Jasper Maskelyne.

Maskelyne was a renowned magician used by the British during World War II to help them defeat the Germans. Maskelyne took the art of sleight of hand and transformed it to a whole new level. In Africa, he used paint, canvas and plywood to make tanks look like trucks, trucks look like tanks and he even created an entire army that didn't exist. His largest and perhaps most famous illusions were concealing the city of Alexandria and the Suez Canal from German bombers.

Pike mulled his idea over and over and knew that to escape he would have to create his own illusion. He had to make the guard see what he wanted him to see and *not* to see. Being tossed into the room while it was still dark was big plus; he was betting that his captor wasn't familiar with the room nor did he really care, which meant he could paint the scene with a blank canvas, so to speak.

Pike headed straight for the pile of tarps to see what props he had to pull off his own vanishing act. Much to his delight, he found an old toolbox buried underneath the pile. It contained a hammer, a couple of screwdrivers, some nails and a pair of pliers. He unrolled the canvas tarps, and all three of them looked clean and unused. He spread them out, took the hammer and a few nails out of the toolbox, then grabbed the ladder.

He took the first tarp and hung it on the far wall, being careful to cover the head of the nail with his sleeve to keep the pounding as quiet as possible. It fit the wall perfectly except for a small overlap at the bottom that he just folded under. He did the same thing on the other two walls and when he was finished, he stepped back and admired his handy work. The room looked empty and nondescript. Phase one was now complete.

He put the chair back in the middle of the room where it had been then he laid the ladder on the floor in the right corner and tucked the toolbox under it. He took out the hammer and the screwdrivers and hid them in the hem at the base of the canvas on the left and right walls in case the guard saw the box and decided to take it.

Now for the first test. Pike took a deep breath, then pounded on the door and shouted. He quickly stepped back and stood in front and just to the left of the chair. He heard the door unlock, then the door swung open and the guard came in. Pike studied him carefully as he walked in. His cold, dark eyes darted about the room, too fast to really take in any detail, all his attention was being focused on him. Perfect.

"What do you want?" the guard said in a gruff voice.

"It's very cold in here. May I please have a blanket?" Pike stood there with his arm at his side trying to look as docile as he could. The man stared at him for a moment then just turned around and shut the door without saying a word.

That went well, Pike thought to himself; the guard saw just what he expected to see. He had to work fast now before the guard came back. Pike quickly unburied the ladder then moved the canvas coverings on both sides of the room out six inches out from the wall and re-hung them from the ceiling. He quickly put everything back exactly the way it was originally, then sat down on the chair and waited. Phase two was done.

Pike had waited thirty minutes when he heard the lock rattle. He sprang to his feet and stood exactly where he was when he had asked for the blanket. With slightly less caution than he had before, the guard opened the door, saw Pike standing there and threw him the blanket.

"Thank you," Pike said. Just as the guard started to leave, Pike spoke again. "Would you please tell Mr. Cain that I would like my last meal. Being a civilized man, I'm sure he will understand. I would like a Porterhouse steak, bone in, please. It gives it extra flavor, I think. A whole lobster tail, baked potato with the works, tossed salad and a mug of root beer. Thank you." Again, the guard failed to say anything when he left.

As soon as the door shut, Pike grabbed the ladder and repeated his routine by moving the canvas walls out another six inches. After he finished, he returned everything to its exact location then sat down in his chair and waited. Forty-five minutes later, Pike's head was nodding as he fell in and out of sleep when he heard the keys turning in the lock. Instantly he was awake as he jumped to his feet and stood again, only five inches further to his right this time. With his heart pounding in anticipation, he watched as the guard opened the door and shoved a tray in then left. Pike let out a huge sigh of relief as once again the guard paid no attention to his surroundings and hadn't noticed the walls.

He picked up the tray and returned to his seat. Even though getting the food brought in was just part of his plan, it didn't mean he was going to let it go to waste. As he ate, he reviewed his plan. Like Maskelyne, his plan depended on deception. First, he gave the guard exactly what he expected to see; a beaten and broken man and an empty room. And each time the guard entered, the room looked just the same as it had the visit before. What he had failed to notice was that the room was now smaller. He had created a false wall that he could now hide behind and leap out and surprise the guard, which brought him to another point: could he kill the guard if he had to?

That was a question that had no easy answer. Could he kill another human being so that he could live? He knew without hesitation that if someone broke into his house and threatened his family, that person was gone. Was this the same type of situation? His mind wandered to K.D. and the way she looked laying on the bed. She had no part in this; she was just an innocent bystander. Suddenly, the emotions of seeing her like that and the feelings of his own loss overwhelmed him.

But instead of breaking down and crying, which he knew he'd do later, he let the emotions strengthen him. The feelings of loss turned to anger, then resolve. If Cain were successful with his plan, then the emotions he was feeling right now would be multiplied ten thousand times over. He could live with his own personal loss and grief, but what he could not live with would be that thousands of other people would feel exactly like he did now because he failed to act. He would not allow his own indecision to affect others.

He knew it wouldn't be easy but at least now he knew he could try. Downing the last swallow of his root beer, he set the tray down and grabbed the hammer, then shoved both screwdrivers into his back pocket. Time for phase three, all or nothing.

Pike set up the ladder where he usually stood, draped the blanket around it then put his parka over the top of that. A cursory glance by the guard and he would see what he expected to see, a man in a parka standing where he always stood. Next he set the food tray on the floor by the door and piled the dishes into a precarious pyramid.

Pike stood by the door and played the scene out in his mind. The irritated guard would carelessly open the door to see what he wanted. As the door opened, it would hit the tray of dishes and send them crashing to the floor. He would look down to see what happened and would probably become angry, narrowing his senses. He would look up at what he thought was Pike, start to look back down at the mess on the floor but then his mind would react to what he saw and he would do a double take. All the distractions and similarities would last only for a second, but that's all the time he would need to spring from behind his false tarp wall and attack the guard. What could possibly go wrong?

Pike stood in the middle of the room, surveying his vulnerable house of cards. To say he was nervous would be the understatement of the century. His stomach was twisting and turning like a tilt-a-whirl and he could pick enough cotton out of his dry mouth to knit a sweater. Everything was in place.

With his arms feeling like lead, he raised his fist and pounded on the door and called out to the guard, then quickly slid behind the tarp. He peered out between the crack where the wall and canvas met and waited for what seemed like an eternity. As the seconds fell away, Pike felt his resolve slipping away as he began to hear the whispers of self-doubt. *Who do you think you're fooling? Do you really think you can pull this off? Do you really think that you're the* Blast from the Past, *Hot Shot?*

Hot Shot.

Suddenly a collage of memories and images flashed through his mind. Images of his family, growing up, but mostly images of K.D. There were no monumental or life changing moments, mostly just everyday things. That's when he realized that while life does have its big moments, it's usually not those big events we think of but rather the day to day moments that we remember and that really shape our lives.

Pike tightened his grip on the hammer, feeling himself growing angry. He didn't know if he and K.D. would ever have been an item. Who knows, they may have broken up when he found out that she left the lid off the toothpaste or she might have left after he left the toilet seat up one too many times. He was angry because now he would never get the chance to find out.

Suddenly the lock clicked. Pike's heart was pounding so hard now he was getting a headache. Peering through the edge of the canvas, he saw the door swing open and the guard walk in. He wanted to leap out and attack, to get this over with but he knew he had to wait, he had to be patient or else everything would be lost. The door hit the tray and the dishes went clattering on the floor. Just as he had hoped, the guard stopped and looked down, muttered something, then glanced up to where Pike was supposed to be.

His timing was perfect, just as the guard's eyes were registering that something wasn't right and his head was turned, Pike attacked. He raised Thor's mighty hammer ready to vanquish his foe, but when he brought it down, the hammer got tangled in the canvas.

The guard spun around, surprise filling his eyes, until he saw the hammer stuck in the canvas. Pike managed to bring the hammer down, but by then it was too late.

The guard easily brought up his right forearm to block the blow, then jabbed Pike in the ribs with his left fist. Pike doubled over from the blow and dropped the hammer. His jailer rushed forward, grabbing Pike by the neck and pinned him against the wall.

Pike remembered hearing about people getting super-human strength in times of crisis, like lifting a car off a trapped loved one after an accident, but the strength of Samson was failing him here. Gasping for air, he struggled to break the vise grip the guard had on his throat but couldn't get free. Instead, he felt himself growing dizzy and his vision was beginning to fade. He knew he was dying and couldn't do a thing about it.

Suddenly he could breathe again. Then he felt himself floating. Was he dead? Was he winging his way to heaven? His question was answered as he slammed down hard onto the floor of his cell.

The guard roared with laughter after having thrown Pike across the room.

"Nice try," the big man said as he walked over and stared down at Pike. "It's lucky Mr. Cain has other plans for you." He viscously kicked Pike in the stomach and laughed again. He examined Pike's redecorating, then tore all the canvas from the walls and dragged it outside. When he finished, he walked back to where Pike was lying on the floor and went to kick him again, only this time Pike caught the boot in his hands before it smashed into his ribs. The guard stared hard at Pike for a moment, laughed again, then turned and walked out the door. Pike felt more beat up than a Seahawks' lineman. With great effort, he pulled himself onto the chair and just sat there, resting. It hurt to move but he knew if he sat there too long, his muscles would stiffen up and the pain would be even worse, but for now, it was a chance he was willing to take.

Plan A had failed, but where there's a plan A, there's always a plan B; he just hadn't thought of it yet. He squirmed in his chair trying to get comfortable, to find a position that didn't hurt, but there was none. With great effort, he struggled to his feet then bent down and picked up his parka. With even greater effort he put it on. By the end of his ordeal, he wasn't sure if the pain was worth the warmth.

Semi-reluctantly, he started shuffling back and forth, not only to help him think but to keep his sore muscles from stiffening up. Looking around, he was happy to see that in his fury and feeling of self-confidence the guard had ignored the other items in the room, taking only the tarps, his hammer and screwdrivers.

He paced back and forth, staring at the corkboard insulation on the walls and floor, racking his brain for an idea. He knew that the next time the guard came in he would be wary, expecting something to be up. He looked up again and saw that a small section of the corkboard had peeled away when the guard ripped down the tarp.

Pike began to pace faster now; an idea beginning to form. The guard would be suspicious now and he could use that. He nodded now, his brain moving at full speed even if his body wasn't. This could work, it had to work. The only question now was did he have the time?

Pike worked as fast as his broken body would go and after nearly an hour and a half, he was finally done. He collapsed in the chair, he was going to relax for a few minutes before he called the guard back but suddenly he heard the key in the lock.

Panic washed over him as he looked around the room. Was he ready? Did he have everything in place? He wanted to scream I'M NOT READY YET! But instead, he sat silently in the chair and put on his winning poker face.

The door flung open but instead of a rushing guard filling the doorway, it was empty. Pike fought the urge to yell hello and just sat quietly. A moment later the guard appeared.

"Can't be too carful now, can we? I told Mr. Cain about your little trick and he told me to keep an eye on you, that you're a real crafty one," he said, wearing a devilish grin. "Like they say, fool me once, shame on you, fool me twice, shame on me. And no one makes a fool out of me." The devilish grin turned into a hateful leer.

"Come on *Hot Shot*." He smirked. "Ms. Mallory said you liked to be called that."

Pike want to jump up and rip the smugness off the man's face—no, pound it off—but nothing would be served if he didn't stick to his plan. He was the one in control here, not the guard. Refusing to take the bait, Pike remained silent and still.

Seeing no reaction from his jab, the guard walked in. He was eight feet away from Pike when he suddenly stopped. "What's this?" he said and bent down, still keeping a watchful eye on his prisoner. He was looking at a thin wire running three inches above the floor. Examining it, he traced one end attached to the left wall and the other end was wrapped around the leg of the ladder that was leaning against the right wall.

"What were you planning on doing, crushing me to death under the weight of a stepladder? Guess you're not as clever as Mr. Cain gave you credit for." He laughed.

Pike remained impassive in his chair, not showing any disappointment in his trap being discovered. The guard just shook his head, unimpressed with his prisoner's meager escape attempt. He carefully raised his right foot over the wire and was about to put it down when he suddenly stopped, a coy grin forming on his face.

He brought his foot back over the wire then knelt down and examined the floor. The corkboard on the walls came in four-foot wide rolls that were simply unrolled and attached to the wall like paneling. The floor covering however, was a little thicker and came in one foot squares that were laid down like tile.

"Maybe you are a little brighter than I thought," he said, standing back up. "But you should have taken more time to lay the squares back down the way they were after you dug them up."

This time Pike couldn't hide his disappointment.

"First you try to ambush me with a ladder and now you booby trap the floor? What, did you manage to dig a hole in the ice and hope I'd step over the wire and break my ankle? What do you think I am, stupid, *Mr. Hot Shot?* Mr. Cain said I couldn't kill you, but he didn't say anything about not hurting you."

Wearing a self-satisfying, triumphant grin, the guard stepped over the wire and over the suspect panels. His smile grew even bigger as his foot touched down on the other side on a solid floor. For effect, the guard puffed himself up to his full height, glaring down at Pike as he locked his fingers and cracked his knuckles. "This is going to be fun."

He took another step forward and suddenly the smugness on his face fell away, following the rest of his body. He cried out in pain as his right foot punched through the thin corkboard tile and his leg fell into a 15-inch deep hole Pike had dug out of the ice. As he fell, with one fluid motion Pike sprang out of the chair and released a kick that any Radio City Rockette would be proud of.

The guard's head snapped back and Pike heard, with great satisfaction, a loud crack as his foot connected with its target. The force of the kick flipped the guard over, landing him on his stomach facing the door. He groaned and struggled to prop himself up on one elbow but was quickly silenced as Pike grabbed the chair and hit him over the head with it, denting the chair.

Pike stood triumphantly over the guard like an ancient warrior over his vanquished foe. Pike's chest heaved, adrenaline coursing through his body as he looked down at the guard.

"And as a matter of fact, yes, I do think you're stupid," he said, then let out a muffled yell, then kicked the man in the side. He knew he shouldn't have but it seemed like the thing to do at the time. His muscles protested at the kick, but it still felt good nonetheless. HOT SHOT!

He stood there for a minute, letting his pounding heart return to normal, letting his mind clear. Thinking more like himself now instead of Conan the Barbarian, he quickly laid out one of the plastic sheets on the ground, then dragged the guard over and wrapped him in it like he was making a burrito. When he was done, he grabbed the roll of duct tape out of the tool box, tightly wrapped the guard's feet, put several strands around his shoulders securing his arms, then wrapped one long piece around his head, covering the guard's mouth.

He then dragged the guard over and placed him behind the ice holes, then replaced the cork tiles and reset his booby trap. Pike shrugged his shoulders; *you never know, I might get lucky and get two birds with one stone*, he thought.

Earlier, he had cut up one of the canvas tarps into long strips using a Stanley knife he'd found in the toolbox and had twisted the strips into a makeshift rope. He grabbed the ropes he had hidden under the plastic and threw the coils over his shoulders like a mountaineer and headed out the door.

He rounded the corner and going straight to the escape hatch, grabbed the sledgehammer off the wall. With swings worthy of the great Babe Ruth, he punched through the thin ice with just five strikes. Immediately he was hit with a blast of cold arctic air and a shiver ran down his spine. He hadn't noticed just how much he'd been sweating until the cool air hit him. The sides of the ship were still nearly six feet thick at this point of the hull, so he had to crawl through a short tunnel to get to the outside.

Pike popped his head out into the night air and looked around. He was about eight feet above the waterline, which meant he was about twenty feet below the main deck. A quarter moon cast just enough light to see that the ocean was flat and the winds felt calm.

Looking forward, he could see the lights of the *Rachel B.* as she struggled ahead with her massive burden. But what really caught his attention was what was beyond the stout tug. He could see patches of light on the horizon, glowing faintly like embers from a dying campfire. They were the shimmering lights of the big cities on the eastern seaboard and the brightest beacon was New York. Time was running out.

CHAPTER FORTY SIX

With a new sense of urgency, Pike took stock of his situation. Looking around, he guessed he was just below the VIP living quarters. Right outside their door, the VIPs had a large outdoor commons where they could enjoy the fresh air and do a little sightseeing.

He ducked his head back inside, took the rope off his shoulder and tied it around the handle. His plan was to use the hammer as a grappling hook, catch it on the railing then pull himself up. He just hoped that no one was outside enjoying the scenery.

Lying on his back, he scooted out as far as he dared, looking up at the railing. Listening carefully he couldn't hear any conversations coming from the deck above so he started swinging the rope like a lasso.

His first attempt went straight up in the air and came straight back down, nearly hitting him on the head. He wondered how the cowboys made this look so easy. Roy Rogers he wasn't. The second throw was better, landing just shy of the bottom of the railing. The third attempt met with the same results but on his fourth toss, he heard a clank and the hammer didn't fall back down.

Excited, he gently pulled on the rope to set the hammer. When the line went taunt he slowly pulled harder, making sure the line was secure. With one last tug, he eased himself out of the tunnel, pulling himself up with the rope. Slowly and deliberately he placed one foot against the side of the hull, then hoisted himself up and planted his other foot.

Taking tiny, deliberate steps so as not to slip, his progress was slow and tiring as he pulled himself along. Panting heavily halfway up, he vowed that if he survived, he would cut back on the mochas and the Kripsy Kremes and use his exercise bike in the spare room for something more than just hanging his laundry on.

Ten feet from the top, Pike heard a noise. Looking up, he saw a pair of arms magically appear and come to rest on the railing. He couldn't see the face but the arms belonged to a blonde wearing a heavy dark overcoat. She had a distant look as she gazed out over the ocean and though he couldn't see her expression clearly, the shadows from the moonlight seemed to cast a sad light on her face.

He stared at her intently for a moment and thought she looked like Tabatha but couldn't be sure. Should he call out to her for help? Could he trust her? Sadly he shook his head because he knew he couldn't; he just didn't know how much she had sold out to Mallory. He wrapped the rope around his arm several times then lowered his feet and hung by his arms, pressing himself against the side of the iceberg. One thing for sure was that if she looked down, he was done for.

"You're up late." Pike heard a male voice say. Pike shook his head in frustration. What, are they having convention? *It's freezing out here people, take it inside!* he shouted in his head.

"Man, that was some story we broke huh?" He heard the man continue.

"Yes, it was, Pete," the woman replied.

Pike mentally snapped his fingers. It was Tabatha and she was talking to Toupee Man, Peter Wright! He let out a small sigh of relief that he didn't trust her and call out, it sounded like these two were working together. He looked up and saw that she had turned around to face him. "Thank the Lord for small favors," he whispered.

"That story will flash around the world before we even reach New York. Can you believe our luck catching Pike red handed standing over the senator with a knife in his hand?"

"Yeah, pretty lucky." Tabatha's reply was flat and emotionless.

Pike could hear the smug arrogance in Wright's voice but he heard no joy in Tabatha's, instead he heard more doubt than triumph.

"Doesn't it seem odd that we just happened to walk in at exactly the right moment with our cameras rolling?" she questioned. Pike nodded; it sounded like she wasn't buying everything Mallory had told her.

"Hey, I'm not looking a gift horse in the mouth. If Lady Luck wants to smile on me, who am I to question? Speaking of luck..." Pike heard Wright moved closer, then saw him lean against the railing with his back facing the water. "You were pretty lucky yourself tonight, catching the story with me. You know," he said, moving closer to her, "I can help you in your career."

"Oh please," Tabatha replied. Pike couldn't see her face but having known her for just this short a time, a smile crossed his lips as he could just image her rolling her eyes at him with a sarcastic give-me-a-break look.

Pike heard a scuffle as Wright reached over and grabbed her in his arms. "Listen Tabby," he said forcefully, "I've been making and breaking cub reporters like you for longer than you've been alive. You want me as your friend, not your enemy."

"I don't want you at all," Tabatha answered. Pike heard a grunt then saw Wright collapse to his knees and a second later, something hit Pike in the face. He had to stifle his laughter as he saw that it was Wright's own toupee! Tabatha had kneed her esteemed colleague in the groin then ripped off his hairpiece and thrown it at him. Pike smiled; he still didn't know if he could trust her but he had to admire her style. He heard her storm across the plaza then heard the door slam. A few minutes later he heard Wright shuffle to the door and enter quietly.

Pike felt like a slab of beef hanging from a butcher's hook, his arms aching beyond belief. With the drama gone, he carefully he got his feet back onto the iceberg and painfully pulled himself up the rest of the way.

With a desperate swipe of his arm, he reached up and grabbed the stanchion and just held himself there, too weak to pull himself up. Summoning his last ounce of strength, he swung his leg up over the side and rolled under the wire railing. Half walking, half crawling, he made his way to the corner of the building and collapsed behind a small forest of potted trees.

His arms and shoulders were on fire from the pain and his legs felt like rubber. He knew he didn't have much time but he had to rest. After a very short ten minutes, it was time to move. He had to get to the one place where they would never think to look for him, but the only trouble was is that it was on the other side of the iceberg. It would be too risky to go inside, so his only other option was to go up onto the roof.

Wearily, he climbed onto one of the pots and standing on his toes, he could barely reach the edge of the roof. With a slight jump, which was all he could muster, he got a firm grip on the roof then heaved himself up.

The light cast by the quarter moon was both a blessing and a curse; a blessing because it illuminated all the vents and piping on the roof making his journey faster and safer, but a curse because Cain, looking down from his Tower of Mordor, could see him scurrying across the rooftop. Keeping a wary eye on the tower, Pike moved from heating duct to ventilation tower to electrical box, staying in the shadows as much as possible. Once when he looked up, he could see Cain, silhouetted in his perch. A moment later he was joined by another shadow, which Pike could only assume was Mallory. She handed him a drink and the two of them talked for a while. At one point he thought they were going to come together in a lovers' embrace but after thinking about it he knew that wasn't the kind of relationship they shared. It was more like a teacher-student relationship but with an almost religious reverence. Mallory didn't worship him per se, but her devotion was undeniable.

As he was watching them, he saw Cain's head turn sharply, then he and Mallory disappeared; he knew his escape had been discovered. He moved as quickly as he could, weaving in and out between the obstacles on the roof. With time running out, Pike picked up his pace. In his haste, he tripped twice over low lying ductwork that lay hidden in the shadows like landmines. He had to be careful: not only did he not want to hurt himself but he also didn't want to alert everyone to his presence by thumping around on the roof like a drunken Santa trying to land his sleigh.

He made it to the other side of the roof and peered over the side at the windows below. The rooms on this side of the iceberg were for the staff and last minute guests... like K.D. His luck was holding. He passed only three until he found what he was looking for: K.D.'s window sticker for the Mariners.

K.D. was a Mariners fanatic and could even quote stats from players who played years ago that no one had ever heard of. When the Mariners announcing great, Dave Niehaus, died, she said it was like losing a close friend. She, like so many other people, credited him for their interest in baseball and in the Mariners. He made the game come alive for her, she said as she would listen to her tiny transistor radio stuffed under her pillow when she was a kid, listening to the game instead of sleeping.

Ever proud of her team, she brought the window sticker with her because when all the cameras were showing pictures of the iceberg, they would see her mighty Mariners logo.

He took his makeshift rope and tied off one end around a larger heat exhaust blower and tied the other around his waist. He walked over to the brink and looked down at the rushing water below and tightened his grip on the rope. He was just about to lower himself over the edge when all the lights on the roof suddenly came on. He really hadn't noticed it before, but all the glitzy casino lights that were window dressing for the cameras had been off.

Brightly colored lights began glowing and flashing, and at any moment, Pike half expected carnival music to start playing. If nothing else, Cain was thorough, so Pike knew the roof would be searched soon. He quickly slipped over the side before he was spotted.

He came down just to the left of the window and took out the flathead screwdriver he had taken from the toolbox and slipped it under the window panel and started prying. Just as the pane popped out, a gust of wind caught it and it spun him around like a wind chime. He slammed into the side of the iceberg with such force that the impact caused the window panel to slip out of his hands. He watched as the pane sliced through the surface of the water and disappeared. He wanted to save the glass to replace it once he got inside to cover his tracks, but there was nothing he could do about it now.

Grabbing the lip of the windowsill, he hoisted himself in and slipped into the room. Suddenly, here he was. It had been one thing to sit in his makeshift cell and plan on coming here but an altogether different thing to actually be here, to be in the room where K.D. had died.

His eyes shot directly to the bed with bitter sweetness, glad her body wasn't there, but sad because he didn't have time to say good-bye. Next, his eyes darted to the spot where the senator had been slain. There was a large, dark stain on the carpet; thankfully his body was gone too.

He let out a long sigh and clenched his fists, a thousand different emotions swirling inside him; anger, rage, pity, loss, but the ball on his spinning roulette wheel of emotions didn't land on any of those. Instead it landed on resolve. Like the throwing of a switch, he now knew that nothing and no one would stop him. He would succeed, not only for himself, but as he looked over at the empty bed, for her too.

He threw open the curtain to gain as much light as possible, not wanting to turn on any lights. He started going through her dresser trying to find her cell phone. He felt like a thief sneaking around like this but he had no choice. He had to warn the authorities about Cain's plan. He quickly found the phone in the top drawer but his joy was short lived as he got no signal.

Disappointed but not totally unexpected, he quickly moved on and found K.D.'s laptop on the table and turned it on. Not as good as a phone call, he thought, but an emergency email would still work. He waited impatiently for the desktop screen to pop up, and as soon as it appeared, he tapped the Internet Explore icon and... he got the message, 'unable to connect to the Internet at this time.' Cain must have cut all outside communication the moment he'd learned of his escape.

Out of frustration, Pike pounded the table with his fist and instantly regretted it. The sound of his fist slamming into the table echoed like a clap of thunder. Immediately he spun around and faced the door, checking to see if the shadows of approaching people would darken the flow of light creeping under the door jamb.

After a few tense moments, he gasped, not realizing that he had been holding his breath. He relaxed for a moment, knowing he was not in any immediate danger but he also knew he was far from being out of the woods.

He was just about to turn off the computer when one of the desktop icons caught his attention; it was labeled *Hot Shot*. Pike felt a stab of pain when he read it. With mixed emotions he clicked on the icon and opened the folder: he was amazed at what he saw.

K.D. had collected all the news articles and interviews that he had done since he had become the Blast from the Past. There were dozens of photographs and news stories ranging from the major papers all the way down to his hometown newspaper with interviews of people he didn't even remember claiming to have grown up with him and how they were the best of friends.

He had to laugh. It was amazing; everyone they talked to knew that he would grow up to be something great one day. He just wished they would have told him that sooner and saved him a lot of time and effort.

Looking at the pictures, he saw that she had taken a great deal of time to arrange them all in chronological order. He smiled, that was the engineer in her, always putting things in their proper places. He closed the file and was just about to shut it down when another file caught his attention; it was labeled *DD*. It was a Word document but it was pretty good size; maybe she was writing a book. Then it struck him... *Dear Diary.*

He started to move the mouse, but the closer the arrow got to the file, the more his hand started to tremble. When the arrow was resting on the icon, he suddenly let go of the mouse as if it were electrified. He just sat there and stared at the file. He could feel the floodgate of emotions beginning to open. These were probably her last thoughts before she was... killed. He desperately wanted to know them, to know what she thought of him, but that would never happen now.

These were her thoughts and he felt like he was invading her final moments by opening them up and casually reading them like the Sunday paper. As much as he wanted to know, needed to know, he just couldn't bring himself to open the file. He hadn't had time to grieve over her loss yet and as much as he wanted to, now was not the time either.

Taking several deep, sobbing breaths, he moved the mouse to shut the computer down then stopped. He noticed that the icon for the internet was still running and he could have sworn he'd closed it. He opened it again and the window popped open with the progress bar blinking, showing it was still trying to connect, but there was something else too.

There was another progress bar below the first one and it indicated it was 50% loaded. Pike's heart leapt as he watched and the bar moved to 60%. He would soon be able to send his message and warn the authorities, then all he had to do was to hide out until the cavalry showed up. With a smile, Pike sat down and waited: perhaps Cain hadn't thought of everything after all.

Pike stopped, suddenly the sight of the bar moving to 73% didn't excite him anymore. This was Cain he was talking about here, the man didn't make too many mistakes. Then with the reality of water being thrown in his face, Pike realized that he was the one who had just made a mistake—a big one! The computer wasn't connecting to the internet, the second progress bar was a tracking signal, Cain was tracking the location of anyone trying to connect to the internet after he had shut it down.

Frantically Pike pushed the keys trying to turn it off but he couldn't. The bar read 93% complete when he tossed the laptop out the window. He wasn't sure if the trace was complete or not, but he couldn't take that chance, he had to get out of there now! He had no other choice; he had to get to the *Yankee Clipper*.

He stuck his head out the window and listened for sounds of anyone tracking him from the roof. He couldn't hear any voices over the churning water so he was just about to climb out the window when something caught his eye. He hadn't noticed it on the table before because it was hidden behind the laptop.

He smiled as he reached over and picked it up. It was one of K.D.'s most prized possessions, a team autographed baseball from the Mariners 2001 season when they set the American League record for the most wins with 116. He put it in his pocket as he climbed out the window and grabbed the rope to climb back up onto the roof.

CHAPTER FORTY SEVEN

The Blast from the Past was beginning to fizzle out as he barely managed to get his legs up over the side and roll onto the roof. As he was surveying the roof, he noticed that the glowing lights from the distant cities were getting brighter.

Tick tock.

Taking several deep breaths, the cool air felt good, helping him refocus on what he had to do. He forced himself onto his feet and quickly and cautiously made his way toward the stern. He had just reached the edge of the roof and was overlooking the driving range and sunning area when he heard a clunk. His heart stopped as he spun around and saw the legs of a ladder coming up from the pool area just fifteen feet away. Frantically he searched for cover but this section of the roof was clear of any ductwork. He had no choice but to go down.

He lay down, then swung his legs down and slipped over the edge, hanging on with his hands. Dangling for a second, he let go and fell to the deck. He landed hard in front of the golf pro shop but managed to break a little of the fall by rolling when he landed. Pike scampered behind a golf cart, and watched and waited to see if anyone had heard his fall. He had thought the idea of having a golf cart a bit much since there was no place to drive it, but Cain had reminded him that image was everything and right now he was sure glad Cain felt that way.

When men in black didn't come storming around the corner of the building or rappelling down from the roof, he slowly crept along the side of the building until he came to the corner. Crouching down and peering around the edge, Pike saw a man holding a ladder while a pair of legs disappeared onto the roof. As soon as his partner was on the roof, the other man followed his partner up and he too vanished on the roof.

Pike had heard the term "killing field" before, but now he fully understood what it really meant. He was trying to get to the *Yankee Clipper* but to get there he had to run across twenty to thirty yards of slippery ice, all open area with no cover. If they saw him, he would be the proverbial sitting duck. Once again he chanted the mantra *desperate times called for desperate measures*, trying to psych himself up… that and the fact that he really didn't have any other choice.

Taking several deep breaths, he looked up and saw no one on the roof and he was just about to make a mad dash for the *Clipper* when a guard suddenly appeared from behind the plane, and he wasn't alone. With him was the largest German shepherd he had ever seen; it was big enough to pass as a Shetland pony at a kids' ride.

Pike spun around and sat down on the ice, his back leaning against the wall, shaking his head. What was he going to do now? He *might* be able to sneak up on the guard, but not the dog. Just then a blast of wind swirled across the deck and Pike shoved his hands in his pockets to keep warm. As he put his hands in, he felt the baseball he taken from K.D.'s room and he took it out. Immediately he had a flashback to the charity ball where he had thrown the baseball and hit the gumball machine, stopping the jewel thief. As he held it in his hand, a crazy thought came to him. He shook his head, thinking that his idea would never work and he tried to push it away, but the idea refused to go. He grasped the ball firmly in his hand, looking at it. He hated to do this with K.D.'s treasure, with *his* new treasure, but with what was at stake, he knew she would understand.

Standing up, he peered around the corner. The guard was facing the other way, out toward the ocean, smoking a cigarette and the dog was sitting patiently next to him. Pike took a cleansing breath to clear his mind then stepped out into the open. Immediately the dog saw him and Pike held up the ball for him to see. The dog now stood to its feet, his ears up and head cocked to one side. With a quick prayer, Pike wound up and threw the ball.

The ball flew straight and true, up over the head of the guard. The dog watched the ball sail over head as it bounced in the VIP courtyard. As the ball landed, the dog barked and took off after his new toy. The guard was spun around and was nearly yanked to the ground as the leash was ripped from his hand by the bounding dog. He started chasing the German Shepherd, yelling at him to stop.

Pike half ran, half shuffled across the ice in a mad dash toward the *Clipper*. He felt like a penguin waddling across the ice but it was the best he could do without falling flat on his face. Close to the launch platform he slipped and fell and started sliding. He reached out to grab the corner but missed and kept on sliding. He looked between his feet and was horrified to see the railing coming up fast with the waiting ocean thirty feet below.

As he was sliding across the ice to his doom, Pike was thinking how ironic it would be to be done in by a simple fall and not by Cain's master plan. Sliding on his back like a hockey puck, Pike raised his feet and managed to catch the bottom cable of the railing. The force of the impact bent his knees up to his chest. He heard his knees pop but at least he had stopped.

Wasting no time, he flipped over onto his stomach and wiggled his way back to the cover of the launcher. He lay still, listening for shouts of his discovery and hoped his pounding heart didn't send shockwaves that would crack the ice. He peered around the corner and saw the roof was still empty and the guard was still in the VIP courtyard, yanking on the German shepherd's collar, who was barking adamantly at the railing where the ball had gone over the side. With the coast clear, he knew it was now or never.

Pike scrambled to his feet and had just put his left foot onto the launch platform to climb into the cockpit when he caught a flash of movement out of the corner of his eye. He had seen the reflection of the sliding glass door open as three men who he knew weren't pool attendants came out.

He quickly dropped to the ice like a dead man, which he knew he would be, if they came his way. He watched as they paused and turned their backs on him and for a brief moment he thought his luck would hold, but that thought was shattered as he realized they were just adjusting their coats against the cold and they turned back around and started walking toward him. Panic shot through him like a bolt of electricity; what was he going to do? He couldn't take on all three men, plus the fourth guard and Rin Tin Tin.

Frantically, he looked around for a place to hide but his options were severely limited. When he glanced at the hole he had burned through the ice, he had the oddest thought; he remembered watching Bugs Bunny cartoons as a kid and whenever Bugs was trapped by Elmer Fudd, he simply disappeared down his hole. If it worked for Bugs...?

Remaining on his hands and knees, he scampered to the hole then lay down on his stomach and spun around, lowering himself down, feet first. He was halfway down with just his head sticking out of the hole when he lost his grip and fell. Staring into the abyss, he expected to fall forever but in reality he only dropped about a foot. He knew that when they were draining the pool to fill the hole, they had run out of water, leaving a two foot gap between the ice and the ceiling of the anchor room.

He dropped to his knees and was plunged into near total darkness as he started crawling toward the back. He moved cautiously with his hands in front of him, not wanting to smack into the wall face first.

When he reached the wall, he flipped over and leaned against it, trying to get comfortable. His plan was simple; wait until things blew over then come out and radio for help, but as he sat there, a heavy weariness pressed down on him and drove him into a fitful sleep.

Pike awoke to his teeth chattering like castanets at a samba contest. Even though he had his work parka on, it wasn't designed to keep a person warm when wedged between two giant slabs of ice.

Shaking away the cobwebs, he noticed a bright shaft of light shining down through the hole. He stopped for a moment: something was wrong. He rolled over and held his watch up to the light. It read 12:30pm. He had been asleep for nearly eight hours! He only had three, four hours tops before Cain carried out his deadly plan.

Hurriedly, he started to crawl out of his cocoon when he noticed a dark form lying in the far corner. Odd, he thought, he didn't remember leaving any tools or anything else down here after they filled room. He slithered his way over to investigate and when he got within arm's length, he reached up and grabbed the object and pulled it toward him. To his utter shock and horror, he found himself staring into the dead eyes of Marilyn Talbot. For a moment, he was frozen as solid as the block of ice he was lying on.

He looked up and over her and saw another body and guessed it could only be Tony. Poor kid, Pike thought as he shook his head. Why would Cain have had them killed? Then it came to him, first rule of assassination: always kill the assassins. No wonder no one had found him. Cain knew the bodies were here and told everyone to stay clear.

As he lay there staring at Marilyn, he knew he should feel something for her, but what? Should he hate her for what she did? Should he feel sorry for her because she had fallen victim to Cain's plot and now she was dead too? He rolled her back over, and turned around and started back toward the entrance. He felt nothing at all for her, and that's what scared him the most.

Pike squinted as his eyes adjusted to the brightness, then he stuck his head into the shaft of light and looked up and saw a circle of beautiful blue sky. He listened intently for any sign that trouble was near. All he could hear was the muffled sounds of a busy harbor, people going to and fro, oblivious to the fact that their world was about to change forever.

Reaching up, he found that he was about a foot short of grasping the edge of the hole to pull himself up. He ducked back down to take off his coat. As he did, he noticed something glimmer near his feet. He bent down and found that it was a small puddle of water reflecting the light. Thinking nothing of it, he continued to take off his coat, then stopped dead in his tracks.

Looking around, he saw several more puddles from water dripping from the ceiling. There shouldn't be any pools or dripping water, everything should be frozen, unless... Cain had already turned the juice off and was well into his plan. It was already hitting the fan!

Pike stood in the center of the shaft, bathing in sunlight as he looked up to the edge. As a kid in high school, he was able to jump high enough to stuff a baseball in a basketball hoop; now, he only hoped his old legs still had a little spring left in them.

On his first jump he didn't feel like the Man of Steel, more like the Man of Lead. His legs were sore and stiff from the cold and he only made it halfway to the top. He rubbed his legs and jogged in place to get the blood flowing. His second attempt was much better. His fingertips just touched the rim. When he landed he thought he heard a small crack but considered it just his cold joints protesting.

Third time's the charm, Pike hoped as he leaped. His hand cleared the edge and for a moment he managed to hold on until his hands slipped and he fell back down, landing hard on the ice. When he hit he heard the crack again, only this time he knew it wasn't from his tired body.

It was a loud snap at first and then silence. He stood quietly listening and was about to jump again when he heard faint snaps and pops, almost like aftershocks to an earthquake. At first, just one or two snaps echoed through the room but soon the room was filled with a chorus of sounds, none of them good.

Pike jumped for all he was worth and watched the floor fall away beneath him, not from the height of his jump, it just fell away. Pike hung there watching in horror as the entire chunk of ice that had been the anchor room, including the anchor, popped out the side of the iceberg and plunged into the harbor below.

Looking down between his dangling legs, Pike saw the anchor chain being dragged along by its 60 ton master. It looked and sounded like a rushing freight train, the sound of the clanging steel, trapped and amplified in the tiny room funneled through the hole like a geyser. Watching the chain rumbling below him in a blur, he knew that if he fell, the only thing left of him would be a memory.

Then, as suddenly as it had started, the chain fell silent as the anchor came to rest on the harbor floor. The sudden silence was almost as unnerving as the roaring. Still dangling ten feet up and hanging on by a thread, Pike knew he wasn't out of danger yet. The chain was directly below him and there would be no way to avoid it if he fell. The fall might not kill him but his legs would certainly be shattered to pieces landing on the steel links.

CHAPTER FORTY EIGHT

He raised his right arm to pull himself up but instantly stopped as he suddenly started slipping. Pike's ears were ringing from the heavy pounding of his heart; despite the cold, he could feel the sweat rolling off his forehead.

In one quick motion, Pike put the sole of his right shoe on the ice in front of him then jammed the sole of his left shoe behind him on the ice, holding himself up with his legs in a very awkward position. A second later, he summoned all his strength and in one massive push/pull effort, he shot out of the hole onto the ice like a penguin shooting out of the sea.

Wasting no time, he quickly scurried under the launch platform and lay still, watching and waiting to see if he had been discovered. He knew he had been extremely lucky so far, he just hoped his luck held out for just a few more minutes. With no immediate sound of rushing feet or gun fire, he pushed himself up on his forearms and scanned the area. Despite the crashing of the anchor through the side of the iceberg, no one seemed to be paying much attention. He shrugged; maybe sleeping late was a blessing after all, allowing everyone to be long gone.

Pike thought it odd: here he was in the middle of New York harbor fighting for his life in full view of the world. He could hear the rumbling of the traffic in the distance, honking horns, and squealing tires. He looked up and saw several airliners pass, along with a couple of police and news helicopters.

But what concerned him most was that the harbor was swarming with boats. Boats of all shapes and sizes were milling around, surrounding the iceberg like a pack of kids swarming the neighborhood ice cream truck. If they only knew the danger they were in.

Pike scrambled from under the launch chassis, looked around one more time, then climbed up on the wing, opened the canopy and quickly slipped into the cockpit. Slouching down as low as he could, he put on his helmet, flipped the master switch, then turned on the radio. "Mayday, mayday, this is the *Yankee Clipper*. Do you copy? Over."

Static.

"Mayday, mayday, this is the *Yankee Clipper*. Do you copy? Over," he repeated. He tried several more frequencies but the only answer he got was more static. How could Cain jam his radio in the middle of New York harbor? Someone would have noticed... unless it was extremely localized and extremely short range.

"Hello, Gabriel."

Pike nearly jumped out of the cockpit, hearing Cain's voice over the radio.

"May I ask you what you think you are doing?"

"Hello, Nigel. Thank you for your hospitality but I really must be leaving now."

"I must say, I really do admire your cleverness and ingenuity."

"I wish I could say the same."

"Oh come now, Gabriel, we can still come to an equitable solution, don't you think?"

"Sure," Pike said, stalling for time as he studied the new controls for the launcher Cain had installed. "You and Beth can just turn yourselves in, then we can talk."

Cain laughed. "Now you know I can't do that. But we can talk. Seriously, tell me what you want and maybe we can come to some sort of terms."

"What do I want? What do I want!" Pike shouted in anger. "What do you think I want? I want K.D. back! That's what I want!" Pike could feel himself going blind with rage. Cain's arrogance was unbelievable. He had had second thoughts about having to kill the guard during his escape if he had to, but he would have no such thoughts if Cain were in front of him right now.

Suddenly he caught a glimpse of motion out of the corner of his eye. He turned to see two men with guns drawn coming out of the spa area and another two scrambling their way across the roof. Pike was not a swearing man but he was cursing himself now for letting Cain distract him so his men could get the jump on him. He didn't recognize the first gunman but the second one he did. He had a bandage on his nose and his face was badly bruised; it was the guard from his cell. Orders or no, Pike knew the guard would kill him this time.

He turned on the engine and pulled the throttle back, letting it idle and warm up. In a military emergency, the Sabre could go from a cold start to takeoff status in three minutes. He had never attempted to do this before, but as with many events of the past 24 hours, he was about to learn.

Just then, a news helicopter zoomed overhead then made a low pass, then hovered slightly in front of the *Clipper*. Pike looked up and saw a cameraman hanging out the side, filming, and Tabatha Amies in the copilot seat broadcasting. She looked down and smiled, then gave him a thumbs up.

Whether by design or just trying to get a scoop, the effect was the same. The closest two men coming from the spa slowed and tucked their guns under their coats, not wanting to be seen on national television with weapons in their hands.

The lead man stopped, then put his hand to his ear, receiving instruction through an earpiece. The first guard stopped his partner and the two of them argued stubbornly. After their brief exchange, the wounded gunman shoved his partner aside, not willing to be denied his revenge. He drew his gun and fired an unaimed shot toward the helicopter as he continued toward Pike. The news chopper banked up and away, out of the line of fire. That was very good idea.

He said a quick prayer then flipped the switch for the Zero Length Launch rocket and shoved his throttle to the stops. With a deafening roar, he was thrown back into his seat as he went from zero to over 250mph in only four seconds.

"WWWWHHHHOOOOAAAA!" Pike heard himself yell. A film Cain had showed him said the G-force at takeoff was about the same as a Navy pilot taking off the deck of an aircraft carrier. After this, he was ready to sign up for the Navy. What a rush! Now he knew what the term "bat out of hell" felt like. He was so exhilarated that he almost forgot that he still had a job to do.

He shot out over the harbor sixty feet above the water, barely missing the mast of a passing tug. He gently pulled back on the stick, slicing between two high rise office buildings as he slowly gained altitude, circling back over the iceberg. Pike noticed that the *Clipper* was handling sluggishly, so he looked back to see that the booster rocket hadn't fallen off like it was supposed to. He knew he could still be able to land with the rocket attached so he wasn't overly concerned. At this point it was just a minor hindrance and no real cause for alarm.

"Mayday, mayday, mayday! This is *Yankee Clipper*. Alpha Whiskey seven-niner-niner-two-one, declaring an emergency. Does anyone copy?" The only reply was static interrupted with an occasional faint voice that was too garbled to understand. He tried several more frequencies with the same result. He was circling at

2,000 feet and decided to climb to 3,000 to see if that would get him out of range of Cain's jamming signal.

"Mayday, mayday, mayday! This is *Yankee Clipper*, Alpha Whiskey seven- niner- niner-two- one, declaring an emergency, does anyone copy?"

"*Yankee Clipper*." The voice cut through the static so cleanly, it startled Pike. "This is Lt. Colonel Douglas Madison of the United States Air Force. I read you five by five. Is that you, Mr. Pike?"

"Colonel Madison? Am I ever glad to hear from you. What are you doing over here?"

"We're a four ship heading to Lakenheath, England, then on to Afghanistan. Look to your high four o'clock."

The F-86 Sabre was circling over the iceberg counter-clockwise. Pike strained his neck as he looked over his right shoulder and saw a flight of four F-15 Eagles descending.

"What is the nature of your emergency?" Madison asked.

"You are not going to believe me," Pike said, shaking his head and feeling his entire body trembling slightly as a sense of relief came over him; it was finally over. Before he could finish, the radio came to life.

"Blackjack Three to One, I have a man on the iceberg, he appears to have a hand-held missile launcher, could be a stinger, sir, I can't tell at this range. He's tracking the Sabre, sir. I'm getting a targeting signal."

Tracking the Sabre? A targeting signal? WHAT! It finally registered in Pike's mind; Cain was going to shoot him down with a missile! "No, no, no," Pike said, shaking his head frantically in disbelief. "This can't be happening!"

"I have a launch signal... and visual confirmation."

"WHAT!"

"Blackjack Three, Four. Dive behind the Sabre and execute flares and chafe. Pike, cut your engine."

"Three."

"Four."

Both pilots acknowledged.

Pike, still in a daze, watched in fascination as the two fighters banked hard and dove in behind him. In a lighting fast pass, they dipped in behind him and then it looked like both planes exploded.

"Cut your engine now!" Madison ordered again, his voice raised but still professional.

Pike was slow to realize what Madison's plan was but then it hit him as he shut down. The stinger was a heat-seeking anti-aircraft missile and would zero in on the heat from his engine's exhaust. Madison had sent the two fighters down to decoy the missile and save his life.

He looked down over his left wing and instantly wished he hadn't. He saw the trail of smoke rising from the iceberg and watched with morbid intensity as the deadly missile streaked toward him. He'd heard stories of people who were about to die and were overcome by an overwhelming sense of peace. His life didn't flash before him and he didn't feel very peaceful at the moment. It must be a lie, he thought, because watching that missile coming at him, he was anything but peaceful. Instead he felt angry. He was angry at everything that had happened and angry that everyone was trying to kill him. His fate was in God's hands now. God's hands, with a little help from the United States Air Force.

Fueled by his anger, he regained his wits and banked the *Clipper* down and away from the missile, trying to put as much distance between him and it as he could. In a blur, the outline of the two F-15s went streaking by followed by a series of bright flashes, then a split second later a brilliant explosion. Before he even had time to think, the *Yankee Clipper* was buffeted violently as the missile detonated, hitting the flares instead of his plane. Pike felt and heard several pieces of shrapnel pelt his plane and he prayed that nothing vital was hit.

He glanced at the altimeter: 2,700 feet. He had plenty of time to restart the engine, he hoped; again, something he had never done before. He quickly went through his start up procedure and then flipped the start switch.

Nothing.

He was down to 2,100 feet. Taking a deep breath and trying to keep his trembling hands steady, he went through the steps again. His ears were met with deafening silence instead of the deafening roar of his engine.

His air speed had dipped beneath 200 knots and he was below 1,400 feet. If he couldn't get the engine started this time, he knew he would have to start looking for a place to put her down. An emergency water landing in open water was a feat unto itself but it would be nearly impossible to do safely without hitting anyone in the confines of the harbor, not only crowded with the normal flow of commercial traffic, but also filled with hundreds of smaller boats, all out to gawk at Cain's monstrosity. He shook his head, just one more thing to add to his list of firsts today.

Taking a deep breath, Pike nervously went through the startup procedure for what he knew would be the last time, one way or another. As he reached over to throw the switch, he noticed that the bypass valve to the auxiliary fuel tank was on. It suddenly dawned on him, that's why the engine wouldn't start—because there was no fuel in the auxiliary tank. He must have hit it accidentally when he shut the engine down.

Feeling like an idiot, he quickly switched the fuel to the main tank. Belching like a giant who had eaten too many villagers, the engine roared to life. Pike pulled back on the stick and leveled the *Yankee Clipper* over the busy harbor at 500 feet.

"Excellent, Gabriel," Pike heard Cain over the radio. "I bow to your resourcefulness."

Pike was now circling over the iceberg again and back up to 3,000 feet. As he looked down, he could see that Cain was wearing his grandfather's coat from the *Titanic*.

"Give it up, Cain, it's over."

"But, Gabriel, I thought it wasn't over until the fat lady sings," Cain mocked.

"I see you're still wearing that old rag," Pike taunted. "They say clothes make the man, but definitely not in this case. Your grandfather would be rolling over in his grave if he knew that his grandson had grown up to be a monster."

After a long pause Cain simply said, "Goodbye, Gabriel."

Pike allowed himself a satisfied grin, pleased with himself for having cracked the armor of the mighty Nigel Cain.

"Two to lead, it looks like he's got another missile," Lieutenant Packard, Madison's wing man, reported.

"Blackjack Three and Four, cover the Sabre. Two follow me in. Going weapons hot, selecting air to ground missile."

"Negative! Abort, abort, abort!" Pike screamed into his radio.

"Stand down, Mr. Pike," Madison replied in a calm, professional voice. "We'll handle this."

"Colonel, you can't fire a missile. The iceberg if made of methane hydrate."

"Made of what?"

"Methane gas! The explosion of the missile could ignite the whole thing."

"What are you talking about?" Madison replied with slight irritation in his voice.

"The entire iceberg is one gigantic floating bomb."

"The subject has dropped the missile launcher and has entered the building," Packard reported.

"He's probably going down below to detonate it himself. If that thing blows, it'll take out half the harbor."

"Do you have any proof, any evidence of what you're telling me Mr. Pike?"

"We've got to break up the iceberg, Colonel," Pike continued. "There's a large cavity in the center of the iceberg where thousands of cubic feet of the gas are trapped. If we can release the gas safely, then the greatest danger of explosion would be over." Pike's voice was full of anxiety and frustration: anxiety because he knew how real the danger was, frustration because he didn't have the time to explain it to the colonel.

"Let's just say for the sake of argument that I believe you, Mr. Pike," Madison said. "If we can't fire our missiles, then how do you propose we attack it?"

Pike shook his head. "I've been thinking about that a lot and this is one of those situations where the solution sounds crazier than the problem."

"You're not instilling a great deal of faith in me here, Mr. Pike," Madison replied.

"Funny you should mention faith, Colonel, because I'm about to ask you to take the biggest leap of faith in your life." When Madison didn't reply, Pike continued. "Do you know how I became known as the Blast from the Past?"

Madison nodded in his cockpit. "Yeah, you stopped a car full of bank robbers and protected a bunch of kids by taking your..." His voice slowed, then trailed off as he figured out what Pike was getting at. "You don't mean to tell me you want to try and break that thing up by hitting it with sonic booms do you?"

"Think about it, Colonel; it's the only way to stop Cain without blowing up half of New York. The sound waves from the sonic booms will resonate throughout the ice, cracking and shattering it."

"Do you realize how many office windows we'll shatter and how many people might get hurt if we create a sonic boom in such a populated area?" Madison argued.

"Do you know how many office *buildings* will be destroyed and how many people will *die* if we don't and Cain succeeds in detonating it?" Pike countered. "Think of the largest conventional bomb you've seen, then multiply it a thousand fold. Do you see where Cain has strategically placed the iceberg? Putting it in the narrows between Battery Park and Governor's Island is the perfect location to wreak the most havoc and destruction.

"Within one mile of ground zero, there are eight major ferry landings, the Brooklyn Bridge, the Manhattan Bridge, City Hall, Federal Hall, and across the bay the Statue of Liberty. Nearly every structure within that one mile radius will be destroyed or severely damaged and any person not sheltered directly from the shockwave will be torn apart. Do you know how many people alone are in Battery Park for 9-11 observances today?"

Madison was quiet and Pike took that for a good sign. The longer he thought about it, the more Pike hoped Madison would believe him. Finally Madison spoke. "I'm sorry, Gabe, I need some sort of proof before I can act."

Pike felt a tiny pin-prick in his heart. He knew that his story was as farfetched as they come and that Madison wouldn't understand, that with his training he couldn't understand, and that was all right. "That's okay, Colonel." Pike interrupted, not allowing him to finish. While they were talking, Pike had been circling over the harbor, slowly gaining altitude, climbing to ten thousand feet. "I understand, Colonel, I really do... and I hope you understand too."

Pike smiled to himself as he looked out at the harbor below, he guessed it really was true after all, because right now he had a calm and peace about him that he couldn't explain.

CHAPTER FORTY NINE

"I can't let you do what I think you're going to do, Mr. Pike," Madison replied quietly.

"Well, sir, unless you plan on giving Lieutenant Packard a second shot at me, I'm going to put my money where my mouth is."

"You'll never make it. You still have the rocket assembly hanging off your fuselage. You go anything much past 300 knots it'll rip your entire tail section off."

"You're probably right but I can't sit by and do nothing. There's simply not enough time." Pike looked out his canopy at Colonel Madison and gave him a salute. "Keep 'em flying, Colonel!" he said, then tipped his wing over.

"Wait!" Madison ordered.

"Colonel, I told you…" Pike started to reply.

"Shut up, Mr. Pike. Lieutenant Packard, take Blackjack flight and return to Langley. Mr. Pike, any man willing to put his life on the line for others and for what he believes in, no matter how crazy it sounds, well..."

"Form on me," Packard ordered quietly. The other two fighters formed on their new lead and when they were ready, Packard gave each of them a hand signal.

"Follow my pass down and let me know what the damage result is," Madison ordered.

"Roger that," Pike replied, "and thank you, sir."

Madison lined up his F-15 on the iceberg and slowly pushed the nose over and watched as the iceberg began to grow closer. Madison loved being a fighter pilot flying at Mach plus and there was nothing better than defeating an adversary in the air, but he also enjoyed the dying art of dive bombing.

The age of smart bombs and laser guided munitions had all but made extinct the need to actually place the bomb where you wanted. At 7,000 feet, he hit the after burners and almost instantly the iceberg zoomed up to greet him. He misjudged his speed and the sonic boom hit when he was at 4,000 feet, much higher that he intended. Still, the results were sensational.

Every window on the iceberg shattered as if a giant foot had stomped on the roof, and like a stunt from a movie, the glass in Cain's tower blew out in spectacular fashion.

Pike followed Madison down in a low-speed, low-level pass to evaluate if there was any structural damage. Zooming down the side, he could see several spider veins running down the length of the hull but nothing that looked very significant.

"Clear the area, Mr. Pike."

"Blackjack Two, I gave you an order to return to base," Madison said.

"Yes sir, but you didn't say when."

"Don't split hairs with me, Lieutenant."

"You're going to need all four ships."

"Lieutenant!"

"Sorry sir, starting our run now. Can't talk." The three fighters were flying line abreast and at Packard's order, all three pushed over at the same time, diving straight down on top of the iceberg. By diving straight down they would be concentrating the force of the sonic booms directly onto the iceberg for maximum effect and at the same time, minimizing the effects of the blast on the surrounding area.

Despite the danger and what was at stake, Pike felt like he was a spectator at an air show who had the best seat in the house. Learning from the colonel's experience, he watched as Lieutenant Packard's flight waited until the last moment to use their afterburners. Suddenly, intense blue flames erupted from the back of all three jets in unison. With a visible burst of speed, he saw them accelerate downward even faster.

By now, all the pleasure boats that had been circling the iceberg realized that something was wrong and they were scattering like cockroaches on a kitchen floor when the lights turned on.

At an altitude of what Pike guessed to be no more than 700 or 800 feet, the sky exploded in a thunderous boom that he felt even in his cockpit 5,000 feet above. In air show fashion, Packard, who was in the middle, pulled straight up while the other planes split out to the left and right. Pike knew they were pushing their planes and themselves to the limit with that sharp of a pullout.

When the sonic boom hit, it looked like the Breath of God had smashed into the iceberg. Large chunks of the roof flew off and Pike could see Cain's tower swaying back and forth like a giant tuning fork, but other than that, nothing appeared to be happening and he was beginning to have his doubts about the success of his plan.

Deeply discouraged, he surveyed the city. Madison's prediction was all too accurate. There was so much shattered glass in the streets, the buildings looked like they were floating in a calm blue lake of shards.

On one of the closer skyscrapers, there were windows scattered over the face of the building that didn't break, starkly contrasting against the hundreds of others that did, making the face of the building look like a giant version of the *Wall Street Journal's* crossword puzzle.

The city was taking a pounding, but Cain's self-proclaimed legacy was still intact. At least with everything happening people would be evacuating and would, he hoped, make it to safety before the iceberg blew up. Pike tried to console himself with this thought but it offered little comfort.

Pike circled back by the stern, starring down at the seemingly undamaged chuck of ice when he let out a long, loud cry of frustration and slammed his fist against the canopy.

"Are you all right, Mr. Pike?" Madison asked.

"Sorry, I forgot the radio was on."

"Yes, sir. A little warning next time might save a few ear drums."

"It's just that I'm so damned frustrated right now. I would have…" Pike stopped in mid-sentence as something caught his eye. As he was flying down the side of the berg, he saw a flash of light like a lightning bolt running its entire length. It took him a moment to realize what it was: a fracture had formed and was slicing its way through the ice and the sunlight was reflecting off the edges: his plan was working.

Pike smiled inwardly: had his scream been at just the right pitch to be the wings of the butterfly that caused the fissure in the ice? Cain would have loved the irony.

He flew over the bow, just in time to see a large chunk fall off its port side, leaving a gaping hole. As it fell away, the towing bridle tumbled with it, yanking out the left tower support, bending it halfway down. It looked like a hook dangling out of the mouth of a giant fish.

When the support tower collapsed, it basically ripped the entire bow section off the iceberg. Flying by, Pike could look into the huge cavern and see the buried support ships nestled together, but more importantly, the gaping hope meant that the gas was escaping, effectively disarming the bomb.

Pike was about to pop the champagne and pat himself on the back, congratulating himself for having defeated Cain, when he suddenly stopped.

"What the hell is that?" Madison asked.

Music was coming over their radios, filling their cockpits with grand operatic music, backing a soprano's singing. Pike was busy trying to identify the song when it suddenly hit him—the fat lady was singing!

"Pull up, pull up, pull up!" he shouted. He watched as the blue flames erupted from the four fighters as they shot upward faster than he could ever hope to go. He shoved the throttle to the stops but his normally responsive bird was sluggish, still carrying the bulky rocket assembly. The *Yankee Clipper* banked hard to the right and started to climb.

Pike was at about 2,000 feet and pulling away from the port side of the iceberg when it exploded. The flash of the explosion was like looking into the sun and he could feel the searing heat from half a mile away. Blinking away the sunspots, he looked back and saw flames shooting out of the bow like exhaust from a jet engine, and it had the same affect.

In disbelief, Pike watched as the giant iceberg slowly moved into the middle of the harbor, propelled by the flames. With great satisfaction, he saw Cain's tower sway, then topple backwards, crushing what was left of the casino. As odd as it sounded, he viewed the fall of Cain's tower as a symbolic fall of Cain himself.

By now, the entire iceberg was engulfed in flames. Not only were the buildings burning on top but so were large sections of the ice itself. As the blazing iceberg slowly drifted through the harbor, it reminded him of a funeral pyre. An appropriate end to Cain's dream, he thought.

Several cabin-cruiser size chunks of ice had fallen away and were bobbing in the water, flames burning low but steady. Pike looked up and saw a fleet of fireboats come streaming down the Hudson River to the rescue. Pike smiled, he bet this was the first time they had ever been dispatched to put out burning ice.

As he watched, he didn't feel any sense of triumph or victory, what he did feel was a sense of relief that it was finally over. He unexpectedly felt drained, both mentally and physically. His body felt like it weighed a thousand pounds and the simplest of tasks, like movement of the stick, suddenly took a great deal of concentration and effort. He wondered if this if how soldiers felt after a battle? Coming down from the adrenaline high and crashing back into reality. He felt like he could sleep for a hundred years. He had always respected the military and the tough job they had to do, but his respect for them just jumped off the scale; he knew that some did this on a day to day basis.

"Mr. Pike?" His thoughts were interrupted by the voice of Colonel Madison.

"Yes, Colonel?"

"A job well done, sir."

"Thank you, and to your men."

"Form up on us and we'll all land at Langley together."

Pike drew in a deep breath through his nostrils then let it out slowly and nodded his head. "There's nothing I'd like better, sir. Lead the way."

He had just swung the nose of the *Yankee Clipper* around and started to climb to join up with the Air Force fighters when his engine suddenly sputtered. First thing he did was to check the fuel transfer toggle to see if he'd accidentally hit it again but he found it in its proper setting. Instantly he surveyed his instruments and to his horror, his fuel gage was nearly at zero. How could that be? He hadn't been flying long enough to use that much fuel. Did he take shrapnel from the missile? He shook his head—he didn't think so, he would have noticed a leak sooner. Then it hit him. He must have used more fuel than he'd expected when he was melting a hole through the ice above the anchor room.

The engine coughed one more time then quit, filling his canopy with an eerie silence. He quickly leveled out and frantically started looking for a place to land, but where? He was still in the middle of a harbor. He was hesitant before about making a water land because of all the normal harbor traffic but now it would be impossible because the harbor was choked even more with rescue vessels and chunks of debris were scattered on the surface, bobbing everywhere like land mines, making it impossible to land.

Panic had not set in yet but he could feel it banging on his canopy as he scanned for a place to land, finding none. It was looking more and more like he would be going swimming. At least the Coast Guard would be close to fish him out. If he survived the landing.

"Mr. Pike, what's the problem?" Madison asked, seeing the vintage fighter falling away.

"You're not going to believe this, but I ran out of fuel."

"You're kidding, right?"

"Wish I were, sir."

"From the frying pan into the fire," Madison said.

"That saying does seem rather appropriate, considering things below."

"Have you ever done an emergency water landing before?" he asked.

"No, but I suppose there's a first time for everything," Pike replied, trying to sound more optimistic that he really was.

He was looking up the Hudson thinking he might have enough altitude to get away from some of the river traffic when something caught his eye. Suddenly a thought crossed his mind and at first it sounded so ridiculous he couldn't help but chuckle. But the more he tried to toss the idea out the canopy, the more it stuck, and the more it started to make sense. It was crazy to be sure, but then again, this week hadn't exactly been a normal one either.

"But I may not have to." Pike slowly banked the plane to the left, maintaining as much speed and altitude as he could to get a better look. He had fallen to 4,000 feet and was gliding at 180 knots.

He was flying dead stick and would have only one shot at this. He had the altitude but did he have the skill *and* the luck needed for this? This was literally one of those do or die moments. Pike sat up a little straighter in his seat and steeled himself.

"Time to put up or shut up, Hot Shot," Pike said, smiling to himself. "Time to join the Navy and see the world." He nudged the stick forward and picked up a little more speed.

"You're not seriously considering doing what I think you are, are you?" Madison asked, seeing but not believing what his civilian friend was about to do.

"Well, sir, since you don't have any KC-130s flying around to top off my tank, I'm afraid I'm going to have to join the Navy." Pike was not a very good actor because even to himself his false bravado sounded pretty lame.

"Good luck, Mr. Pike. Godspeed," was Madison's simple reply.

Suddenly Pike felt rejuvenated, alive and ready. Not from the danger of his idea, though there was plenty of that, but from the sheer challenge that it offered. He didn't approach this with wild abandon like a daredevil just to see if he could do it. No, he calculated the risks involved and looked at the different options and pushed himself because he *had* to do this.

He thought back to an interview he'd heard from a WWII fighter pilot talking about combat and all the training he did. The pilot said that training was important to be sure but that he'd rather be lucky than good. Those were Pike's sentiments exactly because he was going to need all the luck he could get as he swung the *Yankee Clipper* around and lined up to land on the deck... of the aircraft carrier.

The *USS Intrepid* was an Essex class aircraft carrier launched in 1943 during WWII. During the war, she survived numerous bomb hits and kamikaze strikes, and she was credited with sinking two Japanese battleships and downing over 600 enemy aircraft.

The *Intrepid* went on to serve three combat tours off Vietnam and twice as a NASA Prime Recovery Ship, recovering spacecraft from the Mercury and Gemini space programs. She was decommissioned in 1974, but was moved to New York where she has served as a maritime/aviation museum since 1982.

Standing on the dock looking up, the 900 foot, 33,000 ton ship looked huge. From his cockpit looking down, it looked like he was going to try to land on a Band-Aid.

Landing on the deck of an aircraft carrier has often been referred to as a controlled crash, a theory he was about to put to the ultimate test. To launch a plane, a catapult was attached to the front wheel and it was shot into the air. To land, there were four guide wires spaced across the aft end of the flight deck. When a Navy plane lowered its landing gear, there was a hook that extended down from the tail of the plane. The idea was to catch the tail hook on the wires, which would slow and then stop the plane. Being an Air Force plane, his Sabre didn't have a tail hook. What it did have, however, was the remains of the rocket booster still attached to its belly—he hoped would act like a giant tail hook.

An ideal landing was to catch the number three wire but he would be more than happy just to snag any of them. He knew it would probably rip his tail off but he prayed it would be enough to stop him before he slid off the end of the flight deck and plunged fifty feet into the waters below.

Normally the flight deck of the great ship was crowded with up to thirty different aircraft on display, but fortunately for him, they had been removed for maintenance and restoration work. Pike was circling counter-clockwise above the big ship, flying down the portside at less than 700 feet, passing over the submarine *USS Growler* that was moored on the other side of the dock and a British Concord supersonic airliner on a barge right behind it.

Swinging out wide, his glide path toward the stern of the ship was perfect, coming in over the water on his final approach. His speed was a little faster than he wanted but he also knew that if he didn't maintain his forward airspeed, he'd drop out of the sky like a rock. Normal landing speed was around 125mph and he hoped he could bring her in at around 110mph, just a little over stall speed, but right now he was doing close to 140mph.

He came over the stern of the flight deck too high and too fast. He would need to tap the stick forward to get down to the deck then pull back on the stick to flare the landing, easing his contact with the deck and bleeding off airspeed.

Both maneuvers worked, only not as well as he had hoped.

He brought the nose of the *Clipper* down a little too hard and he had to yank back on the stick and overcorrected. The nose popped up, but the tail hit hard. The rocket assembly actually caught the number three wire, but because of the plane's speed and force of the impact, it dug into the deck. The assembly stayed put while the *Yankee Clipper* popped off and skidded down the flight deck.

Pike could see sparks flying out from under the fuselage, just behind the wings, as bare metal scrapped against bare metal. The sound was like a thousand fingernails scraping on a chalkboard. But it was more than just the sound that was hurting him; his beautiful plane was being torn apart. He knew he should be worried more about himself than his plane but couldn't help it.

Looking ahead, he suddenly became more worried about himself. He was rapidly approaching the end of the flight deck and was still going too fast. With twenty feet to go, part of the aluminum skin scraped off and part of the metal airframe caught on the decking. The runaway plane stopped so suddenly, it snapped Pike forward, slamming his head into the instrument panel. Then the whiplash snapped him back in his seat.

Pike was dazed from hitting his head on the instrument panel but he was still conscious: everything was blurry, blending into one giant kaleidoscope of sight and sound. He was vaguely aware that the plane was still moving but he had no sense of how fast or even in what direction. He suddenly sensed that he had stopped, and yet the plane was still moving, not forward, but up and down.

In a brief moment of clarity, he realized that he was on the very tip of the flight deck and that he was actually teetering back and forth like a seesaw.

A wave of nausea swept over him and his world began to blur again. The last thing he remembered was watching the sky flip upside down and then being swallowed by darkness.

CHAPTER FIFTY

He raised his nose up in the air and took several whiffs. "You still stink," Nathan Grant said as he waved his hand in front of his nose.

"Very funny, Nate, very funny," Gabriel Pike replied, taking a sip of his root beer.

"I can't believe your luck," Grant continued. "Only you could land a sixty year old plane on the deck of a seventy year old aircraft carrier, then slide off the end and flip over onto a garbage scow that was supposed to have shoved off earlier that morning but was still there because the captain's wife delivered her baby a day early because a fortune cookie she ate the night before said that good things would happen in the morning," he finished, taking a deep breath. "Unbelievable!"

"My new motto: I'd rather be lucky than good." Pike took another sip then tipped his head to one side in thought. "Have you ever heard of the butterfly effect?"

"The what?"

"Never mind," Pike said, smiling.

Grant just shrugged his shoulders as he took another sip of his beer and finished off the last French fry. "So how's K.D. doing?"

"The same," Pike sighed. "The doctors say that she could come out of the coma tomorrow or she could be under for years. They just don't know."

"Speaking of luck, looking back, it was sure lucky that all those reporters burst in when they did and one of them checked her and found she was still alive. If there hadn't been all those witnesses, they would have quickly finished the job."

"How's George taking all this?" Pike asked.

"Hard, really hard," Grant replied, shaking his head. "I mean, what do you say to the man? I think he knew she was fooling around on him but he still loved her. But how can you handle the fact that she killed someone? It's tough."

There were a few moments of silence as each man was alone with his thoughts.

"So are you home for good now?" Grant finally asked.

Pike shook his head. "No, there are still a few more hearings and review boards I have to attend. I'll be leaving tomorrow and staying about a week."

"Nobody's charging you with anything are they?"

Again, Pike shook his head. "No. All the investigations have proven me innocent. They just need to wrap up a few more details."

"Are you taking the *Clipper*?" Grant saw his friend's eyes light up at the mention of his beloved air plane.

"She's still up at Paine Field being restored so I'll be flying commercial. But by the time I get back she should be good as new, even better they tell me. I can't wait to take her up."

Grant scoured under a piece of lettuce on the plate, searching for more fries. "Do the cops or FBI have any leads on the whereabouts of Cain or that Mallory woman?"

"Mallory left the iceberg earlier in the day and no one has seen her since and Cain's body hasn't been recovered yet."

"You don't think either one of them will try to come after you do you?"

"Cain was on the iceberg and I don't see how he could have survived, and with all the money Mallory has, why would she waste her time on me?"

"True. I don't know why I waste my time on you." Grant smiled.

"Thanks, old buddy, I love you too." They raised their glasses in a toast. After their glasses clinked, the waitress came up to clear the table.

"Excuse me, sir," she said looking at Pike. "I see you don't have any ice in your glass, would you like some more?"

Pike just smiled and shook his head slowly. "No thank you. I've had just about all the ice I can handle for a while."

Both men laughed while the waitress walked away in confusion.

"Excuse me," Pike said as he heard his cell phone ring. He reached down and didn't recognize the number and a frown shot across his brow. Since everything had happened, he had been constantly hounded by everybody and his brother for an interview, all wanting a piece of the Blast from the Past. He sighed and against his better judgment, took the call.

"Hello?"

He heard a soft, frail voice on the other end. "Hey, Hot Shot."

Please enjoy a sample from CATALYST

Paul Byers first novel, available in
eBook and trade paperback.

ONE

THE car drifted slowly to a stop with its engine and lights off.

The driver hesitated for a moment, his eyes darting back and forth, surveying the area for any hidden dangers that might be lurking in the shadows. He knew this had been planned out to the last detail, but even with the best-laid plans, things could go wrong. A cold shudder traveled the length of his spine because he knew what the deadly consequences would be if this plan went wrong. He took a deep breath to calm his fears, pushed his glasses up off the bridge of his nose, and opened the door. Even before his feet touched the ground, two figures emerged out of the darkness and moved toward him like specters.

Both men were dressed in military uniforms, but in the dim, pre-dawn darkness, he couldn't tell if they were American, British, or German. The taller of the two phantoms spoke as he held out his hand. "Good morning, Doctor Strovinski. If ya'll just step this way, we'll have you outta here and back in England in no time at all."

As soon as the soldier spoke, Strovinski knew: American. He hated the way the Americans had butchered the English language with their slang, but this American was even worse. He had a . . . what did they call it? A Southern drawl? He thought the man sounded like one of those cowboys from their shoot-'em-up western movies.

Doctor Nicoli Strovinski was on the high side of his fifties with thinning brown hair, and his large waistline reflected the fact that he was a man dedicated to science and little else. "Let's be quick about this," he said in Russian. Let the Cowboy try and figure that one out.

The Cowboy replied politely in perfect Russian, "Right this way, sir."

So what? Strovinski thought. The cowboy can understand and speak Russian.

He followed behind them in silence, clutching his worn leather briefcase. The night air was cool and clear, washed clean by heavy rains earlier in the day.

In the stillness of the night, their shoes crunched against the gravel, sounding like a column of marching soldiers rather than just three men walking. They rounded the corner of a small building that he guessed to be a barn because of the foul animal odors coming from inside. Strovinski stopped dead in his tracks. It was a peculiar sight to see two fighters and a bomber parked behind the barn. But it was an even stranger thing to see a cow grazing peacefully under the left wing of the bomber and a goat rubbing its head against the propeller of one of the smaller planes. These cowboys must be smarter than he gave them credit for, he thought, getting three Allied aircraft this deep behind enemy lines.

Strovinski was a little disappointed with the small two-engine plane that was taking him out of Germany. He had expected to be whisked away by one of their big B-17 bombers. Although he didn't know much about American aircraft, everyone in France and Germany knew what the Flying Fortress looked like. After nearly three years of seeing the big plane dominate the skies over France and Germany, it had become the symbol of the advancing Allied forces. To those in France, it represented their impending liberation; to the German Army, it represented impending defeat. For Strovinski, perhaps it would mean a new life.

He followed the two cowboys around to the back of the plane and watched the shorter one climb up a small ladder and disappear into the black abyss. The taller cowboy motioned for Strovinski to follow. Drawing a deep breath, he realized that this was no longer a dream but that it was really happening. There was no turning back now as his foot came to rest on the first rung of the ladder.

He froze in mid-step, a cry of terror on his lips, as another apparition appeared from the black void in the form of a disembodied hand that reached out to grab him. The phantom materialized into a round, baby-faced crewman who was reaching out to help him up the ladder. The blond young ghost looked to be only eighteen or nineteen years old, barely old enough to wear long pants, let alone fight in a war. He wondered if he had made the right decision.

The young man reached out to take his briefcase, but Strovinski refused to give it up. It contained the culmination of nearly twenty years of work and he wasn't about to trust it to a child who didn't know the meaning of life. Not even for a second while he boarded the plane. Grunting, and feeling a little foolish for letting his vivid imagination get the better of him, Strovinski managed to hoist

himself up through the small hatchway with one hand. Once
inside, he let the boy lead him through the bowels of the plane.

He thought that a bomber by its very nature should be big and
spacious, but reality proved him wrong. He struck his head twice
on the short trip from the hatch to his seat. He quickly sat down
and nervously fastened his seat belt.

The plane had a dusty and oily smell to it. He could also smell
the telltale odor of gunpowder, sweat, and something else . . .
Was it the faintest trace of fear that mingled with the other aromas? But was it the plane crew's fear or his? His stomach
answered his brain's question by rumbling and reminding him of
just how much he hated flying.

"GOLDILOCKS, Papa Bear, Mama Bear, and Baby Bear are ready
for takeoff."

Captain Jack Lofton of the Royal Air Force, or RAF, shook his
head at the radio message from the bomber as he flipped on the
ignition switch to his Supermarine Spitfire, waking up his sleeping warhorse. The bloody Yanks and their silly code words, he
thought. When he'd been asked to volunteer for a joint U.S.-
British mission, he immediately agreed; but he'd signed on to
fight the Germans, not recite nursery rhymes. He was "Mama
Bear," and his wingman, Lieutenant Reginald "Reggie" Smyth,
was "Baby Bear." What next? he thought. If they got in trouble
over the channel, were they to land on the Good Ship Lollypop?

At twenty-six, Lofton had a soft, youthful smile and bright blue
eyes that were in contrast to the premature weariness which now
fit him like his uniform. He had been barely more than a boy
when he'd joined the RAF, but after nearly five years of fighting
he appeared to be the age of a man ten years his senior.

He looked over to Reggie, whom he imagined wore a grin from ear to ear, eager for the adventure to begin. A sad smile crossed his lips as he shook his head. He wondered if he'd ever been that young. With one last good tug on his harness, he signaled Baby Bear to take off.

The fast, steady rhythm of the British Rolls-Royce Merlin fighter engines joined the loping sound of the twin Pratt & Whitney eighteen-cylinder radial engines of the American's Martin Marauder B-26. They combined for a mechanical harmony that reached a pitched crescendo when full throttle was applied.

"Papa Bear to Goldilocks, Papa Bear to Goldilocks: the package is in the basket and we are on our way home."

CAPTAIN Griffin Avery of the Office of Strategic Services, or OSS, took off his headset and dropped it on the table. He let out a sigh of relief and rubbed the back of his neck. He pushed himself away from the table that held a fifteen-hour collection of cigarette butts, empty coffee cups, and several stale, half-eaten sandwiches and doughnuts. It had been a very long day and night.

From his basement office in a nameless government building in London, he had monitored the flight of the Three Bears and their pick up of Dr. Nicoli Strovinski. He had watched them since they'd left England in the pre-dawn hours, followed them across the English Channel and over occupied France. Now at last, they were on their way home.

Avery stood and stretched. At forty-five, his hair was already turning gray, but he took comfort in the fact that he at least still had all his hair—unlike his father, who was bald on top with only a fringe of hair running around the side of his head. He preferred to think that his graying temples gave him the distinguished look of a gentleman and not that of an old man.

He heard sharp, fast-paced footsteps coming down the hall and wondered who could be coming here at this late hour. The door opened and Avery sprang to attention. "Good evening, General," he barked with as much enthusiasm as he could muster.

"At ease," came the reply. At sixty-two, Brigadier General Arthur Sizemore carried himself like a man half his age. He was a short, barrel-chested man with the personality and face of a bull-dog that liked to chase parked cars. Like his height, his demeanor was short and direct.

"Got a hot date, sir?" Avery asked, seeing his boss was wearing his dress uniform. Immediately Avery cringed, regretting his choice of words. *Got a date?* What was he thinking?

Sizemore ignored Avery's feeble attempt at humor and sur-veyed the messy desk. He scrutinized the room like a father visiting his son's college dorm room for the first time and not liking what he saw. "My 'date' is with the chiefs of staff at a late-running state dinner—a damn waste of time, if you ask me," Sizemore replied, plucking at his collar that vanity wouldn't allow him to admit was two sizes too small. "This is the fourth scientist this month we've nabbed. Who is this guy again?"

"Doctor Nicoli Strovinski, one of Germany's top nuclear physi-cists. It's been suspected that for the last year or so he's been work-ing closely with Werner Heisenberg, head of the Nazi atomic program. He's also known in the academic community for his work in quantum mechanics and—"

"Right, he's some sort of hotshot egghead. Didn't he also work with Von Braun at Peenemunde on the V-2s?"

"Yes sir, that's why we decided to grab him. If Germany could develop some sort of atomic weapon with the V-2 as the delivery system, then they could hold the world for ransom. We have no defense against a V-2."

"Man, I'd love to tell Ike that we bagged this boy." Sizemore paused then grunted, his face even more serious than usual. "If he's so damn important, you'd better not screw this up. And remember, Captain"—he pointed his stubby finger in Avery's face—"it may be my butt, but it's your neck on the line here." Sizemore turned to leave and stopped when he reached the door. "And clean this mess up." He tugged at his collar again and disappeared.

As the door slammed shut, Avery collapsed in his chair. He wasn't sure if he was more relieved that the mission was almost over or that Sizemore was gone. He grabbed a pack of cigarettes out of his front pocket and lit one with his Ronson. Avery leaned back, took a deep drag, and put his headset back on. He would continue to monitor the flight until they were halfway over the channel. Only then would he relax and go to the airfield to collect the doctor.

Avery began foraging through the scattered doughnuts on his desk, searching for one that wasn't stale enough to use as a doorstop. He found an edible morsel buried amongst the greasy rubble and held it up as if he had discovered a nugget of gold, a look of triumph filling his face. He took a bite and sighed. It wasn't the freshest he'd ever had; if only he had some fresh coffee. He was devouring the last bite when the radio crackled to life.

"Break left Baby Bear, Baby . . . oh, bloody hell, Reg! Break left!" the voice on the radio shouted. "You've got two bandits behind you!"

Avery sprang up and checked the channel on his radio.

"Bloody good, lad," the radio blared again. It was the voice of Captain Lofton, and it sounded like they were under attack. Avery heard the roar of the airplane engine and the unmistakable sound of machine guns firing. How can this be, Avery wondered. How could the Germans have known about Strovinski?

"Goldilocks, Goldilocks, this is Papa Bear. We are under fighter attack! I say again, we are under attack. Mama Bear and Baby Bear have engaged."

The sound of the bombers' distress call shook Avery out of his stupor and he grabbed the microphone. "Papa Bear, this is Goldilocks, do you copy? Where are you? Do you copy? *Answer me!* Papa Bear this is Goldilocks, do you read me? Mama Bear, do you read me, over?"

"Breaking left. I'm going to flip over and bring him back in front of you," Smyth replied. Avery could hear and almost feel the tension in the young British pilot's voice

"Roger, swinging around now to line up." By contrast, Avery could hear the calm voice of the seasoned Lofton over the drone of his engine.

"You've got two more coming down on you, Reg, eight o'clock high!"

"I can't see them. I can't see them!" Smyth shouted desperately in the radio.

"They're right above the bomber, swing back to your left, behind the bomber, NOW!"

His mission was falling apart, yet Avery could only listen with morbid fascination as the battle unfolded before him. He was reminded of Halloween night back in 1938. He was home on leave and had just come back from the corner grocer. His mom had wanted fresh corn on the cob to serve with their steak in celebration of the return of their long-gone son.

When he walked through the front door, he found his mother hysterical, glued to the radio. She kept shouting about being under attack. He dropped the bag of groceries on the table and rushed to the front room. On the radio, the reporter was saying something about people being killed and that the Army was on the scene but the enemy had some sort of new weapon, some sort of death ray. Avery could hear yelling and screaming in the background and something that sounded like gunfire. The reporter shouted that they were under attack, and then there was silence.

His mother was on the verge of crying, and his father just sat there and held her, not knowing what to do. Avery was reaching for the phone to call headquarters when the radio came back to life and the announcer said that he hoped they were enjoying the broadcast of Orson Welles and his Mercury Theater production of *War of the Worlds*. It took some convincing, but his mother finally realized that it was just a radio show and not the end of the world. Upon pain of death, she threatened him and his father against saying a word to anyone that she had believed the broadcast.

Now Avery sat and listened as his own radio played out its own scene. Only this time, the sound effects weren't made in a studio and those weren't actors. Real people were going to die.

"My left aileron's hit, I can hardly turn!"

Avery could hear the rising fear in Lieutenant Smyth's voice.

"Steady, lad," Lofton calmly responded over the radio. "I'm almost there."

Then silence.

Avery leaned forward in his chair as if that could help him hear better, but there was nothing to hear. The only sound was the pounding of his heart. *"This is Goldilocks! Does anybody read me?"* he yelled in frustration shaking the microphone as if he could bully it into working. Why won't this damn thing work? "Jack! Do you copy? He broke the rules by using Lofton's name, but he didn't care. "Jack, where are you?"

Silence.

Avery was resigning himself to the fact that the entire mission had failed and eight lives were lost, when the radio blared again.

"What the bloody hell! Is that a red star? *REGGIE!*" Even through the roar of the fighter's engine, Avery could hear a faint explosion and he knew that Smyth was gone. Sitting in his warm and comfortable office, it was hard for him to comprehend that he had just heard a man die.

Avery sat like a statue, his chest barely moving as he breathed, a thousand thoughts bounced around in his head.

"Papa Bear, this is Mama Bear. Do you copy? Papa Bear, this is Mama Bear. Do you read me? Over." Slowly, like the incoming tide, Avery felt hope creeping back into his soul as he heard Lofton's voice on the radio. Perhaps Lofton had fended off the attackers and Strovinski was safe.

But the incoming tide quickly turned into a tidal wave as the radio blasted another warning: "Break right, Mama Bear, break right!"

"Look out, Mama Bear, there's another one coming down on you! Break! Goldilocks, Goldilocks, this is Papa Bear. Mama and Baby Bear are both down, repeat, both fighters are down! Am under heavy fire. Wait . . . top gunner! Watch that one coming down, nine o'clock high! He's in behind us, swing it around *now*! Tail gunner report! Report! Goldilocks we have—"

Silence: total, deafening silence now invaded his office. It smothered the room like a thick heavy fog, driving everything else out, all thoughts of reason, any lingering feelings of hope and, oddly, even of despair. The silence was so consuming that Avery found it difficult to breathe.

What had gone wrong?

Avery placed his elbows on the table and buried his head in his hands, trying to think. After a moment he leaned back and ran his fingers through his hair and noticed a small mustard and mayonnaise stain on his sleeve. His desk that looked like a high school cafeteria. He shook his head and sighed. Given the way the room looked, his stupid date joke and stains on his uniform, it was no wonder General Sizemore didn't have much confidence in him.

But Sizemore was wrong! He'd planned everything, down to the last detail. It had taken him three weeks to go through each phase, step by step, and to finalize everything into a complete plan. He'd checked and rechecked it all at least a dozen times. Each of his two assistants had gone over it with a fine-tooth comb to see if they could find any flaws. And there had been none. He'd seen to the security precautions personally to prevent this very thing.

He didn't know how long he sat there, seconds, minutes, hours; it didn't matter. He fumbled mindlessly with a cigarette and burned his fingers before he realized that it was already lit. What had gone wrong? They should have been in and out before the Germans had even realized that Strovinski was missing, yet they had known and had been waiting . . . but was it the Germans? Something that Captain Lofton had said over the radio, something about a red star. The only aircraft he knew that carried a red star were Russian. In the dark of night and heat of battle had Lofton confused the swastika for a star? Not likely. He doubted that a man with his experience would make such a mistake.

Even though the Americans, British, and Russians were all allies, as they pushed further and further into Germany, it was becoming a race with the British and Americans against the Russians in an effort to capture German technology and resources. Did the Russians somehow find out about their plan and shoot Strovinski down themselves, Avery wondered, rather than let the Americans have him? Or was it just a case of blind luck? Had the Germans just been in the right place at the right time and stumbled across the three allied planes?

It didn't matter now. They were all dead and it was his fault.

Avery stood and tilted his head from side to side, trying to get the kinks out of his neck. His mind was as numb as his body. He couldn't think straight. He needed to get some fresh air. This was the first mission in which he'd been directly responsible for the deaths of those under him. He'd sent men and women into France before to help the resistance and he'd found out later that some had been captured and even killed, but this was different. The Three Bears and Strovinski were dead because *his* plan had failed!

He grabbed his coat and wandered down the hallway, ignoring the few early birds arriving to work, then climbed the stone staircase up two flights to the street above. Wearily, he leaned against the heavy wooden door and summoned all his remaining strength to push it open. Avery squinted his eyes as he stepped out into the street. It was one of those rare, bright sunny mornings in London.

Across the street was a small tailor shop with a bouquet of colorful flowers in the window, a splash of color that seemed so out of place in war-weary London. Half a block down there had been a little family-owned bakery. They made the best glazed doughnuts he had ever tasted. Each time he went in there, the sights and aromas took him back to his once-a-month family trips into the city when he was a boy. On the first Saturday of each month, providing his father didn't have to work, he and his brother would ride in the back of their old Ford Model T as it rambled and rumbled down the dirt road twelve miles into Portland, Oregon. His mother said that his eyes always grew to the size of the doughnuts themselves as he gazed upon row after row of the delectable delights. And the aroma . . . the warm, soft smells of the flour and butter baking made it an almost magical experience.

Sometimes when he felt homesick, he had gone into the British bakery just to remember; his own little personal escape from the war. Yesterday, before all this had started, he had stopped in and bought half a dozen.

Sometime during the night, he had heard the rumblings and felt the impact of what he guessed was a V-2 rocket that had slammed into the ground nearby, shaking his old building to its cornerstone. The V-2s were Hitler's *Vergeltungswaffen,* or Vengeance Weapons. It was a 46-foot-high, 3500-mile-per-hour monster designed for pure terror. They weren't extremely accurate, but by carrying over a ton of explosives, they didn't have to be.

Today, the bakery was a burned out crumpled ruin. It must have taken a direct hit last night. How ironic, he thought, that yesterday, like the bakery, he had been busy and full of life and hope for the future. Now, both the street and his spirit were a pile of broken dreams and rubble.

TWO

THE laughter was loud, drowning out conversation, music, and tonight, even the war. At the far corner of the bar sat an old man known to everyone simply as The Colonel. He was in good shape for a man of 81, too old to fight but not too old to proudly serve his country in the Home Guard, ready to rout the Huns if they dared to stick their noses across the channel. The Colonel had flaming white hair, a large handlebar mustache, and a passion for life still burned deep in his bright, clear eyes. His skin was a tough and leathery brown, reflecting decades of service for king and country.

Tonight, like most every night, he sat at the bar, reliving the glory days of his youth to whoever would listen. He often spoke fondly of the lads of the 24th Regiment of Foot and those fateful days in South Africa at Rorke's Drift in 1879—the time of the great Zulu uprising.

He reminisced about how he was just a lad, only fifteen at the time, and of how he had run away from home seeking adventure.

He could think of nothing more exciting than camping out all the time, so he lied about his age and joined the army. He would describe the smashing old uniforms—how good they all looked in their bright red coats, white helmets, and bandoliers! He recounted how he and the lads had stood toe to toe with nearly four thousand Zulu savages and held them at bay.

One day, Avery remembered, a drunk British sailor had called The Colonel a liar and said he had never been in Africa or fought against the Zulu. The Colonel was silent for a moment then slowly stood and unbuttoned the top two buttons of his tunic. With great care and reverence he pulled out a Victoria Cross that hung from a tarnished chain around his neck.

"Twelve medals were awarded that day," The Colonel said slowly, "but only eleven officially. It was the most ever issued to a unit for a single engagement. When the army found out that I was really only fifteen, they couldn't acknowledge that they had let a boy fight, so they let me keep the medal but made me swear never to reveal my true age at the time."

After that, no one ever questioned The Colonel again.

SITTING at a table, Avery noticed, off to one side, was a group of women—girls, really—from RAF headquarters. They were with the Fighter Command. Some had helped direct the magnificent Spitfires and Hurricanes which had fended off the Luftwaffe in the dark days surrounding the Battle of Britain. They were young and pretty, but several, those who had been around since the beginning, had a few more worry lines and a few more gray hairs than the newer girls. They were seasoned veterans at the ages of twenty-three and twenty-four. Few people knew of the hard work they did or just how close the Germans had actually come to winning the battle and invading England.

There were several small groups of British and American soldiers scattered throughout the bar, telling tall tales and swapping lies in hopes of impressing the local girls. There were also a few civilians about doing their best to set aside the war for a moment. But most of the patrons that night were American airmen. It was easy to tell the bomber crews from the fighter pilots, Avery thought. The fighter pilots usually flocked in groups of three to four, while the bomber crews stuck together in packs of seven or eight.

At the far end of the bar were four flyboys, fighter pilots. One gestured with his hands, describing in great detail his latest aerial victory. In the back of the pub sat a group of eight flyers sur- rounding two empty chairs. They were much quieter than the rest of the patrons as they raised their glasses in a silent toast, a scene that was often repeated. They were a bomber crew who had lost two of their own and were now saying good-bye. Next to them was an empty table with ten chairs stacked on top of it. The crew that didn't come back must have been well known and liked, Avery thought, for the pub to hold a table in tribute to them on such a crowded night.

Captain Avery sat in the back of the pub taking it all in. It had been two days since his report on the loss of Dr. Strovinski, and General Sizemore had not been pleased. He'd had dreams of mov- ing "upstairs" and working with the big boys on major planning projects. But with the war winding down in Europe, his chances of being transferred to the Pacific and being involved with the inva- sion of Japan were all but gone now with the loss of Strovinski.

His less-than-glamorous nine-to-five job involved working with the resistance cells in France, gathering information about German troop movements, and aiding the recovery of downed Allied pilots. With the rapidly advancing Allied forces, he'd also been assigned the task of locating top German scientists and grabbing them before the Russians did.

With certain technologies, the Germans held a slight edge. In some cases, however, their advantage was monumental. Though the British had a jet powered fighter in the Gloster Meteor, it was no match for the German Messerschmitt 262 . . . and the Allies had nothing to counter the dreaded V-2 rockets. While Russia was an ally, the United States and Britain still wanted to make sure that they were in control of these new technologies. It was Avery's job to get the scientists, a job he had now failed at miserably.

Avery took another sip of his beer—or his pint, as the Brits called it. It was his third, and he was nearing that place where he felt no pain, a place that suited him just fine.

The Three Bears had been his plan. His operation from start to finish. It was supposed to show General Sizemore that he could do more than just pass messages back and forth between head-quarters and the resistance. It was to prove that he belonged upstairs with the big boys.

But none of that mattered now.

He'd gotten good men killed. In three large gulps, he downed the rest of his beer and waved his hand at the waitress for another.

"Griff, my boy, why the look of a man who's just found out his mother-in-law is coming to live with him?"

Avery looked up from his empty glass and watched The Colonel spin the chair around and sit backwards in it, holding his beer in one hand and leaning forward on the back of the chair with the other.

"Do you know what I had to do today, Colonel? I had to write letters to the families of the men I lost on a mission . . . a mission that I planned. I planned it down to the last detail, but somehow it went horribly wrong. I knew one of the men personally. I even ate with him and his family. He had a wife and two little girls, four and six. We don't even have a body to give back to her to lay to rest. She has no grave to cry over, only this lousy piece of paper saying her husband was a hero and is missing in action. For God's sake, I can't even tell her what happened to him or where he went down. They died for nothing."

The warmth and humor in the old man's eyes drained. "We were in France," The Colonel began, "in the early spring of 1916 during the war that was supposed to end all wars. The nights were still cold, as Mother Nature still hadn't taken off her winter coat yet, and the rains that April were unusually heavy, turning our trenches and the no-mans land into a sea of mud, muck, and mire."

A humorless smile slowly crossed The Colonel's lips. "It's funny what you remember, but what I remember most, other than my lads, was the smell. The rich, earthy smell of the soil was invaded by the musty stench of everything rotting and covered in mold from the continual rains.

"We'd been stalemated for most of the month, neither us nor the Huns taking more than a few yards of ground at a time, when some general back at headquarters decided that he wanted the stalemate broken.

"Our platoon was handed the nasty assignment of taking out a German machine-gun bunker on a slight rise that controlled nearly the entire line in our area. If we were to advance at all, those guns had to be destroyed." The Colonel paused and closed his eyes for a moment. Avery couldn't tell if he was trying to remember or trying to forget what happened that day.

"It was particularly cold that morning," he resumed, "and a thin layer of ice covered the mud. We were all cold so were stomping our feet to keep warm, and with each stomp of our boots, you could hear the crunching of the ice breaking. I think that the Germans must have heard the crunching and knew something was up because they were waiting for us.

"When the whistle blew, we all charged up over the top of the trench with our best war cries . . . straight into the teeth of hell.

The war cries instantly turned in to screams of agony as the Kraut machine guns opened up on our boys.

"Johnny Biggelow was a scrawny mutt of a lad, but what he didn't have in size he made up for in heart. He was the first one over the top, and the first to die. His foot hadn't even cleared the top of the trench when he was hit. He was blown back and landed on top of me, and we both went tumbling down into the mud. He probably saved my life, because the whole first wave was wracked by machine-gun fire. I'll never forget the emptiness of his eyes as they stared back at me."

The Colonel paused.

"We eventually took those machine gun nests that day, but I lost three quarters of my squad. Three days later, we abandoned that field and the Germans moved right back in. It was my whistle that sent my lads over the top, my orders that got them killed. And just like you I had to write letters home to their loved ones. And to this day I remember each and every one of them. Did they die for nothing?" The old man silently shook his head. "No, they sacrificed themselves serving their country and serving their brothers; they died doing their duty and so did your lads. Don't take that away from them. If you forget that, then their deaths truly have no meaning."

"I guess you're right," Avery said. "I was feeling pretty sorry for myself and that's not what it's about."

"Good! Just remember the lads and their death won't be in vain." The Colonel raised his glass in a toast and Avery followed suit. "To our boys!" He said as their glasses came together. Both men drank, and Avery put his glass down, still distracted. The Colonel followed the gaze of his American friend until it stopped on a table across the room.

A smile reclaimed its rightful place on the old veteran's face as he saw that the center of his companion's attention was focused on a table with two girls sitting at it. "I see you have other things on your mind too." A spark of mischief ignited in his eyes. "Hm, is it the lassie with the short, dark hair? What is it with you American chaps and skinny women? She doesn't have enough ballast on her to hold her down in a stiff breeze. I prefer my women with a little more meat on their bones. When I put my arms around her to give her a hug, if my fingers can touch on the other side, then she's too skinny! Why, I remember this one lassie in Liverpool, she was—"

An American Army officer came walking up to the table and The Colonel stopped in mid-story. "Well, you have company here, lad, so I'll be talking with you later." He got up from the table and turned as he left. "Just remember what I said about your boys."

"Thanks," Avery replied with a small smile.

"There you are."

Avery looked up to see First Lieutenant Jason Peters. Peters was Avery's right-hand man and had come to work for him shortly after he'd arrived in England two years ago. He was a tall, lanky twenty-six-year-old drink of water from Alabama with curly blond hair and deep blue eyes. Jason had a bumbling country boy charm that the English girls found irresistible.

"I've been looking for you, sir," Peters said.

The waitress dropped off his fourth beer, and Avery downed half of it in a single gulp. He set it down and wiped the foam from his lips. In all the time he'd been in England, he still hadn't acquired a taste for English beer. He took another gulp and shook his head. What he wouldn't give right now for a hot dog and a *real* cold beer, like he used to get at the Dodgers games!

Peters sat down and put his hand on his boss's shoulder. "Still beating yourself up, Griff? You did everything you could to make sure things went right. Anna and I couldn't find any mistakes when we reviewed the plan."

"Anna," Avery said letting out a long, heavy sigh like a school-boy with a crush on his first grade teacher. He looked around the room and his eyes stopped when they reached Anna's table. Anna . . . she was the love of his life, only she didn't know it. Anna Roshinko was a second lieutenant who also worked for Avery doing clerical duties. Over the last few months she had been helping him more and more, planning and assisting with her own French resistance cell.

"Look at her, Jay. She's beautiful, and she's as smart as she is good looking." Anna Roshinko was thirty-one with short, ebony hair that framed her heart-shaped face. She was a petite five-foot two inches tall and had a doll's figure that even the Army uniform couldn't hide. Her eyes had the piercing blue color of a northern glacier. Peters chuckled at his tipsy boss, glad for the distraction that took his mind off Strovinski and the failed mission. Roshinko was not bad looking, Peters thought, but not as beautiful as his boss was professing. Then again, he knew Avery was seeing her through a different set of eyes.

Anna sat at a table with her friend, another clerk from the office. The two of them had been there an hour and had been approached twice by American servicemen and three times by British officers, but had politely turned them away.

"Look," Peters said, "Anna's getting up. Looks like she's get-ting ready to leave. I think she lives somewhere around here. Why don't you go over and ask if you can walk her home? You know, be the gallant gentleman and all."

"I don't know," Avery hesitated. "She'd probably just say no."

"But she might just say yes."

"You think so?"

"Yup. And besides, this isn't the best part of town, you know. Look, there she goes. You'd better hurry."

Paul grew up in Oregon on the shores of the mighty and mysterious Columbia River, and spent endless hours daydreaming on the beach in front of his house, making up stories about the ships from exotic ports all over the world that steamed up the river – what secret cargo might they be carrying; did they harbor spies who were on dark and exciting missions?

Later in adult life, he moved to another mysterious and provocative city – Las Vegas, just outside the famous Nellis Air Force base. After work he would sit on his porch and watch the fighters take off and land, igniting his imagination with visions of secret missions and rich speculation about what could possibly be hidden at Area 51.

After moving back to his native Pacific Northwest, Paul worked for the Navy and took every opportunity he could to speak with veterans from WWII to the Gulf War, listening to them swap stories and relate the experiences of a lifetime.

So it is this combination of a passionate love of history, a vivid "what if" imagination, and a philosophy of life that boils down to the belief that – *there are few things in life that a bigger hammer won't fix* – that led Paul to become a writer of exciting, fact-based action-thrillers. His greatest joy is leaving his readers wondering where the facts end and the fiction begins.

www.ingramcontent.com/pod-product-compliance
Lightning Source LLC
Chambersburg PA
CBHW051934240626
47153CB00005B/1490